De

Also by David Hancock

Jackalope Hunting

Dewpoint

David Hancock

Released by 5119, LLC

5119, LLC

First published in the United States in 2023

This edition published in 2023

ISBN 979-88-404820-63 (paperback)

Titles, margin text, and front matter set in Century Gothic

Running text set in Garamond

Acknowledgement

With my love for my wife who gave me the space and quiet I needed to write this novel, listened intently as I read the entire book aloud to her (twice), gave me a pass on diligently putting away my laundry for many months so I could focus on this, and who I hope looks forward to the books that follow. And with great gratitude for my friend Michelle whose feedback helped set the tone and tenor of this book.

Foreword & Prologue

Dear reader, thank you for purchasing this book and I hope you find it enjoyable, engaging, and moving. *Dewpoint* is the sequel to my previous novel *Jackalope Hunting*. Plot elements from *Jackalope Hunting* are referenced in this work. Knowing that book's story arc will help parts of this book make more sense. Thank you again for the time you spend with Merak. I hope you find his world immersive and compelling.

<>

August 1997

High beams appear in my periphery, around a turn and in my lane, moving fast. A horn blares and behind the lights a brown Cadillac comes toward me. The driver's highs turn off and his arms move the wheel. His eyes are wide; his face is terror and I know now that I am about to die.

The brown Caddy's rear end begins to slip and the whole car turns sideways. Everything slows as it hits my Volare's front end. The air baffles below my bumper crumble, fender and hood bulge in and up. Glass from the Cadillac's driver's window slides over my car's hood. He was moving too fast, no question. I was in my lane, well under the speed limit. My car, grabbed by the swinging momentum of the other car, is pushed sharply back and to the left and my head hits the passenger headrest. The world goes starry but they blink off, and the horizontal layers of the canyon I had been driving next to are vertical. A piece of guardrail falls with me. In the other car the man stares at me through his broken window and I can hear him scream through my shut window, or maybe I hear myself scream; he holds his arm.

My car yaws hard when it hits the water. His car rolls upside-down. At the seams around my doors, water comes in. The Cadillac sinks in a bouquet of bubbles. The Volare hits it and rocks up, over, and is pushed backwards by the river. My car takes on a thin brown broth which deepens as we sink. It smells like fish and biomass and the inside of a mildewy Airstream. Water creeps up the front of the car and the grill sinks; the engine stops.

I undo my seatbelt but the water is already over the window. It streams in through the edges along the window, the doors, a small branch lodges in the louvers of the rear window. The car grows dark as what little light the day provided is cut off. When I turn the dome light on, the river's true nature shows itself. Gravel, sand, and rocks are carried by my window. The ping off my car like the hail in Saint Louis.

Contents

1
Purple

No one survives a near-death experience. Almost three years ago, I should have drowned in a river, brown and churning like sloshing hot chocolate. My mind drifts, often, many days, to the moment my car's water-filled passenger compartment cabin light failed, trapping me in lightless black so dark my eyes burned like coals. Thinking of my life before my Volare 'Colander' and I fell off a cliff feels like another me died and the person who walked away, well, I still don't understand him. I feel like a reflection, there but not real, an opposite version staring from the other side of silvered glass: as though the me who limped away from that crash left the other to drown, and sometimes, like now, he stares back at me in the mirror.

Brumby's, one of Cold Harbor, Illinois, college-town dives, smells of acrid wood imbued with three decades of stale cigarette smoke, sweat, cheap perfume and cologne, failed pickup lines, successful pickup lines, spilled and spoiled beer, brawl-bloodied noses and lips, and ozone made by a new smoke-reducing box that hangs over the high tops crackling like a bug lamp in a deep-south swamp. The front and back doors propped open, late-June southern Illinois humidity hangs inside, makes the air tacky; the smokers' smoke sticks to skin like tape. The ceiling fans move the sticky like children playing with clay. At happy hour, the usual crowd orders their usual drinks, cheap beers, hard cocktails made with low-end spirits, and flat pop. Their drinks taste like little more than the minerals in their ice cubes or the dishwasher soap residue in the glasses. Some order food, inasmuch as it can be called that – warmed fries the menu calls beer battered, narrow slices of happy hour cheese pizza with pools of clear-yellow grease in divots, and deep-fried mozzarella sticks with large cavities inside. These are not healthy people; this is not a healthy life.

The regulars, I know their faces but not their names. I am one of them, but not really, and that, if anything, makes me happy. Students call the regulars 'townies': those stuck here because they failed out of school or had the misfortune of being born nearby; they are different than us, trapped. For them, Cold Harbor is not a four-year experience they will look back on with fondness derived from remembering friends and forgetting the town. For students, we will remember the times in bars as fun nights punctuating evenings of study and homework, laughing and playing games with friends, and the careless times that come from comfort and assurance that an ambiguous better future awaits.

Fifty weeks until I walk, funny hatted, to a rolled paper baton and that ambiguous better future. Until then, this is my padded bar stool. It spins rough and squeaks and wobbles. My feet push off an old iron pipe along the bar's base. In any other town, a seat like this doesn't cup the butts of those with bright futures. So yes, I am a temporary, short-term regular. Across the bar, behind my friend and bartender George, a dirty bar-length mirror reflects the backs of cheap liquor bottles and my face, framed between bottles. I make eye contact with my mirror-self, an opposite and reflected me, maybe the me who stayed behind out west when I returned, here now to try and rejoin our lives. He looks like me, but his dark hair is a bit shaggy, longer than the tips of my ears, combed but not clearly parted. Black acrylic glasses, the tops block his eyebrows. The frames are wide now, too wide for his face, gaunt, high-cheekboned, and thirty-six-hour stubbled. I pick up my camera, a Nikon F3 with a fast fifty, from the bar top, set the lens wide, the shutter to automatic, focus on my face, peer over the camera, and hold it steady for three long shots, hoping one photo turns out.

George sets up his drink prep near me, slices limes with a too-dull paring knife; they smash a bit and after a dozen or so he drains juice off the cutting board. He's lived in and around Cold Harbor for almost fifteen years, tended bar at most of the bars here, and many in other small southern Illinois towns. He once said to me, over a bottle of beer just before last call a couple of years ago, "Merak, knowing me, it's not six degrees of separation, it's four. Maybe two in this part of the world." George, somehow, knows everyone and every secret this town holds.

The smattering of regulars around the bar, a few stools away, single or small groups at high tops, friends playing pool or darts and wasting a day's perfectly good light, I know their faces. They live in a found, comfortable routine of waking, working, never advancing, cheap and foamy beer, and sleeping a few hours to repeat. I see them every day. I made up my own names for many because I don't know any of them.

A few tables behind me, I see her in the mirror every day. She sits at the same high top in the same seat. I called her Mona for six months before George called her Chrissy. I still think of her as Mona; I want to believe that Mona is someone different from Chrissy, and that Chrissy is a better and stronger person. She keeps her hair back with a wide athletic band. Dark brunette, stress-graying roots, she's only twenty-eight, seven years my senior. George dated her for some months, and they stayed friends after. George has that way, somehow staying friends with girls he dated, often also the first name they call when they're single again.

Chrissy, a hospital orderly, wears blue-teal scrubs every day, an old denim jacket, too, when it's cold. She sits in the same seat, pulls the table's ashtray to her, or grabs one from another table, lights up a slim 100 menthol cigarette, smokes it to the filter for about ten minutes, and then orders the same drink and meal – a twenty-two-ounce Natural Light, two slices of happy hour pizza, and a side salad with extra croutons. Today, though, no scrubs, instead the old denim jacket looks limp, dingy. The denim, threadbare at the elbows, frayed at the wrists and hem, two metal buttons lost, wears the scars of mileage, concerts, and hundreds of trips in the wash. From a side pocket she pulls her cigarette pack, soft pack; her hands – I've not seen this before – shake like an unbalanced ceiling fan. She tamps the cigarette pack on her left palm five times and pulls out a long, thin, white cigarette with two gold bands at the filter end. Her hand, shaking, drops it on the floor. She stands, stoops and holds the table for balance, picks it up and the overhead light casts hard, strong shadows along her cheeks, ponytail flopping over her shoulder and blocking my view of her eyes. When she stands, holding her cigarette, she turns and faces the mirror, makes eye contact with herself, eyes red-lined like a badly-written essay, the corner of her right eye twitching closed twice, face and mouth slack in exhaustion. After a moment seeing herself, she turns so fast her pony tail whips outward, and she faces the back of the bar, face down, lighter's red-orange glow dancing in her cheek's soft peach fuzz.

Chrissy smokes slowly, more than usual, long drags and holds that release in thick, sigh-exhaled whisp-plumes rising around her head, tendrils wrapping her cheeks and hair like long, skinny fingers embracing her face with tenuous, brief caresses. Chrissy closes her eyes when the smoke touches them. Chrissy's eyes look like a void and she stares past the wall and at the moment space became time, the place where our minds go to hide from thought. She takes measured, long drags and waves away the waitress multiple times. Chrissy holds the smoke in her lungs, sometimes blows it out her nose and it moves down her neck and wraps around her shoulders.

George scrapes lime slices into a metal bin for service, grabs a glass and a rag, walks to stand across from me, and, seeing me watch Chrissy in the mirror, pretends to clean the glass: "Family of five was in a camper that caught fire and the fire, where it was in the thing, trapped two of the kids in the back. She had a rough day." His voice is soft, calm, a lower alto that sounds like a tuned, harmonious pipe organ. His voice inspires calmness that, combined with good drinks and a patient ear, makes him a good bartender. George, almost forty, moved here in 1986 to start school. He grew up poor, worked his way through semesters, gave up, started again, changed majors, floundered and found interests, made enough money on student tips to keep living, and, some months into my first year at Cold Harbor, started trading me beers for tutoring. His eyes' fan-like creases, formed from fifteen years of smiling at drunks' jokes and being out-facing-happy no matter what, now give him a look of someone rewarded with the character-rich face of a happy man. His temples, gray-streaked against light-brown hair kept a few inches long and combed neatly, stand out as one of his few age indicators. Usually, his face wears his rich smile, a smile that turns him from a forgettable-looking average white guy into someone who everyone wants to talk to.

"I haven't seen hands shake like that in a long time. She usually doesn't change after work."

"Merak, you gotta do something better with your life than this. You are the only person here who notices anything about anyone."

"Besides you."

"Bartender. It's the job. Speaking of jobs, I had something land in my hands today that might be up your alley."

George, always a good friend, wants better for me. I'm not looking for a job, really.

"I know you're not really looking for a job, but man, it's better than sitting in a bar being literally the only afternooner who orders beer in a bottle, and getting second-hand cancer every day."

George twists off the cap from a bottle of Killian's; it makes a soft pop and carbon dioxide fog fills and overflows the headspace. "Let's hear it," I say as I lift the bottle. George hands me a small flyer for a job at the college as a note-taker: minimum wage, course auditing credit for notetaking if not enrolled. "Really?" My voice, high-pitched and flat with skepticism, my face almost certainly mirrors that tone. I take a long swig of the Killian's, letting the slightly bitter lager linger on my tongue.

"Hear me out on this. You pick up on things, man; you could help someone who needs this better understand their courses. You could learn something new that you never planned to."

I spin my barstool; it squeaks and wobbles, makes almost half of a third rotation before stopping with a jolt, forcing me to scoot and shift to finish the revolution. "Nah."

"Take the flyer, fold it up, put it in your pocket, think about it tonight. Look, you tutored me and because of that I got to graduate last month. Seriously, that happened because of you. You can do that for someone else."

I lock eyes with my mirror-self, also holding a slip of paper. We look, now, the same: shaggy hair seems shorter, hazel eyes focusing quickly around the bar, cheek bones triangling toward our mouths, and a horizontal jaw that our childhood dentist said looked like George Reeves seem like mis-matched scrapbook remnants. We look at each other and, for a moment, maybe this is just beer and humidity and smoke in my brain, I feel as though, again, two of me exist and we're about to walk very different trails.

‹◊›

For two days the flyer sits folded, halved and resting upright, on my dresser beside some change and my watch, a Fossil chronograph, black metal-link band and housing with a blue face, scratches on the metal and crystal from incidental impacts. For two days I set my keys, wallet, and sunglasses next to it, read it a couple times, and set it back down.

Wanted: Note takers. $5.15/hour. Earn audit credit for courses you aren't in. YOU CAN BE PAID FOR COURSES IN WHICH YOU ARE ENROLLED. Must have good attendance and good note quality. Bring samples of course notes when you apply. Apply at the Student Center, Room 43, M-F 12-4PM.

It's 11:45. Why not.

Student Center Room 43's air mixes staleness, basement must, and toner dust from an overworked copy machine. The space, a generally typical tutoring center, has textbook-laden particleboard shelves that bow in the middle like old mattresses, five round study tables, old plastic chairs from the seventies or eighties – the type with a large triangular opening in the back for ventilation, each plastic chair a different, primary color, tube-steel single-piece legs formed into rounded trapezoids – and the old copy machine placed too close to the wall for it to ventilate properly. Student-tutor pairs sit at two tables, and a lone student sits at a third. At the near one, a math tutor works on geometry with a girl whose hair is purple on the left and black on the right. The next table has a boy with a buzz-cut and metal-frame glasses that pinch his nose bridge enough to make the red spots visible from here, and they read from a book of contemporary American plays and discuss the meanings of key lines. At the far table a girl with straight-ish dusty-blonde hair to her shoulders and dark aviator-style sunglasses sits and listens to headphones while she runs her fingers over book pages, her head moving and bobbing slowly in cadence with her hand's back-and-forthing over those pages. She wears a red and black flannel with use-worn blue jeans that hold permanently-mashed-in dirt stains down to her boot line. Her jeans fit snug, but her flannel loose and a bit long, the bottom two buttons undone and the ends hang at her thighs. After a moment of waiting, a student worker walks out of an office and asks me, in the soft voice a favorite stuffed toy might have, if I need help.

"I'm here to apply for the note-taker position." The student worker looks like a freshman, black hair and small, round, red-framed glasses, a wide nose, some whiskers that might someday be a moustache, and an Iron Maiden tour t-shirt. His eyebrows twitch and he hands me an application. This kid loves his job.

I sit at the table nearest the girl with the headphones and fill in the application. Her fingers slide across the page's texture, slowly with a soft paper-on-fingers sound that reminds my brain of light rain on the roof of a parked car. Though her fingers on paper are quite quiet, it seems louder than the soft conversations about triangle types and the meaning of a streetcar's name. Her fingers press more firmly on a part of the page and the sound changes from gentle rain to an empty paper bag pushed over the sidewalk by a breeze; something in the book warrants added attention. No sound escapes her headphones; a glance at the tape player and I notice the volume set to four, and I admire her hearing. Her old, flannel shirt, covers a plain white T-shirt. Her jeans' permanent dirt stains, mainly around the calves and ankles, and the added wear on the inside of her jeans' thighs come from walking for hours in dirt or mud and riding horses. She wears old cowboy boots, worn in with soft, heavily creased brown leather and a stamped inlay of flowers. She's cute, definitely what I would call cute. Her jeans and white shirt fit a little snug, flannel a little loose, and her shoulder and thigh muscles come from work, not working out.

University of Illinois at Cold Harbor draws students from two places – Chicago and southern Illinois' farming communities. Girls here who dress like this come in two varieties: the legitimate farm girl who wears these clothes for their practicality and cost, and the suburban girls who wear similar but spendier clothes to look cute. This girl: the former.

Standing, glancing again at her, I set my application on the front desk. "You need notes?"

He points to the photocopier then hands me a sheet with class names and times. "Pick some out while you copy your notes and write the classes you can do on your application, and how many you want."

The photocopier clicks and whirs like an old car engine that receives too few oil changes. A moving light spot seeps between the copier top and platen with each scan. None of the listed classes are mine; only a handful occur during my free hours. I pick three – two high-level geology and a geophysical engineering – that are in the building next to the one I frequent, and in timeslots adjacent to my courses. $5.15 per hour, nine hours a week, that's beer and a pizza every weekend.

The student takes my notes and application and tells me to wait as he walks them to an office. Not two minutes pass and a woman in her late-sixties, gray hair with pink highlights, short, upright, frizzy, framing black and gold horn-rim glasses that magnify cataracted brown eyes in a network of crows' feet that look like a river delta, and the jowls that people who spent their lives very overweight until a recent and rapid

8

weight loss carry below their chins, steps from her office and waves for me to come in. "I'm Dr. Peters, and I head the tutoring center. Any reason you picked these three classes?" Her voice sounds like a rusted cheese grater dragged on a stone, weak in the consonants and strong in the vowels, hinting at damaged lungs.

"I, well, I mean," I don't understand the question. "They're near my computer science courses in Deckenger Hall and in the times between my courses."

"Geologies 430 and 435 and Engineering 455? I have a notetaker for 435, but the other two are yours. I need you to start on Monday. Every day after the last class, come here and drop off your notes. Photocopy them and place them in the mailbox with your name on it. We're open till nine each night so there's no reason for you to miss any drops. Miss three drops or three classes or any combination thereof and you're fired. If the student you take notes for is unhappy with your work, you'll want to quit; trust me on that. This job needs you to be timely with your notes and they need to be good. You're not supposed to know who the student is, so if you figure it out, keep it to yourself and don't engage. The student will likely know who you are, and she knows better than to approach you. Start the first class by letting the professor know who you are and why you're there, just in case they don't see my memo. Any questions?"

Besides what have I gotten myself into and why did I listen to George, "no. I understand."

〈◇〉

Notetaking is one of the easiest jobs a school offers. No dirty dishes, carrying sacks of food, or delivering baskets of mail to offices. The job requires that I sit, listen, write, and maybe learn. I sit in a corner, the back, take a few mechanical pencils out of my backpack, and write out a heading with the course name, date, and my name. Students enter and filter to seats without looking around much. They know where they chose to plant themselves for the semester and, as people thrive on routine and habit, return to the same seats each class, likely using the same or similar seats in all their classes without realizing it. As the professor begins writing note outlines on the board and as the room is about half-full, I hear a click-tak-click-tak like a metronome in the hallway and I imagine that whatever makes that clicking must scan or tap back and forth. Sometimes it sounds flatter, duller, like a stick on a rock. Other times metallic and hollow, like a doorbell hammer striking a chime that's pressed and muted against the doorbell housing. The clicking rounds the corner and enters the room. The girl with the red flannel from the student center last week, face pointing upward slightly and her right ear slightly forward, walks down my aisle and stops at my desk, her cane click-taks against the legs of desks and chairs, gently, and she nods as she takes steps, likely counting each step to know when she reaches her seat. At my seat her cane hits my foot with a soft, dull, 'tud' sound.

"That's usually where I sit." She faces forward at the rear wall, not looking my direction. Her voice is restrained projection, strong and in any other setting stentorian. Her tone carries no hint of a capability for softness or delicacy. She sounds like strong, sustained wind against an old door. She wears a different flannel, white and blue striped, jeans with patterns decorated into the pockets with metal studs, and the same brown boots. Over her shoulder she carries an old, tan rucksack with a single remaining strap. Her hair is tied back in a loose braid held with a black fabric band. I notice, her nose free of her aviator sunglasses, a scar above her left nostril, a smooth arc of skin that look like a deep cut left to heal unstitched. She folds her cane into a bundle and the wrist loop wraps around it.

"Just a sec, I'll move. I'm sorry." I grab my notebook and move over a seat. "All yours."

"I know." She sits in the seat, and wiggles a bit, seemingly uncomfortable. "You're very warm, notetaker. What's your name?"

… How does she know? "I, uh, I'm not supposed to engage with you, Dr. Peters said."

"Class hasn't started. You're just another college student for two more minutes." Her face points in my direction, but her eyes, eyelids closed, point slightly past and over my shoulder. Her head moves slightly and, at first, seemingly randomly. But no, I realize, when her right ear turns to the point where chalk meets blackboard when the professor starts writing, that she hears very well, and that her head had moved not randomly but with the undulation of room sound as it grows and lives within the space. Her head points reflexively at a dropped book a few rows over, again moving to a pencil rolling down a desk a few seats away. Her ears drink sound like camels at an oasis; she knows more about this room and what's going on than I do.

"Oh, um, okay. I'm Merak."

"Like the star?" She points her face back in my direction, mostly, and tilts her head.

"I was named after a model of car."

"That car was probably named after the star then. Merak is one of the stars in the Big Dipper. But you pronounce it wrong. The star is ME-ruck."

Well that's the first I've heard of that. "I, is it?"

From the front of the room, "Class, let's pick up from Friday's lecture on plastic deformation in sedimentary rocks. As you'll recall, tectonic pressure during early-stage rock formation when sedimentary layers had not yet hardened…"

She leans over toward me and says quietly, "I'm Amber, and I recognized your voice."

‹◊›

Engineering 455, hydrogeology and hydroengineering in Karst regions, whatever that means, meets in a room laid out identical to the other geology room. Amber sits in the same seat and unpacks a tape recorder and braille textbook from her rucksack. I should sit on the far side of the room: Dr. Peters said not to engage. My legs move me like a train on tracks, helpless to choose a direction, able only to advance along a predetermined route to an unavoidable destination, and I sit next to Amber.

"Merak, are you taking notes in two of my classes?" Amber's voice is different now, not calm, still filled with a force, but smooth like oiled gears.

What? "Oh, hey, Amber, I just thought I might say hi before class."

"You're not supposed to engage me." Amber opens her rucksack and puts her cane into it, and the side of her face hints at a wry smile, the sort carried by a mischief-maker actively causing some mischief.

"Well, I mean, I'm just another student for three more minutes."

Amber leans back in her seat, turns her whole body to face me, and, yes, she smiles. She leans her shoulders back and rotates her head, hair tips gliding around her shoulders like distant rain from a single cloud crossing a valley.

"You're curious how I knew you sat next to me. You may use more fabric softener than needed."

I look forward at the blackboard a moment, mouth slipping from smile to neutral, then look at Amber. "Well, um, yes."

"So tell me about you. If you're going to take notes for me, I want to know more about you."

"I'm a computer major, networking and hardware. I graduate in forty-nine weeks, not that I'm counting. I build machines, set up the physical structures of networks."

"Any plans for the Fourth?"

"I'm going to have burgers and beers with my friend George."

We sit in silence for a moment. "Do you always struggle a bit with conversation?"

"Sometimes. I can get stuck in my head and forget what I was about to say."

"Well, let me help. I'm a geology major. I also graduate in forty-nine weeks, and I am counting. I specialize in mineralogy and studying what mineral compositions tell us about the subsurface. No one ever knows to ask the benefit of that, but it's used in mining and other fields to find precious metals, oil, and sometimes underground water. For the holiday weekend I'll probably hang out at Campus Lake Beach and listen to an audiobook. I hope your notes are better than your conversation."

Well, of course. "I think so. I just try to copy everything and describe all the diagrams on the boards. I'll be right back. I have to let the professor know who I am." I stand and, first, "Amber, we'll catch up some more after class?" Amber sits in her chair, smiles and happily agrees, puts her hair into a braid and adjusts the buttons on her shirt sleeve to no benefit. She undoes the end button, re-does it, runs her fingers along the seams on her sleeves and the hem of the collar. When the course starts, I take the notes, draw the diagrams, write the student questions and answers, and occasionally look over at Amber. She moves a pen in her hands, around her fingers, clicks the tip out and in, and gestures and slides it as the professor talks.

◇

When I was a cub scout, this must be ten, twelve years ago now, our troop held a volunteer event designed to teach us the value of helping others. Our troop leader decided we should, before our July Fourth troop picnic, visit a hospice and spend time with, and cheer up, the residents. She meant well. Our youth and the sheltered life suburbia delivers meant none of us understood that hospices mean the residents had limited time and no possible recovery, so we volunteered with the tact of wrecking balls. My assignment: room A-22. The room number, mounted in black plastic characters next to an unilluminated red lamp, stays in my memory clear as snowmelt water though everything in the building leading to that number rests now behind layers of memory sediment, hidden like a lakebed under moonlight. I remember the hallway's musty smell, old linens and illness tinged with sharp, nostril-destroying tones of disinfectants. I remember the room entry, door closed, an industrial door with a long bar-type knob, horizontal scratches in the paint just below the knob. I looked down the hallway; all the rooms had the scratches, the black lettering, the red lamps. I wondered why everyone needed red porch lights.

I knocked quietly and opened the door. "Mr. Garret?" I peeked my head into the room. The hospice had smelled musty, but nothing prepared me for the room. The room smelled of spoiled chicken and a harsh, burning, painfully sharp smell I didn't recognize. The room, quite large, defined by darkness from the drawn blinds and dimmed lights, felt empty and seemed to echo. The room seemed drowned in permanent night, the only clue that the sun existed at all arrived as thin light lines dust-drawn in the air and stretching from holes in the drapes to small ovals on the floor. I drew the blinds, opened all four windows, and a breeze drew in fresh air that, in some minutes, helped the smell begin to dissipate.

Machines kept the man alive. Only his face escaped the sheets, which clutched his body, swathed like a mummy. They were tucked tightly around his frame and created a topography of his bones. Some large, round lumps on his legs and chest, apparent like the texture on a globe, stood in a relief far different to the harsh angles of his skeleton. A monitor on the wall beeped quietly in a slow rhythm. Tubes from his nose connected to a breathing machine made mechanical, forced breaths with a quiet clunk and a wheeze-like air movement as an accordion filled and slowly emptied air into the man's nose. His face: loose skin thin like rice paper hanging on a wooden frame, mostly pale, cavernous cheeks with dark bruises and a handful of spots of thin and sparse black and white hair. His face's bruises looked like cooled lava solidified mid-way as it traveled toward the floor. Though his skin hung loose on his face, it lacked many of the wrinkles of old age.

"Mr. Garret, my name is Merak Snyder. I'm a cub scout from Troop 78. We're here to talk to some patients today."

I sat for what seemed like minutes or more but was, probably, five or six seconds. No response. No movement. No eyelid shake. The room held almost nothing aside from the machines, the bed, the man, a nightstand, and a chair. No flowers or cards sat on the nightstand, only a tube of some yellow lotion and an old book, Huckleberry Finn, finger-worn purple-edged pages, spine-creased, and dog-eared throughout. The mechanical lungs breathed their thunk-and-wheeze; the monitor beeped slowly. I picked up the book and paged the purple edges to the last dog ear.

"I'm going to guess this is where you left off, Mr. Garret," I said, flipping the pages to the final dog ear, fifteen from the end. "It looks like you've read this a bunch, but maybe need to finish it?" Outside the room in the hallway, our troop leader looked in quickly, gave me a thumbs up, face a wide smile.

I started reading from the first full paragraph on the left page. As I read, the machine beeped, sometimes faster, sometimes back to the old cadence. I glanced up at Mr. Garret on occasion and sometimes his eyes pointed at the ceiling through slit-open eyelids. When the machine beeped faster, his eyes opened slightly. Sometimes his mouth made a dry wheeze, not sounding painful or forced. Dying must be painful until the end; then it must become pleasant, like falling asleep and realizing you're having a good dream, only it doesn't end. Reading the final pages, with which I struggled some, took the entire visitation. When my troop leader returned, she gave us five minutes to finish the last page. When I closed the book, I looked at Mr. Garret, his head stationary to the ceiling, eyes turned to me, dark-pupiled and wide open with near-gray whites and a stare that felt like icicles on my back. I dropped the book and stood, the chair falling over backwards and slamming into the tile floor with force and the sound of a meteor. The noise destroyed the rhythmic pattern of silence, beeping, wheezing, and thunking that had accompanied the reading. Mr. Garret met my eyes again, this time eyelids lower and gaze softer, his stare feeling like a dryer-fresh blanket. Now, some years later, I assume his looks were fear of again being alone and then gratitude for the stranger who read to him. My troop leader, hearing the clamor of the book and chair, ran into the room to see me standing next to the bed. She must have assumed that Mr. Garret had died. I kept eye contact with the old man, feeling the moment's importance like a pair of hands on my shoulders, yet unable to understand it, and after a handful of seconds the beeping slowed and returned to normal and the man's eyes looked up at the ceiling and closed. I set the book back on the table by the bed while my troop leader set the chair up. Two nurses stood in the doorway.

‹◊›

The copier in the student center makes a soft thunk and a mechanical wheeze with each page as the copy bar hits the end of the rails and the motor pulls the rubber drive belt over tensioning wheels. Each cycle takes three seconds – twenty pages per minute an old, finger-dirty sticker says. It takes my notes from a feeder, one page at a time, copies each page, and then spits them into a chaotic stack. When it finishes, I staple the notes and put them in my mailbox. The originals stay in my folder for later reference, if needed.

At a table on the other side of the room, Amber sits with a tape deck and headphones. This is my third week taking notes for her classes and we've been pleasant and conversant before and often after each class. The general process after my work is someone takes my notes and records what they and my diagram and process descriptions say. They also type the notes in braille. I watch, every day when I copy my notes, her fingers slide over pages as she listens to the recorded notes. The times watching her, the five or seven minutes that I get to do this twice a week, have become a periodic and distracting happiness.

As the copier finishes, Amber raises her hand. The kid at the desk says, "Amber, yes?"

"These notes are awful. Get me Dr. Peters. I want him fired. This is three weeks now and they're incomprehensible."

A rock falls from my throat to gut and tears apart my lungs as it passes; this is failure; this is me. Dr. Peters, hearing Amber, comes out of her office with a sigh. As she does, another notetaker, a blonde-haired and somewhat-short boy with particularly young features and the general, but slight, plumpness typical of sophomores who added some weight their freshman year, walks to the copier.

"Done?" he asks while he roots around in a messenger bag for a notebook.

"Yeah, sorry." I step aside, sighing that I'm about to lose my beer and pizza money. The other notetaker sets his notes on the platen, Geology 435.

Dr. Peters stands behind the chair across from Amber, arms crossed with exhaustion bred from impatience and repeated frustration. "Tell me what's wrong."

"This notetaker has been taking notes for three weeks. They're consistently incorrect, lack detail, and are abjectly terrible. The other guy needs to do these."

"I can't just assign like that."

"You can. You need to find a notetaker who can do his job. Just fire the guy who does 435 and assign Merak."

"Excuse me, what?" asks Dr. Peters. Coincidentally, I have the same question.

The tutor next to me stops and looks up at the pair at the table. "What?" The notetaker picks up his notebook, flips a page, and the copier thunks and whines when he pushes the copy button.

"Taylor, is that you, my 435 notetaker?" Her voice is full-power, stentorian and shaking those of us in the room, indifferent to the others studying around us, like a buffalo stampede.

"Amber, you're not supposed to know who they are," Dr. Peters says with patience, but turning and looking at the wall, her jaw square, stretched lips pressed slim.

"Dr. Peters, the problem with Taylor is that he doesn't care at all about this. Merak at least does, and it shows in his work. I want him taking notes in all my classes," her voice slows as she says this, calmer slightly, but still overpowering the copier, "if he can."

"I just don't really get geology, Amber," Taylor says.

"Amber, Taylor cares, and he's doing his best." Dr. Peters looks at Taylor. Taylor's expression: horror; his mouth hangs open and his breath smells of cheese crackers and fruit-flavored pop. He glances at me and then at Amber and then at Dr. Peters. He has a rock tumbling from his head to his gut and, right now, it is mid-chest and wreaking havoc.

"Taylor, you're fired," Amber says turning around to face us, pointing a trembling index finger. Her voice shakes and she points somewhat off to his side.

"Amber, you can't fire your tutors," Dr. Peters slams her hand on the table so hard the books on it bounce. "I apologize for being angry just then."

"Taylor, describe the color purple for me," Amber says, still facing us. She turns her chair and brushes her hair behind her ears, takes off her metal-rimmed aviator sunglasses, eyelids pressed but not squeezed shut, and she rubs the bridge of her nose.

"What?" Taylor asks.

"Describe ... purple ... for ... me."

"Amber, what does this have to do with anything?" Dr. Peters asks.

18

"It's, I dunno, halfway between red and blue?"

Amber turns to face Dr. Peters. "He can't take good notes because he can't put himself in my position. He just described a color with other colors to someone who has never seen color, or seen anything at all. I bet you that if Merak were here he could do better."

"I'm here." Dr. Peters drops her head, sets her hands on the back of a chair, and looks at the table. She hoped I would stay quiet. I don't know why I didn't.

Amber turns and faces me, her cheeks flushed slightly, maybe with embarrassment. Dr. Peters mumbles something about not knowing who the notetakers are or who they're taking notes for.

"It's like the texture of a soft fleece blanket, but a cool blanket, like it's been in a closet for a week waiting to be used, not fresh out of the dryer. Purple is the taste of grape pop becoming one with your tongue in fizzy happiness, and the way the sweetness and flavor dissipate almost immediately. Purple is the sound of crickets as a fresh and cool summer's night breeze wraps around your face and hair, taking the day's heat and humidity away." What did I just say and where did that come from?

Amber's hands on the table's edge loosen, the left dropping to the side of her seat, guiding her as she sits slowly into it. She slouches, takes a corner of her lower lip under her canine, face red and a few sweat drops on her forehead. She runs her right fingers along the plastic bead on the table's side. "He gets it." Amber's voice is mellowed, has become the hoof-flattened soil after a stampede. "Everything he described I can feel and sense. That's why he's a good notetaker, because we talk before and after class and we like each other and he can put himself in my mind and he writes notes that I follow. Give Merak 435, please."

"I can't just –"

"No need, Dr. Peters. Minimum wage ain't worth this." Taylor drops his notebook at the front desk without copying all the pages and walks out the door, messenger bag in front of him, zipping it as he steps, fast enough to mis-step and let the inside edges of his shoes scrape together. He slings his bag over his shoulders and strikes his hand downward at the air in front him, "stupid, stupid, stupid" under his breath. I think everyone tries to do and be their best with the tools they have. We fail or succeed, and, if we listen to the lessons both outcomes have, improve. Taylor and I have the same lesson: we work for and with others the best when we try to understand their perceptions and perspectives.

Dr. Peters looks back and forth at the both of us, a thick vein at her hairline pulses out and in rapidly, two or maybe three times a second, flexing and distorting a liver spot slightly. "Please just pretend that you two don't know each other when you're here."

2
Brown

I don't really have a head for understanding geology. Rocks, layers, underground rivers and lakes, oceans growing and receding, pressure and heat changing rocks' structure and nature, metals floating on metals and rocks floating on rocks, and the scale of mass movement over many eons exceeds what I can understand. Our world exists in a time its own, our brief moment not even an instant to a mountain or ocean. Geology, as timelapse, shows a quickly changing, ever-mutating land and ocean orb alive in uncontrolled chaos like desert sand in the wind. Nothing stops it and, for all we do, Earth doesn't care that we exist. I sit in Amber's courses, write geological processes, mineral formations, and how to read the earth's past, and I feel tiny, inconsequential, unimportant, full of wonder, and terrified by my meaninglessness.

Over the past weeks getting to know Amber in ever-longer after-class chit-chats and hallway conversations, I've not learned geology. I have learned the topography of her expressions, the way her face forms emotions, her joy for learning and trying things, and I am crushing. Notetaker rules be damned.

Four minutes before class, as always, Amber's cane starts its rhythmic click-tak click-tak back and forth. The regularity and cadence calming. Soon, she will sit next to me, say my name, smile in my direction, and spin a ballpoint pen in her fingers. In the entry, her fingers linger on the braille room number. She knows this is the right space, but checks every class. She steps steadily forward, cane close in front, which she told me last week avoids tripping people in crowded spaces. At her row she turns, cane tapping the desk legs on each side; she aligns with the middle and walks confidently to her desk. Amber reaches out her hand, finds the desk corner, step-turn-sits into it, and sets her rucksack between her boots.

Amber folds her cane and secures it with the elastic loop that pokes out the handle. Its folds like a tent pole, compact, and she stashes it in her rucksack's water bottle pocket. "Hey, Merak," she says, scooting a bit in her seat to center herself. She smiles large, and warmly, bright teeth, one canine slightly misaligned. Her lip, a bit dry, catches on it when her smile ends.

"You knew I was here. I must still be using too much detergent," I say, and Amber smiles with her lips only, cheeks and eyes slack as she faces down a bit. "How are things?"

"Things are good." Amber pulls the ballpoint out of her rucksack and spins it between her fingers like a magician with a coin. She taps her left pinky finger on her desk, her shirt's cuff rolled back and my eyes trace the lines of her rounded veins as they move from the spaces between her hand's tendons to where wrist meets muscle and they disappear into her arm.

We sit in the quiet and I tap my pencil on the desk. "Any plans tonight?"

"Going to the game. You?"

"Was just gonna grab a beer or two at Brumby's, my buddy tends the bar there. Who are we playing?" Amber tilts her head slightly as I say this.

"No idea. I just like to go, get caught up in the game. I bring earplugs, though. The games are very loud. Well, I was hoping we'd have time to talk about notes some after the game. Maybe another night?"

"Doing anything tomorrow? We could grab brunch."

The pen and pinky-tapping stop. Amber points her face in my direction. I, also, am confused by that question. "Are you asking me to come over tonight?"

Am I? Maybe. That would be nice. "Oh gosh, no, I just meant we could grab brunch, maybe Mary Anne's, catch up, still have our afternoons free. Maybe just get coffee, not even brunch, if you want. I

22

know their coffee isn't great so maybe just a coffee shop instead," I backpedal.

Amber sits back and looks at me, expression blank as the chalkboard before class. Her hair, braided into pig tails, rests above and in front of her shoulders. "Is this a date?"

I stammer and stutter and manage "I had hoped, but it doesn't have to be if you don't want it to be."

"No no," she says, "it definitely is. I've been hanging out after all our classes to give you this chance. Honestly, I started to think you were gay." Amber crosses her left leg over her right as she speaks, puts her arms on her desk and chair back and twists her shoulders and hips a bit. Her shirt and jeans flex and move, fabric weave adapting to her shifting curves as she cracks her back. "I want you to do me a favor, though. I liked how you described the color purple a couple of weeks ago. Tomorrow, will you describe brown?"

"I won't lie, I'm confused a bit but let me see what I can do. I'll try. But why?"

Amber shrugs, "I just liked purple. I want to see what you can do if I don't put you on the spot."

My expression, I feel it in the muscle tension across my face and cheeks, embodies terror. "I'll try."

‹◊›

George sets a Killian's Red bottle by my hand; he knows me. "Quiet tonight."

George rests his arm on the bar top. "Game ends in an hour. Ninety minutes till the tips start rolling in, less if we're losing by a lot."

I suck down the fog at the bottle top, wipe the bottle's mouth with a napkin, and take a sip. "George, so I told you that I took that job you told me about, but did I tell you the three classes I signed up for, they're all for the same girl."

"You signed up for three classes? So you can afford to buy your beers now?" George picks up a dirty glass and starts washing it in front of me with a rag that, honestly, won't leave that glass any cleaner. "And a girl, you say? This always makes your stories interesting. Tell me about this girl, Merak."

"Well, her name is Amber."

George's rag stops a second then continues. "Go on. Sounds good so far."

"She's feisty."

"Oh this keeps getting better. You could use a feisty one." George tilts the bottom on the glass out and I click my beer bottle on it.

"She's a geology and geophysical engineering double-major."

"Smarter than you, too."

"Dangerously."

"Do tell."

"She has this really good sense of what I'm thinking."

"Your body language gives everything away."

"She's blind."

George stops washing the glass and sets it down. "You're taking notes for Blind Amber?"

"You know her?" Of course he knows her.

George glances around the bar, "Merak, the bartender knows everyone. She's a good chick. You can't really interact with her as a notetaker, but you'd click."

"We have a date tomorrow morning." Record scratch, time stop, and my mind narrates: 'you're probably wondering how I got here' as the seven other people in the bar turn and stare, or so it feels. The mirror doesn't lie; no record, time moves, and no one cares but George.

"That's very against the rules for notetakers."

"How do you know all this stuff?"

"Merak, I've lived here almost fifteen years and spent ten of them enrolled in classes. I know this town, the university, the people, and types of people who live here better than anyone you will ever meet. Now that I have a degree – and thank you again very much for all your help with that – as soon as I have a job somewhere else I'm gone and this town is going to lose a legacy and, if I do say so myself, easily the most important person ever to live here." George sets his balled hands on his hips as he says this, a casual grin cutting open his clean-shaven cheeks and chin. We both know this town, in days, forgets everyone who leaves: no one is a legacy.

"Well," I say, "tell me about Blind Amber and why do you call her Blind Amber?"

"To differentiate her from Redhead Amber and Short Amber."

That was simple. "Does she know –"

"Oh yeah, it was her idea; actually, the Ambers came up with their nicknames. So you two have a date. Dinner?"

"Brunch."

"Meeting her there or waking her up?"

"Dude. Really? Mary Anne's, if you must know."

George looks at the glass, sets the rag in a box behind the counter and grabs a clean one. He rinses the glass with hot water and uses a soapy brush to clean it. "I must know. They have good coffee, you know. Look," he says looking at the glass, "that's exciting. Like I said, she's a nice chick, bit of a rough edge but a good person. You guys will have a great time. I hope you hit it off well. She's cute, too. And not like that fake cute, but that farm-girl cute, the kind that comes from the confidence of hard work. If it goes well, she's going to make you a thigh man."

Thigh man? That's a thing? "Yeah, she's very cute. I, you know what I noticed was cutest?"

25

George shakes his head.

"I got to see her smile on that first day we took notes, a bunch of times, she seems really happy. But this one time, I don't know after a handful of classes, no idea what I said, she smiled and it was so much different. I don't know what it's called. Happiness lines seems a good name. She has these little creases that fan out from the bridge of her nose with big, happy, nose-scrunching smiles. I legit forgot to breathe."

"Don't just fall in love with a cute face and smile."

"I won't. So, here's what I need help with," I tell George about Taylor and the color purple.

"Huh," George holds the glass up to an overhead light, looks through it and, satisfied, sets it on a stack of identical glasses. He starts another.

"So when she asks me to describe the color purple I'm just thinking 'well, it's like halfway between blue and red.'"

"But you didn't say that."

"No. I said," I pause and look at my reflection behind George. Mirror-me seems curious, intent, as though listening to another version of his life. "I honestly don't know what I said. Something about it feeling like velvet and I forget what else. No idea where it came from."

George sets the other glasses in place, grabs a plastic cutting board and knife, and starts smash-cutting lime wedges, which, after just a handful of limes, rest in a puddle of pale-yellow juice. "So, what did she say?"

"Something about my answer showing that I was actually focused on her needs. I was just like a shined deer, man, and I don't remember exactly what she said, but something like that. You know what I do remember, she went from being mad to somber, like a switch flipped. It was like she felt like she was missing out on something."

"Well, she wants a date with you. Must like you a bit. You seem to affect her."

"She wants me to describe the color brown next."

George scrapes the lime wedges off the board with the back of his knife and puts them in a small metal bin with a clear lid. The bin is in a larger, longer bin with separate spaces for fruit slices, olives, and tiny onions. "Well, do a thing well and people want you to do more of it. Hit me with your description." George wipes the knife down and looks at me.

"I don't know. It's mud and delivery trucks. I don't have anything else."

"What did you do when described purple, even the bit you told me?"

"I have no idea how I thought of that."

"That's not the question," George leans in, elbows on the bar top, forearms crossed mid-way, his eye wrinkles form deep crevices as he locks eyes with me, wide-squinting like judgement. "What you did was describe a thing in concepts she could understand – touch, maybe smell and sound or whatever. So maybe think of some things that the color brown means to you, your senses other than sight, your emotions about it, if brown can even stir emotions. If you do well, she's gonna ask you again." George pivots his left arm, hand straight out and resting on the counter in front of me, tapping up and down in time with his words, "So have a formula – touch, taste, smell, sound, and maybe some emotions or memories." He stands back, arms in front, gesturing in a slow, broad arc. "Talk about those things and who knows maybe it works. Your foot's in the door, kick it open."

"Dude. I'm forty-four weeks away from a degree in computer networking – not that I'm counting."

"Not that you're counting," George concurs.

"I'm not a writer. I'm gonna fail."

"Yes you are. Not because you can't – because you decided you'll fail." George washes the knife and starts wedging lemons. "If you decide before you try," I mouth the words as he says them, "that you'll fail, then you will. If you decide to give it your best, you have a chance of succeeding." George starts smash-cutting four lemons into thin wedges.

Two years ago, George, pretending he thought my fake ID was real, told me he wanted to finish college. He had a year of computer networking courses – the same courses I'm completing this year. Every day after class he and I met up, here or at his apartment, and studied. He'd 'pay' me with free beers or a crazy-named, never-the-same-twice, homemade burger. Two months in, when he wanted to quit, I said those exact sentences to him. "Alright, I'll give it a shot."

"Just, you know, this sounds silly, but don't be super nervous, man. She wouldn't have asked you out if she didn't like you. So just go with what you can do. She'll tell you if it's good or not. And who knows, maybe this leads somewhere good for you both. I'm pulling for you."

"I didn't tell you she asked me out."

"I know you, and I know Amber. You have a comfort zone and you only show interest in girls who show interest in your first. You're a girl-wimp. Don't protest; it's true." George scrapes the lemons into their small, metal container, all while looking directly at me with a large, ridiculous, 'I can do this easily' grin. Half the lemons fall on the floor.

<‹›>

My dorm room overlooks Campus Lake. The downside is that it shares a bathroom with the resident assistant Jesse. The upside is that Jesse and I, along with my long-time friend, the brother I chose, and roommate Rick, are good friends and drinking buddies. Rick and Jesse sit on my bed playing a racing video game. Unlike most dorms, instead of four people sharing a suite, because Jesse has a room to himself, only three of us share the space. The dorm's walls, cinderblock painted each year in a new, thick coating of institution-special off-white, bounce sound like the inside of a drum. We adorned our walls in posters not so much because we like the photos or hate the walls, but the posters cover old towels that we hung to absorb our echoing voices. Rick hung reproduction posters of famous 1970s concerts and tours. I hung some large prints I had made of some photos I took some years ago driving through the desert southwest. I hung a photo of the famous bend in the Grand Canyon; one of an Indian girl – I forget her name – standing, placid-faced, in front of her family's diner; another of a cactus with plastic bags and a long length of bubble wrap stuck in the thorns and blown sideways by the wind; and lastly one of a brush-headed boy, shirt tied around his waist and squatting next to a hole in water-wave rocks. Rick and I sleep perpendicular with my bed underneath his on a loft. Our desks face the room's large windows that look outside, out at the lake, at a small concrete pier used for fishing, swimming, or standing quietly and listening to the lake. The lake's water, murky, dark, oil-slicked in places from parking lot runoff, churns in the evening with bluegill feeding on the water skeeters and mosquitoes that dance across and hover just above the water's surface. The lake, shored by cedar trees whose knees reach into the shallow areas, provides homes for cicadas, birds, crickets, frogs, and other things that create an evening symphony of uncoordinated, yet somehow melodic and meandering night music. The cicadas, especially during their active months, create a sound that undulates like waves gently lifting a boat up and down, rhythmically, peacefully.

Outside, that rhythmic sound, quieter than at its peak some weeks ago, backgrounds a gentle breeze that tickles the treetops and brushes leaves into each other. I realize it a bit, but not deeply, that as the sound ebbs and flows I slide my pencil eraser along the desktop in time with it, subconscious, automatic. The breeze brought into our room through the open windows carries the lake scent, a scent with a base of cedar wood and leaves; a sharp, not-quite-acrid overtone of wet mud; and faint hints of the black, decomposing biomass muck that hides underneath lakebeds. The lake smell reminds me of a fishing trip, an old wood boathouse, and the way that old cabins trap decades of fireplace smoke in the walls, drapes, and furniture. I stop my pencil and look out the window. That is brown: that view, those smells, the sounds.

Mary Anne's bustles with the activity of any popular brunch restaurant the morning after a night of town-wide drinking. The diners mumble and murmur, drink strong coffee not caring that it tastes like old plastic and cigarette-ash. The air smells of bacon, most strongly, with a hint behind the bacon of Mary Anne's house-made hot sauce, a slightly sour, thin red sauce that tastes of tomatoes, garlic, onions, apple cider vinegar, and floral hot peppers. The diner only serves brunch, five till one, four days a week and some holidays. The tables, original from when the diner opened, Formica with a boomerang pattern and ribbed metal fascia, rest, some propped with shims, between two, three, or four chairs, much newer, metal and slightly industrial with red-vinyl-covered padding. Mary Anne's walls, in places wood paneled and in others mono-colored drywall, display flags and pennants for the successes of the university's and local high schools' past sports teams. The oldest, from 1964, has hung in place since the year the diner opened. Mary Anne sold the diner, retired, and moved somewhere back in the early nineties, but her name and recipes remain, apparently pretty well untouched, by the couple who bought the diner from her.

I arrived a bit early to get my name on the list and peek at the clipboard and notebook by the front door as names are called. In time, only one group is ahead of me and for a moment I worry that I arrived too early. But, perfect timing, Amber's cane taps flat and dull on the sidewalk a block away. She keeps her cane pointed in front of her, tapping and sweeping the sidewalk. Each rightward sweep, the cane brushes against and stops at the concrete joint between the sidewalk and gutter. She uses that joint to stay a couple of feet from the street, safe from gutter-tripping into the street and clear of a fire hydrant, signs, and parking meters.

Amber, hair back in a ponytail, braided like a horse whip, loose-banded and adorned in fly-aways, moves her head sideways and up and down in a rhythm as she walks, and I notice, now that I can watch her walk some distance, that the movements follow a pattern, and that she must count the times she repeats the pattern rather than her steps to track how far she walks. She wears blue-mirror-lensed aviator sunglasses and her cheeks have some light rouge, lips shine with pink lip gloss. Amber's face is cute, the kind that welcomes a stranger's greeting, shaped kind of like a wide arrowhead with a blunted tip, a strong and straight jaw with defined and inward-bowed cheeks, her philtrum mirrors a small counterpart on the tip of her nose, and, when she smiles, creases at the corners of her mouth hint at the happy face she will have in some decades. She wears a lightweight brown shirt with a herringbone pattern woven into the fabric and blue slacks. For the first time, she's not wearing boots but instead black flats with brown socks. She stops in front of Mary Anne's and feels around the area with her cane to see if any benches in front of the diner have space.

"Heya," I say.

"Merak!" Amber's face brightens into a smile, her cheeks rise and the slight red rogue in them pops in the sun, the happiness ridges along her nose bridge pop into relief and I reflexively gulp. I could spend my whole life looking at her being happy. She pulls her cane apart at the middle union and folds it in half, repeating to collapse it fully and then she wraps the elastic loop on the top of the cane around it. "I hope you haven't been waiting long," she says, even though she's a few minutes early.

"Only two or three minutes," I lie, "long enough to get our names on the list."

"Well, perfect," she says. We stand quietly for a few seconds. "Lovely morning, isn't it?"

A few clouds move across the sky, pushed leisurely by summer winds, and the air carries the hints of today's coming afternoon humidity. I concur that it is, in fact, a lovely morning, and as I do the host calls out my name.

"Oh that was fast," Amber says. "I thought they usually have like an hour wait on Saturdays. I'd been looking forward to sitting out here talking to you for a while."

Goddamnit, Merak. "We ... lucked out?" I lie. Amber pretends for a second to accept this, her lips turned upwards but flat, a disappointment smile, and I turn to walk to the door. Amber stands where she was. "Oh, oh yeah, of course. Um, how do we do this?"

"It's pretty narrow between the tables, right?"

"Yes."

"Turn around and stand in front of me. I'll put my hands on your shoulders. Try not to stop suddenly. Slow down as we get to the table."

I do and Amber puts her hands straight into the back of my shoulder blades.

"You are a bit taller than I thought," she says, which makes me smile. Amber takes a step toward me, reaches up and puts her hands on my shoulders. Her thumbs and index fingers land inside my shirt collar for a moment before she repositions them. "Are you wearing a blazer? This feels like blazer fabric and shoulder pads."

I nod.

"Merak, I felt you nod. If I weren't holding your shoulders, that would be useless to me."

"Ha ha, sorry. Reflex. I am wearing a blazer."

"It's nice of you to dress up. You didn't have to. I mean, I wouldn't have known either way."

"I know, but what would that say about me?"

Amber's hands slide inward and, for a moment, rest on the bare skin at the back of my neck, linger there and my spine tingles from my lumbar up with endorphin joy. My veins pulse. Her hands and fingers are warm, skin a bit tough but not calloused or rough. She slides her hands sideways and wraps her fingers over my shoulders till her fingertips touch

32

my collar bones. The muscles in my back tremor slightly, reflexively; this is the first time she's actually touched me, and she giggles when the muscle shake passes through my shoulders to my neck. She presses her hands slightly and steps closer.

The host looks at the seating chart, across the room at the seat she picked for us near the counter, and then looks around the restaurant. In the back, another table opens. We wind through tables, the alleyways of crowded brunch diners everywhere, ever-moving and changing paths that shift like the Labyrinth as people stand, groups rotate, and tables are pushed together or moved apart for larger or smaller groups. This must terrify Amber, knowing that the way we entered will differ from when we leave. At the table, I stop slowly and Amber walks out from behind me, dragging her right hand down my shoulder to lower back as she does. Amber faces me. "Merak, do you need some guidance on being a gentleman?"

"Oh, yes, sometimes," I walk around behind her, pull her chair from the table, put my right hand on her shoulder and guide her to her seat, which in a quieter room would cushion-wheeze as she sat. Amber feels the table's edge and, lifting and scooting her chair, turns it in to the table.

The host looks at her and says "I have to bus this table quickly. I'll be right back to clean it." Amber thanks her.

"And thank you for getting here early enough to get our names on the list. We have plenty of time after this to talk more, I hope."

I smile at her.

"Merak?"

"Oh, sorry, we do. I was just smiling."

"Well, that's not gonna work. I need you to speak your smile." She says and her lips pull upward slightly. "We'll work on that."

"I was happy to get here a bit early. It gave me a chance to have a cup of coffee and relax."

"Oh, is my date a bit nervous?"

"Maybe just a bit."

The host removes the last group's mimosa flutes and coffee mugs, plates of biscuit crumbs in gravy, potatoes and sausage, and French toast all scraped as clean as possible without the help of a tongue. Few, if any, plates here ever go back to the kitchen with food.

"So are you nervous because I'm blind or because I'm cute or because I asked you to describe the color brown?"

My head rocks sideways a couple of times, enough that I suspect Amber feels it in the table. "Not that you're blind. Yes a bit that you're cute. A good deal more about what I came up with for brown. Mostly because I don't want to mess this date up." I tap my left fingers on the tabletop in a rhythm from pinky to index. "I – cards on the table – I have had a crush on you for a while and didn't know if you felt the same so I'm nervous that I may be more into you than you are to me."

"You've had a crush on me since our second class. It's okay. Same here. I like that you were willing, just then, to tell me what you're nervous about. I'm nervous that you might think dating a blind girl is too much work, or," Amber exhales and inhales, "that you just want to experience it. I'm nervous that if this goes bad then I lose the best notetaker I've had." She lets her head tilt to left, up again, left, an repeats the pattern a few times. "I'm terrified that if this goes well, I'll lose the best notetaker I've had."

Our waiter, too old to be a college student so definitely a townie, thin and as well aged as a sausage patty left under an old fridge for a week, walks to the table and asks if he can get us anything, maybe coffee, water, or mimosas to start, and we both order coffees. He sets a menu down in front of me and starts to set one in front of Amber before seeing her cane on her lap and stopping. "Oh, we don't have a braille menu. I'm sorry," he says, in a passing tone like a person commenting on a sidewalk crack.

"We'll manage," Amber says. She turns her head at me and smiles.

"You know what I hate," I say to Amber after the waiter leaves, "when people say 'I'm sorry.' Not all the time, but like that back there. It means they don't, won't, or can't understand someone or something."

"Was he a don't, won't, or can't?"

"Can't."

When our coffee arrives, I put it to my nose and quickly take it away; the stuff smells like a distant tire fire. I am a coffee snob, no reason to downplay that. I make good coffee and I judge harshly those who don't. I wish that were my biggest flaw. Mary Anne's coffee's cigarette ash taste comes from plastic instead of metal drip baskets. No cleaning fixes this because the plastic degrades in acidic coffee, from hot water, and because of alkaline dish soap. The plastic, as it breaks down, releases, like old brick mortar under a finger, chemicals into the hot, brewing coffee. The coffee carries an undertone of burned dirt, because the drip-maker's water spreader hasn't been cleaned for some time. Vanilla-flavored creamer helps mask the taste. The creamer separates, curdles a bit. The coffee-creamer swirl looks gray as my spoon does two laps around the cup. My upper lip curls downward as I sip it. Amber picks up her mug and sips it black. "They have good coffee here."

Oh dear. Previous summers at home I worked at a local coffee shop owned by my father's business partner. We roast our own beans in house, test the beans for flavor and color before selling, and use precise measures and temperatures for each cup. I have learned that I like city roast – heated to the first crack, the hardest roast to get right. When brewing coffee for our customers, the water must be 195 degrees. We burr-grind each cup or pot on the spot and the grinder must be set at different, specific coarseness settings for different brew types. Three for French press, four for the percolator, five for flat-bottom drips, seven for cone drips, and eight for Turkish and espresso. We check our filtered water output with dissolved metals readers to ensure water purity, and we wash many of the coffee-making components, such as steam wands and the water spreaders, in hot distilled water. I don't know if all that matters, but the coffee is truly good, I am truly spoiled, and the techniques I can use in my dorm for coffee lead to many compliments. I tell Amber just that I worked at a specialty coffee shop and agree that Mary Anne's has the town's best restaurant coffee.

"Some time when we hang out," she says, "you'll make me some coffee. I've never been to a really high-end shop. I'd like to see what the fuss is about."

I would like that, and I tell her. I would like to make it for her some morning, many mornings, but I leave this part out.

"So, while we wait for our food, I gave you some homework."

"You did. Want to just jump right in?"

Amber smiles, takes her coffee mug in both hands, brings it up to her mouth and takes a slow drink. "Coffee is brown, isn't it?" Her eyes are closed and when she takes the coffee away she tilts her face up and left slightly and nods.

"Brown is the color of playing cards with friends at sunset by a farm's fishing pond, trees on the far shore, some horses drinking the water, bugs flying over that water, fish eating water skeeters off the surface, crickets chirping in the grass. It's the tree leaves on the pond's far side brushing against each other in the breeze. It's the smell of fresh soil on your hands, of sweat and work on and in your skin. Brown is dew-wet sand, still warm from a day of absorbing the sun's heat. Brown is an old wood boat, retired and used in the garden for a planter box, and the way age has textured the grain until the paint peels up in long, thin pieces. It's wood-burning-fireplace smoke that's worked its way into a cabin's walls, carpet, blinds, and furniture over decades of winters. Brown is the happy memories of drinks and meals with a close friend, the pad of butter melting in hot gravy, and laughing at each others' anecdotes."

As I start describing brown, Amber sets her coffee down, holds the mug, the warmth transferring into her fingers. She leans back a bit, eyes closed, and smiles a flat, content smile. When I finish, she keeps smiling and it seems like minutes before she leans forward. "I had hoped you weren't done."

"I, uh, this was hard to put together as it was."

"Oh, I know. I would have just said something like 'it's a warm cup of coffee on a cold morning.' You really did better. Thank you."

"It's a fun thing to do."

"Good. I'll think of more fun things we can do." Amber smiles again and drinks her coffee. The mug is thick, off-white ceramic with black flecks like fancy vanilla ice cream. It narrows a bit in the middle and has a thick, but small, handle. Amber's hands wrap around the mug like her fingers are cold and she needs the coffee more for them than to wake up. Her nails are short, but smooth at the end, filed and buffed until the nail shines. An ex-girlfriend had a series of nail files she would use, sitting on the bed in her dorm room in the evenings, to form her nails and then polish and shine the surfaces. Every week she would sit and polish and shine. Amber's nails look similar, polished, shined, cared for. Reflexively, I dry-swallow looking at them.

Our waiter brings our meals – Amber ordered eggs benedict with crispy home fries. I ordered two sunny-side up eggs with an English muffin, hash browns, and a sausage patty. I start to make my own open-faced breakfast sandwich. Amber closes her eyes puts her head down slightly. I stop making my sandwich until she finishes. When Amber raises her head, she asks me to help her.

"Like with cutting your food?"

"What?" I asked the wrong question. "No, where is everything. Reference a clock face."

"Oh, yeah, of course. Home fries on the right, from about one to five. They look, by the way, incredible. Very crispy and fluffy. Then your benedicts are in the rest of the plate."

"Can you do me one favor, Merak? It's a pet peeve of mine. I'm not mad; I need you not to, if you can, use words like 'look' and 'see'."

Amber slides her hand onto and around the tabletop to find her napkin-wrapped silverware, unwraps the paper band and sets it by her plate, places the napkin on her lap, and uses the knife to feel out the height and shapes of the food. She cuts her first benedict in half and the yolk runs out of the egg and over the ham and English muffins, filling the muffin's voids and mixing with butter and hollandaise.

"I will try. It will take some time."

Amber nods and says she's patient, or at least will be with me. "You know, the first bite of every meal is always the best." Amber cuts a small piece of benedict, puts her knife next to it, and presses her fork through it. She traces the food on her fork with her knife before putting it in her mouth and chewing slowly, deliberately. "Your nose smells the food from the plate, then as it gets closer. Your tongue starts anticipating the flavor." Amber sets her silverware down on her plate, handles pointing outward. "And then, bam," she claps as she says this "the food hits your tongue and it tastes all the flavors it had anticipated. The rest of the meal, it's downhill after that. Your tongue, it knows what to expect and it gets kinda bored after a few bites. It's kind of like dating."

"So this is like the first bite, this date?"

"Oh goodness no. Purple, that was your first bite. I kinda know you now. I, my cards face up here, kind of like you, more than a crush. This is more like bite four or six – the 'this meal might be worth finishing' bites. You don't just take a bite and pitch a whole meal. But thinking of that, and with a terrible transition, why did you decide to be a notetaker," Amber, picking up her silverware again, feels around on her benedict with her fork and knife, feeling the shapes of the cut pieces, and cuts a wedge perfect for her fork from one of the benedict halves. She lightly presses the muffin into the yolk-butter-hollandaise mixture before lifting it to her mouth and eating. She chews slowly, enjoying her second bite.

"My friend George, he's the bartender at Brumby's, suggested I would be good."

"You know Bartender George?"

"I do, very well. Why do you call him Bartender George?"

"To keep him separate from Stock Clerk George over at Schnucks."

"Yeah, he said he knew you, too."

"I would think so. And the other Ambers."

"He handed me a strip of paper with the notetaker info, said I should look in to it, that I might be good at it. Your classes were at some of my free times. Why do you ask?"

"You know what I like about your notes? You write them trying to think of what I need to know. I mean, it's pretty obvious you're no geoscientist, and that's okay, but you work at it. Most people, they don't try to actually get to know other people. Most people like to talk a lot, listen a little. I don't think you're that way."

"That's just because I don't think I'm all that great," I joke, I think, and smile.

"Is that a joke? I can't tell. You have a very dry delivery. Did you smile when you said that?"

I do. "Oh yeah, I meant that as a joke." I cut into my open-face sandwich. Mary Anne's makes their own sausage, George once told me, with fresh pork, bacon, and beef, not high-end cuts, but flavorful cuts like shoulder and skirt. They grind those together with a secret spice mix that Mary Anne developed, a recipe the owners never share, and it all gets run through the meat grinder twice, never more than twice because the meat's texture would be ruined. Then they form patties or stuff links, leaving them to chill in the fridge overnight. That chilling part is vital: it lets the flavors enhance in the sausages; they just don't taste right if they're cooked immediately. "But to answer your question, I want to do something that makes a difference for someone."

"What about money? You're a computer major, right?"

"Yeah, I work on hardware and networks. But we're, like, a fourth-tier school for that. I'm not going to make tech millions. I'll be happy to get a job working at some mid-cap, honestly."

"Is it good money?"

"I mean, it'll be okay money. It'll pay the bills. Honestly, I wish I could just move out west and make a living as a landscape and portrait photographer, but market's saturated and I'm not good enough. But, okay, so I'm curious. How did you get into geology? And what are you going to do with it?"

"Well, I'm a mineralogist. I like to identify minerals and the subsurface stratigraphy to determine what's below ground. I can do some low-level subsurface engineering, soil sheer strengths, compressive strengths, things like that. It all helps me figure out where to find stuff worth digging up."

I sip my coffee, wince, and set it off to the side.

"So I got into it by digging holes in our fields. I grew up on a farm, you guessed or knew. I would dig holes and I would find rocks. I didn't know what they were. Farm soil can be pretty homogenous, most of the rocks tilled out. So I couldn't figure them out. And I asked Grandpa Arn, my grandparents raised me, and he'd explain what they were and how rocks and soil and sand and clay all feel different. I was hooked. He bought me a sandbox, I was like five or six then, and I found the difference in the sand texture on my hands versus the soil just amazing. Did you know that sand is just tiny rocks? Anyway, the sand was drier and warmed in the sun. Soil would always be a bit cooler and damp. But anyway, rocks I always liked the most. Grandpa Arn bought me a rock set and I learned how to identify different rocks by their weight, shape, cleavage planes, textures, and even the sounds they made when I tapped them on different surfaces. There are things about them I don't really understand and never will, because some aspects of minerals just require sight, but I learned that if I knew what was subgrade then I knew if something interesting was underground. So I went into mineralogy to get into mining or petroleum. Out west that's a big industry. Southern Illinois, it used to be, but the coal seams are pretty well known here, and the coal industry is dying. Out west, petroleum, precious metals, coal, and water have a future, especially water. All I need to do is convince some mining company or exploration firm or something that, with some help, I can be as good or better than anyone else. Grandpa Arn says that no matter what I do, it's better than farming, retail, or working as a church secretary. There's not a lot here for a blind girl to do. Can I try your sausage patty? It smells amazing."

"Can I have a couple of potatoes?"

"That's fair."

"I did, by the way, know that about sand. I heard it once, out west."

I cut a quarter out of my sausage patty and set it on her plate. "Midnight." I take two of the potatoes and immediately eat them, one at a time. They are the best thing on the plates today, and easily the best potatoes I've ever had. The outside, so crispy it crunches as I bite down, yields to warm, soft, and fluffy potato inside flavored with a hint of beef.

"So where are your folks?" I ask after finishing the potatoes.

Amber, cutting a piece of benedict, stops and faces her plate, "not really a usual first date question."

"I forgot we're on our first date. This feels like at least three or four." Amber nods when I say this.

"My dad isn't in my life. My mom died when I was three. My Grandma Helen died when I was sixteen. Grandpa Arn is the only family I still have. No aunts or uncles but one of Grandpa Arn's close friends, Tad, is like an uncle. He's over for holiday meals and once or twice a month on top of that. You?"

"Well, my folks are married. I knew my dad's dad and both my mom's parents are still alive. I got to see my grandfather a bit, a few family reunions on an island, a fishing trip once. No actual aunts or uncles, but my dad's business partner Todd has been good to me. We see him six or ten times a year. He owns the coffee shop I work at. I can see you want to ask. My dad is an architect, partner in the firm. They design mid-rise buildings, bridges, commercial spaces, and mixed-use – commercial on the ground and apartments above."

"Oh that last one," Amber sets her silverware down and puts her hands flat on the table, leaning in toward me, "could you imagine living above a pizza place? I'd totally have to be buried in a piano crate." A couple next to us, both of whom are fairly overweight, look at Amber. I glance awkwardly at them, face Amber, smile, but don't want to laugh. After a few seconds, "Are you still there? I didn't mean to offend you."

"I am. I smiled."

"Merak, when I say something, please react vocally. It kind of pisses me off when people just smile or nod or whatever." Amber leans back in her seat and tilts her head toward the wall a moment.

"I will do better."

The waiter comes out to check on our food, asks if we need anything. Amber and I eat and talk, less intently, and when the couple next to us leaves they face Amber and scowl, their lips and eyebrows close together like fingers in a clenched fist. I point to my eyes and shake my head and point at Amber. They walk away, no less upset.

Amber asks what happened and I explain, and add that, barring them, I would have laughed earlier.

"Oh. Were they mad?"

"I would say very, yes." This part of life must be hard for her, to say something meant to be funny, to incidentally offend someone, to never know it, to never know why, and to almost never know in public when it's safe and not safe to make a joke that could upset someone. As we start to finish our meals, the waiter again stops by and sets the check on the table with a quick 'no rush' before walking away.

"We should get going," Amber says.

"He said 'no rush.'"

"Merak, some things I may be more aware of than you. Listen to the noise here. It's louder than when we arrived. There are more people, and probably a longer line." A glance out the front door confirms this. "And he said 'no rush' while he walked away, which means he really wants his tip and to turn this table."

"Huh. Never thought of that." I finish my last few bites and leave a twenty under the bill. "Can I walk you out and back to your dorm? I feel like I owe you at least an hour, you know, from before we sat down." I stand, grab my blazer from the back of the chair, and put it on.

"I would like that," Amber says, blotting her mouth with her napkin after finishing her coffee. Amber stands and I step in front of her. "Ready." She reaches her hand up and grazes it over my butt.

"Sorry about that. Didn't see that there," she says, a stutter in her voice says it was an honest mistake.

I chuckle and let her know it's fine. Her coffee-warm fingers grip my shoulders through my blazer and I lead her through the tables to outside.

"Which building are you in?"

"Tower two, seventh floor."

"Nice views?" I pause and realize what I asked. "Sorry, force of habit." Amber's face is a frown.

"I hear that they're okay, but that on fifteen they're great." Amber puts her arm in mine and walks next to me for a half block. "And you?"

"Oh, yeah, of course. Sorry. I was just beating myself up mentally and spaced out. I'm in The Point, Burns Hall, top floor facing the lake. It's quiet. Not so many fire alarms as The Towers."

"Oh, The Point. You mean The Country Club. It's where all the rich Chicago kids live."

That's not unfair. "Well, I mean, anyone can live anywhere."

"Yes, yes, you can tell me that."

Amber and I walk the sidewalk down to Cold Harbor's main drag, her left hand on my right forearm, past the bars all closed for the morning, stools on high-tops as the cleaning crews prepare the spaces for the night, stock workers unload the beer and bar food resupplies from trucks in the street, and the owners sit in their offices tallying revenues and profits. Cold Harbor sleeps on weekend mornings like a bear in the winter, waking at night hungry and ornery. I let Amber know when pavers are uneven and where she should step.

"Anything you want to know about what it's like being blind?"

"Well, yeah, I guess. Sure. I know that this is a stupid question, but what do you see? Like, is the world just darkness?"

"A lot of sighted people ask that. I don't know what I 'see'. I was born blind, so I can't compare it to anything else. My optic nerves didn't form properly. A common question is if I could have it fixed with surgery and the answer is no. I will always be blind."

"If you could?"

Amber's stride falters a moment. "That … somehow I haven't been asked that. It's not an option. I stopped wishing for it when I was in grade school." Amber's lips purse and relax, her eyebrows move like worms on a fishing hook. "I think if I could have it fixed, if it were a real possibility, I might. But I would miss a lot of the life I have now. You've lived here, in southern Illinois, long enough to know that there are some people who just hate other races. It's not so much overt as a quiet festering, an expected separation. I have no idea what race is. I don't know if you're white or black or whatever and I don't know what that even means. I get to decide what I think about people based on how they behave, how they treat others, not how they look. I would not want to lose that."

That catches me off-guard. "I—" It strikes me for a moment that where I grew up everyone is white and relatively affluent, that almost no one in our subdivision mows their own lawn, and that the people who do are all Hispanic, and hired. Some casual waves hello, choppy Spanish greetings, and polite small talk about Mexican food or soccer is the sum total of my interaction with them, and that's more than most people in my town. This thought flits into my mind and then away like a leaf blowing past a window: maybe I haven't tried enough to get to know people different than me, just glanced at their lives. Maybe on my road trip some years ago, talking to the girl at the diner, to shop clerks, that crazy old lady Watersharer, and Michael with his scrub-brush hair, they're all people with whom I exchanged moments only, and I never tried to learn more than just tidbits about them.

"What?"

"Well, I hadn't thought that there would be things about blindness that would be helpful or good. I guess, yeah, it would make it easier to interact with people sometimes."

"Not all the time. I can't see; I can understand. Understanding who a person is, that's both hard and rare." Amber pauses a moment, her grip on my arm tightens slightly. "And it's fair to them, too, to try."

"Most people," I say, "I don't think they even understand themselves."

"You're right. It's easy to sell ourselves on a self-lie."

"As you were walking down the street, you moved your head in the same repeating pattern."

"I remember and associate things with shapes and patterns. So when I walk, I have a head motion pattern that counts off ten steps. So each step when I'm tracking my movement I move my head a different way. Then I count how many times I've done the pattern. It's easier to count to ten patterns than one-hundred steps. It's like the ballpoint pen. I move it, click the pen, tap it on the desk as professors talk and then I

45

remember what they say with the pen's pattern. When I need to recall it, I start moving the pen in my fingers and it helps."

That is, honestly, genius. "How do you match your clothes?"

"I have a friend, Kerry, back home who helps me pick out clothes that match and then," Amber rolls up her right shirt sleeve, "I have shapes stitched into them all right here and I can feel from those shapes what goes with what. I also keep it simple. Blue jeans go with brown boots and then it's a matter of figuring out some shirt colors that complement both."

"Huh," I find this very clever.

"I try to buy clothes with different textures. So mostly my red shirts feel one way, blue a different way, same is true for white, gray, and so forth. How clothes feel, that's important to me, far more than how they match. Scratchy socks, or wool blankets for that matter, I don't have them. Clothes that are too tight bother me. So I find clothes that feel comfortable and trust people to help me pick ones that match. Honestly, though, as long as I feel good in them, I wouldn't care if they match or not."

I smile. "I wish I could say the same." Amber walks a bit closer to me and I think she realizes that what I want to say, what I wish I had the vernacular to express out loud, is simply that I like who she is and wish that I could be more like her. "What's something you'd like to do that you haven't?"

Amber stops us walking and stands facing forward down the sidewalk for some moments. "Let's walk again," she says, taking the first step. "I want to stand on a mountain, to hear rocks fall in a couloir, feel thin and clean air in my lungs, run my hands over the weather-stripped summit, and, I hope, put my face in a snow drift in the middle of summer."

I want to be there for that. "That's better than any dream I have. I'd have just said something like 'get a good job, own a home, and be happy'."

Amber chuckle-huffs. "That would mean missing out on a lot of life. Are we going right back to my dorm?"

"Detour through and around Tolliver Forest? If you have time."

"Yes, let's," she says, with a smile and raised eyebrows.

Tolliver Forest is a small forest, really just a large stand of trees. Home to many of the area's small animals – fox squirrels, various tortoises, chipmunks, voles, and racoons – Tolliver Forest is a favorite place for locals to forage for mushrooms and for drunk students to sleep off hangovers.

"So what do you do for fun?" Amber's pace is sure-footed and confident. She knows the trail we're on well and having my arm to hold gives her some added comfort that she won't walk into a stump or bush.

"I photograph. I, um, I don't use my camera a lot because of how expensive film is. I like to plan out photos and then go take them. I try to make the most of the shots I take. The planning part, that's the fun part. That's where the photo is born. If I don't have a plan, then it's just going to be a snapshot. My best work are images I spend weeks or months planning."

"Well, I don't really know much about that. I ride horseback."

My pace slows and it catches Amber off-guard. "Really? How? I mean, that's impressive. I tried that and never took to it, but how do you know where you're going?"

She faces me, blue sunglasses reflecting my torso and head back at myself. "The horse knows where we're going. It's not going to run into a fence or a wall. If it can't make a jump it won't take it. If there's an obstacle, it won't hit it."

"You jump them, too?"

"Of course. That's the most fun thing to do."

My mouth is open, wide, jaw dropped like the muscles have let gravity win. I close it. "That's unexpected. I'd like the photograph that."

"For proof?" I can't read Amber's expression or if she thinks I'm being skeptical.

"Not at all. I've never photographed horse jumping. I think it would be fun."

Amber and I walk on in silence for a bit, listening to the forest. In the canopy above us, fox squirrels chitter as we walk near their trees. Leaves and pieces of bark fall to the ground as they run and jump between branches. Small rodents rustle leaves around the path, scurrying away as we walk close to them. A box turtle walks next to a fallen tree hollowed by decades of rot. "Oh neat, a box turtle." I stop us and look at it walking for a moment. Amber rests her head on my shoulder and I say, "it's slow."

"I assumed."

"Its shell is very dark yellow, almost black, with yellow patterns on the scutes that look like Rorscach blotches. It walks slowly, putting a rear leg forward then the same-side front leg, then the opposite rear and then the opposite front. Each step pushes it just a bit forward with intention, slowly. It's not running away from anything or particularly worried, probably just looking for some leaves or grubs to eat. Man, what a cool animal." Amber and I stand there and I watch the turtle walking away from us.

"I can hear it," she whispers to me, "moving leaves with its feet as it walks."

With some concentration, I can, too, after she points it out. When the turtle stops to munch a mushroom, we walk on, enjoying the forest sounds, air and shade coolness, and the way that air makes our face skin feel taught. Our walk after the forest becomes sidewalks to a footbridge over Highway 50 and a short stroll to her building.

At the door, Amber unfolds her cane. "I can take it from here."

"Oh, of course. I really enjoyed this and our walk. I'll see you on Monday?"

"I hope so." Amber pauses, smiles in my direction, tilts her head slightly upward, and her collar bones take definition behind her shirt collar. When Amber nose-scrunch smiles, my chest twitches; a small muscle somewhere contracts. And I, when I smile back, am glad she can't see my slightly crooked, always what I feel is weird and uncomfortable smile. Her smile lifts my cheeks, wrinkles my eyebrows, makes my face feel light and lifted.

"I'm gonna come in for a hug," I say.

"Uh, okay?"

I give Amber a gentle, loose hug and her hands land on my lower back. My back muscles tighten and Amber lets go. "I had a lot of fun. Can I see you again outside of class?"

"Sure, yeah, I guess."

"Okay, great, have a good weekend. I'll see you Monday."

"See you Monday." Amber turns and walks into her building and I walk back across campus to mine, smiling, wanting to skip but not actually skipping, and excited for Monday.

3
Red

At Brumby's, Rick, Jesse, and I sit at the bar and George pours and pops our beers. Rick likes a Heineken in the bottle, Jesse a Budweiser draft, and George joins me with a Killian's. Rick and Jesse both look at me like I have something to say but only George asks "so how'd it go this morning?"

"Went great," I say. I tell them about breakfast, and my description of the color brown and then walking Amber to her dorm building.

"And the first kiss?" Jesse asks.

"I gave her a good hug."

"Didn't she want a kiss?" George scrapes the foam off the top of Jesse's beer with a metal bartender spatula.

"It was just a first date."

"Did she tilt her head up a bit?" Rick, at five-foot-six and the shortest boy I know, asks with the understanding of someone used to hinting at those much taller how the date should end. He and George click their bottles in a toast.

I pause a moment and look at myself in the mirror. Mirror-me, eyebrows raised, looks back with curiosity, anticipation, tilts his head slightly downward without breaking eye contact. I run through the memory like a movie scene. "A bit, yes."

"OH!" "Dangit!" Merak!" Rick, Jesse, and George all say at once. "She wanted a kiss and you blew it, man," says Jesse, taking a drink from his glass.

Red

I stare wide-eyed at my mirror-self and suddenly it feels like the room spins, like the falling sensation in that brief moment that marries sleep with wake, and I jolt. "Goddamnit."

‹◊›

Monday. Hallway. Students and teachers walk past me quickly, like movie footage from a hundred years ago. The hallway clock seems to tick in half-time, then third-time, every second taking longer than all the seconds that have come before combined. I tap the heel of my shoe, in time with some silent music made of the extraneous noises that surround me, on the wall outside Amber's first class and wait to hear Amber's cane. The hallway echoes footfalls but my ears focus on the overhead clock ticking, the fluorescent fixtures above me buzzing. I fixate on the clock's second hand, letting it hypnotize me and as it spins so do I, my feet walking me up the wall, across the ceiling, down the other wall, and across the floor over and over with each passing minute until, finally, from the top of the stairs: a click-tak click-tak backbeat to the hallway music.

Amber walks down the hall, close to the wall, then next to it, left fingers on painted concrete, hand rising and then dropping to avoid a fire extinguisher. Her hair is tied back in a loose ponytail secured with a black bow and she wears pink lipstick and light-red cheek rouge. Her red and black flannel top, a personal favorite of mine, I learn as I notice where it fits snugly above her hips, fits with the two buttons under her bust angled sideways and the fabric forming fan-lines out from them. Her black jeans and black cowboy boots blend into each other, separated only by texture and faded-denim seams. When she's a few steps from me, "Hey, Amber."

She stops, drops her cane but the wrist strap end keeps it from falling. "Merak. I thought you'd be waiting for me in class. Are you quitting as my notetaker?"

"No, definitely not, but I wanted to stop you before class. I had a great time on our date, so great I forgot to ask if you wanted a kiss at the end."

51

Amber's cheeks turn redder. "Your timing is as great as moldy pizza." She reaches out and pushes my chest with both hands, partly playfully and partly decided not playfully. "Of course I did. I spent all day Saturday and yesterday trying to figure out what I did wrong. When did you decide you wanted a kiss?"

I look at the floor. "Saturday night I realized I'd made a big mistake."

"You could have called Sunday, come over, made up for it."

My heart stops a moment and my pants get very tight. "Uh, um, could I maybe make up for it in part right now?"

"You want to kiss me, right here, in the hallway, in front of everyone else who's here?"

We are off to the side of a large herd of students, moving in undulating, opposing flows, like currents in an estuary. "It's only us."

"I'm blind, not deaf. Did you forget?" Amber steps closer to me and lifts and tilts her head. I step right in front of her and put my hands on her cheeks, cupping her chin where my palms meet, my fingers reach up to her hair and around her ears, thumbs resting gently just behind her mouth. Her face, warm and soft, relaxes in my hands like muscles after a deep massage; her head lilts slightly as her neck muscles go limp. I run my lips on each other's underside and touch them lightly onto her lips, pink and shiny, slightly dry. Her mouth tastes of apple-pie-flavored lip gloss and a drop of salty sweat from her upper lip that follows my own lip to teeth and tongue: her kiss tastes like sunshine and summer desserts. I press my lips onto hers and when I close my eyes the crowd's passing footfalls fade away, clock stops ticking, overhead lights' buzzing melts to silence, and all is a brain-exploding light and warmth, her pulse under my fingers, slightly dry lips on mine, sweat salt taste lingering on the tip of my tongue, and in time that I already know is too short I pull away, taking her top lip between mine and pulling gently as I do. The crowd around us claps and hollers, someone shouts "my man!"

"I want to see what your face looks like," Amber says. "Can I touch your face?"

"Let me take off my glasses and yes."

"I definitely didn't think you have glasses." Amber puts her hands on my arms and traces up toward my shoulders.

"First, what do you think that I look like?"

Amber stops. She tilts her head slightly. "I know you have thinner, which I wouldn't have guessed, soft lips and not a huge nose. That's new information just now," Amber's right cheek bends up. "I think you have longer hair, maybe down to your earlobes. Probably parted in the middle, a bit wavy." She traces her right fingers across my upper chest in a wave pattern. "I know you're clean-shaven, but I figured you had a goatee before, you know, a moment ago. I think you probably have a strong jawline, horizontal and flat, sharp angle at the back." She reaches up and runs her fingers from my forehead down to my collar bones. I close my eyes as she feels over and around my eye sockets. Her fingertips warm the ever-cold skin on my cheekbones and then trace lines around the side of my face to my ears, and she gives a gentle pinch to my earlobes. My body shivers slightly when she does and Amber tries to hide a smile by biting her lower lip. Her hands run up and into my hair, around the back of my head, and then to my jaw, where she pulls them forward along the underside to my chin. When she takes her hands off my face, running them down around my neck and feeling the contours of my neck tendons and the union of collar bones, I feel a cold tingle trail down my spine from the base of my skull into my feet. She tilts her head again. "I got your jawline right. You're much, much thinner than I expected. You have very pronounced cheeks. I kind of thought you'd be a bit pudgy. Your face is very warm, except your cheeks. I like that your hair is only a bit longer than my fingers, and very soft."

Amber wobbles slightly. "Want to skip class?"

"I have to take notes for you. And I only get three warnings before they fire me. This would be two – missing class and missing notes."

"How many warnings do you have?"

"None."

"So you'll have one more strike. I want to see your dorm room."

"It's really boring, and a bit of a mess. It's kind of the same as all of the others on campus."

"You are so clueless. It's kind of cute, but don't ride that horse too far."

Oh. Ohhhh. "OH! Yeah, I am. That's me, in a nutshell. Clueless and kinda cute. Yeah, for sure let's do that," I say, my teeth starting to chatter uncontrollably in excitement. I grab a stick of gum and chew furiously to hide that loud clacking from my molars. I feel my heart in my neck and throat, like a constriction, like a panic attack, like the fear and anticipation at the top of the first hill on a new rollercoaster.

"Are your teeth chattering?"

"They are."

"That's very flattering. I'm also very excited for this." Amber's face tilts up at me as she wraps her arm in mine and pulls me close to her side. "Who was that who shouted just then? Do you know him."

"Nope. No idea who that was."

"… Good?"

I nod. We start walking to the stairs and she holds my hand.

"Merak, did you just nod or shake your head?"

"I nodded."

"It's not helpful when you do that."

❖

Amber twists her hips under the sheets, stretching her arms up at the ceiling. She turns her body next to me and runs her fingers over my bare chest and stomach, down to my legs, back up and to my arms. "You have a lot of small scars, and some not so small. What happened?"

"I was driving home about three years ago, dark, late, rainy, on a road with no lights and next to a flooded river. Another driver took a blind turn too fast and took his and my cars through the guardrail and into the river."

"Oh my God. How did you survive?"

"Luck. My car survived the fall and filled with water slowly enough that I got my head back while it filled up. I was able to use my camera case as a float. I broke the window and my case floated me to the surface. The scars came from glass in the window frame and rocks and sticks in the river. I still dream about it, often. Once in a while I stand in front of the mirror and look at the scars just to remind myself that it actually happened."

"They feel interesting," Amber says, her index finger tracing up and down a long scar next to my navel. "Does it bother you if I do this?" she says when my muscles twitch as her fingernail catches on a puffy spot on the scar.

"It'll be okay," I say. "I don't mind." My head rests on my locked fingers, Amber's in the space where my elbow bends. "My first roommate, he hated them, said the bruises I still had made him nauseous, demanded that I wear long pants until the cuts healed and bruises faded. When Rick came here our sophomore year, I made sure to request him as a roommate, because of that."

She flattens her hand and stretches her fingers over my left hip. "I'm going to take a shower, skinny man," Amber says, standing, and I learn about myself that I am a thigh man. She has toned, strong legs with definition in the gentle valleys between her muscles and a curve at the top.

"About seven steps forward after you let go of the desk, then a foot to the left, that's the door. My towel is on the lower half of the door. I'll make some coffee when you're done."

I change into clean clothes, getting my belt buckled as Rick unlocks the door and walks in.

Rick nods, stops in his tracks, looks at me, looks around, points at the bathroom door, "who's in the shower? Jesse and I were just at lunch." He looks at me, at the shower, back at me, at Amber's clothes on my desk chair. "Amber?" He smiles wide and sly, leans in to me a bit and raises his eyebrows. Rick's face is thin and lean, oval like a party balloon. He keeps his hair, brown but lighter than mine, longer, down to the tops of his ears and over his forehead. His eyebrows, thick and full, and his gray-blue eyes together express his thoughts uncontrollably. Rick has a slender nose with wider nostrils, pale skin that shows dry-air redness around his nostrils in the winter, and a medium-wide mouth with puffy lips that, I have heard, are considered quite kissable. His eyes are wide, excited, mouth open in a large smile.

"Shh," I say, as though she might hear over the sound of the water on the other side of a cinderblock wall, "and yes, and can you come back in after she gets dressed?"

"My man," Rick says with a fist bump. "But hang something on the door. I don't want to walk in on that."

When Amber leaves the shower a cloud of steam follows her out of the door. She's wrapped in my towel, just in case my roommate was here, she says. I let her know the coast is clear, walk her to the bed, and explain how I laid out her clothes for her. "Can I just change into some spare PJs until dinner?" I swallow reflexively and she hears me, chuckles, says my name with a laugh.

"Sure," I hand her some pajamas from my closet.

"Are you watching me put your PJs on?"

"I am."

Amber smiles and puts on my boxers and thin, blue pajamas and matching top while she faces me.

I knock on the door three times and Rick walks in. "Hey, Amber," he says.

"Who's that? Are you Merak's roommate?"

Rick introduces himself, says he's heard a lot of good things about her, and sets his backpack on his desk chair. Jesse knocks on our bathroom door, peeks his head in, dark brown hair, thick and straight, matching eyes, skin the color of a paper bag. His face, nose, cheeks, brow, and chin are round, flat, but slightly plump from a year of gaining weight. A year ago, when we met, he was thin and toned, dating a very attractive girl and visiting the gym regularly for her. When they broke up, he stopped working out and made a friend in cheesecake.

"Everyone decent," he asks, opening the door slightly. When I tell him to come in, he sits next to Rick on the foot of my bed and fires up the room's TV and Nintendo 64. Jesse says hi to Amber, gives her a slower up and down than I would like, and I introduce him as our friend.

Amber sits on my bed and tracks the sound of Rick and Jesse walking, sitting, Jesse holding up the Goldeneye game cartridge, Rick nodding, and the opening music playing. "Merak, where are you?"

"I'm over at the sink, next to the shower door. I promised you coffee."

"Yo, us, too," Jesse says, not looking away from the TV.

Rick and I built a shelving unit for our sink counter from bricks and scrap pallet wood that we found at a construction site dumpster. We cut the wood to size using an old, rusted handsaw that we found at an antique store. The shelves are a bit cupped and the whole thing wobbles like a child that's been spinning in place for five minutes. It holds our microwave and my coffee supplies, and as long as we aren't rough with it, don't bump into it, or, honestly, breath too deeply on it, it doesn't fall over. Amber, now beside me, puts her hand on my lower back. "Tell me what you're doing," she says, before letting go and taking a step back.

"So, first up I'm grabbing coffee beans. I keep them in a dark-red ceramic container." I hand her the container and she holds it, feels around it, unlocks the clasp and opens the lid. Amber holds the top of the coffee container to her nose and takes a deep breath. Her eyebrows raise and her shoulders drop. "From the fridge I'm getting a filter pitcher with cold, filtered water and I'm filling an electric gooseneck kettle with it. Here, it's not on yet." I stand behind her and take her hands, setting them on the kettle so she can feel the contours and the long, winding pour spout, which she traces up and down between her fingers.

"Why did the game music get so quiet?" Amber says.

Rick and Jesse stare at us, faces tilted downward some, Jesse's mouth open slightly and a thin string of saliva between his lips, connected like a millennia-old stalagmite and stalactite.

"Are they watching us."

"They are."

"Go back to your game, boys." Rick and Jesse turn and face the TV, the music starts up again, my bedsprings squeak under them as they shift. "What kind of kettle is that?"

"It's for coffee and tea, for pouring slowly so the coffee develops flavor."

"A special kettle for coffee? Can't you just use any old kettle," she says, not asking.

"Oh of course, but this has a slower flow and that's better for the grounds. Sometimes I think I want to own a coffee shop someday, one that roasts its own beans, sells them online, be something like a local attraction. Maybe that will be a thing. I take my coffee seriously, find the process of making it calming. Making coffee, the process, the routine, kind of quiets my brain. I like to make it well for myself and others, at any rate." I fill the kettle with filtered water and push the heating button to start it. While it heats, I fill two coffee mugs with tap water and microwave them a few minutes. "Heating the mugs because that helps the flavor, no temperature shock."

"Well, I can't wait to try your serious coffee." Amber leans against the wall and faces me, and I realize the pajama top is a more-than-a-bit see-through.

"I hope it's good. Your mug has a cartoony drawing of a hippopotamus on it, head just peeking out of the water, and the word 'Peanuts' above the hippo's face."

"Is Peanuts the hippo's name?"

"No idea. The rest of the hippo mugs at the store said Hippopotamus. My mug has my name on it, a gift from my coffee shop last year because nothing has my name on it. Stay just like that for a second." I grab an old, soft Colorado Rockies t-shirt with mis-aligned print from my closet, walk back to Amber, put my hands on her shoulders, "let me walk you over here a second," I walk her backwards into the bathroom, "you might want to put this on under the pajama top." She kisses me and closes the bathroom door part way.

"Keep talking."

"I'm grabbing a quarter-cup measure I keep in the coffee bean container and am putting three scoops into the grinder. It's a burr grinder, which does a more even grind than other kinds and it doesn't heat up the beans while they're being ground, and that prevents bitterness." Amber walks out of the bathroom and stands against the wall again. I grind the coffee and for almost a minute our ears fill and echo and ring with the angry screech of my grinder's motor. Amber covers her ears while it runs.

"Here," I hand her a ceramic pour-over coffee top. It looks like a small, angled coffee cup permanently affixed to a saucer with some holes in the bottom. She moves it around in her hands, feels the insides, drainage holes, the saucer.

"What's this do?"

I take the pour-over back, rinse it, put in a filter and some grounds. "This is where the coffee actually brews and drips into the cups." I grab my second one and set it up to make both our cups at once.

"So that goes on top of the cup?"

"Yup. It's like a regular drip coffee maker, but for one cup, and you get all the different flavors of the coffee. With a pot, if you pull a cup at the beginning and very end of the brew, the cups taste different. Single-cup pours combine the whole brew, makes each cup more interesting, a more complex flavor.

"The pour-over makes the best cup. The water goes to 195, much lower than the boiling water that percolators and standard drip coffee makers use. That keeps the water from making bitter coffee. Also there's an art to the actual pour. I begin strong, fill and saturate the grounds so they bloom early, and then slow and keep a steady flow until the grounds stop bubbling. This brings out the most flavor they can give." I put some half and half into my coffee. I remind Amber her mug is hot and she holds it in her hands, fingers in the loop. My mug warms my fingers and we stand next to the sink and sip our coffees, smiling, warm, cheeks red, video game gun shots, explosions, and music in the background. We are pleased and content in this moment.

Everything except Amber drops and spins away and is replaced by a diffuse, light-gray fog beyond the small circle of dorm room floor where we stand. We exist on a small pedestal of floor and sink, hands warmed by good coffee, the sound of sips, isolated and alone as though a spotlight circle shines from above, breaking and pushing back the surrounding fog, and I feel as though all that spins and rotates and repeats in the universe is us, coffee, and a warmth that expands from my throat into my chest, arms, legs, and face. I want more of this, more Amber, more coffee, more standing by my sink with the last of the water in the kettle bottom popping into steam and the pitcher filter drip-refilling slowly. I want more of nothing else existing except us.

"Where's our coffee?" Rick calls out, and the world spins backward up and around us pushing away the isolating fog like a reversed video of a building collapsing.

I look at the sink and counter, tile, the same tile as the surround and wall, old, from the building's last remodel, maybe forty years ago. "When the pitcher refills, Rick."

Rick pauses the game and Amber cocks her head, ear toward the TV.

"Just use tap water."

"Tap water does not touch the inside of this kettle."

"Not while you're home it doesn't." Rick unpauses the game and Jesse shoots him in the back of the head.

"Was that music the game?"

"Yeah, Goldeneye has a fantastic score."

"I thought video games were all beeps and boops and silly ditties. That's great music. I should play more video games, just to listen to the music."

"We can make that happen," I start making two more cups of coffee.

Amber sets her mug down and hugs me from the side, her hands on my belly at my navel and where my back transitions to butt. She presses her mouth to my ear, the air moved by her breath is as loud as her words, "this is the best coffee I have ever had." Amber lets go, her hands dragging downward over my clothes. "Why are you a computer science major, and not a coffee major?"

"I need to get a job. It'll be some years before I have enough capital for a business loan. I need to build to it. Maybe in ten years? Until then, it'll be a hobby I keep working to get better at." Amber walks over to my bed and sits on it, facing the TV. She looks over at me and a triple hand-to-mattress pat says for me to sit down. I do when Rick's and Jesse's coffee is ready.

"Tell me about this game they're playing."

"Okay, so Goldeneye. It's a first-person shooting game, which means they're playing from the perspective of their character. So they play a character just walking around like in the real world, only there's shooting. They have different stages, three-dimensional mazes, just like hallways in a building. And they just go around shooting each other. When one of them dies –"

"When Rick dies," Jesse says.

"– when Rick dies, he respawns." Amber faces me, lips pursed. "He re-appears in another spot. Jesse is so good it's like he's cheating."

"It's not like he's cheating," Rick says, finger up in protest. "I haven't gotten to pick up a gun yet."

"It's bad programming," says Jesse. "Programming flaws need to be exploited; it's the only way that lazy programmers will ever learn to do better."

"The game re-spawns people in the same spots in a pattern. Huge flaw in the design. Jesse memorized all the stages, all the patterns, and he knows where each of the types of gun they select will be in each stage, as well as extra ammo, based on the order in which the selected guns appear on the weapon selection screen. Before the game starts, he knows how to win and every move he's going to make. Jesse has won the game before we leave the title screen. When it starts, he goes straight to the nearest gun, grabs it, goes to the other players based on how far they are from him. He knows from his starting point where they will all be, kills them, and then runs to their re-spawn location. He knows the patterns so well he can run a circle around every stage with all three other players in play and do the same to all three of the other people. As soon as they re-spawn, their screen turns red. Boom – dead. Jesse has never even been shot the whole year we've been doing this. One time, in a seven-minute game, he got 114 kills against three other people, none of whom even got a single shot off. That's sixteen kills per minute, something like ten seconds per life per player. It's, honestly, kind of incredible to watch. So what we do is first place rotates out after each round and second place chooses the stage. The new player gets to pick the game parameters like weapons set. Every other game is competitive."

"Kind of," says Rick. "Merak is no slouch. He usually beats me by a handy margin."

"Have you ever killed Jesse?"

Jesse laughs.

"I have done the best and managed an occasional shot, but have never killed him. Missing him, no second chances. The other games we play, different story. Top Gear is my game; Mario Kart is Rick's." Rick and I spent high school afternoons playing racing games. He excelled at game-like ones while I, ever the driver, took to realistic ones. I learned the racing lines rally drivers use to flatten corners and how to brake and shift to keep speed in turns. Some of that applies to real-world driving, too, and I often visualize race lines on the road and plan multiple turns in advance when I drive my Saab.

Amber sets her coffee cup under the bed and asks if she can hold a controller. I hand her a spare; she feels the shape, the joystick, the buttons. When the game ends, Jesse shows Amber how to hold the controller and explains each button's job.

"Can I play?"

"Sure thing." Rick plugs in her controller and sets up a third player. "Jesse, no shooting Amber. Let her get a feel for this."

I sit behind Amber, my legs around her. I hold her hands, help her feel how the joystick responds, and when she says she has it, I rest my hands on the insides of her thighs and watch over her shoulder.

"Caves, Rick?"

"Good learning stage. For sure."

63

Amber's character spawns and I guide her through how to walk around, pick up a gun, arm herself, and shoot. She walks, mostly in circles, shooting the walls. At the end, she earns the Mostly Harmless award.

"Can I go again?"

"Of course. Jesse, sit in for me," I say. "I'll be on Amber's team. Let's do Caves again with random weapons."

"Gloves come off," Jesse says.

Amber spawns and I tell her to walk forward. She picks up some body armor and I explain what it does and guide her left to a narrow spot in a tunnel with a weapons cache. She picks it up and her screen turns red.

"Jesse."

"That was Rick."

"Sorry, I need a kill. My stats are terrible."

"Am I done?"

"Nope. You're in a new part of the stage," Jesse's character runs past. "Jesse just passed you, so he's giving you a fighting chance." I direct her to a weapon and the shape of it gives me a smile. Amber picks up and arms a rocket launcher. I explain what she has. I look at Jesse's screen and watch as he turns and heads back to our room. I tell Amber to turn left and fire. She turns and squeezes the trigger and her screen turns red. And then I see it, the most beautiful scene in video game history unfolds on Jesse's corner of the TV screen. A rocket appears, distant, grows larger, smoke trail billows behind it, Jesse says 'damn,' and it cruises straight into Jesse's face, turning his screen red. "You killed Jesse!"

"What the shit?" Rick laughs and arms a rifle. He knows where Jesse will re-spawn and he's waiting, ready. Amber re-spawns and I guide her to another weapons cache.

"Gloves off," Rick says.

Jesse appears again and Rick runs past, dropping a hand grenade in front of Jesse, running out of the room, and cackling as the grenade blows up and sends Jesse to a new location in the game. "How's that feel, Jesse?"

Amber picks up a pistol and begins walking around and shooting. By happenstance, Rick walks into her room right when Amber takes a random shot; his screen turns red.

"You killed Rick," shouts Jesse. This gives him the time he needs to pick up a new weapon and start the re-spawn killing on Rick all over.

"I'm gonna kill you once, Amber, you know, as retribution." Jesse walks into the room Amber is in.

"Oh no."

Jesse stands at the entrance, arms a rocket launcher, fires it at Amber, and runs out of the room while it travels toward her.

When the game ends, Rick looks at Amber "I can't wait to tell everyone that Jesse got killed in Goldeneye by Blind Amber."

Jesse looks up at the ceiling. "I can't think of anyone else I'd rather have kill me."

Amber grabs her coffee from under the bed, scoots next to me, puts her head on my arm, and says "Take a guess your assignment this week."

"Red?"

‹◊›

When I get back to my dorm after walking Amber home, Rick and Jesse play Mario Kart, and though it's Rick's best game Jesse keeps it fairly even for wins and losses, and I'm greeted with "did you remember to kiss her this time?" from Jesse as the door handle clicks into place.

"He more than kissed her," Rick says.

"Yes. Thank you both for your concern." My homework for the night is a network wiring diagram that shows physical wiring connections between user access points, ports, and networking servers for on-site and remote setups. I stare out my window as the sunset turns the clouds red and Campus Lake reflects the color in a dark, muddy-red like drying blood. This is going to be hard.

◇

Large rain drops explode on Colander, my Volare's, windshield like dud bombs in the dirt, leaving round water lenses that the wipers clear rapidly, back and forth. Lightning breaks the night's cloud-shrouded black, reflects on the highway center lines, silhouetting trees like giant wendigo heads and hands above the road, flashing so often the dark sky feels like a strobe light. Lightning causes the radio to hiss static and the windshield waterdrops beyond the wipers' reach to shine like diamonds in a store display case. The road has no lights, no white outside boundary lines. To the left, a steep drop into an over-full river, flooded from a dam failure a few dozen miles north, according to the radio, or what I can hear of it.

There's a turn ahead. I know this turn, blind and sharp. I plan out my line, hug the road close to the cliff on my right side because oncoming headlights from around the bend shine through the rain. I slow to take it safely and the water on my windshield alights and glows as an old Cadillac rips fast and straight around the corner. My headlights catch the driver's face, suddenly terrified, contorted as though in pain, and he must be screaming. He's old and afraid and his car hits Colander straight on as I round the turn. The metal in our cars crunches, buckles, the engine fans slamming into the radiators and grills with pained metal twisting. I see an orange flash as my car's hood buckles and a lightning bolt streaks overhead. Colander jerks backward from the impact and my body is tossed like an old toy into a trashcan, legs and arms arrested by seatbelt and the car's hard parts, head onto the passenger's headrest. Out the passenger's window, the man's face flashes with lightning and both cars fall sideways into the river.

The cabin light illuminates Colander – I know for the last time – and we sink to be entombed inside dark, muddy, churning water. When the light dies, I am alone, trapped in my car with only my screams, the blindness of absolute darkness, and the certainty that my eyes will never again see something.

I feel a warmth on my shoulder, a pressure, the car is collapsing, driver's window cracked and flooding and Rick says my name. Rick's study lamp is on, his laptop open as he works on edits to a business plan case study. The lamp casts a dim cone onto his computer and his computer's screen light fills the room in a bluish-white, diffuse glow that pushes back shadows as effectively as a person pushes the tide. I sit up, confused, still half-trapped in my Volare, certain this room is the Volare, the laptop and desk lights Colander's overhead. The first time I had this dream Rick woke me up, almost three years ago. I kept asking where the other driver was.

"It's been months since you had the dream."

"I didn't have anything to drink before bed." Rick, my longest friend, now, too, living with my family since just before college, the friend my father refers to as his 'second son.' He remembers Colander; the weeks I spent out west, Rick spent them at his home worried I would not return and confused, feeling betrayed that I hadn't let him know I was leaving. He told me a year or so ago that those weeks were some of the worst in his life. But, as the closest of friends do, he looked past it. Rick was the first of my friends I told about the accident and the nightmares that have followed. "Thank you for waking me up. I wish I didn't dream at all." My hair feels like a wrung-out floor mop, pajamas and sheets like a Louisiana evening.

I shower in the dark, feel the hot water steam in my nose as I breathe slowly toward calm. Six hours until my first class. After I dress and grab my jacket, I head outside to start laps around Campus Lake. The trail, an infinity loop around the lake's two, large basins crosses a narrow, brick bridge in the middle. It is a bit more than three miles and I can do two laps before breakfast.

Morning around Campus Lake arrives cold and slowly until the sun peaks over the trees of Tolliver Forest and the Tolliver Chapel steeple just east of it. For now, the trail remains a dark and dim blue-gray ghost in speckled moonlight that passes through tree leaves, light that dances on the forest floor and path like grain in old movies. The light's movement gives the path texture and presence. Frogs croak until I approach. Ducks and geese quack and honk at each other. The trees sound like a distant maraca orchestra. On the water, an occasional splash from a fish jumping to catch a bug. And my footfalls, the gravel underneath them grinding a "cush," sound like a mother calming a baby.

Dewpoint, night's coldest point, often arrives before midnight here. When dew forms on the grass and tree leaves, car windshields and anything else that will let it cling there, the air has reached its coldest and evaporated water condenses into dew. Dewpoint is a change, a signal that the night arrived and day left, and that the night will remain until sunrise. Dewpoint signals the end of the previous, a period of coming darkness, but also the promise of an eventual dawn.

At a bend where the trail traces a crescent of beach, moonlight breaks on the water and reflects small, low-energy ripples that lap the sand with gentle, near-silence. I've walked this trail hundreds – literally hundreds – of times and also never before. This time the moonlight dapples the sand and path; pits and mounds of sand cast shadows making the beach appear adorned in large, smooth rocks. I sit on a cold, wet stump where the trees end at the beach. For a moment I am three years younger, bruised, covered in cuts that would later form the scars on my legs, back, abdomen, and arms. My mind tricks me and for some minutes Campus Lake becomes a river, now calmer but once a machine of froth and terror, mud and debris, and a constant switch between my defiant hope and resigned despair. The dream followed me from sleep to this liminal wakefulness, sitting on the stump, trapped in the past, reliving it over and over like the reflector on a bike wheel passes the forks. The younger, bruised and scab-crusted version of myself stands, flexes, bends in pain, shoes and a sock missing, and he picks up my camera case and walks slowly toward a town.

For minutes I sit and take in the memory, the flashback, and let it pass on its own. When it does, I walk again, briskly past the beach, around the lake, and I repeat the loop before breakfast.

I self-serve a half-cup of scrambled eggs, one piece of wheat toast, a ramekin of grits and butter, and sit in a cafeteria corner facing a wall. The cafeteria tables have small, round disc seats that swivel. I twist mine back and forth as I eat. The food is cold and salty, but filling. After breakfast, at my dorm room, I reach under my bed and pull my camera's black Pelican case from hiding.

Every time I open the case: new dirt no longer trapped in the gasket. Three years and still hidden river dirt dusts my black Nikon F3. The F3's brassed edge wear looks like a gilded exoskeleton. I pull it from the foam, put my 24mm lens on, load a roll of film, put it in my backpack, and head to class.

4
Pasture

Amber grew up on a farm in Mariamne, Illinois, she tells me as we drive to her childhood home, more accurately a new, prefabricated home after the original had to be torn down. "My grandparents raised me, you know, and Grandma Helen taught me to rely on myself. She let me get cuts and scrapes. It was hard, she told me more than a few times, knowing that teaching me to cook would mean I'd cut my fingers with the knives or burn my hand on the stove. But she knew if I didn't learn to survive on my own I'd grow up to be what she called 'victim material.' She didn't want that for me."

"My dad's dad would have liked your grandparents."

The farm where Amber grew up rests out of town, well into the area where dirt roads are graded each spring and trucks share the space with horses and wayward cows. Amber tells me she never had a pizza delivered until college, that pizza here meant someone leaving to get it and someone else calling the pizza place ten minutes after they left.

My father named this Saab Federico, F for his sixth car, and he hated Federico, which in turn hated him. I love it. I loved driving Colander, the engine laying seventies muscle on straight-line asphalt. This car, though, it's nothing like that. Small and quiet backward-mounted engine, turbo, hatchback; Federico enjoys straightening curves. Federico will carry furniture, let two people sleep in the back comfortably, and kick gravel dozens of feet when I take a dirt turn too fast. Empirically, he's a driver's car. Federico, my 1992 Saab 900 Turbo hatchback, black paint, tan leather seats with some cracks at the seams, 104,862 miles, stick shift that's a bit wiggly in park, rear flip-out windows (this is a big deal, father told me multiple times, when he gifted me this car), and the 2.4 engine. It's zippy, launches hard, and he will be fun to drive up a mountain someday. And I need to stop calling it he. It's an it. Bad habit from my father; all his cars are he.

We turn off the main dirt road onto a thin, winding back road, the kind defined by small, old farmhouses spaced about a mile apart, old tractors parked to rust where driveway meets road, signs for eggs or honey for sale (honor system), and fences penning cows or sheep that pay my car no mind. This road, only a few more houses to her home, is dirt and rock, large gravel and gentle washboard corners. We pass under vibrant trees that, where they shade the road, keep it slightly damp and less dusty than the early-August heat has made the barren and unshaded dirt. Small rocks ping off my car's undercarriage and body panels. A dust plume hovers behind us in the rearview mirrors. The road's straightaway ends at a series of tight winds in a forested area that Amber says is her family's. Back on straight road, she says "Look for a bright red mailbox on the right. That's us. Grandpa Arn can be hard to understand. He has a thick accent, but also 'cause he lost the right side of his jaw to cancer a few years back. He used to chew."

And, sure enough, as she says that, we reach a bright red mailbox. The gate is open and I drive slowly up a gravel driveway, parking behind a rusty, heavily-dented gray Chevy pickup. Amber's home, a ranch style, has a brick façade exterior, white shutters around the windows, and white gutters beneath a brown asphalt tile roof. The design reminds me of the church I grew up in. These pre-fab homes, I recall my father saying when he worked on a project in Florida, are very nice, better made than most stick-built homes because of Hurricane Andrew. Most have whirlpool tubs inside and huge living rooms.

Meeting Amber's family is, I know, a big deal. Nervousness sweat has made the small of my back its home all day, worsening as we drove here. Meeting her grandfather is not my worry – making a mistake that costs me this relationship, driving her home in an angry silence, sitting on the far side of her classes to take notes, and her likely and eventual outburst about me to Dr. Peters, those are my worries. Meeting someone new, though, that's a chance to learn something new, a chance for both of us to have some small bit of them planted in us that, either now or at some unknown future-time when it's needed, can make us better people.

An old man walks out the front door. His face is dark brown from sun, wrinkled and creased like linens left in a bundle in the dryer for a week. The right of his face, where his jaw would be, is slightly caved in. He has gray hair, gray stubble around his face and mouth. His lips are up in a smile and his cheeks warm and welcome. He wears an old, gray trucker cap with no logos or markings, gray overalls on top of a dark blue t-shirt, and black work boots well broken in with leather and soles that move and bend freely as he descends the three steps that lead from the front door to a small concrete pad at the driveway.

I stop the car, park, turn off the engine, remove the key. "I'm guessing that's your grandpa."

Amber puts her hand on the door's handle, "give him the firmest handshake you can muster," and she opens her door, stands behind it, puts her hand on my car's roof, and shuts the door. Her hand traces the car's roof and hood line until she reaches the front. Her grandfather walks up to her and they hug. He tilts sideways like a tree in wind.

"So gud' tuh' see yuh', chip'punk."

"Grandpa Arn, please, Merak is right there."

Standing next to my open door, I wave, smile, introduce myself.

"Ah'nold," he says, reaching out his hand as he walks toward me. "Cah' me Gand'pa Arn." His hand is muscle and a single, whole-hand callous: the hand of a physical life turning time and muscle into money. His grip makes my right eye twitch and I grip back more firmly than usual. Grandpa Arn nods and turns back to Amber. "He might do."

"Grandpa," Amber protests her embarrassment, hands fisted on her hips, elbows out wide.

I'm invited in and Grandpa Arn holds the door for us. Inside, sock-footed, shoes on a rack by the washer, the home is large. This door,

I learn, is the backdoor. The front, a wooden double door with inlaid glass windows, faces the other side of the home, the side with a large patio overlooking the fields and neighbors. The door we use opens to a kitchen, tile floor, propane range, electric oven, and white-painted appliances. The living room is large, a couch against the wall, a recliner and small end table next to it. On the end table, a small radio spits out crackling, muffled words. Two voices talk about a cow loose on a road.

"Ambuh', kin yuh' tuhn' 'uf 'aht scannuh'?"

Amber does, explaining there is no TV in the house, satellite being expensive and, Grandpa Arn explaining he "nevuh' did ha' it growin' up, and whenever Ambuh' was growin' up we di'n't need it; nevuh saw no gud' come 'ut one," so he listens to the local police radio just to hear about cows in roads, kitchen fires, and the occasional Friday night drunks fighting at Growlers, the local bar.

"What do you do in the evenings?"

Amber says "we play board games or cards, talk about our days, plan out the next day, discuss the farm animals' personalities. There are a lot of things to do other than TV, Merak." She puts her hand on the kitchen counter. "Is that what you grew up doing? Watchin' TV?"

It was a big part of my life, yes. "Well some nights, sure. News." We planned our evenings around that night's shows, and seeing Amber and Grandpa Arn, how they interact so seamlessly, I understand that I have missed out on every game, conversation, thought, and laugh I could have had instead of three sitcoms a night five days a week. Those chances, gone, can't be reclaimed: The greatest value we have is our time, once invested or lost we cannot have it back. I don't remember any of the TV, really. Some show names, sure. Some moments, but no full episodes. And most of the shows I don't recall at all. I think, however, that Amber and Grandpa Arn remember a lot about their lives. My forehead is heat, sadness, and jealousy.

"Well ther' sum' things an' chores. Did yuh' bring sum' work clothes, Merak?"

"Those are his work clothes, Grandpa."

Grandpa Arn looks at my jeans and long-sleeved shirt, which does have a small hole at a seam on my shoulder. "We'll try not tuh' ruin 'aht"

As we walk out, I hear Amber whisper to her grandfather to be a bit nicer.

Amber leads me to her horse barn, which has room, she tells me, for five horses. They only own one, and to help it be less lonely since it's a herd animal, they make sure to have some goats, sheep, and a few cows it can be friends with. Her horse, Sandstone, named because, to her as a kid, his short fur felt like sandstone, neighs as he hears her voice.

The barn's red walls and white trim, painted maybe in the last few years, mark out doors that slide open sideways, window shutters, and entries from the pens inside to small areas outside. Amber slides a door open and five pens line the right side, the left housing some small equipment and animal feed. The floor, mostly dust and stray hay, meets the stalls at small gaps under the doors that hold back piled hay and bedding. Sandstone peers his head into the hallway above his pen door and, seeing Amber, starts walking excited, hooves-up-high circles in his pen. He is tan and white blotches, a mixed-color mane and tail, and when I reach the pen he looks at me, curious maybe, before putting his head over Amber's shoulder and down her back in, what Amber explains, is a hug.

"I ride bareback exclusively," Amber says, opening his pen door and walking in, "but with a bridle instead of using his mane for turning. I mean I could go without the bridle, but I want more space between my face and the back of his head when we're at full gallop."

I nod, say that makes sense. I have no idea if that makes sense. Amber knows what's best; I trust her.

"When a horse gallops, his head, especially if he jumps or something, can rear back. I got a good split lip once. Bled for a couple of hours. Not something I want to repeat." Amber asks me to grab a couple of hand brushes and large combs from a bucket by the pen door, then, holding Sandstone's chin, waves me in. "We'll take opposite sides. Just brush his fur. He likes it a lot, all horses do. Brush with the fur." Her left hand is in her brush's hand loop. My brush fits in my palm. The brush is stiff-meets-lightly-pliable plastic, black, and has short, thick tines in rows. The tines are smooth at the tips, rounded. I run the brush through my hair and my scalp tingles as it passes. "You can use some pressure, too," Amber shows me how she presses on the brush, where it leaves lines on Sandstone's fur as she brushes. She uses long motions, from his chin, running at the line where his mane meets the fur on his neck, to his shoulder. She repeats, slightly overlapping, her hand moving confidently, practiced. Her middle finger hangs slightly over the end of her brush and her fingertip guides her next brush motion, slightly lower, slightly overlapping. I mimic on my side, long brushstrokes, press a bit, gentle lines. Sandstone makes noises that, I assume, are happy horse noises.

"This is nice," I say. My eyes and nose burn with hay dust, which hangs dense in the air around Sandstone, catching light from outside and alighting like a cloud filled with lightning.

"I was debating, right up until you dialed my call box this morning, if you'd show up."

"Why?" I stop brushing.

Amber points her face slightly to my right. "Suburb boys don't do farm stuff."

Brushing again, a few strokes a bit quicker than the first ones, "this isn't what I dream about at night, or when my mind wanders. I want to know what your life is, and was, like." Sandstone shakes and his mane smells faintly of dirt and grass. "I assume you want to know about my life."

"Generic suburban?"

I stop and look over Sandstone at her. "Listen, missy, just because that's the best and most accurate description doesn't mean it's not interesting. There's conflict, like when Mrs. Durgin forgets to separate her recycling. There's drama, like when crotchety old Mr. Harris found the neighbor's kid's soccer ball crushed some of his squash plant's flowers before they could be pollinated."

"Oooh, so much controversy."

"Someone saw a coyote once. People locked their patio doors and carried baseball bats for days."

"Such terror. How many yippy dogs did it eat?"

"You should have seen the literal outrage when my father trimmed the hedges himself instead of having a gardener do it the year we moved in. There was an angry letter from the H-O-A."

"Sin and scandal!"

"Oh yea, 'generic suburban' is full of excitement, intrigue, and thrills." Amber and I work our way down Sandstone. She hands me a gigantic comb which looks like a comically large moustache comb, and describes how to untangle his mane while she works on his tail. When we finish, Amber walks Sandstone out of the barn and lets him run around his pasture. Sandstone runs, trots, canters, walks, kicks his rear legs, waves his head, and gallops. He kicks up dirt and grass, runs circles around Amber, his hooves clomping loudly and she laughs and reaches out to pet him when he stops and stands in front of her. Horse girls. I get it now, George; that's happiness I've not known.

Behind me, three small goats stand and hop in a pen. They walk in the dust and chase a few chickens that wandered in. Some feral-looking cats stalk around rocks, my car. In a far pasture some sheep graze, and a cow, and they look up between bites to watch Amber and Sandstone. Animals are amazing, and I say this to Grandpa Arn.

"Yup."

This must mean he concurs. I look around the pasture, at the barn, at trees that lead to a forest behind the house and barn. "Can I do anything else? Feed the chickens, or, um, bail some hay or something?"

Grandpa Arn turns slowly and looks at me. "Bail sum' hay?"

"You might know I didn't grow up on a farm now."

"Now?"

As I sigh, my shoulders fall, defeated like a helium balloon with a small hole that refuses to pop, just letting out gas slowly. "I know I won't be a lot of help. I thought I might be some, or learn."

"Lirn 'bout what?"

I watch Amber hoist herself onto Sandstone and ride him in a slow walk around his pasture.

Grandpa Arn pushes himself off the fencepost with his elbows and looks me up and down, seems to measure my skinny, weak frame against some concept of what a man should be. His eyes get a bit thin for a moment as his head tilts left. Like many men who work alone, he is not easily read. "Let's feed 'aht chickens 'n' chop suh wood."

"Like with an axe?"

"Maul."

Feeding the chickens is pretty easy. We take some crushed, dried corn and feed and fill some pecked-up plastic troughs not much bigger than dog bowls. The hens, Grandpa Arn explains, also eat grubs, so we don't want to feed them too much. We want them eating grubs, which helps the grass and gives him healthy eggs. He tosses some feed into thick pasture grass, tempting the hens to where grubs might be easily found. In the barn, Amber rides Sandstone back to his stall and Grandpa Arn grabs a large, what I assume to be, maul from a hanger on the far wall. It has a wood handle, dark black at the base from use, thick metal head blunt and flat at the back, shiny and freshly sharpened at the front cutting edge, the rest of the metal dark and use-stained.

"Grandpa, what are you making Merak do?"

"He volunter'd."

"I did. We're going to chop wood." If Amber could see my goofy grin.

"It ain't 'aht fun." Grandpa Arn walks out of the barn to a pile of wood. Amber walks next to me.

"I don't think it's going well," I whisper, walking next to Amber and holding her elbow.

"Oh, he hates you."

I stare at her, mouth dropped.

"Are you staring at me, like with your mouth open, again?"

"Sorry, yes. Hates me?"

"Not really," Amber slaps my shoulder. "He's just testing you. Go chop wood. You'll suck at it. Maybe not. I'll be a safe distance away. I took a large piece to the forearm one day from a guy trying to show off for Grandpa Arn. Don't show off."

A large, flat stump rests in the middle of a small clearing behind the barn and house. Firewood, short, triangular, is stacked between two trees, which Grandpa Arn explains when I ask is because putting it against the house gets mice, rats, and snakes inside. "Yuh ev' used a maul b'fore?"

I shake my head.

Grandpa Arn sighs. "What chya gun' do is put yuh' right han' undah' 'aht head like 'aht, yuh lef' at 'aht grip. Not too fah' dun' the grip. Yuh dun' want 'aht dang-ol' thing flyin' away. Lif', ben' at yuh waist, slide yuh right hand down the shaf' as yuh swing, wood splits. Like 'ihs," he demonstrates on a round piece of wood slightly smaller around than the chopping stump. The maul slides into it as his hands come together at the base of the handle and the log splits, not the whole way, but he twists the maul and the halves separate. "Yuh kin' do 'aht?"

"I can try, yes, sir."

"Yuh kin' call me Gand'pa Arn, please," he picks up one of the halves and sets it on the stump, points to where he was standing, hands me the maul and walks to stand by Amber.

"I will, Grandpa Arn." I look at he and Amber standing way off to the side. "I am not strong enough to split this thing and have it go flying."

"We 'ench wurrahd about 'aht log flyin'; wuhr' wurrahd 'bout yuh' flyin'."

Amber holds up her hand and they high-five. Their fears are justified. I lift the maul like Grandpa Arn and swing. My hands don't meet; the maul has no power behind it, bounces off the log and back, takes me to the ground beside it. Grandpa Arn laughs, explains to Amber as he slaps his knee, and she laughs. Everything inside me turns to porridge; I am useless. My car is just a short sprint away. As Grandpa Arn starts to walk toward me I stand and hold out my hand. I am not useless. Federico can stay where he is.

Grandpa Arn steps back, leans back against the barn wall next to Amber. "He's doin' 'aht uh-gin'."

Amber's eyebrows raise, her eyes closed, cheeks up and lips in a downward smile. The maul feels more balanced in my hands than last time, lets me know that in time it can feel like an extension of my arms. Under my hands, the handle wear feels smooth as a glass vase and the boundary of smooth-to-texture tells me where to find the grip I need. I lift the maul high, bring it down at the log; my hand slides and I bend at my waist and put all my strength behind the swing. The maul slides into the log, rests almost halfway through.

"Lif' it."

I lift the maul a couple of feet and the log comes with it. A second, shorter swing finishes the job. Amber claps and cheers. Grandpa Arn points to the quarters. "Uhn' mor' each 'uh those, then 'aht othuh haf', then 'aht pile," he points to a pile of around twenty logs about the same size as this had been at first.

I nod.

"I'm going to stay out here with Merak, Grandpa."

"I'll be uhroun', doin' stuff, Chip'punk."

"Grandpa, please, I'm 21 now."

"Yuh'll always be Chip'punk."

I set the smaller pieces on the chopping stump and cut them in half and repeat until I need a new piece. The wood chopping space rests in the shade of old maples that dapple afternoon light on Amber and the barn wall; dancing light shapes frolic on her face and body. I imagine that in some months when the fall colors come the leaves will be alight in warmth and leaf-fire for all-too-brief days.

"He's warming up to you," she says, walking to her home's back door and sitting on the steps.

"Did we just live the same last few minutes?" I look at the wood. The bark differs from the trees around us.

"How did you end up back here?" Amber asks.

The light on the walls around Amber line dances as the sun passes between moving leaves. "He asked what I wanted to learn about," I say looking back to Amber, realizing that when Grandpa Arn asked that, my eyes went to her. Our eyes bely our minds and when Grandpa Arn stared at me by the fencepost he wasn't sizing me up against some ideal man, but against what he wants for Amber. My back makes a soft pop as it straightens and I wonder how I measure up.

"You're doing well. What did you want to learn about?" Amber stands, shakes her leg, and walks to me.

"Chores."

"What chores?"

"Feed chickens, bail hay."

"Bail hay?" Amber laughs. "Oh, Merak, I guarantee Grandpa Arn is on the phone right now calling his friends to tell them about my city boy with his funny-looking car, who wants to bail hay." She sets her hand on my shoulder.

"I am so silly aren't I?" It feels good to say that out loud.

"Did you get dirt on your clothes when you fell?"

"It'll wash out."

Amber walks back to the stairs. "How much wood did he leave you?"

"About twenty of those round pieces, so a hundred-and-sixty logs."

"Better get chopping."

◇

The last log takes time, three chops per split. My arms are spindly twigs of permanent fire; what biceps I have force my forearms into an "X" and my hands reach for my shoulders when I finish the last cut and drop the maul. Around me, 160 pieces of wood, triangles with round backs, scattered around the chopping stump. I force my arms straight and start piling them on the ground on the opposite side of one of the trees with the other pile. I can carry a few at a time and the stacking, walking, repeating, takes a bit. I set the rows down, nested point-to-point side or round-to-round side, matching the other pile.

Sitting on the stairs next to Amber, shoulder-stuck fingers, cross-locked forearms. "I'm done."

Behind us, "Ambuh', yuh' din't have tuh' stack 'em"

"I didn't stack them, Merak did. And I didn't even ask him to."

"Why'd yuh' stack 'em dere'?"

"I didn't want to mix the vintages. I know they have to dry a bit."

Grandpa Arn's eyebrows lift, his chin curls. "It's a gud' stack." Grandpa Arn motions for us to come inside. I hadn't noticed this; dusk has come and the sun set. I don't know what time it is; we swim in the texture and sound of late-evening music. Crickets chirp loudly from the forest, the log pile, the barn, and under the house. Mice or voles scurry under leaves around the trees, sounding like small newspapers being folded on themselves for easy reading. A gentle breeze creaks branches and tussles leaves in a soft white noise. Inside, the mantle clock reads just after eight. We had started chopping wood at four.

Grandpa Arn cooks a dinner of macaroni and cheese in a cast iron crockpot, smooth inside and out, glossy black inside, matte-soot-stained outside from when he was a boy and his mother cooked all their food over a wood-burning stove, he tells me. Amber nods and backs up the story. "We didn't have propane here until I was ten. I remember that wood stove. Heat and cooking," she says, and shows me a small smooth patch on her elbow that she got bumping into the stove when she was seven.

Amber and I sit at a small, round table in the kitchen. It has three chairs set up in a triangle. I sit next to Amber and she rests her hand on my thigh. I do the same, run my thumb on the groove between the muscles on the outside of her leg.

"Yuh wan' hear summin', 'aht house Uh grew up in, din't have 'lectric. 'Aht firs' 'lectric system, bare coppuh' wiyuh' strung at the ceilin'. Wuh had 'lectric in 'aht kitchun', muh folks' room, an' 'aht bathroom. The 'lectric stuff, it had long, coppuh' hooks yuh' jus' hang over the wiyuh'. Muh mah, she'd sit in 'aht tub an hang 'aht radio wiyuh' ovuh 'aht bare coppuh' line." Grandpa Arn looks at me. "Yuh don' believe 'aht?"

"I do. I just had never heard of that."

"Commun way uh' it on 'aht loca' fahms."

"Life is a lot better now, Grandpa."

"Owe it to 'aht coal mine."

"We do," agrees Amber. "We do." Amber stands and walks over to the stove, where she hugs Grandpa Arn. "Let me serve." Amber reaches into a drawer and grabs a hot mitt, and then into another for a spoon. She lifts the cast iron lid off the crockpot and steam rises from the top. I sit upright a bit, my stomach growls loudly when wafting scents of cheese, pasta, heavy cream, and breadcrumbs hit my nose. Amber doles out three portions, heaping yellow piles mounding the tops of three bowls to near-overflowing, cheese dripping over the rims onto small chargers. She brings them over one at a time and serves Grandpa Arn, me, and then her. Then she grabs three glasses, fills them with water, and sets them in front of us. "We're on a well, so it might taste funny to you. If it's a bit brown, it's still safe."

The water is clear, but a different kind of clear than city water, maybe a very faint brown tint. It certainly tastes of minerals and rust, but I am parched and it feels good in my throat. "It's good," I say.

"Merak, wud' yuh' do us the honuh'?"

Of what? I glance at Amber and Grandpa Arn, and they hold hands and reach out to me. Every prayer I have ever heard at every meal, every reverend's blessing, every kind and Godly word in my brain defenestrates my mind like convicts seizing a moment. My memory on praying aloud is black and vacuous like a never-used chalkboard. Oh dear. Grandpa Arn looks at me; Amber turns her face toward me.

"Heavenly Father, thank you for this meal that Grandpa Arn prepared. We beseech you to fill our time together with your love and grace. Amen."

"'Aht was gud', Merak."

"We beseech you?"

"I just completely forgot everything about praying. My mind went blank, completely empty —"

"Like your stomach?"

Grandpa Arn laughs as he chews, snorting.

"Yes, Chip'punk, like my stomach."

〈◊〉

83

While we wait for Grandpa Arn to come outside and see us off, Amber and I sit in the dim glow-cone of an old incandescent light above her home's porch. Moths fly in the light, bump into the bulb with a tink at each hit. A spider's web above the bulb has holes from the bugs it caught already tonight.

"Close your eyes, Merak."

I do.

"Here's a bit of my world. Listen. Focus on the sounds you can hear and then listen past them."

The moths and their tink. A faint electrical crackle and some soft hissing, the lamp in the evening humidity. A mechanical whir starts soft in a wood box nearby, the well's water pump. Some animals, maybe Sandstone in the barn, a horse on another farm, the goats or chickens or cows, make quiet whinnies, moos, or footfalls. Their sounds carry far and undisturbed in night's quiet air. A high-pitched, short and repeated sound, many of them, moving fast. Flutters of air. Mosquito buzzes but not at my ears. Leaves brush against each other like fingers softly feeling the contours of a new lover's hands. A barn owl calls out from the forest.

"Did you fall asleep?"

"What, no, I was just listening."

"For ten minutes?"

"Really?"

"Did you hear anything?"

I tell Amber about all the sounds. "I couldn't identify the high-pitched sound, though."

"Bats. If you focus enough you can hear their sonar."

"Oh yes! I should have known. I heard those out west on quiet nights in the desert." Amber's hand, when I grab it, feels cool on the back, warm on the palm. "I feel like a moth in the dark."

"Like you're looking for a light or like I'm a bat?"

As I chuckle out some nerves, the house door opens, the squeak and of hinges and tensioning of springs in the screen door, the hydraulic arm with a couple of loose screws on a mounting bracket settling into place, I stand quickly, startled by the loudness.

"Yuh' okay?"

"He was just listening with me, to the bats." Amber hugs Grandpa Arn goodbye at the home's back door. He shakes my hand, his left hand firm on my shoulder. He smiles, but tries to hide it with a flat face. His cheeks and the curl in his eyes give it away.

"Yuh' drive safe."

"I will, Grandpa Arn." When our handshake ends, I smile at Grandpa Arn and walk Amber, who locks her arm in mine and rests her head on my upper arm, to her door. She climbs in, buckles her seatbelt. "Fingers," I say, and she puts her hands in her lap. I close the door and walk to my side. Federico fires up quietly, his headlights shine against the back of the old truck. My arm around Amber's seat, we back toward the road and from the end of the gravel drive, where it crosses a length of metal drain for the roadside ditch, I see Grandpa Arn waving and I turn the headlights off and back on twice.

We drive down the dirt road back the way we came, through the winding tree limb overhangs and back to the long, straight road that leads to pavement. I press the gas pedal down slightly and let the rocks clang against the undercarriage. Federico loves this and his tires dig into dirt.

"Grandpa Arn really likes you, Merak."

"Oh?"

"He has never asked a boy that I brought home to lead prayer. He had some fun with you about the wood chopping."

"He called you Chip'punk in front of me a bunch."

"You got to do that once, that's all. That was my nickname when I was a baby and a really little kid."

"Okay, I won't do it again, Chip'punk, after that extra time."

"He knows I can't stay here and I think you must have made an impression on him with helping me groom Sandstone."

"It was fun to watch you ride."

"See, that, too. Most boys, they go out of their way to try and please Grandpa. They want to be polite, say nice things to him, but they don't really focus on me. You did, and then you volunteered to do chores. You don't even know. I don't remember a time when he hasn't had to tell a boy to get to work."

"How many boys are we talking about?"

"Quit being insecure. I'm trying to tell you good things. It meant a lot that you stacked that wood and wanted to feed the chickens. He approves. He was skeptical that I would be interested in dating a suburban boy. He told me when we talked yesterday that he really thinks I need a good southern boy, but, I'm gonna guess, that when I talk to him in a couple days that'll be different."

"I'm glad to hear that, I am. And I like Grandpa Arn. He's a good man." I rap my right fingers on the back of the steering wheel until we reach the washboard turns through her family's forest, bounded by an old barbwire fence tied at irregular heights to heavily weathered wood posts, most of which lean. "We should probably have a quick chat about our pasts."

"Why are boys so obsessed with numbers. Is it a competition?"

"What, no, it's just better to know. No judgement, just interest."

Amber crosses her arms and faces out the window. "I don't really want to. It's going to make you mad. You need to convince me that you won't be mad."

"I really like you a lot, okay. And you are who you are because of everything that led you to this point in your life. I'm not going to judge it. I want to understand how you got to be you. I'll go first. You're my third.

A friend my high school senior year, another girl here during sophomore and junior years, and you."

"Three? I'm your third? And after a year-long dry spell? You're definitely going to hate me. I'm not saying," Amber's face, pointed away from me, on the side lit by Federico's console, reflects dim in her dark passenger window, glows like spring tree leaves in early-dawn light on the illuminated side. I sit in silence and drive and almost three minutes tick by on the dash clock before Amber tilts her head down and forward. "You are number seventeen."

Jesus. "That's more than I expected."

"See, you're mad. I shouldn't have said anything. Are you going to dump me now? You seem kind of like a prude about this."

"What? No. I had guessed, I don't know, like nine. I was, honestly, just curious. As long as that stays at seventeen, I'm never going to be mad or jealous. Those guys are in your past."

"Are those other girls in your past?" Amber, arms still crossed, turns her head toward me quickly and says this with fast, harsh-ended syllables.

"No one ever stops thinking about the first person we fall in love with, the first person we say that to. No one ever forgets the first person they make love with, either. So they're in my past but, sometimes, they pop into my head, at the times of the year when we dated, did things like go to the high school's spring play or drive home for break. I don't think about my high school friend so often any more. It's been more than three years. I do think about the other, around spring break, my birthday."

Amber's arms loosen and her hands rest on her knees. She seems to accept this. "I try not to think about the other boys, mostly. One other was decent to me. The rest, I try to forget."

For some moments, counted off by gravel pings under Federico, my mind wanders to Amy and the last time I saw her, just days before Colander and I drove out west. She asked me not to go to college; she didn't get in to one, asked me to stay in Deer Lake, marry her, said we could both get mall jobs and that we'd be okay. I said no and she screamed and hit me at least five times with the candy-colored brush on her nightstand. After my trip, I learned she had been in two 72-hour holds during my time away. I blamed myself, maybe still do. "I like to think that, in time, we all get to forget the problems we had, the people who hurt us, and, if we're lucky, that we hurt people, too. Feeling bad for mistakes we made before means we're better people now."

In my rearview mirror I see my father. He reaches forward and pats my shoulder, smiles. And through him: red and blue lights. "Dangit."

"What?" Two quick woops from a siren. "Are we being pulled over?"

"We are." I pull Federico into a safe, flat spot at the roadside, and then realize it's the entry to a driveway. Two figures, silhouetted, stand on the front patio at a large bay window, watching the excitement out front. Window: down; engine: off; hands: steering wheel.

In my driver's side rearview, a dark figure with a bright flashlight walks toward us, slowly, shining the light on the back of my car and through the rear window. He shines the light at the back window, into the back seat, and then, standing next to me, the front seat.

"Evening, folks. License and registration, please."

"Pocket and glovebox," I motion with my head.

The officer shines his light on the glovebox and puts his other hand on his gun. "Slowly."

Slowly. I reach over and hold the glovebox door so it doesn't drop. The officer shines his light in the space and follows my hand with it as I pull out a small, black wallet-sized paperwork pouch and hand it to him. I reach to close the glovebox.

"Leave it." He opens the pouch and looks over the paperwork before handing it back. "Sir, do you know why I pulled you over tonight?"

"I do not."

"Neither do I," says Amber.

The officer looks at Amber.

"Firstly, we're not even going to talk about how fast you were going, but the posted speed limit is only thirty-five, not, well, not what you were doing. The problem, sir, is that this road is only for pickups. Cars are not allowed on the dirt roads in this county."

What?

"Officer, I'm really sorry," Amber says. "I didn't know he was on one of the pickup-only roads. I can't see the signs, you know."

What signs? I look forward out the windshield. Pick-up only roads? Is this a dirt road thing? I and Federico were doing just fine, thank you and very much.

"This is a serious offense in this county, folks. Sir, please step out of the car."

"Does he really have to? What's his punishment? Is it just a fine? Oh, Merak, this is a serious law you've broken. You could go to jail! I really should have warned you."

"Jail? A fine?" I can't afford a fine, or jail. My head drops and my legs, dusty on the seat, quiver.

The officer looks at Amber and sighs. "Alright. Look, you're very lucky that I'm very busy tonight. There is, in fact, a cow stuck in a tree a few miles away and I have to go help it climb back down. As you can imagine, a lot of cows get into trees out here. But there does need to be some punishment."

Cows can climb trees? "What is it?" I ask, tilting my head to look at the officer.

He smiles huge, "ya gotta bail some hay." He stands up and laughs out loud, slapping his leg. Amber laughs, too, drubs her hands on the dash above the glove box. She opens her door as the officer walks behind the car to her side. "It's safe to get out, Amber."

"Tad, it's great to hear your voice," Amber says, standing and giving him a tight hug. Tad lifts her up and her feet kick back. "Cows in trees, Tad? Did he believe it? Does he look like he believed it?"

"He does," Tad says glancing in the car when he sets Amber down. Tad helps her back in the car, tells her to mind her hands, rolls down her window and after he closes the door pokes his head through the window to kiss her cheek. From the house behind him, a man's voice says something I don't understand.

"It's Amber and her city-boy boyfriend. I'm just having them on a bit, Charlie. Ain't no trouble."

"Amber's dating a city boy?" Charlie shouts from the porch.

"Sure is. Arn made him chop 160 logs today and had him lead supper prayer."

"Are they getting married? They must be getting married."

"Are we seriously at Charlie's house?" Amber asks.

"Yup," says Tad, facing us as Charlie walks back inside.

"Geez, Merak, you were driving fast."

I look at Amber and I smile, chuckle. "You guys got me. I approve."

"You two drive safe," Tad picks his radio up from his shoulder and he looks at Amber, smiles at her, then at me, and before he walks away says into his radio "Hey, Arn, wanna hear something funny?"

The side of Amber's face glows in console light, her head leaning back on the headrest. "Boyfriend," I ask.

"Shhh. Don't spoil the moment," she says, closing the glovebox.

5
Siren Song

As often we do, Jesse, Rick, and I spend this rainy August afternoon playing videos games. For the last two weeks, the time between summer and fall semesters when the dorms must be empty, our stuff was boxed in a 'first-month-a-buck' storage locker off campus. Now we live amongst stacked boxes of stuff, the TV and Nintendo unpacked. I'll find my sheets tomorrow, or the day after. Jesse and I play a two-person fighting game while Rick watches and waits for the winner's controller. While he waits, he autopilot unpacks a box and seconds after plugging in the phone it rings.

"Desmond's mortuary and taxidermy. You snuff 'em, we stuff 'em. Desmond speaking."

"Rick, is Merak there? It's important." I hear Amber through the phone, quite loud. I toss Rick the controller and grab the phone.

"Amber, is everything okay?"

"What color is your car?" Amber speaks normally, but the volume switch on the phone was bumped up to high.

"Black. Why?" I turn the volume back to low and Amber sounds normal and relaxed.

"Dangit. Kerry at the feed store said, based on what Grandpa Arn said about you, that she thinks you're more of a red car guy, I said I figured you for blue."

"To be fair, this car was a gift. If it were up to me, I'd like a blue car, a Z, or a WRX."

"Yeah Nissan," Rick shouts.

"My first car was orange, kinda like red, but also a gift. I've never really chosen a car color."

"The car you actually bought was brown," Rick yells, and I look at him.

"Rick, I needed any ride that wasn't a bus, thank you." I sigh. "What brought this on?"

"It was a thirty-second thing; we've already talked about it for longer. Kerry and I were talking about the county fair this year and how much fun it was and the food and the pie baking contest and who had the best pigs and cows at the 4-H show. I don't even remember why it came up. Wasn't that important." Amber tells me to wait for a second and with a muffled voice relays the car info off the phone.

"Are you at the feed store?" I sit, put the phone between my head and shoulder, unpack and setup my computer.

"Yeah."

Rick and Jesse mutually agree to stop the fight for a moment and watch me. I shrug at them.

"Anyway, I'm really calling, not just because of that, but yeah, Grandpa Arn's truck just broke down in the lot. There's some steam coming out of it. Said a hose burst and while he can fix it once the engine cools and he can figure out what part he needs, it'll be a few hours before it gets running again and I have class tomorrow."

"Babe, no problem. Be there in an hour."

‹◊›

I take the turns on the dirt roads about five or seven over the limit, for a bit of fun. The Saab doesn't drift, though it does let me kick the back out a bit, and it can still stop pretty well just having gotten new tires and brake pads last week. I don't, I admit, know exactly where the feed store is, but it's somewhere in Mariamne's two-stop-sign downtown. At the town's outskirts, I listen to the radio's weather forecast – hot, muggy today with an early evening cold front, very high thunderstorm potential and anticipated tornado watches. In town, finding the feed store

on the second block, I park two spots from the pickup, hood up, Arn
bent over the engine.

"Anything I can help with?"

"Yuh' kin' tek' hur' tuh' school. Aht's impor'ant." He points to
the engine. "Aht's jus' gun' tek time." Arn points to the feed store and
Amber stands inside chatting with the cashier. She moves freely and
comfortable, relaxed. They gesture as they talk, both as carefree together
as Amber has become with me and my friends. I watch Amber a moment
longer, unaware that I'm here, and exhale for this confirmation that she
feels as comfortable with me and her new friends as she does with her old
friends.

"Need any parts that I can run over to Marion and pick up?"

Grandpa Arn shakes his head. I nod and head inside to get
Amber.

"I really hope I haven't been more than another thirty seconds of
your conversation."

"You, sir, have not come up once, except for us to ponder why a
renowned lead foot was taking so long," Kerry says, introducing herself
and giving me a hard, long, huge-boobs-smashing-into-my-chest hug, her
arms pressing mine to my sides as she squeezes me like a favorite stuffed
bear. "But it's nice to meet Amber's boyfriend Merak, finally."

"Nice to meet you," it comes out with a breathy pop fading into a
weak falter like an inflated balloon deflating across a room. "So she calls
me her boyfriend?"

Kerry lets go and I feel almost like I might fall over, "when you
and Amber get married and move away, just try and stay close for me,
don't go off somewhere far like St. Louis."

"How's that go?" I ask.

"We've been planning our wedding, Merak," Amber puts her
hand on my shoulder, smiles, faces Kerry, faces me. "And our kids. We're
going to have six boys and two girls and we're going to name them all

Charlie, Charlies one through eight, because I can't remember eight names and then we'll just call them the number and not really their name. And when we get married they'll be there to hold my gigantic train on the wedding dress, and Charlie six, who will be a girl, will also be the flower girl."

I look back and forth at Kerry and Amber, my eyes wide, eyebrows up, mouth open, for a moment, and then, "wait, I think you're having me on."

Kerry, "had him for a second."

"Merak, seriously. We talked about last year's fair's winning pies and how we could make Kerry's better. She makes awesome pies but hasn't placed yet."

Kerry waves her hands up and down her torso. "You can tell I make awesome pies, can't you."

Uh, well, yes. "What did you decide?"

Kerry smiles at me, "it's a super secret, but I don't think you'll tell anyone." She looks down the aisles. "Blueberry-blackberry compote filling with some orange zest and a spritz of lemon for brightness. Then a flakey, butter top with some dark rum and a caramel drizzle, probably a fancy design."

"Flake sea salt, and I'll get that over Thanksgiving in Chicago if you need," I say, "for on top of the caramel and the crust's egg wash. Maybe keep the top traditional, since the filling is fancy. Don't lose the judges."

Amber and Kerry face each other and Kerry points at me and smiles. "I like that idea. You're right, Amber, he is husband material."

Amber shushes Kerry, her cheeks and forehead flush red. "You should have Merak describe it and do your write-up."

I look at Amber. "If you're going to sell my time, at least do it for a pie?"

Kerry looks at me, plump cheeks, blue eyeshadow, thick and shiny black hair tied up in a bun showing pale, soft, cream-like neck skin that leads into, what is, without a doubt, the fullest bust I've ever been pressed into. Her left finger has a gold engagement ring with a small, clear stone and, I imagine, she makes her fiancé very happy. Joy like hers infects like a virus I would like to catch.

Amber looks at me. "You still owe me red," as Kerry leans in, elbows on the counter, hands pressed into a cup at the palms, chin resting. Kerry looks me in the eyes, raises her eyebrows and wiggles her hips.

"Red, Amber, is hugs from family after an absence, their warm hands around your shoulders and the familiar scents of their clothes and soaps on their skin. It's those moments on a long autumn walk in a warm coat strolling over dried leaves that crunch underfoot in those days between the trees' branches clearing and the first snowfall. Red smells of wood burned down to embers perfect for cooking food and feels like the heat in your mouth of a fresh-roasted marshmallow and that mix of sugar and smoke that sticks in your teeth. When I remember that moment a few months ago at my dorm, when you wore my blue pyjams, touched my arm, whispered in my ear that I had made the best coffee you'd ever had, and I knew I was more than just a notetaker, when I relive that moment, that is red."

Amber and Kerry's eyes are closed and after a moment Kerry looks at me and waves her right hand under her chin, says breathily with a done-up, exaggerated southern word-licking slowness, "Lordy, you make me wish I was a cheat," hand and arm out, finger tips up, tracing them down in a straight line as she talks, biting her lip before licking them. She looks me up and down, eyes linger below my belt line an extra few seconds before scanning up again.

"Kerry!"

"What? That was something else."

Amber slides her hand across the counter to mine and traces her fingers up my arm, my hairs standing up as her fingertips pass. She puts on Kerry's same tone, all breath and south, words lingering in her mouth like time-thieves, "well, I dunno, I'm not the jealous type," Amber says, her face turning toward Kerry, "maybe we could trade for a couple of those pies you're gonna make?"

I look at her, then at Kerry, then back, since when is Amber not the jealous type? "Only two?"

Amber smacks my butt. "Kidding. You are not for rent."

I turn on their voice. "You could join us, Amber."

Kerry runs around the counter, hugs me again, just as tight, shakes her chest against mine and my torso twists and shakes with my arms pinned to the sides. She hugs Amber just the same and before she lets go leans in to Amber's right ear and, maybe intentionally just loud enough for me to hear, "you marry this boy. You and he got a future outta here." Amber hugs her again and takes my arm as we head out of the store.

"We'll miss you when you two move to St. Louis," Kerry shouts as we walk through the doors. Grandpa Arn's head turns up from the engine and toward us, an eyebrow raised.

Amber, again-red-cheeked: "I'm sorry about my friend. It's not so uncommon around here, you know, joking about treating boys like shared clothes, for the pretty girls. But I don't really–"

"Not to interrupt, but I know where you're going." I reach between Amber's arm and her hip, reach to her lower back and put it in my hand, turning her to face me. Amber turns her face to my chest, tilts her head a little upward. "You're better than pretty; you're cute. That's like pretty, but not intimidating."

"Well maybe I want to be intimidating," Amber curls her lip and a few teeth peak from behind.

"Only works until someone gets to know you."

Grandpa Arn seems to smile at that, or maybe he's just making progress on the car. With my car's hatch popped, Amber feels out the space and places the boxes I hand her, sometimes asking for specific boxes that fit generally well. She doesn't have a lot – mostly clothes, notebooks and other supplies, some stuffed animals, her talking clock, and her rucksack. With a hug for Amber, a handshake for me that leaves my hand engine-black, Grandpa Arn sends us on our way over dusty dirt roads, past some slow tractors and pickups, and eventually to a line of cars getting onto campus, a long parking queue, and some distance carrying boxes.

"Personally," I say, carrying her boxes into her dorm as she holds my shoulders and walks behind me, "I'm really glad you're on the first floor this year. It'll be noisier sure, but easier in a fire drill than being on seven. And you guys have a lot of fire drills in these buildings." As I finish, someone with their own large box blocking their view clips my shoulder. I feel Amber get bumped and her hands let go. With a thud, she's on the sidewalk, hands up, hair tussled, right elbow with small road rash. The box's corner hit her right eye.

The student carrying the box sets it down and apologizes over and over. Amber faces him and words leave her mouth like racehorses through an opened starting gate: "not like it'll make me any blinder." The kid looks around at a few bystanders, at me, breaks eye contact quickly, takes his box and walks away.

I pull Amber up and, when we get to her room, she opens the windows and unpacks boxes as they arrive. When I set the last two down, "hey, so, there's tornado watches tonight for all over and this room is a bit musty. Not really where I want to be if there's a tornado."

"You don't have to stay." Amber: wall-facing dismissive, monotone, calm and quiet.

"No no. I was going to see if you wanted to grab dinner at the dining hall here and then come back to my room."

"Dinner yes, but I really just want to get some rest. My elbow and eye really hurt."

"Can I entice you with video games and beers?" I grin large, tilt my head as I speak, hope my tone comes across.

"You guys already set up the Nintendo?"

"We have only unpacked the Nintendo. I don't even have sheets on my bed yet."

"You had me at Nintendo, lost me at no sheets, but got me back at bed."

"That wasn't hard."

Amber fiddles with her hands on her lap. "I am very afraid of tornadoes. If there's going to be a bad storm tonight, I don't want to be alone."

"PJs, clothes for tomorrow," I say as I grab them from her boxes. "Anything else you need for an overnight?"

Amber grabs a stuffed animal, a crocheted jackalope she tells me is named Mr. Sniffles, and her toiletries. "I think this is all."

‹◊›

Rick and Amber sit on the foot of my bed and he guides her jumps, punches, and kicks as she plays the fighting game against Jesse. Jesse goes easy on her, but never outright lets her win, though a couple of times she does. I unpack sheets and my pillow, make my bed, having everyone stand as I put on the fitted sheet. Outside, horizontal rain and small hail batter the windows and roof. Even with the drapes closed to dampen the sound, Rick still has to talk loudly to Amber.

Amber hands Rick her controller with an "I'm done" and knee pat, joins me in the room's desk chairs, set facing each other, her legs up on my lap and feet around me. I reach into our cube fridge, pull out two Killian's, and pop them open.

"Hey, no beer in the dorms. I will write you up," Jesse says, and I hand him one. "You know my price."

"Such corruption and abuse of power," Amber says, holding out her beer, and Jesse clinks the bottles' necks. "So what do you do in a tornado in these buildings?" Amber points her face toward me as she takes a drink.

Wind buffets the windows so hard the panes shake and air seeps through edges of the openable frames with force that rustles the draperies. Rick checks the window locks and the storm's wind through the seams ripples his arm hair.

Jesse answers. "Officially, cram in the stairwell. Unofficially, close the draperies because they're heavy and hide under the beds or in the bathrooms. One of the old maintenance guys told me the stairwell thing makes it easier for rescue and recovery crews if the building gets hit, because we'd all be in the same place. These buildings are sixty years old and concrete block, not cast. They're not standing up to a tornado."

"I remember a storm," Amber says. "When the F3 rolled through campus in 1983 and took out the forest, it also took down the old student center, and I'm told that was built the same way as these buildings. But I gotta say I'd be happier here than in my tower if a tornado hits."

"Fun fact," Jesse says as he and Rick finger-point to different games to decide what to play next, "until that 1983 tornado, Tolliver Forest had flying squirrels. The trees that they lived in all got destroyed so they don't live in our forest any more. The trees that survived are tall enough for them again, but the forest is so isolated because of campus that flying squirrels can't get to it to reinhabit the trees."

Rick and Jesse change the game to Top Gear and I decide to check the weather as the wind picks up, the building shakes in the strong gusts, and the cypress trees around the Campus Lake bend so wildly sideways as to block street lamps I didn't think they could reach. When I power on my computer, the hard drive clicks and whirs, a warning that I may want to buy a new one soon. In time, a weather report opens. "We're in a tornado watch right now, guys, and there's a warning behind it. Radar has a strong cell of dark red with some circular motion forming and heading toward us." I unpack my radio, plug it in, and turn it to a local station. For now, music; if a tornado forms, they'll let us know.

Rick and Jesse look at me. Amber swallows. Jesse, face going a bit wax-like, excuses himself to check in with the other resident assistants.

"Rick is, uh, he's going single-player, against the computer. He's playing a winter stage, ice and snow. Um, it starts accelerating up a hill and then he's in fourth right now and working on a corner to take third."

Amber puts her hand on my knee. "I'm nervous, too."

Rick has a lousy lap and as he starts his second the wind picks up again, leaves from the cypress trees, torn off their branches, batter the dorm window and walls. A branch, large by the sound, hits the building.

"I think we should go the stairwell," Amber says.

Our dorm's rooms line one side of the building. The hallway that connects them has, on the opposite side, a large window wall looking out at Campus Lake. Jesse ushers our neighbors on the hall's far side out of their rooms and toward the stairs.

"The stairs are full," someone shouts from the middle of the dorm.

"What?" Jesse shouts back.

"There's no more room. They're completely full."

Jesse looks lost, like he has no backup plan. Lightning over the lake, dozens of bolts, rapid succession, thunder follows in indistinguishable rumbles that bleed into one loud, constant, warbling and varying sound, as though a timpanist who won't slow down until he faints has trapped us all in his largest drum. Outside, lightning flashes show a cloud spinning, pointing downward, a funnel cloud. That could be a tornado in moments. Last tornado I saw I outran. Colander's engine churned horses and his body shook as the rusty bits that barely held him together rattled and some, I'm sure, snapped. Here I have no escape, only, oh no, a gigantic window wall. Jesse and I make eye contact from across the building and he must see me look out the window because when I look back, he's seen the funnel cloud.

"Back in your rooms," Jesse shouts. "Close the blinds, hide under your beds with your blankets, cover your faces and ears with your pillows."

I spin with Amber and the brightest, longest flash of lightning I can recall in my life fills the entire hallway brighter than daytime and before it even finishes the building thunder-shakes some plastic ceiling light covers free and the overheads go dark. My radio switches to battery and a voice breaks the music to list towns that are now in a tornado warning, where an active tornado has been sighted on radar. The voice names Cold Harbor second. Tornado sirens start.

The hall is a strobe dance-party lit by lighting as the students turn and run into their rooms. They move in flash-broken spasms like low-budget animation, instants of movement bracketed by moments of pitch dark. Thunder like a base line from concert hall speaker shakes the floor and windows. People scream as they turn to run. "Amber, get us to my bed," I hold her waist in my hands and she guides us back to safety through flash-shattered darkness. Rick, staccato movement in the bits of lightning that sneak past our drapes, pulls his blanket onto the floor and hides under his desk. Amber, at my bed, guides herself under as I hand Rick his pillow. I feel the underside of my bed in the dark and Amber's hand grabs mine, leads me under the springs. Dragging my pillow and blankets with me, we swaddle ourselves together and she nests herself between me and the wall. The wind slows and my ears pop like they did driving in Colorado's mountains.

As the noise changes, I hold Amber, my eyes closed, embracing her as the darkness under my bed embraces us, but warm, telling her we'll be okay. The darkness that traps us here has no such assurances, no consolation, and no compassion. This darkness is unmoved by our peril and shows us nothing but indifference. I hold Amber close and she covers her ears saying it hurts, that the pressure changes hurt, and I yawn and pop my ears and try to help her to do that, too, and when she does the thunder dies down, the loud and rushing sound of air like the sound made by an immense waterfall or a crumbling rock cliff face, fades quickly and we are left with Amber crying, Rick shuffling under his desk, and the tornado sirens wailing in a circular drone like the cycle-sound of a forever-accelerating motorcycle. And then the sirens stop, slowly. The sound of more distant sirens across town continues faintly in the background.

"It's okay," I tell Amber. "It's past us now. That was it. I've been through these. It's over for us."

Amber shakes, "so it's safe?"

"They'll fire up the sirens again for all-clear, but we're out of it."

Amber shakes in my arms, in the dark, waiting as our body heat warms the cold tile beneath us and the blanket traps what warmth we have.

"How are you guys?" Rick asks.

"We're good," I say. "You?"

"Also good. I'm just gonna hang out here for a bit."

Amber stumbles, trips on her words, her throat chokes like her speech is dry bread, and through false starts and retries finally says, "my mom died in the 1983 tornado and it must have been absolute terror."

‹◊›

The morning brings some light through the bottoms of the drapes and, stiff-backed, shoulders popping, I put my hand on Amber's forehead. "Wake up but don't sit up. We're still under my bed," and I'm glad I did when she starts to sit up with some force, driving my hand into the bed frame's springs and putting a decent cut in the back. I clench my teeth and suck air. "I'm fine," I reassure her, and we scoot out into the room and I search for a bandage. The water for Rick's shower, probably what woke me, stops and he eventually walks into the room dressed for the day.

"Check outside?" Rick asks.

"No."

Rick's mouth looks like a whistle and he turns his head. "Probably a microburst, decent one."

The blinds open with metal rings on rod, sounding like worn bearings. Tree branches float like a waiting armada in Campus Lake. The overhead lights are still off, no power. Phones work, though, and Amber lets Grandpa Arn know she's fine.

I look at Rick and point to the shower. "Cold?"

"Steam lines are gas-powered, still working."

When we open the door, ready to see what the morning has brought, the hallway is light from the sun and clear skies, windows intact. Our neighbors mill about and read by the windows, some eat energy bars and drink cans of pop for breakfast. These are the meals of those without power. Outside, the bike racks in front of the buildings are bolted down, but the bikes, last night neat and vertical, now rest sideways, some with bent front rims. The cafeteria has a stand out front passing out snacks and coffees. Thank God.

Eventually, coffees and candy bars in our bellies, butts on morning-sun-warm benches, we face Campus Lake, the old bridge that crosses the narrow point, somehow looking untouched by the storm, and the forest's upper canopy, which looks like it skipped autumn into leafless winter. Birds chirp and sing loudly, seeing if their friends survived the storm. Geese and ducks on the lake swim around the debris and turtles rest on the floating logs, sunning themselves. Fish break water and snag insects that hover around the floating branches. No clouds shade us; the sun, warm and punishing, turns the water on the grass and in the mud into humidity as a warning for the day's coming heat, a heat that will turn our dorm rooms into small, cement cookers all day, leaving them hot overnight as well, unless we get power back soon.

We eat our breakfasts and sit in the hot, humid air disturbed only by animal noise, intermittent warm breezes, and the sounds of our chewing. Rick and I lived through microbursts before, just life in Chicago. Deer Lake, our home town, had a couple of them growing up, and running a shingle and siding replacement business there could be a nice living. Rick pats me on the back and hugs Amber when he leaves for class.

"You've been around a tornado before," I ask her.

"Yes, 1983, and small ones not this close in '90 and '95. I don't know where I want to live after college, but I know it's somewhere without tornadoes. Also, no earthquakes. That's my rule for us."

"Us?"

Amber faces the lake, her eyebrows up. "I meant me. Unless you, by happenstance, move where I move, like if you randomly get a job there. I guess maybe it would be cool to have you around."

"I think it would be cool to have me around, too, but I'm not unbiased."

Amber smacks my leg. "I accidentally let something romantic slip. Don't ruin this moment." Small waves on the lake, built of breeze-on-surface, break at the branches on the shore. "And forget I said it, too."

"I don't forget anything my girlfriend says," and I lean in to kiss her cheek.

6
Tongues

Grandpa Arn, on hearing my car come up his driveway, tosses the last of the chicken feed into the grass and scratches a nearby goat behind its horns, "come back tuh' bail sum' hay?"

"It's all I dream about any more, Grandpa Arn," I say through my open window.

Amber unlocks the doors and we walk to Arn, the gravel drive packed and firm. She gives him a big hug and, while he hugs her, reaches out his hand and gives me a hearty handshake, warm, dry and tough skin, not as firm as last time, but confident and happy. "Did yuh' tek' 'dem cah'-only roads heah'?"

"We did, yes," I say as Amber lightly smacks Grandpa Arn's shoulder.

"We're stopping in to say hi before we go to church. Merak wants to know what the church I used to go to is like, even though I haven't been there since I was, what sixteen?"

Grandpa Arn's smile flattens, his face muscles stiff, jaw more angular as he clenches his teeth. He lets us know he has to fix the tractor and that we can make ourselves lunch or just hang out.

We walk in his home, shoes by door, and stroll back to her bedroom, leaving the door open of course, and sit on her bed. Amber's bedroom reflects the space she grew up in. Though this wasn't her actual room, most of her furniture made it in here, an old flat-pack dresser where she kept her clock that speaks the time, a desk with a typewriter with braille keys that she used for homework growing up, a nightstand without a lamp, closet of now-undersized clothes, and her twin bed. The walls are white, devoid of posters and pictures, but they have some horseback riding ribbons on them and a 4-H Club plaque.

"So, Grandpa Arn had a reaction to the church."

"I felt his arm tense up. We haven't gone in a long time." Amber leans back against her wall, pulls her legs up on the bed, scoots back to sit flush and folds her legs under each other. "If you hear all this and want to end this, I understand," she says, pointing her face at her knees.

For no reason, I gesture open hands in circles near my shoulders. "This won't phase me."

Her eyebrows raise above her aviator rims in a hopeful arch, but somehow it seems the same look as a dog at a pound when someone new walks up to their cage, dropping as they walk past; Amber's eyebrows drop the same way. "I don't know who my dad was. That's the life my mom had before I was born. She and Grandpa Arn and Grandma Helen hadn't really talked for about eight years before she got pregnant. Grandpa once mentioned that for three of those they didn't even know if she was alive, in the area, or what. But when she got pregnant, she came back, and like the rich man whose son returned, Grandpa said, they welcomed her and worked with her to get her cleaned up. They didn't have the ability to put her in a program, but grandpa and grandma, with mom's okay, basically kept her locked up in the room that would one day be mine, or under close supervision doing work around the farm, for the five or six months of her pregnancy she was back with them. She stayed here after I was born, too." Amber sighs and sits for a moment quietly facing the wall across from us. I shift on the bed, bring my left leg up onto it, fold it under my right, which hangs off the edge, and I turn to look more directly at her. The living room clock ticks loudly. Amber's hair, tied into two unbraided pigtails that point down and back, secured by one black and one red band, has some stray strands.

"So I was born and they did some standard tests at the hospital and determined I was vision impaired, and in time that I had no vision at all. Mom, she apparently blamed herself and her life early in my pregnancy for that. The doctors, Grandma Helen once told me, reassured her no end that there was no connection, that I have a rare genetic thing that caused my optic nerves just not to form right. And in time, I guess, she came to believe that. And then she started going back to the church that she and grandpa and grandma went to when she was a kid. It's a fire-and-brimstone place. 'Sinners in the Hands of an Angry God' place. The preacher, Reverend Morris, did a whole sermon about how God punishes sinners for their sins by hurting their family, and specifically said 'by making their children blind to show his hatred for our sins.' I don't, of course, remember that. Grandpa Arn does, and he wanted to stop going to church right then and there but mom wanted to keep going, needed I think maybe to purge her guilt and thought those sermons would burn it all away. And for the next two years, Reverend Morris made mom and me a semi-regular example of what God does when people sin."

"Jesus." I shift on the bed, lean up against her wall, put my feet on the mattress, and hold my knees.

"No kidding. A couple years back, I started to realize how messed up that horse hockey is. Mom was working to make her life better. She was feeling clean and not so tempted by her old life, finally. She had a job at Growlers, serving some nights, cooking others. She wanted, I guess, to open her own pie shop, bakery, or dine-in restaurant in town and she was learning how to do the work and the business. And then one night we had a really bad storm. It's the first thing in my life I remember." As Amber speaks, her voice shifts, takes on a vowel-twang, slight pull against the consonants. "Distant tornado sirens, rain on the walls and windows like being trapped in a popcorn popper. The house shaking in wind and thunder, the air sucked out of the basement, gasping to breathe, feeling the air tingle whenever there was a lightning and smashing my hands to my ears because the thunder was right above us and so loud that when it went dust would get shook out 'uh the floorboards and onto us. And I just sat under those basement stairs crying and screaming for it to stop. It took shingles off our house's roof whenever that funnel cloud came over. The sirens were going off and the restaurant was closed but my mom and two other staff were still there cleaning and such. And you don't get in your car in a tornado. So they got into the cooler. The tornado mostly just went through farms and forest, taking out trees, a couple grain silos, crops, a barn or whatever," Amber lets out the last of this non-stop breath and takes in a long, new one, "and then it went through the restaurant. A big enough tornado, ain't no safety. That cooler got picked up and tossed around a thousand feet as the building blew apart. Gas station next door, a shared doctor and dentist office behind, leveled. Mom, the two others in the cooler, two employees at the gas station..." Amber faces me and shakes her head.

My hand touching her chin then up her cheek, I take Amber's aviators and set them over my knee. No tears: This was almost a rote recitation.

"So that very Sunday, not two days after, we're in church, and I guess what Reverend Morris says, he says 'God sent us a tornado to cleanse our town of evil. And he called home his good and faithful servant Lorraine,' my mom. And bam, heel to hero. I only remember Grandpa Arn's teeth grinding. At her funeral, the preacher, he said, Grandma Helen told me, to know that the greatest sin can be forgiven by God if we ask, and that he hoped my mom had asked as that cooler was flung through the air."

Good Christ. "And that's when you stopped going to church?"

"We went less," Amber says, her voice dropping the country twinge. "Grandma Helen wanting to go, Grandpa Arn he was done with it though and only went because we should go as a family, the ever-rarer occasions we went. Grandpa Arn never forgave, as grandpa calls him, Joe. But when Grandma Helen died, this was whenever I was sixteen, Reverend Morris he spoke at her funeral," Amber holds her right arm out in front of her and tilts her head down some and, as she speaks, moves her arm in a flat arc. "He said, 'hope that God understands our weaknesses and forgives our sins of religious infidelity and that he does not cast into the fire those who stray from the fold because their sadness weakens them.' After the funeral, behind Pritcher's, Grandpa Arn punched him in the face. It sounded like a horse landing a jump in damp ground. Officer Tad came around the back as Reverend Morris was falling. Tad walked right up next to Grandpa and when the preacher said 'I want to press charges,' Tad knelt down and says, 'For what, tripping on your shoelace and hitting your face on the doorframe?' Tad's what I think an uncle is like. He and Grandpa Arn are close and he watches out for me," Amber exhales, taps her left fingers in a pattern on her leg. "I know that's a lot to dump on you."

"We don't have to go to church."

"We do. I need you to understand." The living room clock ticks away some seconds. The tractor engine tries to start, fails. Amber turns her face toward me, "do you hate me now?"

My hands find Amber's knee, "I'm sorry you didn't really get to know your mom well and I'm kind of jealous that your grandparents worked so well together to raise you. My parents, not so much. They were distant to each other when I was a kid, then openly hostile as I finished junior high and started high school. I just figured they'd get divorced. Never did. The summer after I graduated high school was the worst. But that fall they decided to work at things. It helped that a divorce would have dissolved my dad's architecture firm. So they got into therapy and, much to my surprise, worked out their issues. They're like kids in love now. That's a good example for me. Everyone is worth another chance; everyone can become better." I tap my index finger on Amber's knee, "we are who we are because of our experiences. If we don't embrace those, we don't embrace who we are as people."

"So, like, grace?"

"Loaded word, concept works. People work to become better. I like to think that the end of our life pulls us, like the gravity of an impossibly large star, ever toward it and that the journey gives us opportunities to be our best self."

This seems to sit well with Amber, "you have a sense of meaning in your life. I'm a little jealous. I do not. I don't know why I'm here, or you're here, or Grandpa Arn, or why God doesn't just start us all off in Heaven and let us be the best we can be there with no fear of dying and no question of whether or not anything even comes after. What do you think comes after this?"

I lean back on her bed, change my legs' orientation as they begin a nerve-pressure tingle. Amber shifts and the sheets move and the bed shakes a bit. "I know we're mourned by those who will miss the shared times and experiences, the mutual growth, and the laughs and memories we won't make together. Mourning really is that, I think, an immense sadness at what we could have had, but won't."

"So you love the experiences you have with someone, not the person?"

"Oh, that's not fair. Like I said, experiences make us. Sharing experiences means we become part of that other person." In the living room, the recliner shifts and I wonder how long Grandpa Arn has listened.

"Well, I need to change into a dress. Pants are a sin for Pentacostal girls, you know. This is an experience you can't share with me," Amber says, kissing my cheek and patting my butt as I stand.

‹◊›

I don't know what woke me. Maybe the conversation in the kitchen. Maybe a dream of daylight and outside games, but I woke confused, unsure where I was. That cabin, bare wood walls and white-tile counters, smelled of filterless cigarette smoke, wood must, fireplace heat, and a tart, nostril-tinge of wall-hidden mold. It was small, two rooms, and my grandfather rented it every year from a friend he'd known since the 1950s.

The kitchen table, a goldenrod-vinyl-topped, tarnished-aluminum-trimmed folding table with rickety metal tube legs, shook and full glasses splashed over when someone played a card too forcefully. Four seats, three of which could be used safely, surrounded it. Right of it, the wood-burning stove burned low, warm, and ember-fueled; a thin smoke tendril seeped into the room through a crack that ran the length of the door's thick glass. Left, the fridge, yellow, dimmed the lights when the compressor cycled. An icepick hung chained to the freezer handle.

The white-tiled counter stretched from the fridge to the sink and then the wall, maybe ten or twelve feet all-in. The grout in the tile, where intact, was black next to the sink. Above the sink, window drapes, pulled to the side and held in place with short lengths of the thick, white fishing line my grandfather used on his muskie rod, danced on the bottom hem as breezes moved alongside the cabin. The glass, too, moved in the air; loose in the wood frame, the old panes announced any slight breeze with a tap of glass on wood, then returned to rest again with another, tinnier tap when the breeze passed.

The bedroom faced the kitchen and had only a bead curtain for privacy. The bed was an old double with spent frame springs and a worn-top mattress. I lay across the foot, eyes open, my right eye peering through the space between the top of the mattress and the bedframe's metal handle, running up to a bend and crossing the bed's width slightly above the mattress' top. The bed frame's paint covered other layers, revealed in divots and scratch-craters that said this bed had, at least, been white, black, orange, blue, pink, red, brown, and purple.

Off to the side of the bedroom was a small bathroom with a thin door. Behind it, the toilet, at regular intervals, dripped and partly flushed. The bathroom window whistled when breezes rattled the kitchen window.

My grandfather sat at the card table with his friend. His friend's robin's egg blue shirt proudly proclaimed in bold, white letters that he was the world's best fisherman. What was his name? Even now I can't recall it. No, wait, he had the name of that laboratory. Fermi? Was that right? No. Livermore. That was it. His last name was Livermore and grandfather called him Liv.

Liv and grandfather played a slow game of double solitaire. When wind moved the tree branches, the pathway light outside shone through the kitchen window over the sink, casting the men as shadows on the far wall. The primary light inside came from the wood stove, a faint, red glow that flickered through the thick and sooty glass, danced a slow, perpetual motion across the walls and around the room. Red-orange light shimmered as the coals at the bottom of the fire brightened and dimmed in waves and rhythm, occasionally flaring bright orange as wood or trapped gasses ignited. Fire: matter, mass, and energy in one – its light moved like a shallow, disturbed puddle across the walls and the men's faces.

"Excited for tomorrow, Quentin?" Liv asked. His voice was deep, and could once have been a choir-worthy baritone, but age had turned it into a cheese grater on concrete.

"Of course. Muskie. Love catching them. Did I show – no, I don't think. Take a look at this thing." Grandfather stood and walked to his tackle box, a brown plastic case that opened like a clamshell and unfolded layers and layers of trays. My father had a matching one, but used it to hold tools for fixing the old MG in his garage. My grandfather retrieved a brass disk with a single treble hook on the end. The disc looked like it could have been hammered over the business end of a baseball bat, rounded with the same diameter and cup. It was polished and my grandfather flicked and spun it from a swivel. The fire light, bothered, disturbed when the cup spun toward the stove, reflected a diffuse, copper-red spot around the room's walls, like a searchlight. The reflection appeared, disappeared, over and over, slowing with each pass. Grandfather handed the disk to Liv.

"That, Liv, was buried in the boat house. It took some doing, but I figured out what it is. No one at any of the bait or tackle shops in the area had any idea what it is. Guess."

"It's a fishing lure."

"The best muskie lure ever made. They were so effective that the Canadian government made them illegal, except for two hours a day, for years. That law is gone, maybe, not sure. Easier to ask forgiveness than permission. Anyway, no one makes these anymore. I polished it and tomorrow it's gonna catch some fish again for the first time in no one knows how long."

Liv smiled as grandfather put the lure away. "What's eating you?" Grandfather asked.

"Do you think a man can be separated from his actions?"

"I don't follow," my grandfather said, shifting the lure in place.

"What I mean is, are we just our actions or are we more?"

"Well," grandfather said looking at Liv and tilting his head, "I know what you're asking and I think we're, yes, the sum of how we treat others. There are times when we're told to be someone we're not. I'm not sure how to account for that."

"I won't be able to make this trip next year."

"Well, your social calendar must be pretty full if you're planning things a year in advance." Grandfather finished his beer and pulled another from the fridge. He handed the can to Liv, who declined with his palm. "How do you even know you'll be busy next year?" He put the can back in the fridge, paused, looked at the freezer door, stood upright, closed the fridge, and watched the edges of his fire-cast shadow dance on the wall. "I'm sorry, Liv. How long did they give you?"

"Four months, at most."

"And?"

"Liver, pancreas, intestines, blood, and just last week in the brain and bones."

My grandfather sat, opened his beer, and let it rest and hiss a second. "Chemo?"

"I've seen enough people cling to life, like death is pulling them off a cliff and they're clawing at the dirt and hoping some of that dust will keep them from going. All they end up leaving behind are finger marks at the end of their road. And for it, their families, friends, and whomever else gets to remember them as pale, gaunt, sunken-eyed and helpless needing a nurse to wipe their ass and dab their bed sores with yellow cream. I don't want that. When I reach the end, soon, and when death comes to get me, I'm gon' let him take me without a fight."

Grandfather and Liv sat quietly at the table. The looked at the fire and grandfather sipped his beer.

"Goddam' I'm gonna miss these trips, Quentin."

"Same here, Liv," grandfather set his jaw, blinked in a rapid series.

I watched these men through the gap between the mattress and frame. Just minutes ago they seemed invincible until, on my grandfather's cheek, a shiny, red-lit trail grew toward his stubble. They sat in silence for what seemed minutes. A log in the wood stove cracked and broke, ash-spark-light glimmered on the wall except where the mens' diffuse shadows, flame-light-dancing penumbras, moved behind them. A wind tapped and whistled the window pane. The toilet dripped and part-flushed. The fridge turned on and a fan in the back clicked metal-on-metal.

"What do you suppose happens when we die?" Liv asked, looking at the fire.

Grandfather sat a moment, held his beer and looked at the window. He picked up the cards on the table and separated the decks into piles. "All I know is that the people we love will miss us; the people whose lives we improve will mourn us. I hope that after everything goes dark that I'll see a growing light, like the way the sun rises over Lake Superior at the first of spring: a steady lightness and then a burst as the sun crests the horizon. And I hope that then God will put his hand on my shoulder and say 'you were wrong about a lot of things, but that's okay'."

Liv nodded, reached for and sipped grandfather's beer. "What do you believe happens?"

"Everything I just said up to the part where everything goes dark. I've lived 'bout half this life a good church-goer. I like to hope there's more, but I believe this is our one life."

"I hope that you're right. About either." Liv finished what was left of grandfather's beer in a single take. "I hope, if there's more, that we forget. Everything. This whole life," Liv said.

"I hope you can forget it all, too, Liv. I hope we get to be friends anew again, too."

"Do you think that after people die they forgive the ones who wronged them?"

"Grudges don't benefit the dead."

"I want to forget it. All of it, Quentin." Liv looked at him, cheeks shining like red mirrors, edges rippled as new tears moved to his chin. "I don't want to see their faces when I sleep no more. I don't want to hear them, smell them. That burning smell. There's no escape. Nothing in this life set me free." Liv pushed the empty beer can in circles on the tabletop, making a sound like distant, large waves breaking on beach rocks. "I hope that eternal sleep isn't like this life's sleep. That's all."

My grandfather pulled two more beers from the fridge and sat with his feet on an empty chair, resting his soles toward the stove. "For whatever I believe, Liv. I'm pretty good at remembering the Bible. Isaiah 65:16 and 17 read 'For the past troubles will be forgotten and hidden from my eyes. See, I will create new heavens and a new earth. The former things will not be remembered, nor will they come to mind'."

Liv opened his mouth dryly, held his right index finger up, but didn't challenge. Their next beers popped open under their fingernails, not quite in sync, metal shearing and beer fizzing. The men tapped the rims in a toast. When Liv tilted his beer backward, my grandfather looked at me, lowered his index finger over his eyes. I blinked and the sunrise lit the kitchen window, stove fire faded to gray smoke. The cabin smelled of coffee, beans, and bacon.

"Grab some bread and a peeled egg, Merak. Make a sandwich to eat as we walk to the boathouse."

The trail to the lake was a quarter-mile sinusoidal dirt path through wild berries and tall conifers, around boulders left carelessly by retreating glaciers, and down a steep hill to a slanted wooden shack half over the lake and half not. The walls: weathered, gray wood slats that aligned, generally, on at least one plane. The ragged-bottom planks over the water provided a home to moss and lichens where the wood had not fallen away. The roof: a bow-crested hodgepodge of different shingles sported patches of thick moss and trapped, fallen leaves.

Our boat was an old, metal job with dented and paint-chipped sides and a steering wheel where my grandfather would steer from the middle. Beat-up old seats, torn padding and low backs, were tack-welded to the boat's bottom. It was still one of the coolest things I had seen because who knew boats could drive like a car.

"Indian fill the tank and leave us some extra?" Liv asked.

"Charlie always does."

"I need to visit a tree quickly."

I waited until Liv was behind the tree, "what people was Liv talking about last night?"

Grandfather looked at where Liv went. "Liv is a vet," he said. "Not the animal kind. He was a soldier and spent almost three years in Korea. That's where he, Charlie, and I met. He was also in another country, Vietnam, some years later. I was not. The things he saw, I only know a few; he does not talk about them with anyone. You don't need to worry about these things. And don't ask Liv about them. Pretend last night didn't happen until after this trip, okay?"

"Why did you say you'll miss Liv next year?"

116

Grandfather turned from the path Liv took and knelt in front of me. "Merak," he said, holding my shoulders firm like ladder rungs and staring in my eyes, his eyes red with exhaustion spider webs, "everyone at some point faces the moment they die. It's an important part of being human. Some of us have seconds or less, others some weeks or months. How we face the end says a lot about, and comes from, how we lived. You're too young to understand this now but, I hope, when you need to hear this again you remember it: We have to forgive the people who wrong us and ourselves for the wrongs we do others. If there's another point to life, I don't know it. I hope you don't have to learn this next lesson like I did, maybe you learn it from me now, but never wait to tell someone something important."

The boathouse was an engineering marvel. The doors opened along sliders made out of pipes that doubled as gutters. The lake lapped inside. My grandfather pulled on a chain inside the boathouse and far doors over the lake opened inward. He looped the chain to a metal hook next to the door and pulled a second chain, this one around a gear near the roof, and the boat lowered into the water. The chain screeched like a train on an old bend. A musty, damp breeze came through the boathouse from the lake.

We stepped into the boat and grandfather pushed us out of the boathouse as Liv started the motor. Grandfather steered us into the lake, "Grippins shelf off Peers Point, Liv?"

Liv nodded and, in seconds, the boathouse shrank in the distance as a narrow triangle of small waves spread behind us.

‹◇›

Amber's childhood church is a small, white, old-timey looking chapel named "Forever Pathways Pentecostal Church at the Madonna of the Caves Mine Chapel." Amber explains that the chapel is a historical landmark and that the chapel name must be kept. It has a double-door entry, a narthex no deeper than a coat closet, the sides of which are used as one, and an immediate entrance to the chapel. Only seven rows of pews stretch front to back. Maybe a bit more than eighty people can safely fit in here, but Amber explains that well more than double that attend each service. Above us, two ceiling fans on high, one rocking and clicking, move the hot, humid late-august air; I don't know what I'm in for, but it will be hot. At the chapel's front, a simple, wooden lectern rests on the podium and serves as the pulpit. A high school kid in gray pants and a white polo shirt pulls a projector screen down. He joins three other kids, dressed the same, who connect cords to musical instruments and test audio levels on their speakers. Services are mostly music, modern Christian rock anthems played, generally, either as power ballads or bubblegum pop, depending on that week's service's theme, Amber tells me. This week would be a power ballad week where the church band, the high schoolers with any musical talent, will play their favorite Christian praise and worship covers while the preacher's wife sings.

Amber wears a long dress, to her ankles, light blue with gray stripes, a personal favorite she explained because it has pockets. The dress fits her chest a bit snugly and, as we head toward the church I notice one of her bra straps has slid from under her dress strap. I correct it and, in my periphery, see someone pass, eyes angled down and lips frowning. At the entry, Amber takes my hand and starts to lead us up the aisle. "Whoa, hold on," I say. "Where are we going?"

"I sit in the third row."

"Is it assigned seating?"

"No, that's just where I always sat. Where do you sit?"

"The Snyders are a back-of-the-church family. Back row, exclusively."

"That is the lamest thing you've said. 'The Snyders are a back-row family.' What does that mean?"

"Let's sit in back. That way we can leave iffin it gets too loud."

"Did you really just say iffin?"

I did. "Not on purpose."

When I was around ten or eleven, my father explained to me that my family sits only in the back row of the church. I asked why and he said that maybe when I was older it would make sense. I am not, I don't think, old enough yet to understand what draws people to the back or front of a church. Knowing, though, that Amber's mother chose to sit at or near the front, to make herself a target, to choose fire from the pulpit, maybe that's the difference. Maybe those who sit at the front want or need to feel judged and those who sit at the back, no less sinners, prefer to judge.

Service warms up when a woman, wearing her gray hair in an older perm-style, walks to the front past some casual hellos in the pews. Her blazer, a fine-thread broad-line-pattern weave and gold buttons, hangs fitted well over her shoulders and age-dropped bust. Her blouse moves like silk and her skirt, pattern-matched to her blazer, hangs from her hips with straight, pressed lines that lead to black, lizard-skin heels. Her fingers are a multitude of rings, silver and glittering in the lights that point down at her from above.

She stands in front of us all, a white projector screen behind her, a small band of high schoolers playing guitar, bass, drums, and a keyboard antipode her via the pulpit. The projector reads Live Out Loud and "Brian Crawley" in two lines. As the music starts, the lyrics replace the song name on the screen. The guitarist starts to play loud and slow the poppy, catchy chords that feel as though played on a tape timed by pinched fingers. The chords repeat a few times and then the drums join, the bass and keyboard join, and the woman on the other side of the stage starts singing.

"That's Meredith Morris," Amber says, and confirms her marriage to the preacher.

Meredith launches in slowly, timed to the power-ballad music, with lyrics while the pews start to pack and people talk amongst themselves. The woman who glared at us sits in front of us, turns around, sees Amber, greets her enthusiastically, and asks where she's been lately.

"College."

"Don't let your school interfere with your education, if you know what I mean. Them elites'z just a bunch tryin' tuh' make you think like 'em."

"I'll be careful, Betty. Thank you."

The music at the front is loud. People around us talk over each other, ignoring it. I put my hand on Amber's leg and she slides it to her knee, "do people always talk over the music?"

"Yes, people talk and converse until the sermon. Don't they at your church?"

"What? No. That's super rude. Second note of the opening music and everyone is silent, facing forward."

Amber's head recoils a bit. "It's silent?"

"We say 'amen' when we're supposed to and recite The Lord's Prayer. There are some hymns we sing and Bible verses we recite. Don't they," I gesture broadly to the crowd, though I have no idea why, "sing the standard hymns?" I notice the pews backs have no hymnals, no Bibles.

"What hymns do you sing?"

"*El Shaddai; How Great Thou Art; Holy, Holy, Holy;* and some others come to mind. Standard hymnal."

"I've never heard of those songs."

I sit with my back against the pew, neck and head straight up, wall pressed against my hair: what, exactly, did I get in to. Around us, people have turned in their pews to talk to others, and started to notice Amber. They look at us, point. The music overpowers their voices, but their mouths make clear shapes with their words – circle to wide to thin smile to open and pressed closed – someone asking who Amber is with. Open, wide to small circle, not so wide, quick open and close, lower lip curl in and lips out – gotta be 'I've never seen him before.'

"People noticed you, Amber. They're pointing at me."

"Merak, this is a small town. This is big news. Everyone assumes we're going to get married."

The music stops and a man a few years older than me, sitting in the next pew, in jeans, a large belt buckle with a pattern I can't make out, and a button-down shirt, mid-conversation, not dropping his voice volume any, says "ain't never seen a car like that before, no. Who's is it?"

I lift my right hand and look at him. "It's mine."

Amber gasps.

"What?"

The next song starts and I miss the name of it before the screen shows the lyrics. The man gets up and walks over toward us.

"His name is Terrance, Merak. He and I dated. About a year, off and on."

Terrance stands in front of us and holds out his hand. I shake it, like I would Grandpa Arn's, and Terrance grinds my metacarpals like he wants to make them powder. "I've not had the pleasure of seeing you around he-ah."

"You have not," I shake his hand and clench my jaw so I don't cry out, force my name through my teeth: "Merak."

"Call me T-T, all my friends do."

"Nice to meet you, T-T." When he lets go of my hand, I want to flex my fingers, re-align my hand, but I don't; I won't, not until he turns away.

"Lovely to see you, Amb," T-T says.

"Same," Amber replies, facing forward.

T-T walks away and I give my hand a bone-cracking flex.

"You two –"

"Please don't"

Too late, "– it didn't end well."

"Did not."

T-T spoke two sentences and managed, in both, to say 'see.' Since Amber asked me not to use vision words, like starting sentences with "look," as Chicagoans do without realizing, now when others do it the words fill my ears like headphone heat. All I know about T-T: he knew how to cause pain and chose to do it.

The preacher's wife sings to a bass solo filled with long, low notes that drag like vowels in a drunk's two-AM words. I lean over to Amber, "You don't ever have to tell me. Also, we can leave if you want."

"You don't want to see the sermon?"

"Honestly, I really do." Whatever it's going to be, it's gonna be a spectacle.

After some more songs that compete with ongoing conversations, people milling about in the pews, a few locals coming to say hi to Amber and ask about this nice guy-friend she's brought, people smiling politely when learning that I am from Chicago, and expressing surprise that Amber is dating someone who doesn't drive a truck (this is a major conversation topic,) a man milling about in the front row walks to the lectern. He taps a few times on the microphone, which is quite obviously on and sends painful static shockwaves through the room. Conversations mostly end as butts shift-squeak the pews. Amber and I, pressed together closely, share our pew with at least one-too-many people and our hips and legs press into and share sweat with those next to us.

The man at the lectern is slight with a dyed-black hair crown and shaved-bald scalp on top. He wears older glasses, round-lenses, submarine-style temples, weathered brass that may once have been gold-plated. Behind his bright orange tie he wears an ill-fitted light-gray suit; it looks second-hand and of an older style. I feel; this feeling defies description – not pity, that's far from right. I understand for a moment the differences between my life, not rich but comfortable, and the lives the people here lead. I have a good suit, have never been without since I was around twelve. I may have only worn each of my childhood suits once or twice before outgrowing them, but then a thing would arise and my dad would simply have a new one tailored. This man's suit is not tailored to his frame, could not have been given the leg and sleeve lengths. Our differences are not how we worship, what we believe, or what we want from our lives, but the opportunities life afforded by lottery of birth. We share the same desires: a better life for ourselves, for our current or future children, to live with less fear, more security, and in those desires we are one. Our wants align, tools and opportunities do not.

"My brothers and sisters, let us give great praise for the lovely music we heard here today so far, and the other lovely music we will hear before rise, as sung by Meredith and the Forever Pathways Church Band!"

Someone in the audience shouts "Preach it, Deacon Tidings!"

"Let me lead you all in prayer," Deacon Tidings says. He reaches his arms out wide, shakes his hands like a magician, his coat sleeves waving like line-dry laundry in the wind, and he slams his hands together in a clap so loud and sharp that Amber and I jolt in our seats, shaking the pew and earning some flash-quick stares from our neighbors. The congregation bows their heads and closes their eyes, and Amber does the same. I bow my head but glance around the room and at Deacon Tidings as he talks. "Heavenly and ever-loving father and our Lord and Savior the Baby Jesus, please give our beloved Reverend Joseph Morris the words you want him to speak, the message someone here needs, and the ears of those who need to hear it." Deacon Tidings clasps his hands together so hard his fingers start to go white. He shakes as he speaks into the lectern microphone, his high-alto voice bounces around the room, both from the mic and his mouth, like a social butterfly making the rounds at a party.

The congregation shouts "Amen."

"Lord and loving God, please fill Reverend Morris with your Spirit so that your Truth, your Justice, and your Word may flow from his mouth today like the waters of the great Amazon River into the ocean, and allow those of us here to be that ocean to hear and absorb the words you give Reverend Morris." Deacon Tidings' clasped hands shake like he's holding dice; he brings them in circles around his head and shoulders, shaking and spinning his hands, pulling them in close when he gets to the microphone stem, as though he has hit it before doing this.

"Here here!"

"We beseech you, oh Lord, to fill Reverend Morris with your Presence so we may know the nature of your Will."

"Amen!"

With this final sentence, Deacon Tidings unclasps his hands and the color returns slowly up his fingers. He flexes his fingers and looks out at the crowd. The band begins to play something that sounds like it could be a hymn, right beat and cadence, but it's definitely not a standard. As they play, the crowd turns and watches the slow, handshake- and smile-greeting-filled up-aisle stride of a man in a dark navy herringbone-pattern suit, fitted, tailored, new in the last six months, no lose button threads, pattern-matched at the seams of both the coat and pants, white-silk button-down shirt and black-silk tie, gold tie clip with a pair of opposing black-triangle inlays by the engraved letters "JM", and gold bar-style cufflinks peeking past the surgeon's buttons on his coat. I turn to Amber and whisper "How rich is Reverend Morris?"

"What are you talking about?"

"He's wearing a tailored suit, probably about four grand." Then I see his shoes, dark brown; I know that pattern. They are shoes I wanted with my last suit, but my father coughed reading the price tag and said a firm 'not in this lifetime.' They're hand-sewn in Portugal. "I could not buy his shoes if I sold my car," I whisper. Betty hears me over the music and holds her finger to her lips.

Amber's mouth moves like she wants to say something and can't. Reverend Morris stands at the lectern at the front of the crowd and clears his throat. The sound booms through the audio system and he reaches slowly up to the mic and turns it off.

"Sorry, Reverend Morris," says Deacon Tidings from the front row.

"Deacon Tidings, God's good and faithful servant, no sin was committed here today," Reverend Morris says with a bright, full smile filled with impossibly white, straight, and perfectly square teeth. His voice fills my soul with tremble in its depth and rich bass. His words carry around the room like birds of prey circling on a hillside thermal and I feel like a field mouse eating grass.

Deacon Tidings thanks him and sits quietly. Reverend Morris stands tall at the lectern, above it like a broad cliff face over a river. He has a belly, large and round, six or so inches of belt overhang, and his coat button does not strain. I look anew at his wife's also-tailored outfit, rings, and shoes; their well combed and healthy hair, and bleach-white and straight teeth stand, to me, in stark contrast to clothes, jewelry, hair, and teeth of the congregation.

"I have warned you. I have tried to prepare you, for the times they are coming," Reverend Morris booms loudly and with no warning. The entirety of those attending reel back in their pews, which lift and scoot with the movement, wood-on-wood landings sounding like synchronous foot stomps at a concert.

I lean in to Amber "I know this song." Betty turns around and scowls.

"Be prepared at any moment for the coming of Lord God for you do not," he yells the 'not' and slams his hand into the lectern, "know when the Lord God will decide to call you home. Only God knows the hour of his coming for you. Can I have an Amen."

"Amen!"

Reverend Morris looks around the room and he sees Amber, and then our eyes lock. He looks me up and down. Is he gauging the quality of my character, my soul, or my suit? If only I had a better one. This man needs to be challenged someday.

"You all here," he stares me in the eyes as he says this, "are sinners. Love the sinner and hate the sin, you have heard this, and only through God's endless Grace for the repentant, for those who sought to separate themselves from their sin, for those who practice His Word every day of their lives, practice His Word through the singing of His songs, the giving to His church, the loving of those within His flock, only you few will know the wonders of Heaven. All others are to be cast into fire to burn in their sin." The congregation nod and someone near me says 'so true, so true.'

"Sinners, repent!"

"We repent!"

"Sinners, did you repent?"

"We repent!"

"It is never too late to repent." Reverend Morris leans on the lectern with his right forearm; the wood creaks as he turns his body slightly sideways and looks across the congregation. He speaks with a smirk and just loudly enough so the whole room can hear, "well, it's never too late until it is too late. There is no repentance, no forgiveness, no mercy to those who stray from God's path without repenting in life. When you are dead, it is too late. When will God come for you?

"We don't know."

"Who knows when God will come a-knockin' on your door, let himself in, open the book of your life, and ask you where you think you are going next?"

"Only God knows."

In this round of recitations I hear Amber in unison with the congregation. What the heck? I feel like I'm trapped on a carnival ride, as though we all spin and gravity pulls at me from behind, the same feeling I get from breathing dentist's gas. For a moment I see only a circle of world through a long, black tube and Reverend Morris' voice becomes hollow, tinny, and distant and the floor spins underneath me as I whirl around opposite the spin with the rest of the room and I swallow back an urge to vomit.

"We know only that God will come for us someday," Reverend Morris says, calmly, standing upright. "You, T-T," he says, pointing at T-T, who sits in the third row back. "You robbed a grocery store."

"I did."

"At gunpoint."

"I did."

"How much money did you get?"

"About five-hunderd' dollars."

"How much is your soul worth, T-T?"

"More than five-hunderd' dollars."

Reverend Morris is calm, speaks slowly and with intent, scanning the room and making eye contact with the congregation, like a tree-perched leopard looking at gazelle in the grass. "More than five-hundred dollars. That, T-T, is right. God gave all y'all your souls." Reverend Morris begins to work himself up, shaking his shoulders. "God's gifts are beyond value in this life." He steps from behind the lectern, carries a Bible out from it, held in his left hand, and starts to walk down the few steps to the aisle. "God knows the true Heaven-value of your gifts, of your souls, and he knows when he wants to collect them for himself. He knows who will be rich in Heaven, who will be poor in Heaven, and who will be nothing because they will not be in Heaven." Reverend Morris booms, slamming his right fist into the Bible with key words. "Do you want to burn in the eternal fire, hot enough to melt rock, the eternal blast furnace powered by God's hatred of you?"

"No we do not."

"Do you want to be rich in Heaven?"

Staying for this was a mistake. The air turns thick, feels like dehydration spit. The speaker system rings faint feedback and stops. I am aswirl in chaos and noise and a hundred peoples' exhale and it cups me in this ancient chapel like a baby in hands of heat. My lungs fill as though breathing water, submerged and in growing darkness, drowning and feeling around the slick wetness of vinyl seats and windows in Colander's dimming overhead lamp-light as he flips upside-down and I fall onto the roof and without warning say, "yes we do."

I feel around the back of the pew in front of me, my right leg pressed against Amber, my left against the thigh of a stranger in tight sweat pants and an old concert tour T-shirt. I am pressed tightly between them, and we exchange body heat, inhale others' exhales, shoulders pressing and forcing our arms to our fronts. With a vibration that travels from somewhere in the pew's wood, the room stinks of rancid digestive problems. Like smelling salts, it brings me out of the whirling flashback trance-Wendigo that threatened to eat my consciousness like a lost hiker's soul. I shake my head; the floor stabilizes. The tunnels around my eyes recede; the spinning ends with me upright.

Reverend Morris stares at me as he speaks, "Galena, you have used opiates."

A woman with short black hair looks up at him and around the room, like a rabbit that sees the coyote too late. "I did."

"Your husband left you because of it," his gaze turns to Galena.

"He did," she says softly, looking at her hands resting on her lap.

"Did God leave you?" Reverend Morris' voice turns soft, supple, calm.

Galena trembles; her short, dark hair and the hint of frail shoulders under an old shirt all I see.

"God did not leave you, Galena," Reverend Morris' soft, dulcet tone sounds like a man asking for make-up sex from a woman with a black eye. "He led you here, did he not?"

"He did," Galena nods and speaks fast.

Reverend Morris steps off the stage, walks to the second row of pews, puts his hand on Galena's shoulder and gives it a squeeze. "God forgives you. Stay on God's path, be pure in virtue, and God will still love you." He reaches down to the button holding his suit coat closed, undoes it, and flares the coat, revealing a shiny, purple lining that catches the overhead lights in crescents and waves. "All y'all know this, but I had my first drink of booze when I was jus' thirteen. John Wayne, that was who I wanted to be, and I struggled to drink that stuff, made that scrunched face like they did in the westerns, because the body is God's and the drugs and booze are Satan's and the body wants to reject that which is Satan's. I know you are good and God-fearing people and that many of you have tasted the Devil's sweat. The body wants to be filled with that of God, not that of Satan, and that is why we cringe when we drink."

I face Amber. "That's patently not true. They acted those faces to show that whiskey back then was poor-quality and tasted like turpentine, and a lot of it back then was toxic."

Amber puts her hand on my knee and her finger to her lips.

"I, friends, have been clean now twenty-two years."

"Preach it," someone a couple rows ahead of us shouts.

"I drank every day until my thirty-fifth birthday, when I woke up in the drunk tank, Officer Tad—"

"Boo!"

"—dragging his baton on the bars, that sound a-ringing in my head like God's own angry bells and I thought I was being called home. I don't remember my thirty-fifth birthday. I do remember every day since and how God has kept me," Reverend Morris stretches his arms wide, looks up at the ceiling, lifts the Bible above his head, "on the clean, narrow path with the help of my loving, steadfast wife Meredith." He turns and points to Meredith and the congregants erupt from silence into applause and cheers.

"Amber," his voice is roundness and warmth, but my hairs stand straight, my skin cold, endorphins and adrenaline blaze fear-driven up my spine and through my gut. My mouth goes dry and I feel my lungs stop mid-breath. "It's wonderful to see you again after all this time," he says, bringing the Bible in front of him, listing his head slightly to the right as he speaks. Somehow, this feels so much worse than anything else he could have said. "Are you coming back to the fold and who did you bring?" What I just thought was incredibly incorrect.

"This is Merak."

"Merak," Reverend Morris says. "A pleasure. I'm glad you could join us today and we hope we see you again soon."

Reverend Morris walks up the aisle. He shakes the hands of aisle-sitting congregants, makes eye contact with me while he shakes someone else's hand, before turning around and walking back to the front and setting the Bible back in the lectern.

Reverend Morris: left hand over eyes, right arm shaking like a just-used diving board in front of him, his hand a trembling, pointing finger slowly scanning a half-circle, side to side. "I can hear God telling me that there are those among you who sinned this week," his voice raising as he speaks to damnation-level, bass deep and spewing molten rock with the important syllables. "Do you hear your sins? Do you hear God call out your sins? Do you see them? Touch them? Taste them? Smell them? Remember your sins?" He sounds breathless, exhausted, his voice suddenly on the verge of failure. Reverend Morris, left hand still over his eyes, stops his right hand: the scanning, trembling, and the pointing finger freeze pointed at me as though carved in rock. His voice strengthens anew, filled with the burn and sulfur stench of Hell, "God is calling out to us today, right here, in this room. Do you hear God?"

"We hear God."

Amber sits, arms folded on her lap. She does not respond now. She points her face toward her knees. She and I share the same fear: Reverend Morris will call on her again.

"Do you feel God?"

"We feel God."

"Here? In this room?"

"We feel God here, in this room."

Reverend Morris stands, again, behind the lectern and pulls a small, glass bottle with a yellow liquid and small cork out from the lectern. He removes the cork, places his finger on the opening, turns it over in his hand quickly, and smears and oily cross on his forehead.

"Bohumm numn goladda na hummaka hummaka humakkkala. Grunhy, grunhy, grunhy bohakka. Bohumma hukaba, na na na lalia, bohumm grunhy, HALLELUJAH! I am filled with the Spirit of the Holy Ghost join me to be anointed in God's oil!"

Deacon Tidings stands and as he does the band starts to play another song and Meredith Morris sways and sings. Deacon Tidings points to rows and the people stand and walk up to Reverend Morris who, when congregants stand in front of him and close their eyes, fingerpaints an oily cross on their forehead. As they pass, one of the student band members holds an offering tray in front of each person. The congregants drop money in the tray and form loose circles that dance and spin in the limited space at the chapel's front. Other congregants push empty pews to the walls and more people dance and spin and at the center of this space, moving like an accretion disk around a black hole. Reverend Morris looks at Amber, sitting cross-wristed and face-to-floor, as he paints the foreheads of closed-eyed congregants.

‹◊›

After the service, Amber and I walk back to my car. T-T walks past us, says it was wonderful to see us, and hopes to see us again soon, his stride stilt-forced by crotch-snug jeans, to a large, red pickup with over-sized tires and tailpipes. Betty, politely, thin-lipped, smiles as she passes. Galena and some other congregants talk about how powerful Reverend Morris' message was and how much they needed to hear it that week.

"Mark, Amber," Reverend Morris' voice calls out to us. We turn and he gestures for us to come back to the church where he is.

"Let's just go, Merak. Ignore him."

"Thirty seconds, tops," I say. The parking lot is dirt and gravel, sparse grass at the perimeter. The chapel's front steps end at the gravel. Reverend Morris steps down to us, still towers above. I have never met someone this much taller than I. Up close, he is large with strength from a lifetime of carrying extra weight.

He puts his right hand on my left shoulder, left hand on Amber's right, and gives us each a long, firm squeeze. "May I pray with you?"

Amber nods.

"Heavenly Lord God, please watch over little Amber and her young friend Mark as they return to their schooling. Help them to recognize your way through the temptations of college life. Amen."

We say "Amen."

Reverend Morris lets go of us. "So tell me, Mark, what church were you raised in?"

My head tilts slightly. Does this man know anything except how to work a room? "UMC."

"What do you believe, as a UMC?"

"Orthopraxy," my head tilts upright. I have my answer.

Reverend Morris nods. He looks down at me, eyebrows long and turned upward at the end, bushy and controlled like golf-course topiary. "Fascinating."

"I would love to stay and talk more," I lie. "Amber and I have dinner reservations back in town," I lie. "Maybe I'll see you again?" I hope I lie.

"I would like very much to learn a bit more about UMC Mark and his orthopraxy."

"I hope that opportunity arises," lips-only smile. I have never hoped I lie more than I do right now.

"Careful what you hope for, Mark. It might happen," Reverend Morris says with a large, broad smile that wraps into his eye creases. Something in his smile, some lip twist, eyebrow curl, something I can't identify, fills the air between us with the menace of a coming lightning strike.

Federico starts up quietly and I drive us over the gravel lot to the road. A couple stop signs up, we're in line behind T-T and his large, red pickup. Thin tendrils of black smoke seep from each tailpipe. "We're behind T-T," I say.

"He's gonna roll coal on us."

"What's that?"

T-T must stand on his gas pedal. Through his exhaust, engine compression shakes Federico in fast pulses and a thick, black heavy smoke plume surrounds my car. The air filter falls to this acrid, diesel-filled mess; thin smoke and strong diesel stench, the kind that burns nostrils and eyes, spills from the vents. I pull forward slowly trying to leave the hanging black cloud. T-T, ahead of us, drives slowly, eyes to his rear-view mirror.

"We're in town, Marion and Washington. If I go right on Marion, can you get us home?"

"Yes."

I decide not to follow T-T.

"So, I noticed," I say, "Reverend Morris made you uncomfortable."

"He does."

"No, I mean, like he was trying to."

"He does." Amber fiddles her fingers together.

Oh, of course. Amber tried to let me know that the first time; it's something he intends.

"Some people, and I used to be like this, Merak, need to know fear. Fear is addictive, a drug, and potent. Fear, the irrational type I mean, of things we can't control, it changes our brains and leads us to do things we otherwise would not. Some people, they sleep with a gun next to their bed, or lock themselves away from the world and people. Others need Hell. Fear is addictive because it leads us to do things that give us an illusion of control. That illusion is the true addiction. But our brains, they don't so much separate that, you know? It's a hard, hard addiction to break because letting go means embracing something else."

"Like what?"

"Hope, maybe." She sits upright, twists her face toward me. "Or trust, courage – hoping we will be okay, trusting that others are on our side, and having courage of those things. I guess that's reverse order."

As we drive down a curving dirt road, gravel clicking gently off the undercarriage, I have a moment where I understand what she means. Fear, antipode faith, demands we embrace it like a child does a parent. When I returned to Deer Lake, three years ago, the Nissan I bought in Colorado barely running, smoke from the engine and vents, windows down so I could breathe, my father handed me the keys to this car and decided to set about fixing the Nissan. He had hoped to refurbish Colander to better-than-new glory. Timing worked out, though, and my father fixed the Nissan enough to hand it, the keys, and title to Rick when he moved in with us the next week. It's been his car since. Rick had that, hope and trust, in my family.

134

"You've never known fear, have you?" Amber asks.

"I've been plenty scared, yes."

"Scared's different; it's a moment, fleeting, like the sound of a plastic bag carried in the wind. Fear lingers, present in the back of our minds like traffic on a busy highway. I'm a bit envious, I won't lie, of you for that. You are a wrecking ball finding an old grain silo, Merak. You don't have any worries about the obstacles before you." Amber faces out the window, hands together, fingertips on opposite-hand knuckles, tapping in time. "That is so, so intimidating, and I am afraid of it and, a bit, of you."

"I hope that passes. I'll —" look out for you, watch over you, keep an eye out, "— make sure I'm not scary." I want to tell her that every night I know fear; sleep, the dreams I might have, terrify me. I drown them with beers before bed. After we sit in silence for a moment, those words do not reach my mouth.

"That was a long pause," she says, still facing the window, now fiddling with her dress pockets.

"I needed to figure out good wording. When do I turn?"

"In a few minutes you'll see a four-way intersection, unmarked, old tree on the left, dead from a lightning strike. Probably be a cow lying next to it."

"We passed that a mile or so back."

Amber turns her head toward me, tilted and surprised. "You are admirably in-control of your car. It never feels like you're going fast." As I do a mid-road three-point turn, Amber inhales deeply. "When I was sixteen, right after Grandma Helen died, like a week or ten days after her funeral, Grandpa Arn took me to the county fair. You know, carnival rides, junk food, games and prizes. We were between rides, had just gotten off this little roller coaster called Nitroglycerin. My favorite ride. Anyway, Grandpa Arn sits me on a bench and says he's gonna go get us some chili dogs and a couple of colas. While he's up I hear these heavy footfalls walk up to me and then the bench rocks and settles. It's Reverend Morris and his breath smelled like vodka, fries, hot dogs, and onions."

I finish the three-point turn and, stopped on the shoulder, look at Amber. She seems small, curled on herself, legs pulled in close, knees up, instead of stretched into the passenger's leg-space. Her hands are on, more like around the sides of, her knees. "But he hasn't had a drink in like twenty years." Before she says it, I understand that it's hard for her to know when people lie.

"I can't always tell when people are lying, Merak. I've heard that people's body motions or postures can give that away, but, well, nothing that I can do with that." Her words land in my ears like water on a hot griddle: They sizzle angrily, shrink, and fade.

Amber frowns a bit. I realize in a moment that the fear she has lived with for so many years isn't the fear of the world, of its invisibleness, of uneven sidewalks, street crossings, or being lost. She fears peoples' intentions and her inability for easy recognition. Truly trusting another person must come hard. Amber's fear is of not knowing when abuse is coming.

"So Reverend Morris puts his arm about my shoulder and says he's sorry my grandma died, hopes the best for her. I don't know where Grandpa Arn is, of course, just in line somewhere. But this is Reverend Morris. He's the reverend. And while we're sitting there, he's running his finger between my dress strap and shoulder and he starts telling me what a lovely woman I'm becoming, so fetching, so, I think he said fit. He was massaging my shoulders – I needed help being less tense from everything – when Grandpa Arn came back with our food. Grandpa Arn thanked Reverend Morris for making sure I was okay given the previous weeks, and we walked away to go eat our food elsewhere. I only took a couple of bites. That weekend, well, I had been dating T-T for about two months. I called him up to go out. I slept with him. It was my first time and it was … one-sided. We dated until he was arrested. I just felt like if everyone is going to take advantage of me, might as well have it be my boyfriend. It was so good for me, his time in jail. I finished high school, got into college. I dated other boys, but that just taught me other people want to take advantage of me, you know? I also learned the world outside of town is better and I want it."

We sit for a moment in the quiet of the engine's idle, a small wind-funnel of dust saunters across the road. "I can't promise to be perfect. I can promise I won't lie. The worst thing a person can be is a liar."

"Grandpa Arn says the same thing."

‹0›

At home, Amber rides Sandstone through his pasture, bridle and reins, bareback as she does. She's just giving him a quick ride before grazing; a long ride would delay dinner, and, she explained excitedly before her ride, she's going to make Grandma Helen's beef stew for me. Grandpa Arn and I walk around the pasture to a large, fallow field with some distant white boxes, beehives.

"Uhlergic?" he asks.

"Not a fan of stings, but no allergies."

"Keep calm, dun't move fas'. Ain't got no suits. Iffin' yuh' get stung, dun't swat, dun't run. Suck up the pain."

Grandpa Arn fills the hives with smoke from a smoker. I feel bees in my hair and on my arms. One walks along my face and I stay calm, relax, breath slowly and deliberately through my nose. Grandpa Arn lifts a hive lid and pulls out a rack of honeycomb, holds it out toward me. My hands pass through air with caution; feeling a bee in my armpit, I decide to hold the rack out. Arn looks, eyebrow up, I motion my eye to my armpit and he nods. He pulls out a second rack and holds it while he closes the hive. When we turn to walk my arm gives slightly and I feel the bee sting. I hop reflexively, holding the comb. Arn walks away, as though on a rope bridge, as six then seven, then I don't know how many bees sting my arms, neck, and scalp.

At his house, "sorry about killing some of your bees."

Arn shrugs and uses his fingernails to pull the stingers out of my head and neck. I pull them out from my legs and arm, the armpit being the worst as the bee is still stuck to it, struggling. We drop the stingers, twelve in total, and dying bee in the grass. Arn holds the part of the hive we harvested over a wide, flat canning funnel modified with some welded-on pieces to hold the hive rack. Arn caps the honeycombs with a long, sharp, round-tipped knife. Honey, thin and warm from sun and the bees beating their wings, flows down the comb in large, liquid trails that fill a large mason jar. The wax he puts into a small pot with a lot of charring. He'll cut it with paraffin, he explains, and make emergency candles for the next power outage.

Amber stands at the sink washing her hands. She starts the stew by mixing a biscuit dough, Grandma Helen's biscuits, she explains, noting that Grandma Helen didn't have creative recipe names, but did make good food. Flour, baking powder, baking soda, salt, all go into a mesh strainer on top of a mixing bowl. I ask if I can help and, "I'm making you dinner, Merak. We're not making dinner for us."

"I'll feel weird eating while you two watch."

Grandpa Arn looks up from a magazine and smiles at this.

"Silly boy, you know what I mean. Let me do this for you. I like cooking and I don't get to do it for you."

Amber mixes some water, buttermilk, a quarter cup of the fresh honey, and butter in a pan and puts it on low. She checks the liquid with the back of her knuckle and then puts in the yeast and pours the mixture into a glass bowl to let the yeast bloom. As the liquid rests and builds a surface foam, she grabs some vegetables from the fridge – carrots, celery, yellow onions, potatoes, radishes, bell peppers, and mushrooms – and washes them in the sink. Veggies washed, Amber pours the liquid, all foamy on top now, into the biscuits' dry ingredients and mixes them with a wooden spoon. When the dough can be worked, she sprinkles flour on the table, asks Grandpa Arn if it looks good, he glances past his magazine with an "it duz'," and Amber kneads it into a soft, smooth cylinder.

"I only knead it till I can roll it." Amber rolls it out thin, uses a box grater, and this is a new trick to me, to grate a frozen stick of butter onto the dough sheet, spreads it out, folds the dough onto itself in thirds, twice, rolls it out again, grates on more butter, and then folds the dough into quarters. She places it in a buttered and cornmeal-coated brownie tray and it nests well. "These aren't as crumbly as a lot of biscuits because the butter I just grated in will melt, kinda moisturize the flour. The yeast gives it rise, so it's a bit kinda like a biscuit went out behind the barn with a croissant."

Grandpa Arn raises his eyebrows and looks at me, I think to gauge my reaction.

"I get what she means."

Grandpa Arn looks back at his magazine.

Amber smiles at me. "I'm smiling back and blowing you a kiss," I say, making an exaggerated kiss sound.

She keeps smiling, shakes her head a bit, and puts the old cast iron crockpot onto the range, pours some oil into it, and starts it heating. At the kitchen island, facing me, Amber feels out the carrots with her hands, lining them up four at a time tip-to-rounds on a cutting board. Curling her left fingers back, she holds them in place and chops surprisingly-even carrot coins. She halves two onions and peels the skin. Feeling for the root stub, she cuts three even cuts lengthwise down each, one sideways, and then she chops them into large pieces, placing them into another bowl.

"I am amazed at how well you use a knife."

"Grandma Helen let me learn the hard way. I have cut myself a lot," Amber says, "this finger-curl technique, chefs do it this way, keeps my fingers safe." Amber works through the remaining veggies, methodically creating even pieces, putting them with the carrots. When done, the lone onions go into the crockpot, thin smoke tendrils rising above it, with a sizzle, steaming as Amber pushes them with a wooden spoon stained black with use.

"I know this is going to be an ignorant question," I say.

"How do I know when things cook?"

"Yup."

"Your nose broken? Your ears? Hands? Tongue? You use your eyes too much, Merak. Smell the food, listen to the sounds it makes when it cooks, feel the texture, taste it to see if it's good. You do this stuff with coffee. You can smell differences in different coffee beans."

Grandpa Arn looks up. "Dif'rnt coffee beans?"

"African, Asian, Middle Eastern, and South American beans all smell and taste different. Heck, Yemeni Sana'ani tastes and smells different than Yemen Gurmah. Same is true of all the varieties from all the countries. And, check this out, coffee from a single farm or even a single tree tastes different than general blends of the same variety."

"Citah' folk shuh' do like complex-ah-tees. Is 'ere a p'oblem wih' Fuljahs?"

I lock my fingers together. "Can I make some coffee for you next time we're here?"

Grandpa Arn shrugs.

"That's an excited yes," Amber says, adding the other veggies to the pot when the onions start to brown. While the other veggies cook, she opens a large can of whole, peeled tomatoes and spoons three heaping piles of tomato paste into them. In time, it goes into the stew with some broth, red wine, and a slurry of water and corn starch. Amber turns the boiling pot down to a simmer. "Won't be long now, maybe three hours."

Grandpa Arn folds his magazine, "I'll be in town, feed stuh', gas station, oil change."

"We're gonna play cards," Amber says. They hug, Arn tells us to be good, and Amber takes some braille playing cards from an end table drawer. Her fingers wrap them; the practiced arch, bridge, and clean mix, near-perfect alternation, captivate my eyes. "Are you staring at me shuffle?"

"I am."

"You never talk when you're staring at me when I do something."

"I wondered."

"I grew up playing cards most nights. What do you want to play?"

Arn backs his pickup down the driveway and out into the road. "I'm tempted to say demon, but I think I'd have a distinct advantage."

"Yes. I was going to suggest strip poker." Amber smiles at me.

⟨◊⟩

Amber and I lie in the soft forest dirt and dried leaves of the trees behind the barn, cool dirt on our skin and dappled light on our bodies. "We should get back inside," I say. "I'll find our clothes," standing.

"Hold on, turn around." Amber starts her hands in my hair, tussling it and dust cascades off my shoulders. "That's quite the hive on your scalp." Amber's hands, warm from sun and heartbeat, feel like tiny campfires against my ground-cooled neck skin. She rubs my shoulders downward, loosing dirt and leaf bits, massaging my back. "These little bumps on top of your shoulders always do it for me. Are you too skinny? Maybe I need to cook more food for you."

I smile. "Not too skinny. I have a 28 waist now. Was a 38 after freshman year."

"Freshman forty?" Amber's hands work my lumbar and butt; dust falls back to the ground.

"Bit more than."

Her hands run down to my legs, then upward and brush my butt-thigh curves. "What happened?"

141

"School stress, obsessing about the accident, not sleeping because of nightmares. A little stress; I'll down a box of cereal and a gallon milk at every meal. Lots of stress; I force myself to drink water and coffee. A lack of sleep also destroys my appetite." Amber's hands move down my legs' insides, gently brushing away dust; she turns to face away from me. "I was, still some nights, have a couple drinks or more before sleep. That, um, that helps keep me asleep sometimes. I drank a lot my first year, to keep the nightmares at bay. I'm cutting back."

I run my fingers through her hair, shake them and press the tips into her scalp, feel her slightly coarse hair tangle and slide on the sides of my fingers, and as I do her body shimmies and her head tilts back with a soft moan. Her hair, filled with leaves and dust, seems to pull my hands as though wanting to keep them. She tilts her head forward and shakes, tussling hair into a fishing reel bird's nest. As she finger-combs it out I brush dust, leaves, and small stones off her back, arms, sides, butt, and legs. Her sides have little love handles, part of her freshman forty that never went away, she says, as I give them a squeeze and kiss a line around the back of her neck and shoulders. I put my chin on her shoulder and, speaking chin-restricted, tell her, quietly, as though anyone else were around to hear, "everyone who rides needs something to hold on to. Let's get dressed."

The kitchen smells of warm meat and tomato with a hint of earthy veggies. Amber tastes the stew and adds some salt, a few twists from the pepper mill, and a tablespoon of lemon juice. She mixes some of the fresh honey with a beaten egg and brushes it on top of the risen biscuit dough for baking. This, she explains, gives it a fantastic crust on top. As though on cue, Grandpa Arn drives up to the house. I kiss Amber's cheek and meet him outside and help him carry supplies to the barn. When we finish, Grandpa Arn puts his arm across my shoulder, gives it a squeeze, thanks me, and we walk inside to the smells of buttery, flaky, biscuits, large and golden on top. Amber ladles stew, thick and dark red, shining under the kitchen lights, into old cream-colored bowls with a single, blue decorative ring on the inside. We each have a single large biscuit and butter at our seats. Amber's stew steams and the beef cubes and soft veggies, coated in thick stew broth, taste rich and full, feel like liquid velvet on my tongue. The beef dissolves as I chew. I pull my biscuit apart and it breaks and crumbs, flakes into layers. It mixes easily in the stew, adds some buttery richness. Amber, Grandpa Arn, and I talk and laugh, we listen to Arn's stories about welding broken equipment at the mines, and we are as full and as warm as the now-empty crockpot was when we sat down. We play cards into the night and when I wake in the morning, on the couch, my brain calm from hours of dreams about Amber riding horseback, she is with me, face in my arm, snoring softly.

7
The Camelback Cricket

For those who look, any place provides interest. Southern Illinois offers a wine trail with vineyards making sweet and dry wines grown on hillsides ideal for grapevines. The Lake Kincaid Spillway with its falls and pools, warm summer water, and bonfire pits affords a break from classwork. The hardest places to find, in college towns, are good restaurants. Certainly, Mary Anne's for brunch, but lunch and dinner are typical college food – deep-dish pizza and beer, football-big burritos, chain sandwich shops, and bars that serve 'food.' Resigned to that, at least The Camelback Cricket has games. Tucked into a campus corner two blocks off the main town drag, The Camelback Cricket spills pinball and video game machine noise onto the sidewalk and wraps itself in the meaty, sticky smoke of cooking food. Open early on weekends, its quarter-played arcade games, affordable if unremarkable burgers, pizza, hot dogs, and crunchy tacos fill ears and stomachs, distract from homework.

Amber, Rick, Jesse, and I meet at the front amid the mechanical clatter of metal balls on bouncers and electronic racing and shooting game clamor. Amber, despite the early September heat, held my hand beyond the point where palm sweat becomes unbearable as we walked from her dorm here. Rick and, especially, Jesse wear an overnight video game marathon on their faces like limp sacks of peanuts hanging off shelves, red-veined eyes, dark and baggy eye sockets, slack jaws and face stubble. When Amber and I stroll up, peppy and happy, Amber's cheeks a bit red, hair a bit tussled, Rick points at me and alternates his fingers with each syllable, "someone got laid."

"Rick," Amber protests, adjusting her aviators. "Rude." She faces away from us and, returning, blushing, chuckles. "But true."

"George late?" I ask.

"Only a few minutes," he says, behind me. We grab hands and shoulders, he hugs Amber, puts his hands on Rick's and Jesse's shoulders and we follow the trio inside. Amber, hands on my waist, lets me lead. To the right: booths with napkin and menu holders and a jukebox terminal, faux-wood tabletops and white plastic trim, hard single-piece booth benches curved and contoured in teal. We take the furthest booth, along a window wall that overlooks some outside seating, away some from the arcade area. I guide Amber into the booth by her hips.

Our waitress opens a pair of gray-metal double-swinging doors from the kitchen with her knee, a basket of napkin-wrapped utensils in one hand, tray of waters in the other. She wears higher-than-ankle black boots with thick, offroad-tire-like soles and white laces, fishnet stockings over defined and tattoo-covered legs to frayed-end and hole-ridden blue jean short shorts that her pockets poke out the bottom of. Tucked in behind a black belt with a buckle that looks like an electric guitar, she has a white tank top that shows ink-sleeved arms and tattoos that climb her cleavage and neck. Her face is angular, a chin and cheeks that lead and point away from her cat-eye mascara eyes and platinum hair tied into double bobs. When she looks at our table, her eyes go wide: "oh my goodness, George!" She sets, near drops, the basket and tray on the next table, water splashing from some glasses. George stands, takes a firm hug and longer-than-friendly cheek kiss with a smile that rides up his cheeks to meet his eyes.

"Beth, how long have you worked here?"

"Three weeks, started the first week of classes." Beth looks George up and down while holding his shoulders. "You look great, George." Beth's hair, platinum-bleached-from-dark-brown, around the bob's black elastic bands has loose, intentional strands that splay outward like firework smoke paths. Her high-boned cheeks, now that she's close, prop a freckle bridge across her nose and flush when she smiles. Her lips are thin but pretty. She is hip-and-bust-curvy, waist-thin, fit from walking all day, taking orders, and carrying food. Her forearm tattoo sleeves depict an ocean and ocean animals on one, a grassy plain and a cheetah and a gazelle on the other, and end cleanly just behind her wrists' long-sleeve-shirt tan lines. Beth's left leg tattoos are a cityscape behind an ocean shore, mountains in the distance, and a large expanse of stars. Her right leg has different flowers, all named with their common and Latin names, a bouquet that spirals up from her ankle to well inside her shorts. Those were expensive tattoos.

"Guys, my good friend Beth; we tended bar at Slam Tracks a few years back. Beth, the guys," says George, before introducing us by name.

"George, after I get your guys' order in, step back to the kitchen and say hi. We'll catch up. But I don't want to take you away from your friends."

"They won't miss me," he smiles, and gives her a wink.

Beth exhales happily, asks if we're ready to order food or just some drinks. We agree we can order and when Beth starts with Amber, Amber asks for another minute. Beth continues around the table and when she reaches me, I order a turkey sandwich and a small side of fries. Beth looks at Amber, "your turn."

"Eggs benedict, no sides. I'm not very hungry."

"Can I change my fries to a large side, please?" Beth says I can.

"What's that mean?" Amber says.

"When you're not very hungry, it means I'm only getting two fries."

"Oh no," Rick and Jesse say, almost in unison.

"What?" Amber says

"What? It's true. Doesn't bother me."

"Uh-huh." Amber faces me, her eyebrows squeezed in a bit, a slight frown, my face, all eyebrows up in surprise and a wide what-did-I-say-wrong smile, reflects in her aviator lenses; her closed eyes are faint forms overlaid on my face like an accidental double exposure. "I'll remember that," she's not mad.

Amber drinks her water through her straw and I notice, somehow for the first time, how pristine and un-teeth-worked it is each time she finishes a glass. I, and yes this bothers me, chew straw ends into crinkles and harsh ripples that make their use harder. We all sit and adjust our clothes hems, wearing swimsuits under our shorts and shirts.

A couple sits down outside, just beyond the window next to Amber, with a shorthaired white-and-brown dog with a solid brown head and stubby tail. The dog lays between them and the husband loops the leash around his chair's armrest.

"Huh," I say out loud, thinking I had kept that to myself.

"What?"

"Oh, a couple just sat down and they have a dog. I don't think I've ever been to a place that allows dogs. But, I guess they're outside, so I'm sure it's fine."

"Ever had a dog?"

"I did, when I was young, a small, gray schnauzer named Tiddlywink that we used to play catch and fetch with."

"Oh my gosh what a cute name," Amber smiles.

"I remember Tiddlywink," Rick says. "He was a yappy little shit."

I nod, and, smiling: "A bit, yes, at times. Really, he just didn't like you." Rick concurs.

"What is a tiddlywink?" Jesse asks.

"You know, like the game, that's the best I have," I say.

"You don't know Tiddlywinks? Really?" We all look at Amber. "Basically, you have some plastic discs and you use another plastic disc to press them and make them pop up and into a little cup."

Jesse raises his hand, opens his mouth, and then puts his hand to his lips.

"Quick question," Rick asks.

"Of course I wasn't any good at it, Rick. Grandma Helen and Grandpa Arn taught me it so that I could learn how different amounts of pressure on things have different effects, learn to control hand power. They'd sit at the table with me after dinner, set up some of the discs, and then guide me through which ones to shoot, how much pressure to use, where the target was, and how far off I was. I did learn to get them into the cup. That was never the point. Games are family time." Amber sips her water glass until it drains to suction bubbles and noise.

"I won't lie," this is me, "I'm pretty impressed by that. Not the game, but the family time."

"We had one for a while, a dog that is," Amber says. "It came and went, lived in the barn with the cats. One day it just didn't come back. It had been a stray so maybe it went back to being a stray. Dunno. Had it about six months. Never named it."

"Well," I say, "maybe someday we can get a dog, a little puppy. It'll be cute and it will play a lot and we'll name it Turing, like Alan Turing."

"First, I do not like that name at all. If we get a dog we'll keep the game names, Rummy like the card game, Checkers, or Hopscotch."

"I like Hopscotch," I concur.

"Second, how do you expect me to be safe around a puppy with puppy energy, jumping all over the place, pooping on the hardwood floor for me to slip on."

"I like the sound of hardwood floors. Well, maybe we rescue an old dog. One that sleeps twenty hours a day, snores all time, with constant farts that smell like an abandoned wharf, and it'll climb into your side of the bed at four AM every day to wake you up with sloppy face kisses."

"That ... does not make me want a dog."

"And he'll take short walks with us because he'll be at least ten years old, and we'll just walk down the street to some coffee shop to sit outside under a tree and order our coffee and a biscotti or scone and then go home and fix up the house while he snores."

"Or maybe you own the coffee shop and he's our mascot and every time one dies we find another that looks the same and name it the same thing."

"We can do that, too, I suppose."

"We'll call it Hopscotch's Coffee."

"Yes, for sure." I give amber a kiss on her cheek and nibble her ear a bit. "I like that."

In time, food in our bellies, George mum on how well he knows Beth, some bills changed to quarters, we spread out around the games. George, not really a video game player, catches up with Beth, gesticulations and gestures that seem like he's showing her how to mix different drinks. Rick and Jesse make the rounds of shooting, street-fighting, and classic games.

"So where do you want to start?"

Amber hums a bit. "Tell me what they have? What are these even like?"

The Camelback Cricket's arcade mixes many old classics like Frogger, Pac-Man, and Donkey Kong with new games that have large, bright-colored guns for shooting zombies, parallel foot stands for downhill skiing, a few with steering wheels and gas pedals, and one with two half-life-size crotch-rocket motorcycles, one red and one blue, for a racing game.

"You know exactly which one I want to try."

I look at the motorcycle game. It's a dollar a round, but definitely worth it.

"Are you smiling again?"

"I was. Motorcycles sound like fun." The motorcycles are low but I keep my right hand on her hip as she steps her left leg over the red one.

"I've ridden on the back of one of these before. I know how to get on."

"Oh. I have not."

"Just step over the back, put your arms around my waist, tell me how much to steer."

The small, red plastic motorcycle is really kid-size. And above the game is a sign: "ONLY ONE rider at a time." Amber is my girlfriend, though, not the sign. I straddle the bike and sit on the back, a molded brake light poking uncomfortably, as the motorcycle jolts and makes an unsettling thud. "Hey, before we start," I say, Amber tilting her head to the side, ear toward me, "I'm impressed by how willing you are to try new things."

"Well, you're here to make sure it'll be okay."

I swallow and thank Amber. "Also, um, since you had a good childhood, that's something, well, what I mean is, not forecasting too far ahead here —"

Amber turns her torso and faces me. "Spit it out."

"I'm gonna need coaching if we have kids."

She shakes and nods her head at the same time, a short, diagonal, zig-zag pattern. "Yup. I'll step up. Let's race." Her face lights into a broad smile and she turns around.

Quarters in the machine, motorcycle engine whirring, hands on Amber's hips, the race starts and I tell her to turn the handle, "no, not like steering, turn the handle part forward. That's the gas."

"Oh well that doesn't make sense," Amber says as the video game road accelerates toward us. Holding Amber's hips, I guide her leans into the turns, speak directions and call-out obstacles in her ear, "two racers ahead, tight left turn here, go wide, not that wide, we hit tires, no it's fine we're back in the road so you can accelerate again." At a particularly sharp turn on a race, Amber and I move the motorcycle hard and it turns with a loud thunk and shake as she careens into a tree. We play round after round and Amber, as we do, shifts her weight backwards, shimmies her butt against my waist and I press my chest close to her back and we lean and tilt through the turns, brake and gas together, and in one race she doesn't place last. For the last two rounds, Rick and Jesse watch and cheer behind us, slapping high fives with Amber after each race.

"Shall we head on to The Spillway?" This is Rick.

"Not just yet," I say. "I need a moment before I can stand up. This seat is a bit uncomfortable and my legs are a bit numb."

"Merak has a boner," Amber says.

"Thank you, babe," I say while Rick and Jesse, hands in the air, walk toward the exit. When Amber and I do stand, the red motorcycle rests at an angle, much closer the ground than the blue motorcycle, the metal arm that connects it to the video game machine bent. 'I'm sure it was that way,' I think, walking Amber briskly to the street.

‹◊›

Lake Kincaid, the largest manmade lake in Illinois, I heard once, rests high above its parking lot. There are two ways to get up to the lake, running up the dam's grassy dike slope or climbing The Spillway waterfalls. George's best advice, either take The Spillway or jump right in the water at the top of the grassy dike slope to get the chiggers off your legs. We, exclusively, take The Spillway. I've seen chigger rash and have no interest in that.

The road to The Spillway winds down and then up, a few switchbacks and then the lot. I know this road and the best lines around the turns, plan them five-out and take Federico close to the insides, slowly out toward the shoulder, back inside, making the driving line smoother, losing less speed in each turn. Often, as today, park rangers sit in the lot with binoculars looking for college students with glass bottles. Beer cans are allowed, but no glass. Too many people play in The Spillway in bare feet.

"Amber, lay down," I say. Five of us fit only so well in my Saab. George, being as tall as I, sits up front. Rick and Jesse sit in back and because there's not enough space between them for Amber she lays across their laps. For most of the car ride she had her head in Rick's lap and her feet out the window. We have to drive past the parked rangers. One of them watches us take the last paved spot, his eyebrows up. He watches five people climb out of my car and shakes his head, going back to his binoculars.

In the parking lot I lift the rear hatch and, stripping to our swimsuits, we toss our clothes into the car where some towels and a cooler of waters, burger fixings for George to make dinner tonight, and beers wait for later. Across the parking lot, down a short dirt path, our first water crossing. This time of year the water is low, but present. The Spillway's falls, in late summer, have a steady but quiet sound, water-music made as they slowly wear rock faces smooth. Photos of the falls in late summer look like rocks covered in the long, white tails of enormous Lipizzan horses. Dark silhouettes rest at the bottom of the lowest Spillway falls; tiger muskie, introduced for sport fishing, wait for fish unlucky enough to have gone through The Spillway's falls only to drop into the pool at the bottom ready to be eaten.

Amber wears a black and silver one-piece swimsuit, left over from high school and now a bit snug. Her swimsuit's black and silver diagonal lines hug her hips where the fabric "V"s into her thighs. Her thighs, pale from hiding behind jeans, are defined by muscle lines, and a soft, curving ledge into her butt.

Amber walks behind me up to the first water crossing, her hands on my shoulders. "The water is only a few inches deep here," I turn around and face her. "I'll walk backward and tell you where to step. There are rocks under the water, like pavers with gaps. If you miss one, you'll step into mud." She nods and lets me take her hands. I step backward on to the first rock and then second, straddling the short gap between them, right foot leading left. "Okay, your right foot first, just about a foot and half out. Good." Her foot slides under the water and onto the rock. The rock's form is visible, but the water is murky like creamed gas station coffee. I step backward. "Left, about two feet in front of your right foot."

Amber stands onto her right foot and slides her left foot forward, her toes feeling out the next rock, the water above her ankle bones. Finding it, she slides her foot onto it. "This isn't too bad," she says. The next stones are a bit deeper, mid-calf, in cooler water. Goose flesh forms up her legs and arms, hairs standing upright, mine as well. "I'm doing okay aren't I."

"What did you expect from yourself? I expected nothing less." We walk across the submerged rocks and up a short, damp path of solid rock to the first waterfall.

"How high is this? I can just walk up it, right?"

"Hundreds of feet, pretty much vertical."

"Merak, stop."

"It's three tiers of falls total, maybe ten, fifteen feet each. You can walk up a couple, or climb on all fours if you want. I'll be here, right behind you enjoying the view as you go."

"The view?"

"The waterfalls are quite pretty."

Amber frowns in feigned displeasure. "Of course. The falls."

Amber and I climb up the first falls. "I'll help you put your feet and hands in place. This isn't so steep that you'll fall down it. Just keep three points of contact the whole time and you'll be safe."

"I'm not sure."

"I won't let you fall."

Amber nods. I guide her hands to good holds, tell her where to put her first foot, then her other. "Good, now take your left hand, slide it up the rock, up and left a bit, about a foot. There's another small place to grab there." Amber does and she repeats for her next hand, her feet, and after five or six cycles of this we're at the top of the first falls and she pulls herself onto a flat surface. In the falls here a group of people sit in a manmade rock tub built to catch and deepen water spilling from above them. They applaud Amber when she stands. Amber waves.

This tub is large, can easily hold a dozen people. George once said he didn't recall a time here without it. People rebuild it each spring, and all the similar tubs. There are better tubs up above and I see George, Rick, and Jesse scurrying to find an empty one.

Amber and I walk to the second falls, which are shorter than the first, gentler, and we walk up the rocks next to them. At the third falls' base, allowing us to avoid the steepest climb, Rick, Jesse, and George have staked a small, natural pool with a waterfall flowing into it. It's a good pool, not the best, but top three.

When I put my hands on Amber's waist, her muscles flex, and then relax. My fingertips slide under her swimsuit hem to her thigh-hip joint and she covers my hands with hers. We walk slowly, close together, water rushing over our feet, across a solid rock shelf. At the pool, I help Amber step over the rock wall and we sit in the churning, clear water, kept fresh and cool by the waterfall feeding it. George leans back into the waterfall and lets the water flow around him. Rick and Jesse sit across from us. They point to the people in other pools, rate them on a scale of one to ten, and debate whether or not they would be fun to date.

I sit in the water with Amber and close my eyes, the sun red through them, warm on my face. The water in the pool swirls, spirals, circulates around the center to the perimeter and over a small rock pile that keeps this pool a few inches deeper than the waterfall intended. Rick picks a leaf off a bush and drops it where, captured by the whirling water, it seems like I watch from afar as a large boat fights against a vortex. I imagine sailors on it, adjusting sail rigging, the helmsman frantically holding the wheel and rudder in place, and, as in the books I read as a child, adventure or a monster must certainly soon ensue. Amber leans her head on my shoulder, wet hair draping my back and chest. Her breaths, deep, slowing pace with each cycle, belie her climbing stress. "Merak, how am I going to get back down?"

"Backwards. Where we have to climb, I'll go down first tell you where to put your hands and feet, and catch you if you fall. I'll be there."

"Good," she rests her hand on my knee. I put my right arm around her and run her hair through my fingers, combing it, twirling it loosely and letting it drop, over and over until I fall asleep in the flittering shade cast be an overhead tree moved by a light breeze.

◇

George wakes me up. "It's almost seven, time to head down for dinner." George, standing, taking Amber's hand, and walking her over to me, says, "I'll see you guys down there with some waters ready to go."

Amber and I walk the rock path to the middle waterfalls holding hands, and I crawl down the rocks at the first waterfalls. "Now, sit down and slide your legs over. What you're going to do it put your heels on some rocks. I'll guide them in. Then you'll just turn over like you're about to do push-ups, swing your left leg over. I'll place your foot in a hold." Conversations indistinguishable over the falls' water-music quiet and fade as people watch, most with titled heads or a raised eyebrow. Amber swings her leg out and over, her arm at the same time, and drops into a push-up position, left leg out. I put her foot in my hands and guide her toes to a rock hold.

"Good. Slide your left hand down the rock about a foot, over left, right an inch, and there's a good grip. Nice. Now your right hand, straight down, a few inches below the hold for your left." We inch down the rocks slowly, Amber keeping her weight and grip where she trusts them, me guiding her movements with simple directions. When she steps off the last rock hold, she puts her arms loosely over my shoulders.

"Thank you," she says, and runs her hand on the back of my head, tilts my face toward hers, and gives me a kiss, "for helping me do that."

155

"Okay, so what kind of rock were we climbing and walking on back there?" I ask.

"Felt like, and given our location, should be Pennsylvanian-age shale and sandstone."

"Nice."

"Do you even know what that means, notetaker?"

"That you're a really good mineralogist."

"No, silly, I mean, I am, but the rocks?"

"Shale and sandstone are the rocks. Pennsylvanian is when they were deposited. I don't know when that was. Oh, and they're sedimentary rocks."

"Around 300 million years ago. What else?"

"I don't know the pattern. I heard once that rocks like this tell us if an ocean advanced or receded."

Amber has me turn and face the spillway. "All those rocks," she says, putting her hands on my hips and her mouth near my shoulder, speaking us into a space beyond where we stand, to a time dialed back millennia then sped-up as the changing world she describes grows and morphs around us, "exist because ancient oceans grew and shrank where we're standing now." Water rises, salty and warm, ancient fish and a plesiosaur swim around us. "As they receded, gigantic forests and swamps grew, evolved, died, and fell into the muck hidden beneath water." The oceans drain and tall palms, gigantic ferns, insects the size of large dogs grow and walk around us. "Like modern oceans, rivers carried water and that moving water had sediment. That sediment floated out in the ocean, large pieces like the sand in sandstone, dropping early. Fine particles, like the biomass and dust that formed shale, floating out further and sinking." The oceans return and conveyors of particles large and small cloud the water, spreading outward, dropping, growing, and shifting as the shoreline moves in and out around us, millions of years of oceans passing in seconds. "So the layers – shale below sandstone, or sandstone below shale, for instance — tell us if the ocean was getting shallower or deeper as it aged. The different rock types and the materials that make them tell us how deep the oceans once were. The Pennsylvanian age was at the end of the coal-forming carboniferous period, so the depth of the Pennsylvanian rocks tells us how far down we have to dig to find coal."

"That–" I spin around to face Amber, placing my hands on her hips.

"Don't even say it."

"–rocks.

"With jokes like that you're going to be an awesome dad someday." Amber hugs me close, looks up at me. As she talks, her cheek moves lightly on my chest, rubs against my ribs. "The earth is alive, Merak. It changes, grows, ever-shifting slowly, so slowly that we almost, in our short lives, never see it. But to the earth, if it perceives time in the same proportion we do over our lives, to the earth molten rocks blend and separate like shaken water and oil separating. Mountain ranges may as well be goosebumps that rise and fall in a flash of emotion, swamps a bead of sweat in the sun. All humanity has existed for such a short time that if earth's lifespan were our own it would not even have had time to realize humanity existed. We are ephemera and dust, the passage of a breeze through hair, and we burn like film's silver crystals in the sun. And in that less-than-instant we live, we get the joy and the fortune to breathe in all the endless beauty we can find. The earth is amazing, Merak, but I can't imagine anything as beautiful as life."

Amber turns and stands to my left, holding my arm, and we walk slowly back to my car, letting her words resonate in my mind like the echo of a vibraphone, repeating and cascading into themselves until they become a bridge between neurons.

George, Rick, and Jesse huddle around my car, hopping, shivering, holding their arms to their bodies. "Don't look at me," I say. "No one asked for the keys." When the doors and hatch unlock, everyone grabs

157

their clothes, warm from baking in the car-oven, and they dash into the forest to strip and change. I drink two bottles of water, quick succession, as Amber and I drag our toes and heels through the grass to the forest. Amber holds my arm, slowly across the field to the woods, moving with the pace of the first 'I love you' from brain to mouth. We find a spot with some privacy, behind some bushes, a flat stump for a seat.

"No peeking," she says, from a few steps away.

"Come here." Amber steps over to me, facing me, my face at her chest. "Turn around." I slide my hands under her swimsuit's shoulders and lift them. The suit's straps slide over her shoulders and stop. I stare at her back muscles, run my hand down her spine as I help push her swimsuit off and to the ground. She is pale where her swimsuit was, markedly tan like a gutter penny on her arms, legs, and neck. I stand, walk in front of her, and hand her clothes to her one piece at a time as she dresses. "Oops," I say when I hand her jeans to her. "I peeked."

Amber unties my swim trunks and slides them down. I feel her hands trace up my thighs and linger. "So did I," she kisses me, takes two steps backward with her hand outstretched, still holding on to me, and sits on the stump. I dress quickly and we walk back to the car where George already fired up one of the park's standing grills to make burgers and, when we're done, some kind of dessert thing he calls 'Molten Apple Crunchy Cinnamon Raisin Oats Skillet Cobbler.' Rolls right off the tongue.

Amber sits at a picnic table by my car; I grab my camera, a few rolls of fast film, and a flash. Loaded, I warm up with a few group photos. "Smile," everyone looks at me, flash large smiles, George holds his arms around Rick and Jesse, a metal spatula in his hand that looks like it's poking out of Rick's head. Amber smiles a pleasant and wide grin. The guys' teeth show, mouths open, like they're in the middle of greeting a long-lost friend. "Just be natural until I run out of film, guys. I just, you know, these might be good photos to have some day."

They nod, or shrug. George starts to roll burger patties in his hands. Rick and Amber talk, and Jesse flexes his right arm showing off a three-branched Brigid's Cross tattoo he got just before the semester started. All of George's recipes, especially his burgers, have ludicrous names. Tonight he's making something called "Twisty McGroo's Ferocious Ferris Wheel."

"What on earth is that?" Amber asks, half-chuckling.

"Ah, it's the name of the burger, ma'am" George feigns shock and indignation, his voice short and staccato, as though not realizing that this was anything other than patently obvious represents the greatest insult in human history.

"What's on it?" Rick asks.

"So it's a medium-rare half-pound patty, not too lean, seared with a lovely crust on a griddle alongside bacon, and in the bacon's fat. And then there's American cheese, egg, and some jalapenos I'll fry as I build the burgers."

"Can you make my egg scrambled?" Amber asks.

"I'm going to make them all scrambled. I don't want a messy egg when I have no clean shirts nearby. Actually, can you break and scramble them?"

George grabs a dozen eggs from the cooler. Amber breaks them into a large bowl for him, holding each egg in her right hand, cracking the shell on the bowl's rim, and prying them open into the bowl. While she works on the other side of the picnic table from where George cooks, Rick peels the cheese from plastic wrappers, sets them on a paper plate, and separates the bacon while Jesse slices jalapenos and watches the eggs for shell bits. When Amber whisks them, she puts the whisk between her palms and spins it like a fire-starting stick, the whisk twirling frantically back and forth, the eggs churning in circles and spirals around each other. I ask how she knows when to stop, and why she's whisking them that way. "When they're mixed they feel nice and uniform and there's no differences in resistance. And as for this whisking, eggs get fluffier, more homogenous, when they're sheared during beating. This shears the eggs up nice and George likes them beaten like this because it makes for better scrambled curds."

As George cooks, the beer cooler opens, ice and water inside still cold, beer tops pop, and we clink cans, toast ourselves and our friendships, and let the beer hit our dehydrated brains like a bat to a fastball.

George has us all can-clink a toast to the hamburgers. He pats the raw patties dry with paper towels and salts them. He starts the bacon first, gets the griddle to be a thin puddle of popping, liquid bacon fat. The burgers settle into the thin puddle with a sizzle that seems as loud as a horn. This, he tells us, make a crust that pops with flavor. The burgers, in some minutes, have a thick, brown, hard crust and I've never, I tell George this, seen a similar burger. When they're about to come off the grill, George tops them with two slices of bacon and two pieces of cheese, giving them moments to melt. George lays out the buns on paper plates, stacks the burger-bacon-cheese pile on the buns while the jalapeno slices sizzle in rendered fat. He pours the eggs from the bowl onto the griddle and rubber-spatulas the bowl clean. The eggs bubble and fry in the rendered fat, mix with the jalapenos as he scrapes the griddle, turns the eggs, and they form large, loose curds a vibrant yellow with browning jalapeno rings and flecks that had been burger crust. The eggs smell of bacon smoke and beef. As they clump, he portions them onto the burgers evenly. Finishing the plates with thin potato chips, we eat. But first, I photograph my burger, five times, different angles, placing chips differently, setting the plate on the edge of the picnic table and photographing into the sunset, embraced in blurry warm hues.

"Did you just photograph your food?" Jesse says.

"I did."

"That's ridiculous. Who does that? I mean really. Who does that."

"People who photograph food for restaurants and magazines," Rick helps.

"No one will ever do that except people who photograph food for a living. Who wants to look back in the future at all the meals they ate? Oh look, it's a photo album of why I'm pudgy," Jesse says, swaying his torso back and forth, arms out, bent elbows, hands wide above his head like one of those dancing air tubes at a car dealership.

"You look like an idiot scarecrow, Jesse."

Jesse reaches over the table and hugs me, smacks my back with his right fist.

We force a slow pace. George's food is good. Everything he makes, mixed drinks, desserts, breakfasts, lunches, and dinners, never a miss. These burgers are no exception. The buns, soft from burger juice, hold the bacon in their blanket of melting cheese and eggs, and make the bacon feel the way it should – part of a whole thing, not a side. This burger makes sides of bacon seem cheap and easy. Burger juice drips from the back of the bun onto my chips. The jalapenos add a warm, floral heat. We drink waters and beers; Rick passes a flask of peach schnapps.

"I have a game we can play," Rick announces, as he finishes his food. He pulls a standard die out of his pocket. He points at us and assigns us each a number, one through five. "Six is a re-roll. First number has to tell us something about the second number that they think the rest of us won't know."

"I don't follow," says Jesse.

Rick rolls a one then a three, "so if this were real, Amber would have to tell us something that she thinks no one else knows about me."

"What if you rolled two ones," Amber.

"You'd have to tell us something we don't know about you."

"Oh this game sounds scary," she says.

Rick rolls a two and a three. Everyone looks at me and then Rick.

"Oh boy," I say. "Rick never played video games until he met me and didn't own a video game system at all until he came down here for school."

"But you're really good," Jesse says, genuinely surprised.

"It's true," Rick rolls again, a five, "George, tell us something about," roll, "Jesse."

Jesse looks at George, "I think I know where this is going."

"I agree. So you know how Jesse and Angie broke up six months ago. Do you know why?"

Jesse chimes in, "to be fair, it was never really a good match to begin with. We're just very different people."

"She hated how much he jokes about things. So Jesse, and this is a bit passive-aggressive, decided to just crack wise any time he could. You know, rather than just man-up and break up with her."

"She didn't like my sense of humor, that's true."

"So one day she says she wants to spice things up in bed."

"That was, honestly, the depth and breadth of our relationship. I need someone I can laugh with."

"So what does Jesse do?"

"I walked over to my desk drawer, pulled out a jar of chili powder, and said 'okay, but this might burn'."

"You did not," Amber says quite loudly, setting her beer can down too hard and it foam volcanoes onto her hand and the table. Amber wipes her fingers on her pants and keeps drinking her beer.

"I did, and she walked right out the door."

Rick drops his head to his arm, laughing and slapping the table. "That's, honestly, such a mean way to dump someone. Alright, next up, Amber," Rick rolled a one and all eyes go to Amber, "tell us something about," Rick dramatically rolls the die in his hand and drops it. "Merak."

Jesse and George "oooooh" and Rick confirms it needs to be good and juicy.

"Oh dear," that's me, a hair worried.

Amber smiles and rolls her head, neck cracking, and tilts her face upward a bit, thinking a moment. "Should I do this one?" I reflect at myself in her aviators, face lit dim and red by the fading sunset, my glasses casting circle shadows onto my cheeks.

"If you have to ask, then no." My reflection is calm, lips up but cheeks slack, a calm but fake smile.

"I will. Merak, at least once, usually many more times, farts during sex."

"Oh God." Jesse turns his head and laughs beer onto the grass. George and Rick look at me laughing, and Rick lets Amber know she is really good at this game. I rub my eyes behind my glasses. "No use denying."

When everyone gets over that, Rick rolls "George, tell us something about ... Jesse."

I feel George put one of his legs against the table's underside and he leans back, looking up at the sky, the darkness of the trees. He asks Jesse, "St. Louis, Dunbark Hotel? It's the one I have."

"Oh boy. I suppose that's fine," Jesse lifts his arms and then drops them, defeated.

"So Jesse and I were hanging out with our girlfriends at the time. This was right after he started dating Angie. And so Angie and this girl I was seeing, Chrissy, she's still a regular at Brumby's, they're both very tipsy. We'd gone out clubbing and they kept getting free drinks from guys, it was St. Patty's, and so forth. Well anyway, I forget exactly how we got to this point, because some parts of that night are really a blur, but they said they would make out for Jesse and I if Jesse and I just gave each other a quick peck on the lips."

"We did."

Rick's mouth is a huge "O" and Amber, gasping, says something about a scandal.

"Sounds like you have an opening there, Rick," I say.

"Oh I know," he says, fanning his neck with his hand before rolling "George, again, tell us something about, oh, this will be interesting, George."

"Again? Well, at least I keep the town's secrets." He glances a circle around us, eyes to eyes a moment each, drinks from his beer, drinks all of his beer, and opens another with a metal-pop-top-crack. "Seven years ago, I had a fling with an Aussie exchange student before she went home. A year ago, just shy of, she e-mails me. Married, lovely and kind husband, and a son. He's biologically mine. She wants to know about family medical stuff. I'll never meet him. And, I think, that's okay. He has a good family and a dad who loves him very much. He'll grow up well."

We four sit back and look at George. Amber, in time, breaks the silence, "you've got the right view, even if that's hard." We drink our beers and commiserate with George. He looks past us a few times, to where tree silhouettes meet the pink-to-pale-blue sky, twists his mouth and eyes.

"I asked her if she'd send me a picture, and she did. Cute kid, looks like I did at his age, different chin and eyes." I clink my beer with George's, who says the smoke has made his eye sting a bit. George grew up poor, but loved, and once while I tutored him he said he only wanted to finish school to get a degree so he could afford to raise a family. But, mid-thirties, he thinks it may be too late. He wanted to be a dad, play catch in the yard, fish on Saturdays, teach a boy to shave, and everything else was just a means to that. We all have a thing that motivates us: George, family; Jesse, a desire to be a great programmer; Rick, to live his life as he wants; Amber, to leave and be more than her town ever thought she could be; and me …

Amber brings me out of my mind with a loud: "no fair cheating. The dice say Merak gets to tell us about you again."

"Oh fine. Merak, tell them all something about me."

I look at Rick across the table and give him a wry smile. I take a few slow drinks from my beer.

"Don't give me that look. It means you're thinking."

Jesse leans in, elbows to table, arms crossed and flat. "I bet he has dozens of good stories."

"Dozens," I concur. "So back in our sophomore year, we're driving back down to school and we both, suddenly, we have to go to the bathroom. Like bad. Now, we'd just passed Arcola."

"I was afraid of this. Look, I said I was sorry." Rick drinks his beer and takes a long draw off the peach schnapps. "Can you just pick another?"

"Oh dang there is nothing till Mattoon," George says.

"Long drive, rain pounds the windshield like a heavyweight boxer lands punches, bladders busting. We pull off under that bridge for 1200 and run behind the cement support for a couple very long pees. So I'm just looking off to the side and all and when I glance back, there's Rick, dong in hand, done peeing, just wide-mouthed looking at my junk."

"And Merak just turns, says, 'dude, come on.' And that was that," Rick says, looking down at the table.

"What Rick really said was—"

"Don't do it, man."

"—'damn I wish that thing was gay.' Not his best friend, just his best friend's dong. Rude," I emphasize with a swig from my beer and set it down, watching Rick, face in his palms, elbows on the table.

"Look, it's a nice one."

"Enh, eightieth percentile," Amber says, calmly, sitting and facing straight forward as the rest of the eyes at the table turn from Rick to Amber to me, and stare.

I feel my pulse in my forehead, neck, chest, gut, wrists, and calves. My eyes dart to Rick, Jesse, and George in different orders. They sit, quiet, look at their drinks or the grill or forest. Amber starts to fidget: it's on me to fix this. "Wish all my grades were that good."

After a few moments, Rick drinks more schnapps and keeps looking away from me, Jesse and George finish and open more beers, Amber leans toward me and whispers, "did I say something wrong?"

I want to say 'I don't know. I didn't see the other sixteens guys' dicks,' but instead, "they couldn't tell that you were joking. You've picked up my dry delivery."

"Joke, of course. Yes, joke. Ha ha. Rick, roll again, please," and when he does: Amber to Amber. "I don't have a lot of funny me-stories. Growing up, local kids ideas of having fun were getting me to walk into things. So, kind of serious, but I don't know who my dad is. Grandpa Arn does, but won't tell me."

After a moment with cricket chirps, crackles from other groups' fires, and some music and laughing across the parking lot, I ask Amber if she has any guesses.

"No. Honestly, no idea who it could be."

"Who do you wish it was," George asks.

"I wish," Amber sits upright and puts her arms below the table, "I wish it were Tad. He's always kind of been like my uncle and we see him a lot and he keeps an eye out for me and Grandpa."

George nods, raises his eyebrows, makes quick eye contact with me and looks away.

As the last of the evening's blues blacken, the forest recedes from view, stars begin to shine through gaps in wispy overhead clouds, Jesse finds and drags over to the picnic table a nearby metal firepit that lost its anchor chain. Rick searches unused firepits for wood. A few other groups remain in other parts of the park's open area, their fires give warm, dim orange light to the undersides of leaves and branches, small bubbles of warmth, light, life, and chatter separated by void. These small orbs of warmth are like us, each of us a small life separated from others by space and darkness, but seeking others to bring into our space, for family, for communion. Someone at one of the fires plays a guitar and he and a few other people sing acoustic eighties pop covers. Other groups converse and laugh, roast hot dogs or smores. Beer cans open and fizz. Cicadas sing in warbling, incoherent waves that ebb and dip like the moments before sleep after a day of boat fishing.

Rick and Jesse start a fire in the pit with the wood they found and a pizza box from a garbage can. In time we have our own dim light and a part-orb in orange that pulls the forest line out from the darkness, reflects and shimmers in my car's grill and windshield, and that lights Amber's face in an orange hue that dissolves my friends, the forest, the other groups, the insects, and leaves me, staring at her face, as though all existence has failed and this, now, is the last light of the universe.

My friends laugh about men kissing just to see girls kiss, and Amber presses them to explain why it's gross for men to kiss but not women, which Jesse explains is just because it is. George, older than all of us and raised poor. Rick, my age and through high school he knew no barrier that money could detour, but unable to be himself. Jesse, half-Mexican and half-Irish, dark skinned and black-haired, the one of us not tinted like printer paper. Amber, of course. We are all different but for it find ourselves better and happier. I understand their motivations, our differences, similarities, and that I want to find and know those whose lives I don't recognize, and through that to be better. Amber puts her hand on my cheek and all is noise and nature-music, guitar and firelight, beer cans and laughter. My face feels like an iron under her hand. I take her hand, kiss it, and let her know that I was just thinking I'm lucky this is my life.

George's dessert, a concoction of canned apple pie filling; a long roster of herbs and spices; and granola, raisins, currants, and dried blueberries bubbles on the grill like a penned-up emotion. He pours brown sugar on top to melt and caramelize. The molten apple pie filling bubbles through the granola, softens the bottom of it, but the heat and sugar turn the top into hard, candy-coated oat goodness. We eat it slowly out of paper bowls with plastic spoons, tossing the bowls in the fire when we finish. Rick laments that it needs ice cream.

As the other groups leave, as our fire turns to embers, I roll down Federico's windows, turn the stereo on loud, and put in a CD. We sing in the dimming fire light, wail off-key and miss notes. Amber's feet between mine, my arms trace her back's contours and we rock in cadence. Rick and Jesse and George dance, together and sometimes with Amber, pull me in and we five are dance and joy, motion and sweat, mosquitos on arms, molten apples and beer and burgers in our stomachs. We are full to the brim of food, with drink, and the unique love of friendship mixed with youth.

8
Pink

The couch in Grandpa Arn's home feels like decades of Christmas mornings, a childhood of birthday parties, spilled and cleaned Kool-Aid and snacks, and countless evenings eating take-out pizza and watching VHS rentals. The cushions absorb me like a welcome-home hug. The guest blanket, a red and gray diamond-pattern crocheted by Grandma Helen, is warm enough. Grandpa Arn and Amber move quietly in the kitchen; the living room air fills with brewing coffee, warm and buttery biscuits, eggs sizzling sunny-side up in lard, bacon popping and cracking in the oven, and a gentle heat as window-calmed sun beams move across my face and torso.

"Ah' think ee's uhwake'." Grandpa Arn picks up some large peppers, Anaheims maybe, slices them into spears to toast them in a dry skillet. In moments, their skin and seeds pop; capsaicin tickles my nostrils.

"I am." I sit up and stretch, arms over my head, legs out in front of me, feeling the muscles pull and strain across my shoulders. I roll my head, crack my neck.

"That sounded like a good stretch," Amber says.

I nod and stand up, stretching my back.

"Did you just nod?"

"Sorry, I did."

I sit at the table and Amber brings over two mugs and a coffee pot. "I know it's not up to your standards," she says, sitting next to me. "Next time you stay over, you should wake up early and make it."

"It's going to be good, thank you, and I will." Amber, as I pour our coffees, moves her hand up and down from my knee to mid-thigh. Amber takes her mug, holds it in her free hand and lets it warm her fingers as she sips. Grandpa Arn slices biscuits and layers them with American cheese and the cooked food. He sets the sandwiches in the oven for a few minutes after they're assembled and they come out crispy-shelled with loose, dripping, stretchy yellow triangles that had been the cheese slices' corners. He finishes our plates with fresh, large, and bright apricots and carrots he picked this morning.

"Sammy aht' six, slice' currahts' midnigh' tuh' three, an' apurcots' nine tuh' nun," Grandpa Arn says as he walks breakfast over to us. He places both plates at the same time, arranged in the same way, in front of us and then brings his over. I pour coffee for him and he takes a long, slow, and careful swig, setting his mug down and smiling. "'Aht, aht righ' heah' is nice," he says. "All 'aht I wanted fuh a long time, tuh' see Ambuh' with sumun' 'oo I actually like."

"Grandpa." Amber puts her fork into a carrot and eats it.

"True. 'Aht's a long," he drags the vowel out, "list uh' guys I didnuh' like."

"Not that long," Amber protests, the carrot flying from her mouth and back to her plate.

"It's kinda long," I say, and smile at Grandpa Arn.

"Hey, don't you two gang up on me."

"Sumtimes' pipple' jus' need tuh' make mess-takes' 'fore they dun't."

"And I, for one," I add, "am glad those let you recognize that I'm not a mistake."

"Well, that was a good enough save, I suppose," Amber says, piercing another carrot with her fork, pointing her face at mine and lightly but not angrily frowning as she does.

I take a bite of my breakfast sammy, the biscuit, hot, crunches and cracks and crumbs bounce off my lip and chin. It sounds like dried autumn leaves under my feet. The bacon breaks easily and the fat dissolves on my tongue. The eggs drip dark yellow because Grandpa Arn raises happy chickens, and happy chickens lay rich yolks. The pepper tastes like caramelized, flame-roasted pain that fades quickly to a bitter-fruity accent. I give Grandpa Arn a thumbs up and he smiles.

"Yuh'all stayin' fuh' chores?"

"Well, we're going to the orchard." When Amber says this, Grandpa Arn smiles.

"Gud."

"But yes. Merak can help feed the animals before we go."

I look back and forth between Grandpa Arn and Amber. Grandpa Arn eats his apricots. "Ah' 'sume yuh's takin' San'stun?"

"That's the plan."

‹◊›

Grandpa Arn hands me a quart-size baby bottle full of warm milk. The goat pen gates each lock with a ring mechanism; if I push the lock ring to the side, a gate opens and the ring rolls back into place. Closed, the ring engages a latch and won't open. I find this to be absolute genius. Grandpa Arn calls the sequential gates the air lock, says if the goats want to get out, they can. They don't want to leave, though; he raises happy goats. In the pen, the three tiny goats hop over each other in a mud puddle by the air lock.

"Are they kids?"

"Yus', an' pygmuhs', so extuh' tiny. Keep 'aht grazz' low, eat scraps, gih' uh' bit uh' wool, not much. Dun' much 'ave uh' use sin' Helen pass'. Helen uze' tuh' mek' a cap 'uh sumtin' like 'aht each ye'uh. Coarse, wuhm'." Grandpa Arn explains that to feed the goats I hold the bottle up, let one drink and when it's about a third gone let another drink.

I hop over the mud puddle and sit on a stump in a dry area. Grandpa Arn, wearing rubber boots, walks right through the mud unphased and starts shoveling goat poop into a plastic drum. The goats clamor onto my lap, tracking mud on my pants and shirt. One hops on my back and off, over and over again, and I feed it first, to make it stop. As it eats, a second goat jumps on my back.

"Gud' wuk', Merak," says Grandpa Arn. "Yuh' jus' towt' 'em 'aht jumpin' uhn' yuh' back gets 'em 'aht food."

The goats drink their milk and, I learn, that makes me their new favorite person. They nudge my leg, climb on and off of my lap. I leave the air lock to Federico's trunk, grab my camera, and take some photos. When the roll ends, I rewind, reload, and watch Amber walk to the barn. She runs her hands along the barn wall to a large metal ring, flips a metal latch aside. This routine, daily, practiced, rehearsed – perfected: her hands go to each item exactly, her steps confident and placed well. She slides the barn door open, disappears into the barn, and some seconds later horse feet on hard-pack barn floor herald her riding Sandstone in a trot to the field. Amber and Sandstone speak a language of gestures, gentle brushes, slight rein tugs, and soft words. Amber trusts Sandstone to take her around the open field. When they pass under a tree's branch, Sandstone slows, raises his head slightly. Amber leans forward and puts her ear aside his neck. Past the tree, Sandstone lowers his head and Amber sits upright. I track them as they trot and refresh their vernacular of touch.

I grab my short telephoto from the camera bag and lean against the far goat pen fence. Picking a shutter speed fast enough to freeze her motion, the mirror and shutter curtains click softly open and close, forever trapping her hair sinusoidal in mid-trot-bounce, mouth open in a command, one hand mummied in reins and the other between Sandstone's ears. The photos freeze Sandstone's steps, his mane and tail mirroring Amber's hair's motion. Mud clumps suspended in air behind Sandstone's shoes. I trap light in the silver halide emulsion of four rolls of film, two color and two black and white.

Amber, face pointing slightly upward, left ear to the ground, rides up to the fence and as she approaches Grandpa Arn says "yuh' tuh' ehn't miss uh' beat." Amber slows and stops by his voice, points her face in our direction and asks if I'm here. "Takin' futus' like 'e 'as unlimitud' film," Grandpa Arn smiles.

"Whatever makes you happy, Merak," she shrugs. "Want to go get some apples?"

Grandpa Arn tells me that I do. I put my camera in its bag, sling it around my shoulder; I have no idea how to get on a bareback horse. "Uh." I look at Sandstone, at Amber, at Grandpa Arn, at the goats standing on the roof of their overnight house, and back at Sandstone.

"Yuh' jus' climb on, Merak," Grandpa Arn says. Amber sighs, over-obvious and for drama.

"Like climb the fence and get on?"

"Yes," say both Amber and Grandpa Arn.

Right hand to fence post, I step up the wooden beams, reach my right leg over Sandstone's back. I slide, almost too far, and scoot to the middle. Hands on my thighs, I nod a proud smile for my achievement.

"Put your hands around my waist. Squeeze Sandstone with your thighs, and move up and down with me as we walk. Got it?"

"Sure." I lie. I have no idea what that means. I learn what it means when Sandstone starts walking, however. Grandpa Arn, waving at us, opens a far gate and we walk out.

Amber leans forward a bit and Sandstone turns his ears toward her. "Apple orchard," she says, and she guides him to the left with her reins, a slow walk and stop at the road. Amber listens, points her face in each direction, and then gives the reins a slight flick. Sandstone walks forward and across the street.

"Merak, you need to bounce up and down with me as we ride or your legs are going to be on fire tomorrow."

"I thought I was."

"You're going opposite of me. It's not hard. Just have rhythm, like sex. Not hard."

173

I start to lift and dip in rhythm with Amber; my body moves with hers, up and down slow and slight with Sandstone's walk.

"Better. Not great, but better. Hold on and ride with me." Amber says "Yah" and flicks the reigns. Sandstone starts into a canter and Amber and I ride in something like unison with him along the roadside, his shoes sounding like a small orchestra of tambourines and bright dry cymbals on the road's rocks and hard-pack dirt. I close my eyes and listen to the music, inhale deeply the floral shampoo scent in Amber's hair, cinnamon gum on her breath, a faint barn hay smell from her plaid flannel shirt, feel her abdomen flex and her muscles contract and relax with each bounce, try to align my leg squeezes and body lifts with her. Sandstone moves faster and with more noise as Amber flicks the reigns again and he breaks into a full-on gallop, the melody of his hooves hastening, repeated and melodic and faster and Amber and I move up and down together, squeezing our legs to rise and fall as though a single rider. A white pickup passes us and honks and two people inside shout "Amber" as they drive away.

"Who was that?"

"What kind of car was it?" Amber shouts to overpower our gallop.

"Old white Chevy pickup."

"I really wish that helped," she says.

In time, Sandstone slows to a canter, then a trot, and then a gentle walk along the winding and forested road segment we drive through each trip here, and he stops at a break in a wire fence. "Legs up," Amber says, and we both bend our knees as Sandstone walks through the fence gap, just inches wider than he. Amber puts her head down and I follow suit. Sandstone leads us on a barely-visible path through overgrown trees whose leaves have started to peak in oranges, reds, and yellows, and where thick ferns begin to brown for the winter. The path follows a gentle hill, not high, maybe fifteen or twenty feet, to a clearing and an overlook.

Sandstone stops at the hilltop, long and flat, the trail ending a few feet in front of him. Below us, on trees with leaves starting to brown, yellow apples adorned in red stripes fill the branches of three tall, broad trees with large canopies that, the absence of ground plants indicate, shade the ground well.

I sit on Sandstone and feel Amber's body under my hands, in front of my chest, and between my legs.

"You need to get off first, Merak."

Oh. Oh dear. "How?"

"Really?" She says quickly, too quickly, before I finish asking; she knew I would ask. "Slide your right leg over Sandstone's flank, hold his side, and drop to the ground."

Great in theory, in practice, I smack my chin on Sandstone's hip, land into sharp ankle pain, and fall back-to-fern, my camera bag rolling a few feet away.

"Merak?" Amber slides off Sandstone like a gymnast, lands and turns. "Where are you? Are you okay?"

"Down here. I'm fine." I stand and brush leaves and dirt off my pants while Amber shakes her head and lashes Sandstone to a tree.

The walk down to the orchard is steeper than the trail up. Though Amber holds my arm, she doesn't need to; she knows each foothold and step. "Grandpa Arn and Grandma Helen used to come to this hill when they were dating, weekend lunches, summer picnics. They'd eat apples and toss cores in this clearing." Amber's words keep time with her footfalls, paced, thoughtful, and measured. "They would eat and talk, and then, this was the late fifties, Grandma noticed some trees growing. They had about twenty for a time."

"Only three survived?"

"Apples aren't true to seed, so most trees made small, sour, apples. Grandpa Arn would use their wood for projects. But one tree, it was incredible. My mom, for her junior high science project, she propagated it into a bunch of clones and planted two back here near the original. She wanted us to have more apples." Amber leans her back against one of the trees, rests her head in the crotch of two limbs. "This is the original tree. Can you get me an apple?"

I find a low branch with a number of apples free of holes and spots. They look like still fire, their red and yellow stripes and striations blending. I stash a few in my camera bag and hand one to Amber. She rubs it on her shirt. The apple crunches as it yields to her teeth, lips wrapping the flesh and a drip of clear juice falling from the side. Amber's free hand pulls me and I feel us, pressed against each other, warm, breaths mixing in the air between our mouths, stray hairs dancing on each other's foreheads. Her free hand feels for my cheek and she brings the apple to my mouth. The flavor starts sweet like sweetened apple juice and as I bite it changes to sharp, tangy, and crisp like late-autumn cider. It leaves a lasting, bright and bold tongue-lightning that feels trapped in my mouth for some time.

"I need my camera," I step back from Amber. "Keep eating that apple. Turn your head slightly so I'm not reflected in your glasses." She does and as she eats I take her photo. Over and over I fill the camera's viewfinder with her, shoulders to stray hairs, head resting in the tree, fine-mist apple juice spray glimmering in the sunlight that sneaks past the canopy, a stray drop on her chin, her tongue out of her mouth and licking the stray drip. One shot remains. I step back until Amber fills the viewfinder entirely, boots to head. She leans against the tree and tosses the apple core to the side. Her ponytail tied with a red band at the root, but loose, drapes over her shoulder. Her red plaid flannel, top three buttons undone, her shirt untucked from her jeans, jeans dusty and muddy from riding Sandstone tucked into her brown boots. She lifts a foot and puts it on the tree.

"Where did you go?"

"I'm here. Can you look kind of to your right?"

"Not really, but I can turn my face that way." Amber does, without a smile, but instead content, cheeks a bit flush, nose bridge bright red, and she runs her hand up to tuck some hairs behind her ear. I take my last shot and rewind the film as I walk toward her.

"I think that will be a good photo. I know you don't care so much."

"I do care. It makes you happy." She smiles when I'm close, nose bridge smile-wrinkles fan flash atop her cheeks. They are my favorite part of her face because they only show up when she's happiest.

"What makes you happy?" I put my camera in its case, nest it amongst the apples.

Amber leans forward and kisses me, flicks her tongue on my teeth and across my lips. Her mouth tastes like a warmed cinnamon apple pie. She puts my hands on her hips and reaches a hand down the front of my pants. Her voice smiles "I think you have some ideas about that."

‹◊›

Amber and I lay naked, the orchard sun warm on our skin, the air-scent of apples around us. I trace my finger on her torso's contours, the lines and creases in sweat-and-dirt relief adorned in small bits of tree bark and dried fern leaves. She takes a bite of another apple.

"How many of those have you had now?"

"Six," she says.

"You are going to be so sick tomorrow." I lay on my back, fingers crisscrossed behind my head, eyes closed, and the world is red, black, red from the sun on my eyelids as the trees sway to block and reveal it. Ground litter pokes my shoulders and butt, my feet rest in some short, soft plants. Birds chirp in the trees, mice or chipmunks scurry around the ferns alongside the orchard, and Sandstone whinnies softly. "But," I say grabbing my third apple, "these are the best apples I've ever had. They're like pink ladies, but sweeter, crisper, and somehow very pleasantly sour. I don't even know how to explain it."

"You should have them in a pie. Thanksgiving? We could do that for Thanksgiving. It's just two weeks and a day away."

"I have to be in Chicago."

"Oh."

"Do you-"

"I can't leave Grandpa Arn alone on Thanksgiving."

"We could all-"

"He won't leave the animals."

Sweat on my forehead dries and my skin tightens like a drum top under now-dry skin dirt. How it is in the seventies and sunny on November seventh? "We will make a time for that. Second Thanksgiving."

A few seconds pass. "I'm smiling, if that means anything," Amber says.

"It does. I have my eyes closed, taking in the sun and dancing tree leaves through my eyelids."

"I don't understand, but that's okay. I like the way sun and trees feel, how the warmth flutters around on my skin with the breeze." Amber shifts and rolls onto her side, arm over my chest, other arm stretched in the grass, her head rests on it. Her body presses against me, right leg over my hips, right hand slowly tracing the relief of my shoulder, neck, and chest. She runs her hand on the rib-stomach canyon formed when I lie down. "So, a pink lady apple? What's the color pink mean to you?"

I inhale and exhale deeply. I haven't ever pondered pink in depth. "I suppose it's like red, but not really. I mean, it is red, red and white, but it's totally different. It's the way the handle of a generations-old cast iron feels warm when it's simmered food low and slow on the stove. Pink is the slightly rough texture and the flowery smell of your hair on my face in bed at night. Pink feels like your hands holding my hip bones and squeezing. Pink is the sudden mental flood of fond memory, the best moment of our life, the moment we would live in happily for an eternity, given the chance."

Amber nibbles my ear and holds my hip. "That one was short."

"That one didn't need anything else."

‹◊›

St. Patrick's Day 1999, almost three years ago, the night I met Meggy. Spring Break. Rick and I, back in Chicago, Club Louis, a trendy bar that Rick got us in to because he had dated the bouncer. Club Louis' ear-ringing, tones-I'll-never-hear-again loudness bounced in pressure waves around the room and made the music an audio oatmeal. The air, less air and more cigarette and clove smoke, pungent and thick like burning spices and dog hair, a dense cloud above the moving, undulating dancefloor body-mass, caught and turned the spotlights into an even haze-halo above the sweating, whirling body movement sea. We had managed a high-top when a group got up. No chairs, black table, corner, no spotlights on us. Rick tipped our waitress well and she returned often.

We didn't talk, too loud, instead sipped drinks, new ones arriving before ice touched bottom. I kept the same drink, not for like, but for the volume preventing a new order. I hated that drink, fake-flavor sweet over cheap alcohol that hit like the pavement the first time I fell on my bike. Rick and I nodded at each other, pointed at girls I would like, boys he would like. Rick saw Meggy first, pointed at her. Meggy's mouth wore thin parentheses smile lines that cupped her lips like an important thought. She pulled a friend to our table, looked at my shirt – Illinois University Cold Harbor – pointed at me then at her and smiled, parentheses disappearing into deep smile, lips pink and shiny with brushed-on gloss, curling uneven with the left side higher, lower lip into a triangle, whitened teeth peeking past. Her eyes, blue, a deeper shade, hued and clear like a mineral spring. She and I, eye-eye, pupils-pupils, maybe a few seconds; however long, no breath, no pulse, my heart rested briefly for the first time since it first began pumping. Meggy turned her hand to mouth, mouth to her friend's ear, and her friend, I don't even remember what she looked like, giggled.

Blue eyes, black hair, long and loose, wild like summer wind. Meggy danced in front of me, hair tracing her head's movement. She slowed time as her hair, black and wrapping her face, back and forth, in long strands of darkness melded with the club. Her hair drew the world around us into its waves and motion, warped me into undulating space, and all the club-motion around us muted into her hair's darkness and my own tunnel vision, me taken entirely, rhythmically, willingly into her bounding and rich dark black hair. And then the music paused, just one second. Meggy looked back into my eyes and Club Louis flashed back to existence from the perception-void to which I'd been taken.

She walked up to me, put a hand on my waist, mouth to my ear, "Meggy, marketing."

"Merak, IT." The music turned back on, pounded and ricocheted, pulverized silence and fought to drown her name. Meggy. Meggy I repeated to myself. Meggy in marketing.

Meggy shouted in my ear "I need your leg," pointed at the ground, "kneel." Rick looked at me, eyes wide, smile reaching well into his cheeks. One knee and one foot to the floor, Meggy stepped on my leg and onto our table. Her hair smelled of expensive, perfumed salon shampoo and bar smoke as it brushed my face, wrapped around my chin, the tips whipping my ears. She wore a pink button-down shirt, black buttons, thin fabric that barely hid a black, patterned bra and a small, silver navel ring with a short chain and black pearl. New black jeans, expensive, no fading even on the seams. Boots, black suede, silver eyelets, thick tread. All pink and black, lipstick and hair, shirt and pants, and two blue eyes like glowing lights in the night. Meggy's friend stepped on my knee and they danced on our table, arms around each other, turning back-to-back, then back to chest, embracing, hands and arms exploring, friend's fingers on and separating Meggy's blouse buttons. Meggy's eyes locked with mine, then closed, and she danced open-shirted and hands above her head. Her hips rotated, right to front to left to back, circling, changing direction, swaying to her sides, knees bent, careful not to step off the round table and fall, she bent at her waist, turned toward me, loose pink shirt hanging open, breasts and gravity, hair swung down over me, capturing my face and I looked up. Blue eyes, a freckle bridge over her nose denser on the right side, left-biased asymmetric lip-curl-smile, and she winked. With a quick, reflex jerk, Meggy flipped her head up, hair following, breathing through open pink lips, sweat on her face and chest and gentle mirror-curves on her stomach around her vertical navel and swinging pearl, dancing with her friend but for me. And just as fast as Meggy and her friend arrived, two bouncers pulled them off the table by their hips and carried them outside. Meggy looked back at me, waved, and held her fingers to her face like a phone. The crowd slowed our chase.

Minutes later, outside, the streets quiet except for the electric humming in my ears that turned car tires to distant and flat echoes, I dragged Rick around the block. Nothing. Meggy had vanished as fast as she arrived. Rick and I took a cab back to our hotel and I contemplated calling George. But no, it was late, he would be going to sleep. Maybe back at school I'll just check the dance club Slam Tracks. That may be her spot. No, that's silly, Merak, she's just cutting loose tonight, I told myself, maybe out loud.

When break ended, I drove to Cold Harbor faster than any time since Colander and I outran the tornado. I parked Federico crooked in front of Brumby's, ran in, and slid across the freshly-mopped floor.

"Dude, I literally just mopped that." It was George. George will know.

"George, who is Meggy?"

George paused. He looked at me, looked to the slide lines, looked at me again. "What?"

I brought him up to speed in a flurry of auctioneer words. "She said I should call her."

Pink

"First, how did you even get in to Club Louis. Second, if she said call, did you lose her number?"

"She never gave it to me."

"This sounds pretty insane." George walked over and mopped away my shoe-slide tracks.

"I want to see if there's a chance."

"She's a deec," George slang for decent, "chick," George said. "Oozes a bit of privilege."

"Okay."

"She kinda runs the table with people." George put his mop into the bucket, rinsed it, and squeezed it to mopping-damp. "Man, I hope this isn't a mistake. She flirts without end, probably was just being cute with you. She hangs at Slam Tracks."

"I knew it!" I made a fist, pulled it toward my hip.

George leaned in, locked his eyes with mine, and spoke very slowly, "that is what she likes to do. Dance and flirt. Why did you even need to ask me, Merak?" Frustration brought out George's age lines, seemed to amplify his graying temples.

"Because you know people and I don't, George. Thank you!" I said in a hurried voice as I ran back outside, back to my car, to the dorm, to unpack, shower, and maybe learn to trust my gut.

9
The Bulbous Otter

Sunday back from Thanksgiving break, Rick, Jesse, and I sit on my bed and race go-karts on the Nintendo. First by only a small distance, the music faster as the last lap starts, I drop a banana peel behind my kart, Jesse hits it with a shell. Rick, third kart back, has three shells. Forty seconds, that's all I need. I have one more banana peel, no more item blocks to re-supply. Jesse has two more shells. Rick has aim. Jesse closes the small gap between us and launches a shell. I drop my only banana. All I can do is sprint and hope. Jesse's shell hits my banana and he launches his second; I dart sharply right, focused on the dodge and not on Rick who launches all three of his shells in a spread. The first hits Jesse and the second hits me; our karts flip. The third passes me, bounces off an obstacle near the finish line, ricochets back, and slams Rick face-on as he passes us. We three, aligned in a neat row, dead-stopped, mash our controllers' accelerate buttons. Rick accelerates the fastest, but it's not enough. A lightning bolt from a computer racer spins us and shrinks us. A computer racer with a super star hits us, wipes us all out again. Computer after computer kart pass us. The kart that fired the lightning bolt tramples Jesse flat. We end in the last three spots, Rick, me, and Jesse, shouting at the TV as we finish.

"Alright," Rick says, exhaling, setting the controller on the TV. "I have to get to work. See you at seven, Merak?"

"Seven. Yes. Ready?"

"I am."

Jesse looks at me as Rick leaves.

"Uh, so, I spend a lot of time dragging Amber into my world. I don't experience hers. Her life, yes, but that's different. I try to describe things in ways she can relate to. But I – well, I don't really know what it's like for her. Since I've never been to The Bulbous Otter, I figured that I'd go with Amber and try to experience her world."

"What do you have planned?"

I reach into my desk and pull out a dark, black blindfold.

"Is Rick going to help you?"

"Oh no. He's can't do anything I don't ask for. I don't know the place's layout, and they don't have braille menus. I want to know … I want to know the worst-case for Amber: new place, new layout, unknown menu, things like that."

I hold the blindfold to Jesse's eyes and he holds it tight, faces the open blinds, "can't see any light."

‹◊›

Federico fires up quiet, idles silent, speaks in combustion and piston cycles when the shifting line nears. Around town, this car drives its best, launches when red flips to go, gives torque to merge or pass as freely as a politician gives handshakes. It doesn't sip gas, but it doesn't drain the debit card. At the nearest gas station, I scrub Federico till it shines as much as a decade-old Saab's paint allows. At the florist next door, a small shop with chillers and fresh flowers in bundles or vases, I pick up a small, mixed bundle, different textures and smells, no thorns. At campus, parking far from trees and puddles, flowers in one hand, I hang the blindfold over Federico's rear view, pat him —it— twice and my stomach growls for lunch.

The Point cafeteria hallway has a large display ad for the new, colorful Apple Mac computers and another for the movies opening at the local theater this month. This time of day, the student workers don't check if we swipe our meal cards or not, and pretending means I have a free late-night snack waiting. They serve scraps these hours: lamp-stale bread, dry turkey or roast beef shreds, wilting lettuce and flavor-void tomatoes make a small sandwich to stave off hunger until we enjoy dinner at Murphysboro's finest fine dining restaurant. Heading out I snag a clean glass, the college student's vase.

Tolliver Forest, damp from morning rain, shades path puddles which linger in the pavement's low-points. Dropped pine needles float in the puddles like boats at a marina and splash out and to the forest floor when I hop and land one-footed, flamingo-like, in the puddles. Behind: laughing each time I hop, and I stop.

"You didn't have to stop," says one of two girls, a redhead with a shorter blonde. They jump up and land in puddles, like flamingoes. They smile and we all hop-splash through the forest. When we split off, the redhead says, "have a good date," and waves. I'm glad they're happy for me.

Most students live in the The Towers; each of the three buildings houses as many students as all of The Point. At Amber's building's door, just a minute's wait and someone exits, I fumble at my pockets, pretending I could open the door, but, being courteous of course, the exiting student holds the door. I thank him, he says it's nothing, we go about our days.

Seven minutes early. When I knock on Amber's door, her desk chair slides wood feet to tile floor a few seconds before the door opens. "Whoever you are, you aren't my boyfriend Merak. He's never early and never smells like flowers."

"Throngs of girls were chasing me for the flowers, so I ran," I put my free hand on hers and Amber pulls me into her room.

This room's door sticks and Amber kicks it closed. "I assume they're pretty," she reaches up the stems, fingers tracing under the petals.

"Ugly as sin, wilted, mostly dead, but the guy selling them on the street sprayed them with cologne."

"Wait, are these different kinds?" She feels the petal shapes, places her nose against each flower.

"A few of each, six different kinds."

"A cafeteria glass."

I nod.

Amber sets them on her window sill. "That's peak-cheap. I approve."

"I wanted to spare many expenses."

Amber shakes her head, rolls it back slightly. "What's our plan for tonight? You've been cagey."

"A walk over to Campus Lake –"

"You asked me to wear nice clothes."

"– then seven o'clock reservations at The Bulbous Otter."

"A walk and dinner? So standard date plus flowers. Look, Merak, I appreciate it's a nice restaurant. Can't we go to a concert, a movie, open-mic? Those are things I like and we don't do them."

"We can. Friday, open-mic at Cellar Door. Music, comedy, people reading their poetry. We'll go."

"Good," she says, sharp and fast from her mouth. "Look, I know five months, now, I know that's a long relationship for me. I'm just not as happy as you. We do things that you like, the same things."

No no, this is, I have this plan. I am doing a different thing. Tonight, even. "I have," I say, sitting on her bed, "not been great at that."

"Why are you on my bed?"

"Look, sit a sec."

"Why did you bring flowers? So I could smell them and appreciate them?"

"Can I have a moment to explain?"

"Explain. Explain so that this doesn't seem like you're just using me for tactile and fun blind sex. That's why boys like me. Tell me I'm wrong."

"You're wrong. My medium requires sight and I am stuck there. If I'm not taking photos, I'm observing. That's something different for us –"

"Different, so I'm different?"

"No, I mean, not like that. I like that you see the world – habit, sorry, I'm trying – differently and that you're who you are because of that."

"Merak, this was a mistake. You have one sentence. Prove this wasn't a mistake."

"When we get to The Bulbous Otter Rick is going to blindfold me and seat us at a table far away from the bathroom and I've never been there so I don't know the layout and they don't have braille menus so we're going to have trouble ordering and I wanted it to be a surprise because it's the first good idea that I've had about how I can do something that helps me understand you a little tiny bit for a few hours, and I thought that might make me a better boyfriend."

Amber stands, turns to face her closet. Her jaw seems to tremble some; maybe I can see something that hints at that, maybe it's just my mind. Footsteps muffled-thud through the hallway. The radiator steam valve clicks and the metal ticks ticks ticks as it heats. Her computer fan turns on. "Please leave."

I stand, open my mouth to start talking, but nothing, and I let my hands drop limp and slap my thighs. Amber flinches. My feet and legs move through numbness to her door, which opens with a hard stick, closes with a pull, and campus passes around me in a mushy mix of color, traffic and footfall noise, and the memory-phantom flower smell.

<(•)>

My walk home detours me around Campus Lake. Last night, a saxophone player was on the bridge again. I don't know if he plays his own music, riffs, or covers songs. I don't know if it's a he or she, even. He plays random nights and I sit with the dorm room windows open until he stops. Right here on this spot on this bridge I cross twice every time I lap this lake, a bridge where fish and turtles sometimes swim beneath, this is where the saxophone player plays. I follow the long path back to my dorm. I play over the conversation repeatedly and try to figure out what went wrong, the exact moment it changed, if it even happened today or if I did something weeks ago that I'm paying for now. I'm too boring, unoriginal with things we can do. I don't make her feel independent, maybe. Amber dumped me about three hours ago. It's almost five and I do not want to go home. But I do and in my room the answering machine light blinks three times.

"Merak, it's Amber. Call me." BEEP. "Merak, please call me. I'm sorry." BEEP "Merak, look, I have problems trusting people and their intentions, and you know that. Call me. Pick me up. Pretend I'm not like this."

I feel like I should be elated, overjoyed at this, and I think I am, and I feel exhausted, too. I drop into my hard, wood desk chair and look out the window at the bridge; repeated, strong exhales from my nostrils move my shirt. My arms and legs feel and hang like damp laundry on a line. I call Amber. "Meet me out front of your building in fifteen?" She agrees.

She knows my car's engine and the sound it makes when I put the shifter in park. She stands, hair straight and draped over her shoulders and behind her head, hiding the silver temples of her aviator glasses. Amber wears a long, black dress with no sleeves, thick straps and short frills along the curved hem around her neck. She unfolds her cane when I park and as I open her door for her she tap-taps the pavement to the door. "Left a step," I say, and she steps left, reaches for the door frame, runs her hands back along it to where the door frame curves, folds her cane and wraps the handle loop around it, holds the door itself, and sits. Amber brings her legs into the footwell and runs her hand along her dress to make sure it won't be caught in the door. "Watch your fingers," and she puts her hands on her lap. I shut the door gently.

In my seat, door closed, "Want me to turn on your heated seat?"

Amber nods.

"Want to talk to me at all?"

"I have trouble trusting people, don't I?"

"Yes."

"Can I explain a bit and you just listen? I know you weren't cutting me off."

I nod.

"Did you just nod?"

"Sorry, I did. I'll listen, yes."

"I've dated guys. And so far every one of them has used me for sex. No exceptions. They all just thought it would be fun to do a blind girl, that I'd have to reach around all over them and, you know, guys like that. I mean, you sure do. And a couple, I've heard them tell their buddies that's the only reason they dated me. So I have trouble believing that someone wants me, the actual me, not just the sex me. And it seemed back there like you want that actual me and I don't know how to understand that." Amber fiddles with her cane's wrist strap, the elastic bit that holds the bundle together. "I think for the last five months I've, deep-down, believed you were just using me. I apologize." She pulls the cane's strap out and lets it snap onto the aluminum over and over for some time. "You might not understand the trust that I have to place in people every day, and you definitely don't know the times that people used my blindness to hurt me, to tell me to walk safely forward and into a sign so they could laugh at me, to tell me there are no stairs when there are, telling me a sandwich has no mustard on it when it does or putting salt in my pop. People, Merak, can be mean." Amber sets her cane on her lap and her hands rub her dress fabric quickly up and down her thighs, bunching and unbunching the fabric underneath as they move. "And yes that's not many people and yes it happens less than it used to now that I'm out of the town I grew up in. And, if I'm honest and fair you are not the only boy I've dated who likes me for who I am. But I still have to trust people, if you excuse the phrase, blindly. I am used to people hurting me and the more I trust people the more it hurts. And I trust you a lot. A lot, Merak. You don't know. You don't even know. The only person I trust more is Grandpa Arn. You're third in line for trust. You can talk now."

"How am I third?"

"Grandpa, Sandstone, you."

That tracks. "I understand. I try and relate. I try when I describe colors to make them really relatable. I want to understand your perspective better. Let me be very clear, though, that I will never do anything to hurt you on purpose."

"Only through your ignorance, stupidity, mishap, accident, and a lack of consideration?"

"Well that's quite the list. I might say on accident, yes."

"You know I honestly don't care about the world of the sighted. And you're the first, maybe second, boy I've dated who really tries to experience my life. Second, yes. And you do it the best." Amber unclicks her seatbelt and twists to face me. "Merak, it scares me sometimes because no one else has ever been like you, and I don't know where that leads. All the rest followed a script. You ad lib."

"It scares me, too, because loving a person is scary." Damn. I was saving that for after dinner.

"You don't just get to drop the 'L' word so casually. How do you even know you're in love with me?"

"Because I've never tried to work so hard to be my best for someone before."

"I don't know if I'm in love with you."

"I know."

"You think you know, anyway," Amber crosses her arm and turns her face to the car window.

"Okay. Do you want to drive around –"

"Take a stroll at a park?"

"I guess. I mean the reservation is for seven. We have some time."

"What is it with you and walks?"

"They're quiet, we can talk, and it forces you to hold my hand or arm."

"I'm sorry you didn't get to surprise me tonight."

"I know."

⟨◊⟩

At The Bulbous Otter, I park in a close spot and let Amber know she has no car on her side. I walk around Federico and Amber, waiting for me with her hand on his little aero wing, takes my arm. At the entrance, Rick is waiting for us, grinning large.

"Welcome to The Bulbous Otter, do you fine folks have a reservation tonight?"

"We do, Snyder for two, please."

"Ah, yes, of course, here you are. Now, special requests, a bottle of champagne is already at your table, and for you, ma'am, a special surprise."

"Oh?"

"It's not a surprise." I hand Rick the blindfold and take my glasses off.

"Oh." Rick leans in as he ties the blindfold and whispers, "why'd you tell her. You're good at running moments."

"Later." I feel the blindfold go on and Rick tie it behind my head. The Bulbous Otter, already dark and dim, ambient light and single candles in small votives on the tables, becomes an enveloping darkness that wraps around my head and senses, like water in pool. The darkness feels like oil on my skin, like cold muddy water, like a car turning upside down, like a cabin light going off. I pull the blindfold up, look at the wall, and pant some hard breaths.

191

"We had a bit of a tiff, Rick. It's alright. Sometimes," I hear Amber slide her hands on her purse, "sometimes it's like a volcano, you know, and things just build up and then they erupt and then after that, if, you know, things weren't too bad you can see that yeah, it's good."

"Are you okay, Merak?" Rick asks. He grabs a cocktail napkin from the bar behind him and dabs my forehead.

"What happened?" Amber asks.

"I'm okay. I just had a moment." I take five deep, controlled breaths, eyes closed. Inhale I am not in the river and that was more than three years ago exhale. Inhale slower darkness is not drowning darkness is just the absence of light; it isn't even its own thing and we only define it by what it doesn't have and that means darkness isn't real or a threat exhale slower. Inhale again yes that was real danger in the river and I survived it this is an experience and not danger and I am doing it because I love Amber exhale. Inhale I am not ready for this but I am going to do this and I am not going to take that blindfold off until we're back in this foyer after dinner exhale. Inhale one last time I am ready for this and I will not succumb to something that cannot even exist except for the absence of something else exhale. "I'm ready."

Rick looks at me with his eyebrows up.

"I'm ready. It's not coming off. There will be no peeking."

I close my eyes and feel the blindfold go on. The panic rises in my spine, spreads outward like a timelapse video of mold on bread. No. No I am okay. No I am not afraid. Rick ties a bowtie, just like shoes he tells me. He's letting me know I can pull the cord and bail out. I will not.

"Sir, if you'll follow me to your booth." Rick's shoes on the carpet are quiet, but he takes some steps away from us.

I pause. "Um, really?"

I hear his shoes stop, he turns, I imagine like a military man on his heels. "Of course, that was silly of me. Reach out your arm, please." I do.

"Now, I'm going to let you put it on my shoulder and I'll lead you to your seat."

Amber places her hand on my back, where my neck meets my shoulders. "You have a train here, so please no sharp turns."

"I understand, ma'am. Thank you."

Rick leads us, as I had asked him to, directly to a seat that is far from the bathroom. I know I will need it and I know I will have trouble getting there. I count my steps. Forty-seven. "Just out of curiosity, where's the bathroom?"

"Over there," Rick says.

"Rick, did you just point?" Amber's voice is calm.

"Oh, of course. I apologize. Simply walk down the aisle to your right, your left, ma'am, and at the wall make a left, the entry will be the second on your right. The first is the kitchen and you probably don't want to walk there. I'll let the wait staff know to watch out when they exit the kitchen tonight, just in case."

"Thank you, Rick," Amber says.

"Of course." I hear the familiar clop of hard-leather-bound menus set in front of us. "Shall I open your champagne bottle and pour you some glasses?"

I pick up my menu. "Do you have one in Braille?"

"I'm sorry, we do not. Would you like me to read you the menu?"

Amber speaks before I can, "Just your specials tonight will be fine."

"Of course." Rick's voice changes, the amplitude, the brightness, as he speaks. He must be looking at, alternating between, Amber and I. How have I never noticed this before when people move their heads and talk? "We have a salt-roasted sea bass tonight. We cover it in a mound of salt, roast it, and then serve it atop a selection of local, fresh vegetables and a side of puree celeriac. We also have a roasted half of chicken, which we truss and then baste in herb butter, inside and out, and roast specifically for crispy skin. It will be served with a buttered pasta and vegetable of your choice. Lastly we have a delightful croque madame sandwich with house-made sourdough bread, uncured local ham, a jumbo egg from a local farm, and a topping of a delectable tarragon-infused béchamel sauce topped with fresh tarragon flakes that we serve alongside any of our fresh, rustic-cut French fry varieties. Sides can also be substituted for a salad, for only two dollars. Would you like me to start you with the champagne, or another drink, while you decide?"

"Amber?"

"Champagne, please."

Rick asks us if we prefer a coupe or a flute, and I suggest a flute, not out of preference but out of not knowing what a coupe is and how I would drink out of it without seeing it. The champagne bottle rustles the ice cubes. One of them tinks back into the ice after the bottle has been lifted. It must have held and then slipped off the bottle. Some minor noises. I assume Rick is undoing the wire binding and then a pop as the cork comes out and I feel myself jump in my seat. Rick pours the champagne cleanly; it makes no sound of air rushing into the bottle, no fizz rising too high in the glass. The glasses set down softly and I can't tell where. "I'll be back in a moment to take your orders."

As Rick's footsteps fade quickly away, I raise my hand, open my mouth. I need to know where the champagne is. I point my face at Amber. "Any ideas where our glasses are?"

"He put mine in my hand. Put your fingertips on the edge of the table. Slide your hand slowly forward. Back and forth. Keep your fingers loose so they wrap around the stem and don't knock the glass over."

Smooth, the tablecloth texture feels like fine sheets with no discernable threads or pattern in the weave. The cloth has no ripples, no hemlines beneath it from being folded over. It rests flat and still on the table. My hand moves, I think, in slow straight lines, but somehow I keep running the side of my palm into the table's right edge. I am not making any progress at all.

"It's probably centered right in front of you, or up and left."

I reach my arm out and slowly slide it left until my forearm feels the stem. I pull my hand back and pick up the glass in my fingers. "Toast?"

"To what?"

"Well, to five months."

"To being lucky enough to have found someone who opens our minds to things we otherwise would never know."

Dang, that's good. "Yes, that's the best toast I've ever heard." I lift my glass. "I assume we're just lifting glasses, not clinking them?"

"Well then I'm just holding my glass in the air in front of you like an idiot."

"Really?" I move my glass slowly toward, I think toward, the table's center.

"No not really. I just lifted it. I'm teasing you a bit."

I get it, a part of it, a bit of it, a hint of what it is like to have someone play a joke or a prank, to exploit a difference over which I have no control. "And maybe to understanding each other a bit better." I bring the glass back to my lips and I hear Amber take a sip and set her glass down. Bubbles pop and fizz on my tongue, leaving hints of grape sweetness and complexities I have not noticed in other drinks before.

"Back there, a few minutes ago, the blindfold, when Rick put it on," I start.

"I was about to ask."

"I had a panic attack. I was suddenly back in Colander, under water. I have nightmares still."

"Not when I spend the night."

"Not yet, anyway."

"I haven't had a nightmare in years. Not a true one, just sometimes a dream that's not as pleasant as others."

"What are your dreams like?"

Amber's hair rustles on her shirt collar. I suspect she's tilting her head. "They're, I guess you'd call them sensory. I dream about textures and smells, sounds and tastes that sort of are normal but sometimes just completely wrap my body all at once. They're filled with the feelings in my fingers, things that move and rub against my hands, sounds around me from different sources and voices. I feel vibrations and used to dream often about walking in new places with my cane, feeling out obstacles, counting steps. But lean in, Merak," the table shifts a bit as Amber leans in close and when I do she says "the sex dreams are definitely the best."

"Wait, you have those, too?"

"Shh, and yes of course. Everyone does. Geez. How would you not just assume that? Do you think there are people around us listening to us?"

I sit up and take a sip of champagne. "Um, let me see."

"No peeking."

"Sorry, phrasing. I mean I'm going to listen closely and try to figure that out." Kitchen noises of silverware and chefs knives carry across the room. Quiet otherwise, just some stray sounds from behind a wall and down an entry off to my right. Oil sizzles. A baking tray drops on a metal counter. An overhead vent fan makes a soft white noise. Someone says 'order up, table nine.' I listen for the sounds of diners, silverware on a plate, a conversation, ice in glasses, footfalls of other waiters attending the section. Hearing none, I declare we must be alone. Someone a few feet to my right coughs.

"Okay," she says. "We'll go with that."

Rick walks back to our table and asks if we're ready to discuss appetizers.

"I think we'll just go straight to the entrees tonight. Amber?"

"I'll have the half chicken. Can the pasta be spirals or tubes?"

"We have both rotini and penne."

"Penne, please. Water to drink"

"Of course, and you, sir?"

"I'll have the croque madame. What are my French fry options?"

"Regular, crispy battered, sweet potato, parmesan, and truffle. The truffle are a five-dollar up charge, but, if I might say, very much worth it.

"Crispy sounds lovely. Also, water to drink."

"Of course, sir. Anything else that I can get you right now?"

"I think that will do it."

"Of course. Please mind the candle in the middle of your table, by the way."

"Thank you." I had forgotten about those. "Oh, one other question, are there any other diners back here tonight?"

"You're my only table in this section but right now there are four other parties back here."

"Dangit. I really thought I was right when I guessed we were alone."

"Nope. And they're all staring at you."

"Really?"

"Nope. No one cares that you're here and it's probably dark enough they don't even see you're in a blindfold."

"Thanks, Rick." I hear his watch jingle and I assume he just gave me a thumbs-up before he walked away.

"Okay, so what exactly is a croque madame? It sounded like a ham and cheese sandwich."

"With an egg on top."

"But they call it a croque madame because this is a fancy place?"

"No, because it has béchamel sauce."

"What is béchamel sauce?"

"Uh, it's a white sauce, like alfredo, cream-based, but I don't think it has cheese, lots of herbs, though. I'm curious about a tarragon béchamel." I slide my hand forward to pick up and sip my champagne flute.

"I know alfredo sauce. It comes in a jar," Amber says and after a pause her champagne flute sets down on the table. "Merak, honest question, how are you feeling right now?"

"I feel like I need to introduce you to fresh Alfredo sauce."

"About the blindfold, I mean."

"I think I'm doing okay. I worry about going to the bathroom. I worry about sloppy eating." A tray clatters in the kitchen and I feel myself startle-jump.

"Feels like you're a bit jumpy."

"You felt that?"

"Yes, in my seat. Our booth must wrap around," Amber says as she pats the cushion with her hand, and I feel the vibration reach my left leg.

"One thing I know, after just these however-many minutes, I am so much more impressed with you because I think I could be quite scared all the time."

"I don't really have a choice. It would be like you being afraid of having ... not having four arms or something like that. You only have two arms. You don't really have a choice to have more. It's just how you are. Are you afraid of life without two extra arms?"

"No. No I'm really not." Amber and I sit quietly for a time. I sip my champagne flute empty and assume Amber has as well. "More champagne?"

"Did you finish yours?"

"Yes. You didn't?"

"No, I'm pacing myself. Am I the designated driver now?"

I laugh a bit. "Do you want to drive a car?"

"I've never driven a car. Honestly, yes. Yes I would like to drive a car."

"Tomorrow. We'll go find ourselves a nice empty stretch of road or a parking lot. Sound good?"

"Sounds illegal. I'm down."

"Your waters, sir and ma'am," Rick says.

"Jesus, man, I didn't even hear you coming."

"They're placed about two-o'clock, near the table's centerline."

"Thank you, Rick," Amber says, and her voice is fluid and a smile.

After I assume that Rick has left, "I'll be back in a moment."

"I'll be here."

I start to turn but realize someone may be coming. I turn slowly, slide one leg and then another into the traffic lane, hoping no one is rushing by to trip on them. Right and left foot, short little baby steps will be safe. What was the route Rick said, right to the wall, left to another wall. Second entrance. Right. Right? Was it kitchen then bathroom or bathroom then kitchen. Aw shit, I forget. I'll know when I get there. One will have kitchen noise; one will not. Inhale, I can make it there, exhale.

I walk and on my third step I hear "Watch out behind you," and it's too late I walk right into the back of someone sitting in a seat at a table that must be next to us. He makes a loud "oof" and I hear his voice change, focus, the direction points to me like a lighthouse beam spinning and stopping in place. "What on earth is this about?" He sounds fat, like the sort of huge old man whose suit buttons are held on only by trust and magic, sleeves too short, and hem lines forming a framework under the coat fabric. He probably has silver and black hair, thin, slicked back.

"I am so sorry, sir. I really didn't see you there." I don't know where I'm looking but I don't think it's at him. "My girlfriend is blind and

I wanted to see once what her life is like every day to be a better boyfriend, so I'm wearing this blindfold. I honestly didn't see you."

"You are very lucky I had set my red wine down, young man. Playing games is dangerous. What if I had had my fork in my mouth, or I was cutting my baked potato while holding it?"

"I am so sorry. Are you okay?"

"He's fine," a woman's voice from across the table. She sounds like she has a perm and not-hard-to-detect dye job to hide her silver hair. "There is space to walk on either side of us. The booths on the right are empty, left are not."

"Thank you very much, I say" walking sideways to find a booth. It has the same tablecloth as our table and I walk forward, holding the booth table's edge.

Behind me, the woman says "Well I think it's sweet that he's doing that for her. Maybe you could be a bit more sweet sometimes."

One step, second and the table ends, third and fourth and a pillar between booth backs. Five and then the next booth's back cushion. Six, seven, eight and the next booth's tabletop ends. I can do this. Five booths, that will be forty steps. Wait. How many booths are there? Do I remember five or am I making-up five? I count my pace and, yes, five booths, just more than forty steps and my hand wraps around the final pillar and touches smooth drywall on the back of the last booth.

The kitchen sounds close, left, loudly left. It smells of fresh, roasted herbs, warm spices, seared steak, and roasting birds sizzling in their own fat. The floor underneath my feet turns from carpet to a raised seam, must be tile on the other side. Three feet, maybe four, to the far wall if it's a normal space. Conversations off to my right, another seating area. I cannot forget how many steps I took here. I hold my hand out slowly and step forward. I feel the wall, find the corner of a photo or painting hung on it, place my hand below the frame and touch the wall with my fingertips, hand slightly in front of me, as I walk to my left, tracing both the wall and the bottom of the frame. One, two, three, four, five, six, seven, doorjamb. Cutlery and plates, fry oil and meat on iron, an oven door slams.

"Walking here," I say, inhale, and step forward into the opening with caution at first, reaching my hand in front of me to feel for the far wall. I feel it and take a fast step toward it, pass the next doorjamb. Exhale. Almost there, right? Rick said second entry; I was right. Four steps, wall ends, what's here? Are there two doors? Is there a hallway leading to two doors? Is this a unisex bathroom for one person at a time? Can I find a sign? Nothing. "Is anyone down here?" Nothing.

I hold my hand out and feel the wall's corner. It does feel like it leads to a hallway, but I don't know how long. It must not be that long. I walk and my knee hits something hard. "Oh my gosh, I'm so sorry," I say, putting my hands down, feeling the stack of booster seats that I just apologized to. The doors must be on the other side. My left hand reaches through the air; it feels a doorjamb, straight and smooth on the left, angled, stepped, leading to a piece of smooth wood and glass textured like a golf ball. The door must be right in front of me. I feel around it for a sign. Dots! Braille! This must be the sign. I need raised letters or a raised shape for a man or a woman. I can tell those apart, the straight lines of the generic man shape versus the triangular woman shape. I need to find those triangular corners.

Nothing. The printing on the signs is smooth. Not raised. Not recessed, either. It feels like paint, too thin to discern the shape. I step right; the door that I found is to my left. My right hand follows the wall to its right. Smooth and flat, smooth and flat, smooth and right angle! Doorjamb!

Okay, I think I'm standing between two doors. I think. Are they both bathrooms or is one an office or a break room? What's usually first in the hallway, men's or women's? Is that even standard or random? I take a step back, then a second, expecting to feel booster seats but I just run into the wall behind me with my back. Can I hold it long enough to wait for someone to come along and ask? No, I don't think I can. Pressure transitions to pain. Time to fish or cut bait. I think that the men's is usually first in shared hallways. I step forward and reach for the left door, find the wood and textured glass. I know this glass, it feels, as I run my hand over it more closely, like it was poured over smooth pebbles. It's frosted, or at least all of this stuff that I've ever seen is frosted. I find the metal push-plate. I had assumed a restaurant this size would have a multi-person bathroom, but this confirms that and I enter with some confidence.

"Hello? Anyone in here?" Hearing no reply I walk in and pick a direction, turn left, hold my right arm straight in front of me and my left down, at an angle. If I run into a sink and counter, my left arm will touch it first and I'll know the toilets are to the right. If I reach a toilet, my right arm will touch the wall and I'll hopefully not stick my left hand into a urinal.

Step and two, three, four, counter. Counter. Sink, what the hell kind of sink is this? Is the whole counter a sink? I wave my hands above it, slowly, feeling around it to find faucets and if they pour into their own basins. Yes, I think the whole counter is a sink. It feels like carved stone, smooth and polished, angled inward. A long, metal grate is in the back of the sink, touching an abrupt backsplash. Alright. Let's find out if this is the men's.

I turn around and listen. Does a wall of stalls sound or echo differently than a wall half of stalls, half urinals? I don't know. Fortune favors the bold, as my father says, and I hold my arms out and walk forward. Ten steps and a cold, damp metal pipe and handle. Urinal. Thank you, God.

My hands trace the pipe down to the top of the urinal. Standard height. I unzip and start to pee, adjusting the placement until the sound changes from a flat splash to the bubbly soft sound of pee on … ice cubes? For a moment I feel safe, and calm, and maybe even a bit magnificent. And then I finish, shake, and zip. I turn, walk confidently back to the sink, counting my steps, and with a hard jam to my gut learn that my stride is much longer when I think I know where I'm going.

"Fuck," I mutter, as I search around for a faucet. I find one and it's a well-pump-style, not that it needs pumping but that the top of the waterway is open. I lift the handle and, wait, which way do I turn these for hot and cold. I don't want to be mid-scrub and suddenly it's hot. I place my hand under the water and start to adjust the handle. Left first, I think that's hot, because most people are righties and so they put the cold on the right for safety. I think I heard that once. In some seconds, it gets warm. Some fiddling finds a good temperature.

Paper towels. Crap. Are they by the sink or the door? I side-step along the sink to the wall, feel to my left and find a paper towel dispenser and when I near it and the sensor triggers it to spit out some of the roll. Some fumbling around finds the paper towel and uncoordinated waving releases a few more sheets.

Dry hands, wall, back to the door, backtrack on the right side of the hallway till it ends, miss the booster seats. Left and then right. Oh no. The steps. I forgot the number of steps. But would they be the same now that I have confidence in where I am? I walk along the bathroom hallway wall, left hand tracing it as I go, kitchen noise growing, someone walks past me quickly with no announcement, food smell and sizzle and heat right next to my face. "Coming through," I say, turning out of the bathroom hallway and walking briskly across the kitchen opening to the far side. Step and step, and how many do I need? There was another dining area. If I can hear that, I can guess.

Frame. I lift my hand along the wall slowly, feel for the bottom of the frame. I find it, the same frame, same texture. I run one finger on the underside as I walk and when it ends I turn right. Forty- wait. How many steps? Dang. Five booths. But where is ours? Our booth is round. Are we in the corner? Usually those are round. But I bumped into that guy, so we must be middle. Did I walk straight or not. Look, Merak, just get close; you'll figure it out.

I step, left arm out and angled away from me, feeling for a wall. I find it. Wall, pillar, booth seat, gap, tabletop, gap, booth seat, pillar, repeat. Five booths. I hear the man I bumped into talking to the woman and I follow their voices to where he sounds like he's in the same place he was before. I feel my way to the second booth. "Amber?"

"Back so soon? Didn't get lost or fall in?"

"I, um, I thought I was slow. If you need to go, it's five booths down and then yours is the second door. Watch out for the booster seats." I feel my seat and slide in.

"I know. I went and came back while you were gone."

"What? How?"

"I asked the nice couple that you bumped into for some clearer directions. I passed you before you got to the kitchen."

"How do you know that?"

"You were shuffling like a ninety-year-old on a cruise ship."

I put my hands on the table.

"Rick refilled your champagne for you, but that was when you stood up. I hope it isn't flat now."

"Very funny."

"For what it's worth, he kept an eye on you to make sure you didn't get hurt."

That, that makes me feel a lot better. I tell Amber so. I feel around for my glass and Rick left it in the center where it had been before. I sip it, big sips, many sips. My hands shake and it translates like the Morse Code of numbing terror into my lips.

"Are you okay, Merak? Did you have another panic attack?"

"No, I just," I lean back. I set the empty flute down in front of me. "I felt powerless."

"Power's an illusion for most of us anyway, Merak. But if you think you get it, pull the knot."

"I know, but I won't."

Amber's water clinks and gurgles when she straws up the bottom-drops. I push my flute out toward the table's middle, to make room for when the food arrives. As I push it, it falls. It's empty, so I reach to pick it back up. I feel glass, a bit warm but probably just from my hand. It doesn't occur to me that the rim is upright and I stick my fingers into the candle flame and hot wax. "Mother of pearl," I say, reaching for my water glass, swinging my right hand wide, I hit it, the glass falls over, my ice water splashes on the table, spills on to the floor. I pick up the glass and shove my left fingers into it, into what ice remains, the wax on my fingers hardening, peeling away from my skin.

"Merak, what happened?"

"I burned my fingers in the candle trying to pick up my champagne flute. It'll be okay. I've got them in ice right now."

"Jeez, Merak, are you all right? Hold on, I'm topping off that glass." Rick pours ice water into the glass and the last of the wax hardens and my fingers start to feel better as they cool. "Let me see it. Okay, it's not actually burned. That's good. Just some wax on them. Your knuckle hair is pretty well singed off. It looks like little, dead fiddleheads. I'll take the candle away and bring you a fresh glass of water with your dinners, which are ready now." When Rick brings our dinners out, back in character with a polite sir and ma'am, the plates rest in front of us and he explains to Amber that her chicken is a full half-chicken, not further separated, breast up and leg down, center plate, midnight, taking up the top half. Then from nine to six her pasta and from six to three her vegetables. He says we should enjoy our meals and walks off.

I raise my hand and start to open my mouth.

"Rick didn't tell you where your food is."

"I think he did that on purpose."

"Oh yes. He did. He asked if I thought that was a good idea."

"You two are ganging up on me, aren't you?" I chuckle. "Alright, so, I just use my silverware to feel around the plate and find the food?"

"You do. I put my fork out first, try to find the major outlines. A sandwich and fries should be very easy."

I place my napkin in my shirt collar, just in case, and slide my fork forward on the table until it tink-finds the plate, and I slide it around the plate to get an idea of the size. The plate's right side has a block, it feels like a brick, but lighter, and it moves. This is the sandwich and the fork tines on the crust confirm that. I use my knife to find the fries and they are laid in a small pile on the left of the plate. Once the mental picture forms in my mind, the actual cutting and eating falls into place easily. Though not hard, I imagine I may be a bit messy and am unsure if béchamel has dripped on my napkin or pants. I use my fork to find bits that I miss and then I spear them and eat them. I put a small piece of bread, ham, and the béchamel on the fork and pass it to Amber, who after taking the bite off my fork and chewing with audible joy, decides that I won dinner.

When we finish, Rick takes our plates and asks us about desserts. We both agree that we are very full and he brings the check.

"Um, how much is it?"

"Forty-seven fifty-six, sir."

I reach into my pocket, fish out my wallet, and pull out a credit card, I think. "Can you add a 25% tip and round up to the nearest dollar?"

"Not with your laundry card."

"Dangit. Here. Thank you."

Rick, returning with the receipt, holds it where I need to sign. "If you'd like, I can walk you to the foyer." We agree and he walks us there, very quickly. In the foyer I take the blindfold off. Though dark, the rooms feel bright, painful even. The features and faces of people are clear and, wait, our booth was literally ten feet from the foyer? The heck? "Oh, you know, I kind of paraded you around the restaurant when I sat you down."

"Dude. It worked. I was completely confused." I give Rick a hug. "Thank you, man. Thank you." I think about all the moments in my life that have needed trust, and how, bar none, I took those for granted without realizing trust's real value and worth. In a second, as though all of human history flashes before my eyes, I realize that what truly separates us from the rest of this planet's life isn't tools, speech, or even intelligence, but the ability to trust others, even strangers, and that our collective work turns trust into society. Trust leads us to ask others for help, and the ability to seek help, to trust the helper, makes us human.

Rick hugs me back and we bump fists. He walks up to Amber, hugs her. "You guys have a good night. I'm closing and cleaning."

I hold Federico's door open for Amber. "Can I take a photo of you?"

She looks down and back at me, "you brought your camera?"

"Just in case."

"Well, yes, you should take at least one, you know, just in case." She winks at me, exaggerated, cheeks up and bright. "Tell me when to smile."

Flash, 85mm lens, best film I own, no, the flash's light will be too strong, wait, I know. I grab the blindfold from my pocket, fold it in half and hold it in front of the flash a few inches. The harshest, direct light will be blocked but side-escaping light will still be enough if I shoot wide-open. I set the focus to the closest point, hold the blindfold in front of the flash, and as I lean in to get Amber in focus, "you can put your hands in your lap, yes and turn your head toward me, and yes, you are the loveliest person I have ever photographed."

Amber smiles wide and surprised, the happiness wrinkles near the top of her nose form points to her bridge. The flash capacitor discharges into light, shutter clicks, and Amber asks if the photo will be good.

"Ask me in a couple of weeks."

‹◊›

Federico is a very easy car to park, turns well, I can see the parking spot lines from my seat. We don't park in The Spillway's grassy lot, too muddy; Federico will get stuck. A few other cars and groups have small gatherings around the grassy parking lot and the paved one, too. When I take the keys out of the ignition, which Amber knows means the car is in park, we both get out and walk to the hatch. Amber runs her knuckles against Federico's window frames and to the spoiler. "Fingers," I say, and Amber holds he hands away as I open the hatch. In the back we listen to the soft cracks and pops of the fires near other cars, the dull murmur of the other groups' conversations, and occasional loud laughter as other people tell anecdotes and jokes. All these sounds, discordant and uncoordinated, merge to build a melody of night, music of youth, and harmony of man and nature. Amber grabs our pillows and we lay with our heads near the back, warm and damp night air coming through the open hatch, accompanying the sounds.

"I think," I say to Amber, looking up at the night sky through Federico's rear window, "that tonight was important for me."

"Not just you."

I turn and look at Amber, us both in dark, the fire light from other groups too dim to light us beyond a warm, red glow. "For us. I like us, you know, what we've been making together."

"Love?"

"I mean, I won't deny that, but more than that. This feels like a solid foundation."

"Even though I can be a pain?"

"It's hard to get to know someone, hard to learn to trust them, when you have to first unlearn what people are like. I'm no piece of pie to live with, either. So we'll work it out and it'll be good because I love you and we'll work together."

"I love you, too, Merak."

The last two seconds linger in the air, obliterate the night breeze in tree limbs, conversations and laughter, and fires cracking and popping. The night's darkness cocoon collapses around us, holds us safely in my car, warm and calm. Amber takes a deep breath through her nose and exhales.

"We really did just say that, didn't we?"

"Yes."

"Did you mean it?"

"I did." Amber rolls into me and puts her hand on my chest. I wait a few seconds. "Did you?"

"What?" She smacks my chest. "Of course I did. I —" Amber's hand is warm, and she runs it under my shirt onto my stomach, finger circles my navel.

"Dude, that tickles."

"I know. Merak, I've never said that to someone, like a boy, okay? You can't just abuse that. And you can't just leave me or something, okay? Because it's not going to be easy, you know, with me. And if you want to bail before it's too late, I would understand."

"Amber," I say, running my left hand's fingers in her hair, tracing the outside of her ear, the back of her earlobe, "I'm not leaving you. Loving someone is never easy, and with you it will always be worth the effort."

Amber scoots next to me and hugs me with her right arm. "Thank you," she says, stumbling over the words as though they are new, uneven ground. They may as well be and I feel it, too, the rocks and the risks, the potholes and the precarious nature of love between people. For seconds I sense our future together, years of continuing to learn to speak with the other, not at, and the risk that defines love: that we may love and the other may, one day, simply stop. Love is, at its core, a willingness to be hurt married to hope that we won't be. Love is also, when the person we love does hurt us, as they will, hoping it's out of ignorance or accident and not malice. Love is looking past the other's flawed humanity and forgiving.

"Nothing that I can think of scares me more than being in love with someone, and trusting myself to be the best I can be. I hope that makes sense."

Amber nods. She scoots next to me and curls, putting her face against my chest.

"I'm looking forward to whatever happens next."

10
Blue

At campus, my room, our Bulbous Otter dinners still in our bellies, Rick still a few hours from coming back, Amber sits on the foot of my bed. She tells me to leave the lights off, and I do.

"Am I the first girl you've been in love with?"

This feels like a trap. This feels like an invitation to a fight. I inhale and trust it is not. "I, well, I, my upbringing, no, that's not right. I need to let you know why this is hard for me." I remember my parents' fights about this same subject in the weeks after I returned from Colorado. My first year at school they attended something called 'Forgiveness Counselling' to re-connect. My father told me that the process, a direct result of my time away and of calling them from Pine Grove Stand, allowed him to see how he had hurt the people he thought he loved, forgive himself, forgive my mother, and how the reverse was true. He lobbied me to reconnect with Meggy when that ended, but I did not. I, more now than before, am glad I didn't. "I was very much in love with a girl down here named Meggy. We met March '99 and it ended October '00."

"Did you love her as much as me?"

The sink water runs hot and I wash my hands, soap, lather, rinse, towel. "Different, yes and no. I did think we might get married, for a while. We had a different dynamic. Some parts of it I miss, others not."

"Why didn't you marry her? Did you tell her you loved her?"

"I did tell her that. She loved me, too, but we defined it different ways. She, what's the best way to put this, saw me as a project that needed fixing. And that came at a time when the mental damage of my trip was new terrain for me, an unfamiliar traveling companion may be the best way to word it." I hang the hand towel and walk to the bed, pull my chair

211

out, and sit on it facing Amber. "I was trying to separate who I am now from my pre-Colorado self and I think Meggy wanted me not to. I trust that she intended to help me be the best I could be, but it wasn't what I needed. I never did reconnect with him, that pre-Colorado me – he's dead. I'm like a second me, like some similar-ish stranger inherited my body and memories. I don't know if that makes sense. I know I like who I am more." Amber, hands in her lap, taps her fingertips on her thighs in time. "Why do you ask?" I stand and sit next to her in bed, my chair squeaks and thunks on the floor and the bed's spring support squeals like train brakes.

Amber turns her head to face me, runs her hand along the bed to find my leg. I sit facing her, my left leg on the bed, bent at the knee, left calf tucked under my right leg. Her hand finds the crevice of my knee, her middle finger rests inside it. "Her loss my gain. I know I'm not easy to date. I've dated a lot of guys."

I nod, agreeingly.

"I can feel you nodding and that was not a window for that, thank you. Anyway, I've always dumped them all. I've wanted to do that to you a lot."

"Is this –"

"No. I struggle with trust. Merak, you are like a deadbolt that can't be shot open. I trust you. I have something I want with you. I mean, our future, I want you, if I get a job somewhere not here, to move with me, not into your own place, not into your own bed. Into my place, our place, our bed. If I don't get a job somewhere else, I want to move with you to Chicago, or wherever you want to go. Do you want that?"

"I do." Weird, to hear that come out of my mouth. I know I want that; I didn't know I wanted to say it.

"Have you ever," Amber takes her hand back. She locks her fingers, puts them on her lap. She faces away from me a moment and looks back. "Have you ever made love without protection?"

212

"I have, a few times."

Amber points her face at her lap. Moonlight reflecting off the lake and through the window shows a frown. "Damn." She breathes through her nose a few times, a faint whistling as she does. "I have not. I want that to change, with you. Tonight. Right now. I need you know this isn't something I just thought of on a whim, or because we had a nice dinner and some time at The Spillway."

My left hand rests on her closed hands. "I understand." This explains her reaction this afternoon.

"No, not yet, I don't think. Humans, Merak, we interact with each other like farmers with a tilled field. What we say, how we treat others, these are seeds that we, I believe, plant to grow in others to help them grow. I –" Amber sets her hands on my leg again. "I don't think anyone ever knows what grows in the soul of another person because of our time with them. But, with you, Merak, with you I see a future outside of Johnson County and more than working at a school or convenience store, slowly growing comfortable in that life, afraid to trust myself to be and do more. You've taught me that I can do and be more because you don't treat me like I'm incapable, or fragile. You just give me the little helps that I need. I am different today than I would be if I had never met you. You are a farmer, Merak, and not just for me for all your friends, and we are all better for having you in our lives. I fear that you will get bored of that with me."

My brain feels like an electric motor caught fire, burning in the idea that I could be a benefit to the people I know. I fight back the desire to believe she's wrong, that she has me confused with someone else. In the moonlight that passes through the window, I watch her face's left side; I pull her hair back and tuck it behind her ear, see the delicate, short blonde hairs on her cheek stand and her left eyelid twitch open and closed.

"Do you know why people, strangers, talk so much to you, Merak? Most people, they don't want change. They want to cruise through their little lives unchallenged and unchanged, convincing themselves with no evidence that they're right and the world is wrong. And the ones who talk to you, they just know it, sense it, that at any moment, without warning, you might say some little, offhand-to-you thing that would sit in their brains, stir, grow, and force them to either examine who they are or become someone else. Growth hurts, and it's hard, and most people can't, or at best don't want, to do it. But you, Merak, you're driven by a need to force yourself to be better. It's just who you are; you can't even help it. You bring everyone with you, whether we signed up for the ride or not. You don't even know how scary that is."

Quiet, no not quite. Faint saxophone on the water, muted by the room's windows. Amber and I exhale, inhale, sit in the mute-music room and our lung-rhythms align to sound that bounces off water.

"Take off your glasses and look away for a moment," Amber says.

I turn away, lean to set my glasses on my desk. Upright again, Amber fiddles in my pants pocket and she puts the blindfold over my eyes. "Let me know if you have a panic attack."

"I'll be okay." A rush of calm drops from my scalp downward while anxiety and fear rush upward. They meet, like great and opposing waves, in my chest, rise up my neck, and I feel my heart pound in the muscles at and above my shoulders. Calm prevails. My pulse quickens in anticipation but the throbbing in my neck relaxes. Amber tells me she wants me to make love to her like she does to me. In the dark of my room with the blindfold on, our hands trace out the braille of our skin's excitement bumps as our hairs raise, vestigial and reflex-driven. We seek the physical dialect of form, the language bodies speak as opposite-side parts align, mingle, and intertwine. I feel the weight of river water try to drown me and the freedom of a late-night road, the thud of falling on hard pavement and the wrap of water when gravity wins at the end of a dive, the heat of a desert sun and the cool breeze of cave air wrap around and within Amber and I.

‹◊›

We sleep through Rick coming home and he sits at his desk typing homework when we wake up.

"Erm," I say to him. "Can we have a moment to dart to the shower?" Amber giggles.

Rick sighs. "After this paragraph I'll step into the hall."

Amber and I shower while Rick finishes his work and heads to an early class. As Amber dresses, I grab a random photo album from the small bookshelf built into my desk and page through it. I watch Amber dress and idly flip the book pages. Not until she's sliding on her jeans do I realize what album I grabbed, and Amber asks what photos I'm looking at.

"Uh, well, I randomly grabbed an old album. It's, this is awkward, some photos of Meggy and I."

"Like naked photos?"

"No, just stuff we did. A weekend trip to St. Louis with George and Rick and Gabby, the girl George was dating then." Amber sits on the bed and listens. "There's photos of the rides, our dinner out, shots I took on the car ride up and back, places we stopped. Just, you know, goofy stuff. George shoving a stack of six doughnuts in his mouth, Meggy dancing on the rusty hood of an old tractor that was in a field, then one with her acting like she's driving it. George and Gabby kissing by a roadside statue of a gopher." I flip a page and Amber drops her finger onto one of the photos, middle photo, left side.

"What's that photo?"

"That's a shot of Meggy wearing my blue pajamas and bouncing on our hotel bed like a trampoline. I wanted to try a new photo technique I had read about called dark room flash. Basically, a camera flash is a super short burst of light, like a twenty-thousandth of a second or something. So very, very much faster than a camera's shutter can do. So in a dark room I can use the camera's standard flash speed, which is way too long to freeze motion, combined with just the near-instant light from a flash to freeze motion well."

"I don't exactly understand, but it sounds neat. What's the photo actually look like?"

"We used three rolls of film trying to get this one shot. A few were okay, but this was the best. So Meggy is frozen in mid-air, wearing my pajamas, which are loose on her, the pajama top's buttons all undone, an open gap down the middle of her body, a bit sheer and see-though, you know, and her navel ring, a small pearl on a chain, frozen like a tiny, curled snake. She's right at the peak of her jump, her head is facing the side and she was whipping her hair around so it's frozen in a disk around her. Individual strands are just hanging there in the air. And because she was right at the top of her jump she's, well, she isn't a particularly bosomy girl but this photo makes it look like she is. Her legs are a bit up and twisted at her hips and her knees bent so she looks like she's kneeling on air. The pillows are a couple inches above the bed, the lampshade cockeyed because she bumped it coming down on a previous jump, and, yeah, it was a fun photo to take."

Amber flips a few pages. "This one."

"Meggy in Federico's passenger seat. We stopped for gas on the way home and she was exhausted, sun-drained, dehydrated a bit. We went in to get some waters, pops, a stack of candy bars that would look like a toddler on an expense account bought them, and when we got out, she was out cold in the front seat. She had the seat back a little, socks and shoes on the floor, her bare feet on the dash, toes pressed into the windshield. She's wearing these dark-blue jeans with the knees torn open, lots of loose threads, and a white top over a navy bra that shows through a bit. Oh, and a black choker. She loved wearing a choker. Her hair is all a mess and tussled like abandoned bed sheets, mouth a bit open.

"Should I be jealous?"

"No."

"Do you still hear from her?"

I look at the photo of Meggy sleeping, white and blue on tan leather seats, my reflection faint in the window. "Meggy set me down a road I didn't, not really, want and that bothered and stirred my mind. My brain would spend hours stuck in those quiet moments when the ghosts of the thoughts that thrive in our mind's ignored shadowy corners pay us their respects. I just kept reliving my crash over and over and she did a lot to break me out of that cycle. Sometimes now the crash just feels like a story I tell people, not even a thing that happened." That's the nature of the pain our minds inflict on us, to bring us back to the beginning, to simultaneously hold us back from progressing while also actively wanting to be better. The brain does both things, always, like a coin, not so much stuck between heads and tails but both at once. "She moved back to Chicago and will finish school at Columbia next spring, Rick told me. They're still friends."

"Does she ask about you at all?"

"Rick said she does, not every time they talk."

I flip back once more to the photo of Meggy frozen in air wearing my pajamas. It, in particular, reminds me of the optimism and joy Meggy had for us, and how her at the peak of this jump, that was the peak of our relationship. I could have been better and I wasn't. "I, um, I learned an important lesson from her, I mean a lot of important lessons. For us, I learned to better appreciate what I have and to better care for a relationship. I hope, very much, that I do that for us."

Amber says I do and after some time in silence together, her arms around my waist, head on my shoulders, we walk out of the building toward her first class. When I let her hand go she stops and asks if I would be willing to tell her what blue is like soon. I would.

‹◊›

Rick hands me the keys to his car. I know it. I bought it. I drove it through states and hills, staving off the engine's desire to burn. Rick, after his father kicked him out, moved in with us, just weeks before I left for college, and it put a deadline on my father to fix this for him. That my father fixed it so it would get him through school, well, I'm not the only one who sees Rick as family. "If you guys crash it, just leave it wherever. I'll report it stolen."

"No one will believe your car was stolen. And it's more likely to catch on fire again." How this car made it back from Colorado, this car's not willing to give up on us.

Rick shrugs; I'm right. I hand him Federico's keys so he can go to work. "She's gonna love this, you know."

I smile. I nod. I know. I give Rick a hug, thank him for trusting us, and head out to the hallway where Amber and Jesse are plotting how to beat me in more video games.

At the Dining Hall, the four of us get our meals, sit, eat, and talk. "Okay, so one of my Geo professors, he's quite the prankster," Amber says. "This one time on a field study at Yellowstone, he and a class, this is some years ago by the way, they were watching a group of tourists and my professor, he just got this inspiration. That night they went in to town to a hardware store for some plastic pipe, a box, paint, and some wire. They made this pipe and box into something that looked like a lever, put it in this box that they painted red, and then glued some coiled wire so it looked like it was coming out of the back of the thing.

"Now, geysers, they don't just randomly go. I mean, some do, but some have timetables and most generally let you know beforehand that they're gonna pop by shaking the ground and sputtering. So my professor, he and a student wear something that he said kind of looked like a construction worker outfit uniform and stood by the lever, wires plugged into the ground, just off to the corner of this tourist viewing platform. Right on schedule, the geyser he was near, it starts to shake the ground

218

and pop steam out the top and so he points to his student who pulls the lever: geyser. The crowd turned and faced him and applauded. He bowed. And he did that all day until some park rangers, laughing about it, politely asked him to stop."

"My first job was at this small used sports equipment store," Jesse says. "I worked there after school with this other guy, nice dude, Mac, who worked there after his shift at the Motorola distribution center. We got along well, and he, I, and the manager Robbie we used to play all these silly pranks on each other, you know the standard stuff like mustard in the straw when the other person looked away, watering down their drink, turning their sandwich upside down —"

"Lots of food pranks," I say.

"— Oh yes. So we'd had this escalating prank battle, lots of random little skirmishes. Anyway, one day I called in sick so Robbie asks me to prank Mac. King of all pranks, he says. Really wasn't, but we got Mac good. Robbie tells me he's going to tell Mac that I'd been fired for stealing. That he caught me taking used tennis balls out of the used tennis ball bucket to give to my dog. You know, clearly just a stupid thing no one cared about. We didn't even inventory those. So Mac totally doesn't believe it. And good on him. But Robbie, over the span of a couple hours, has him starting to think it might be true. My job was to take a quick jog up and down my street so that, combined with being a bit sick, I'd be really breathless and sound nervous and then call in at a certain time to talk to Mac. So I do, and I sound terrified. And I get Mac and ask for Robbie and I hear Robbie in the background telling Mac he's not taking any calls from 'that thieving little crap.' And I'm selling this big time like I'm making it sound like I'm weeping on the phone and everything and begging to have Mac beg Robbie to give me my job back. And Mac does that after we hang up and Robbie just stands his ground, insists I'm fired. We had Mac so strongly believing that I'd been fired. So at the end of the night they're locking up and Mac's all bummed out and after the doors shut, Mac later told me, Robbie looks at him, double finger guns, 'Gotchya' and walks away."

"Rick?" Amber asks.

"Oh, I don't really have any prank stories. Not so much my thing."

"Merak?"

"Oh gosh, no. My idea of a prank is making coffee extra strong for my old coffee shop coworker who liked his coffee extra thin. You know, on accident, because I could never remember which way of normal to go." My friends talk and exchange stories; we sit here months away from our shared graduations, on the cusp of entering an adulthood I know none of us are in any way prepared for. But now we have what life needs for happiness: time, friends, food, and the internal warmth of shared love. This moment now, these memories we're sharing as stories, will be the hallmarks of our shared innocence and the last breaths of our childhood lungs. Mistakes and tragedies with real consequences, successes and milestones that better the lives of others in real and lasting ways, these wait to greet the unsuspecting young in adulthood. But these moments right now, sharing stories, enjoying a pre-paid hot meal with friends, having only time and friendship to our names and making the most of it, I hope that for my life I remember these times most clearly and cling to them like an anchor on rock.

After dinner, Jesse: homework; Rick: real work; Amber: "video games, Merak?"

"I promised you a drive today." I look at Rick as we walk toward the parking lot. Rick smiles; he is glad to be here for this.

"Really? That wasn't just a joke?"

"I thought we might find a quiet back road and let you drive around a bit."

"What? No," she says, stepping back, into Rick, and pushing on my chest with her hands.

Rick puts his arm around Amber's shoulders.

"I get to drive Federico?"

"Well," I say. "Rick's car. I'll let you drive my car someday but it's stick. That's just added complexity." Amber walks back to me and Rick pockets his hands.

"I get to drive Federico to work. Don't tell Merak, but I have no idea how to drive stick."

"Really?" I am concerned. Rick finger guns me as he walks away to where my car is parked.

At Rick's car, I unlock the passenger door with his key and it opens with a voice like a raccoon that's had its tail stepped on. After Amber sits and locks her hands in her lap, the door takes a hearty force to shut, the rusty hinges fighting the whole way. Rick may not have opened this door since, well, ever. When I sit, Amber turns and faces me, "This car sucks, doesn't it?"

"Oh holy cow yes." Rick's family has a whole lot. My folks have done well, especially in the last few years, but "Rick's father, he's in finance and he makes money decisions every day that are bigger than my dad's entire business's value. So," I put the car's keys in the ignition, turn off the radio because I know Rick likes it loud, and with a few tries and a false start get the engine whirring away, the carburetor or pistons, hard to tell which over the rest of the engine's bizarre sounds, knock a bit. "You cannot let Rick know I told you all this, okay?"

"Of course."

The Sentra's engine, once we start to move, is quiet; the ride is not. Over its 185,763 miles, so far, as Rick says, the already-soft springs have given the ride more sway, more slop, and some creaking and squeaking in the turns. The car feels like a badly-designed carnival ride in tight corners, rocks back and forth like a bassinet when it straightens again. The body's rust holes whistle when the air hits just right. Pieces of rust slide around inside the door; body panels, disturbed by the whistling air, sound like a cheap, novelty rattle. The seat springs, never good on these cars anyway, twang when we move and bounce in them as the car rocks and fidgets. This car is the musicality of chaos played by raging madmen using plastic childhood toy instruments. But it's automatic, and for today I need that.

As we drive down the street, "dang, we need gas. That's fine, just a few extra minutes. Moving on, Rick is gay, you know. His dad is anti-gay. When I was on my road trip three years ago, a few days after I got back to Chicago, Rick, he says emboldened by my willingness to take a risk and find myself, decided to tell his folks he was gay. It did not go well. His dad canceled his tuition at a nice, East Coast school. He moved in with us and is essentially the brother I never got to have. He spent that first school year living with my folks and going to a junior college, transferred to Cold Harbor sophomore year.

"Winter, the past few summers, spring break, he spends with us. I know he talks to his mom a few times a year. That's it. Like, all he wants in the world is — I think that he was really hurt to learn that his parents, his father mainly, didn't love him for who he was but for who they thought he was. That's hard. Because love with conditions isn't really love. There's no love in a statement like 'I love you but only if you are who I want you be,' because that's a threat. No one threatens people they love." We drive off campus and into town. I know a perfect back country road, straight and empty, at most maybe one other car this time of night, likely none. This little road runs through Makanda, crosses and parallels a creek with a railroad track on the far side.

"Well, I love you conditionally that you're not secretly a Nazi or something."

"Well, yes, okay, that's different, though. Hate is always a choice," I say, pulling into a gas station and killing the engine. "Who we love is who we love and no one would choose a life where loving someone else causes them to be hated by others. Hating someone for choosing to hurt others, that makes sense. Hating someone for something they can't change about themselves, I don't know how people do that."

As the tank fills, I sit with the door open and listen for the pump to stop. "He, honestly, doesn't care if his dad believes that he didn't choose to be gay. He'd just be happy to hear his dad say he doesn't like the choice, still loves his son." When the handle clicks off, I make some short pumps to round it up to the dollar, ask Amber if she needs anything, water yes please, which I also need, pay cash, and start the car back up.

"You made an off-hand comment some time ago at dinner about me having been with other guys not being an issue for you, about those experiences making me who I am," Amber says.

"I did."

"Is that because of Rick?"

Inhale and exhale, think. "Very possibly. I like to think I was always accepting. Maybe not. I don't really know how others perceive me. My friends stay friends and I think that means something. Rick has been a friend for years and when he needed me I could be there. I don't care who he loves. I know I find the idea of kissing another guy off-putting and gross. But that's how my brain is wired."

"So you wouldn't give a guy a peck on the lips to watch me make out with some other hot girl?"

I laugh out a strong no. "But back to that moment, it demanded that I step up. Rick is my friend, more than a friend now, he is absolutely my brother. And I chose that. And if I chose to love my brother, how can I hate who he is at the core? He doesn't hurt anyone; he chooses care every time, no exception. He's compassionate and loves freely on the terms that others' give him."

"He taught you that."

"I would think so, he and Meggy, yes. And … no, I would hope so. Because what other reason do we have to exist than to help others become better? And I think it is better to hope that we're better people because of others than to think it." Amber's eyebrows are low. "Hoping that other people make us better leaves room to hope that it can happen again, in the future, and that we can return the favor. Thinking other people make us better leads to arrogance, a notion that what we do must be right because we're better than we used to be. I dunno, maybe that's nonsense. I don't know of a better way to express that."

The Sentra starts with less weird noise now, the engine warm and more ready to run, maybe recognizing some old, near-forgotten hands on its steering wheel. We pull out to and in the street. Cold Harbor doesn't have a lot in it south of campus, at least not on this road, and the suburban-style houses and handful of local shops yield to forests and farmland, some hills with small vineyards, and old, small houses built to support coal mines. The drive will take, maybe, thirty minutes until we reach a spot where the road turns to a winding canyon, the final few miles to Makanda.

Amber faces forward and leans back a bit, her seat springs pang and ting as she rests her head on the headrest and sips her water, a few drops splashing as the car rocks back and forth when I straighten after a turn. "I hope I'm a better person now than I used to be. I think that becoming better because of someone else is a huge compliment. I hope you hear it that way."

Brain: misfire. She's saying that I've made her a better person? If anything, it's reversed. She makes me think about the world in ways I never had – how to live in it, describe it in ways that make me see it as others do. I've become more cognizant of her challenges and, I hope, that makes me more compassionate toward everyone's. No, I mean, there's no way I could be making her life better because she's making my life better. That makes more sense, and by the time I say "thank you, and you make my life better and you make me want to be a better person, too," she breathes slowly, her head lolled to the side.

‹◊›

This won't be easy, but also not hard. The road is dirt, straight for almost two miles, built on a flood protection embankment, a short shoulder on the other side of the road marked by old, wooden bollards, a swale between the road and creek, the creek, and an embankment up to the Illinois Central railroad tracks. These are active lines and we had the chance to wait for a long coal train in Makanda a bit ago. It's night, so anyone oncoming will have their lights, which means that this is very safe. Amber sits in the driver's seat, parked, nodding as I explain all of this. I have her put her feet on the pedals – right on gas, good, move your right foot left a bit to the brake, there, and rest your left foot on the floor, excellent. Keep your left foot off the parking brake, there it is, great. I think we're almost ready.

"Now, the shifter is on the floor to your right. Good there. It will shake and vibrate as you drive because the transmission mounts are shot and, also, the tranny gears are probably on the verge of failing. You're in park so you can rev the engine a bit and see how it feels." The little Sentra's engine rages in what, now, is guaranteed to be less than the original sixty-nine horsepower. "You'll want to press in on the parking brake pedal and it'll pop up," the parking brake spring clangs loudly like an out-of-tune harp played in anger. "Now, right foot on the regular brake, and move the shifting lever backward three clicks until you're in drive."

Amber does this and takes her foot off the brake. The car lurches forward slowly and she yells and jams the brake like there's a child in front of us. "Sorry, I got scared."

"It's okay. The car will move us forward slowly in drive. It's okay for now to let it just do that."

Amber does and the car lurches forward slowly. I explain steering, to use the wheel gently and not steer hard or too fast. As Amber steers, the car weaving like the trail of a desert sidewinder across the road, I explain where we are on the road, how to get back in our lane, no turn it less because there's a shoulder there, okay that's good, left a bit to straighten the car, and we amble slowly like a leaf in a creek for almost twenty minutes until we close in on the straight section's far side.

"We're going to do something called a three-point turn. We're going to do it slowly because there's a ditch on the other side of the road that we do not want to drive into."

"There's a what?"

"A ditch," I repeat, "but we aren't going in."

"Why am I doing this?"

"We have to turn around. The straightaway ends here."

Amber taps her fingers on the back of the steering wheel. "I actually meant why am I driving. This is a bit scary."

"Think of the story this will be. Besides, don't worry too much, there are wood bollards along the roadside. I guess we could drive between them, like that's a thing that could be possible, but you'll be fine. The shoulder is wide. We're not going in the ditch."

"Okay."

I explain a three-point turn. It's basically a triangle, and how to turn the steering wheel at each point, and how this is the case where it's okay to really crank the wheel. As she does it, I walk her through the shifting, braking, and I keep an eye behind us. No cars. A coal train with three engines at the front moves slowly up the tracks across the creek in the direction we'll be heading. The engines' noise, loud as it builds speed and power, gently shakes the Sentra in rolling vibrations up from the ground. We start up the road, slowly and straight; at the road crossing with the train a pickup races across it, safely in front of the train and onto the road toward us.

"Keep driving straight, Amber. There's a pickup coming in the other lane. It's cruising." The truck is easily going 50, double the speed limit. The driver's high beams are on and I can't see well out the front. He passes us with feet to spare, engine loud as a fireworks show grand finale, dust and rocks kicked up by knobby tires spray the Nissan like birdshot. Amber screams and in her panic hits the accelerator.

"Brake brake brake brake brake!" Amber jams the accelerator and the car lurches forward, the little, old, tiny-when-new-now-even-weaker engine strains to accelerate as it pulls the car into a wood bollard. Our seatbelts grab us like mousetraps snapping and we both "oof" as the car jerks to a stop.

"Oh god oh no we crashed what happened we crashed."

"It's okay. The truck was going very fast and it just hit us with gravel and rocks that it kicked up. We're both okay."

"Are we in the ditch?"

"No, one of the bollards stopped us. Fortunately, this isn't a fast car so we just kinda tapped it." I look at the hood, which has a bit of a bulge on the passenger's side where it rests at the bollard. Not much, five or six inches high. Maybe it was already there. "The bollard will be fine."

"I don't want to drive anymore," she says undoing her seatbelt and reaching for the door, locked, it won't open and Amber begins reach for things on the door, grabbing the handle and window knob, pulling them back and forth fast and forcefully.

I put my hand on her shoulder and look out the back window to make sure no cars are coming. "Amber, it's okay. Hey, it's okay. The lock is on the top of the door by the window. Just lift it. I'll be right around." Amber doesn't wait for me. She opens the car door fast and walks around the back, holding her hand on the top of the car, the trunk, and over to my door. I intercept her, reach my arms around her shoulders, and she puts her face into my chest. Amber cry-shakes, tears and runny snot on my shirt.

"I thought that was it. I thought that truck hit us."

"It's fine. We're fine."

"Rick is going to hate me."

"Rick does not care about this car. I promise. He's not even planning to take it back to Chicago after we graduate. This car literally just has to take him to and from work three nights a week until May. It's fine."

I help Amber into the passenger's seat, sit by her on the car's doorframe, and put my hand in hers. She breathes deeply, rapidly. I guide her through slowing her breathing down and when she says she feels better I walk around the car to the driver's seat.

Both of us in the car again, I put it in reverse. The shifting makes a new noise, kind of like a rock being pushed over gravel. The Nissan does not want to back out; the engine strains to gain traction in the grass and dirt. I rock it back, let it slide forward, rock it back, forward, the bumper groans and slides between the car and bollard; the grill sounds like uncooked pasta being stepped on. The little Sentra finally, after some tries, backs out and the front bumper falls off, resting on the ground in the headlights, the passenger's side beam noticeably askew.

"What happened? Is it okay? Did I break it?"

"Uh, well, I'll be right back," I say, getting out, putting the bumper in the trunk, then pushing on the light to re-align it as well as I can right now. When I shut the door: "It'll buff right out. Rick's never gonna notice."

"Really?"

"Nope. The bumper fell off."

"Oh my God, Merak, no! It did not. You're joking."

"I'm not. But seriously, don't worry. We'll just tape the bumper back on or something."

The Nissan slides into drive and the transmission feels and sounds a bit stiff for a quarter mile, maybe a bit longer, the shifting lever shaking and spinning like an upright branch in a whirlpool. That's a new combination of feelings. A belt in the engine whines into a soft scream as the car accelerates. That's a new sound.

In the parking lot at campus, I back the Nissan into one of the spots Rick typically uses. No point in hiding the missing bumper. Amber and I walk back to my room so that I can change shirts before we take a couple of laps around Campus Lake. Amber cranks open the bedroom windows to let the night air, lake sounds, and tree branch wind music into the room. The air is cool, a slight touch of humidity that chills my skin and sends ripples of tingling like cold fingertips up my back and neck. I grab a sweater and Amber takes my coat.

She runs her fingers, both hands, up my sweater sleeve. "This is my favorite of your sweaters," she says. "The way it feels, these thick, knitted cord designs that overlap and then the more delicate, pattern between them, sort of like fish scales maybe, or a tight lattice? Hard to tell exactly, but it feels lovely."

We follow the path the way I normally walk it, counterclockwise, through the trees we hear in our dorm when the wind blows, past the day's wave-energy breaking on the cedar knees along the shore. We walk as the gravel beneath our feet skooches and shushes and small rocks trapped in our shoe treads click with our steps.

"Was it at least fun, you know, up to a point?"

"Scary, even before the truck. I didn't ever really feel in control."

"You said it, though. Control is an illusion," and Amber squeezes my hand in hers. "Don't you feel that way riding in a car? Not in control?"

"Well, yeah, but that's different. Especially with you. I never fell asleep in cars whenever I'd ride with other people, not even Grandpa Arn."

"What's different with me?"

"It never feels like you're not in control of the car. You take turns smoothly, even on dirt roads. You don't slide on dirt roads or fish-tail in the gravel when you accelerate. You're safe and I can fall asleep with you driving."

I smile and thank Amber.

"I need you to know how rare that is, how important that is. Usually, yes, I feel stuck in a car, just kind of hoping it all goes well and aware I won't know if it doesn't."

I do, and don't understand. When people drive poorly, I'm happy to volunteer to drive instead. Not having a choice, being in a position where no other option for getting around aside from walking, or having a very smart horse, is truly available, well, I think about that a moment and decide that, no thank you, I would not like it.

The path leads us to the beach clearing where the forest ends. To my left, the bridge over Campus Lake, the light on the bridge on, and under it I see a shadow with a saxophone walk to the center arch.

"Our saxophonist friend is out on the bridge." Amber and I stop and we face across the water. The bridge was built in 1922, making it now seventy-eight years old. The bridge has stone foundations on each side of the lake crossing, foundations repurposed from an even older narrow-gauge rail bridge. That bridge, built in the 1880s, burned in 1918 and the foundations sat unused as the line that had run on it folded shortly before it burned. When the campus started being built-out, the lake became a major feature for student recreation and the school built a footbridge for students to use. They connected the foundations with a stone arch, inlaid with a red granite pattern of small, decorative arches, and built up the railings and walkway in cedar. An iron lamppost in the middle, originally gas converted to electric sometime shortly after World War Two, gives a small, dim light cone to the center of the bridge at night.

The bridge embodies much of the school's mythology, with almost every student who passes through the school having some story about it. That, at least, is part of that myth. Myths are the most binary of human belief and embody only the worst or best of human tendency, both excusing away bad behavior and lauding the good. But myths also ground us in belief – true or not – of things we can't know with direct experience, and they afford explanations that let us develop our perceptions of ourselves and the world. In that way, at their best, myths provide us a seed of self-knowledge that becomes a vine we can climb toward better understanding. The bridge, it's part of that, a distinct and unique school myth. I don't know if anything people say about it is true: I know only that today, in my years in Cold Harbor, a stone-arch bridge with an iron lamppost exists and that on some random nights, like tonight, someone walks to the middle and plays saxophone.

I can't see much of the person under the light. Though the player stands facing us, he or she splits the penumbra cone of lamplight, shoulders-and-up in darkness, torso and saxophone in light. We, bathed in the umbra of crescent moon falling behind thin clouds that slide through the sky to cover it, sink into darkness as music starts.

Saxophone music carries over lake water like a paper airplane in a still-air room. The music moves unimpeded, bouncing off the water, clear and with a round undertone. The player points the sax bell at us, not knowing we're here; this is always the direction the player faces, as though the music is for the forest. Every time I hear the saxophone music, it's different – different styles and different tunes, never the same song, never one that I recognize. Tonight the player has jazz on the mind; music bounces up and down across the scales, short and then long notes, clear, bounding and dropping into them directly, no slide, no smear, no guesswork on what to hit. A few notes over the song hit sour, but find correction quickly. The music only lasts about three or four minutes and then, when it ends, the player walks out of the light and off the bridge, as always.

Amber and I stand on the beach, holding hands after the player leaves, watching the bridge.

"I wonder who that is," she says.

"I don't."

"Do you know who it is?"

"No idea, and that's the way I like it. Knowing would, I think, kinda ruin the experience for me. There's a bliss in not having to know. That lets me enjoy the music on its own merits."

"Do you think that any people know who it is?" We start walking, holding hands. Our walk will take us over the bridge and around the far side of Campus Lake, back across the bridge again, an infinity loop, before we go back to my room.

"At least one."

‹◊›

Before I unlock my dorm door, the light seeping under the door lets me know Rick is home. I let Amber know and she gulps. When I open the door, Rick, working on some homework, looks over at us. "How was it?"

"Uh, fine. Went fine."

"Took my request to crash it a bit seriously I see."

"Rick, I'm so sorry. I really didn't mean to," Amber says, launching in to an explanation of the truck.

Rick laughs when she finishes. "It's fine. But where's the bumper?"

"Trunk."

"Grill?"

"Scattered around the road."

Amber sits on my bed; forehead in hands, elbows on knees. She moves her hand around as Rick and I talk, Rick laughing deeply. Amber rubs the bridge of her nose, the points of her eyes – still red and slightly swollen – her nose again, hairline.

Rick leans in his chair. "I can't imagine a future where this isn't one of my favorite stories. I wish I'd been there."

Amber sits up. "So you're really not mad?"

"I told you so," I say.

"Of course not!"

"The bumper," she says.

"We'll get some duct tape, no problem."

"Hot glue."

"Maybe some rope."

"Probably need it to tie the hood down."

"Oh yeah, I saw that. It's a new air intake, more air, more speed. We'll call it a feature."

"Less weight, more air. You can take it to a race track now."

"See, Amber, thank you! You made my car a whole lot better."

"To be fair," Amber says, "nothing could make it worse."

11
New Year's

Blue is a good mystery that keeps the reader guessing until the last page, the light that penetrates clear lake water to the fish swimming slowly deep beneath the surface, cold vanilla soft-serve on a humid hundred-plus day, and being halfway into a long walk when a warm, springtime drizzle starts. It's playing board games with friends on a Friday night, drinking till dawn, and eating a greasy breakfast to try and outsmart the headache. But blue's shades, more I think than any other color, tell different stories. Dark blue is the low notes of an oboe that blend into an orchestra's harmony unnoticed, but glaring were it absent, the sweetness of a home-made pumpkin pie, the soft and broken-in fabric – stitched and mended from age-wear – of a childhood stuffed toy. Dark blue wraps our minds with comfort and relaxation like the warmth of a family dog sleeping with its head on our lap. Light blue, however, is the rattle of small hailstones on a metal roof, the cymbal clatter of a hard rain on sun-hot pavement, and the steam that rises when the shower passes. Light blue is a sense of the path laid out ahead of us and an idea of the challenges, but no solutions. Light blue smells and tastes like burned toast with marmalade and feels like an itchy sweater on bare skin.

I sit on Amber's desk chair, our Christmas breaks over and school starting again tomorrow, and face her, on her bed, legs crossed and knees bent, back to her wall. Nothing in this room, aside from her private shower – because it's reserved for students with different abilities, as the school says – differentiates it from my room. All the dorms have either an A or B layout, my term, depending on which side the shower entry is at. That's true of all three groups of dorm buildings, even though each was built at different times. It must make furnishing, cleaning, and repairing much easier. Her room, though, is louder than mine. Many more students live here, her placement near the main exit means most of them walk past

234

her door when they go in and out, and the outside foot, bike, and car traffic passes through her single-pane windows without great difficulty. We both prefer my room, even though there's often company, because the lake's placement makes it much quieter.

Amber shifts her hips and her bed frame springs click and stretch, "didn't you say Meggy's eyes were blue?" Amber frowns, holding her Christmas gift, two small earrings, blue glass gems, a small square set in the middle with four small triangles on the sides, all set in and surrounded by thin, polished stainless steel. Not expensive, but pretty, durable.

They were. "I guess I may have. Why?" Why did I just think of this, but today, January 4, is Meggy's birthday. Weird coincidence.

"Well, that's an awesome description of your ex's eye color."

"Dude, I need you to not be jealous of a girl I haven't even spoken to in fourteen months. You definitely think about her more than I do. Look, it's 2001, okay, new year, no more worrying about Meggy."

Amber runs her fingers over the earrings. "They feel very nice. I believe you that they're pretty." She takes the small, round, silver studs that she usually wears out of her earlobes and replaces them with blue ones. She turns them so they look like small, blue letters "X" on her ears, less like letters more like some artistic bit of lens flare from a tiny light in a photograph. She faces me when she finishes, "you inhaled deeply there."

Smiling, "well, they suit you very well. Merry Christmas."

"I didn't get you anything. I'm sorry."

"I don't really want things. I'd be very happy if we enjoyed a nice dinner together and went for a walk, to a movie, or to an open-mic night."

"That's like any old date for us, Merak."

"I guess that makes every date we have as special as Christmas." I lean over and kiss her cheek.

Amber frowns at me a bit. "They do feel very nice. Thank you for picking out something that looks good and feels nice to touch," her right index finger runs along the earrings gently, tracing their shape, feeling their four points, ridges in the centers of the small triangles.

"We're going sledding tomorrow, right? That, for me, is a huge gift. I've been looking forward to it for weeks. I even brought my old tube sled from Chicago and there's some good and fresh snow on the sled hill south of town today, too." I turn away from Amber, my shoes and coat at her door, hers in her closet.

"What do you get out of this relationship? I mean, besides sex. What do you get from me that you can't get from someone else?"

I turn and look at Amber, hear myself sigh, hope that this time I can convince her I'm here for who she is and have it last longer than six weeks. I hadn't expected that, but I hear a small voice in my head tell me exactly, I think, what the answer is. Right or wrong, what's important is that I know this to be true: "You know because you've told me, I'm highly visual. I have to see what's going on with computer hardware, trace networking cables and organize them, read lines of networking code script sometimes, and of course I photograph and that's strictly a visual medium. You refocus me on things that aren't visual and that expands the world I live in. You make my life more full."

Amber smiles and says, "that was more than I had hoped for. And I know. I just needed to hear that again." She puts the silver studs in the earring box and closes it, a loud snap as the hinge springs take over and the top drops fast. "Do you think this will have been the last Christmas that we spend apart," Amber asks, her face starting toward her knees, ending toward me as she asks.

"I hope so, yes."

Amber smiles at me, leans in a bit, a sign that she wants a kiss on her lips I've learned. "Wherever we are next Christmas, I'm going to make you a big steak and some fluffy potatoes."

‹◊›

George's apartment faces town from a small hill to the north. It's a fine area, safe but industrial. Trains shake the floor every hour or so, but the horns are distant because of the noise ordinance, so when they pass they offer a soothing and quiet background rumble. When Amber and I arrive, Rick and Jesse already there at the kitchen table playing cards, Amber lets go of my arm and walks through the foyer, around George's couch, and to the table to join the guys. The table is an old one, plywood with peeling oak veneer, loose bolts from being moved too often, left discarded by dumpsters, reassembled by any number of students and residents over the last however-many decades. It's round, seats five easily, and the top wobbles on its single central support post. When we set our hands down too hard it splashes drinks and, from habit, George keeps our glasses only half-full and paper towels under them.

The apartment is old with brown, trampled carpet that, when we walk on it, spits the dust of the now-powder padding installed with it some time before any of us were born. The stove and refrigerator, dark yellow, make noise and fail to do their jobs superbly. The oven doesn't bake evenly and the refrigerator lets milk spoil in three days. This is, George tells me, standard for this apartment complex. George uses, and has for a couple of years, a portable range instead of the oven's range because of 'a concerning crackling noise' that three burners make. But it is, George once lamented to me, the space he can afford as a bartender. And this is, George once reminded me, the nicest place he has ever lived.

I recall asking him about that. George, the eldest of us by a margin, grew up in a time the rest of us would not recognize. His parents, a now-retired church youth pastor and now-retired church secretary from a small, independent congregation that served a poor area and supported itself, had him when they were into their forties, their last-ditch attempt at a child he told me. Though he grew up well and loved, he also grew up poor in a small, rural Minnesota town with a name I can't pronounce. His parents' church reinvested their offerings into the community, feeding congregants and providing lower-than-cost childcare rather than salaries for the church staff. Both pastors had two rooms in the church for their families. His family fished a local lake every weekend and hunted with loaned guns owned by the congregation members in order to eat well, often supplementing their meals at the foodbank. The church members never knew about the foodbank, George told me once, because of his father's pride. His father loved his work, and his church, and his mission. It introduced his father and mother, kept them guided when they struggled. The benefits were never meant to be financial, however, and his parents live now in a small car and camper, travelling around campsites and national parks on their retirement and occasional checks from George. When they make their way through the area each spring and fall, they stop in and visit for a few days.

Amber, at the table, pulls out her deck of braille playing cards and shows Rick how to split and bridge. Jesse jokes the three of them should play strip poker, which gets no opposition outside of George and I, but never happens.

As they play some friendly Go Fish, George and I grab the food from my car and he tells me how to make his latest burger invention.

"Alright, this is a hard one so I need us both."

"Sweet," George and I each grab three bags of groceries from the trunk and carry them upstairs. I admit to him that the list has me highly confused, and he smiles. "What's the one called?" I ask, as George opens the door.

"The Jenny Peters," George says, and Jesse looks over at us; George looks back at Jesse. "Because, just like Jenny, it's hot and sweet, if you know what I mean."

I glance at Amber, who faces us. Rick staring at Jesse, mouth in a big "O." Jesse nods at George.

"I do not know what you mean," I say, in what must be the most-robotic, most-staccato tone that I've ever used, because it elicits a "nice try, Merak," from Amber.

George runs through the burger with me, a four-ounce smash patty, thin, crispy edges, started in a thin layer of duck fat. Easy to make as a single, double, or triple. Toasted pretzel buns that he made from scratch earlier. They're round and slightly chewy, like a jumbo pretzel at a baseball game, browned with a butter and egg wash, large and coarse salt granules adorning the tops, a decorative "X" in the middle. After slicing, the buns get buttered up and toasted, a thin layer of strawberry jam on the top, a thin layer of some fresh-made chipotle egg-yolk mayonnaise we're about to whip together for the bottom, some white Monterey Jack cheese – a slice per patty, caramelized onions, pickled ginger, and thin-sliced serrano.

George shows me how to separate the ground beef into small balls, cup my hands, and roll the patties into spheres on the cutting board. George chops the chipotle fine, slices the serrano into strips no thicker than a birthday card. When I finish, George and I separate the egg yolks, divvy out mustard, lemon juice, and white wine vinegar, and add some oil, salt, and sugar to the mix. This, George explains, is his grandmother's mayonnaise recipe with the chipotles as his twist. We take turns whisking it with a dervish's fury until thick, and we can fold the chopped chipotle into it. "Resting in the fridge until it's ready," George tells me, "helps the flavors meld. Ideally, it should rest at least overnight. But it's still going to be good."

While the burger ingredients rest, George and I chop potatoes into cubes, rinse them to starch-free, and bring them to a boil on the one range burner George sometimes trusts. George shows me how to roulade basil leaves into decorative strips as the potatoes cook and explains how the potato's heat, when they're done, will release the basil's best flavors. Burgers and boiled potatoes for dinner, beers and bags of chips on the table now. Amber, Rick, and Jesse sit and play cards, Amber sometimes tilting her head to hear George and I.

George heats an ancient but recovered griddle that he tells me he found in a dumpster a few years ago. "It was still good, tons of life, just needed some care. Cast iron, it's like people, put in the time and care and you get a lot back." He tells me, as it heats up, about stripping off the seasoning with hot vinegar and a lemon juice and salt scrub, giving the rusty parts a hand sanding, and then borrowing a neighbor's orbital sander to polish the cooking surface smooth where the pits weren't too deep. He goes through all the different sandpaper grits, the black iron filings that collected on the surface and how they helped the sander work, going over it again and again and refining the cooking surface and how, now, most of it's so smooth he can fry an egg on it with just a quick hit of cooking spray. He loves this cast iron, works the seasoning each time he uses it, cleans it and, if things can share our affection with us, the way that this griddle cooks the patties shows that it loves him back.

As George builds the burgers, melts cheese on patties until the white, hot liquid seeps into the large pores left as the smash burger patty fat melts into griddle juice, I drain the potatoes and stir in butter until 'the outsides look like they're wearing potato sweaters,' as George described it, give them a quick sear in the griddle fat, divvy the potatoes onto our plates, sprinkle basil on top, and as the last burger tops drop into place, patties still sizzling, cheese and fat and jam and mayonnaise mixing in a hot, molten puddle around the buns, George and I take the dinners to the place settings. George takes out a six-pack of beer bottles, standard Coors, not a favorite, but palatable after the fifth, and Jesse proposes a toast.

"To Jenny Peters," Jesse says. "I don't know where you landed after you graduated, but you were the best girl I ever dated."

"Same here," says George.

"The fuck?"

Amber inhales her beer too fast and foam sprays out her nose and onto the carpet.

"Scandal!" Rick shouts.

"What?" George asks, looking around at everyone. "I thought you all knew she and I dated. Why else would I name a burger after her? Wait, you dated her, too, Jesse?"

"For about five months, right before Angie."

"That's when we dated," says George.

"Goddamnit," Jesse sets his beer on the table and the plates and forks rattle as the top shifts.

Amber cough-laughs and pounds her chest.

"Well that's the first I've heard of that," George says.

We all sit and cast quiet, furtive stares around the table at each other. Rick's mouth hangs open, eyebrows raised high like arching doorways. Amber's mouth is slack, but lips closed, probably holding back beer foam. Jesse and George, sitting perpendicular, stare straight in front of them and don't make eye contact, mouths closed, jaws set, eyes wide and unblinking with surprise and an unclear path forward. I start eating my potatoes and, can't lie, they're really amazing, and I tell George that. Jesse glares at me. "Can we get through this other thing first, Merak?"

"You can. I'm eating. This food is good."

"Did anyone know about this?" Jesse asks, and we all confirm we did not.

Amber says "I assume Jenny did, though."

"Amber, not now," Jesse rubs his temple.

"Alright, kimonos open," George says. "If I knew you, it would have been different. I didn't. I'm sorry we both found out this way. I met you literally five days after she moved."

Jesse scrunches his lips, nods his head up and down and back and forth. "Probably won't really care in another year anyway." Jesse reaches his hand across the table to George and they bump fists. "At least we all know you and I are tied for best taste in women here."

"Not a hard contest," Rick says, taking a bite of burger as hot burger juices drip into his potatoes.

"What?" I gesture with a potato on my fork at Amber.

"Merak," George says with the gentleness of a parent putting a toddler to bed, "Meggy is no Jenny Peters."

"So, firstly, Amber is easily three Jenny Peters. Meggy a solid two Jenny Peters, thank you."

"Is Jenny Peters a new unit of measure," Amber asks. "Like, can we all rate each other on how many Jenny Peters we are? Merak, you're like a fifth of a Jenny Peters right now."

"You knew Jenny?" Rick asks.

"I did, we had a few gen ed classes together" Amber says, taking a bite of her Jenny Peters. "George, this burger is very good. I don't like the name right now, but it's very good." Amber spears a potato as she chews more Jenny Peters and, after swallowing, eats a potato piece.

"I'd rate Amber a few Jenny Peters, too," Rick says. "She's cute, definitely more datable than Jenny Peters, but not hotter."

"I agree," Amber raises her hand. "Jenny let me feel her face once, and her boobs, totally exposed. First boobs besides mine I ever felt. She was super hot. I am not anywhere close."

Jesse and George stare at each other, mouths open.

"I always feel like I miss out on the most fun stuff by a year or two," I say. "Wait, first?" Amber's head bobbles as she chews potato and she shrugs a yes.

Eyes wide and looking across the table at Amber, I lift and bite into my burger. The rich duck-fat-and-beef-tallow crispiness filled with the hot and salty cheese and mayonnaise, topped with the fried serrano slices, the rich and soft sweetness of caramelized onions and strawberry jam, and the chewy doughy pretzel bun mixes into a flurry of rich, hot, cold, warm, soft, and spicy sensations that fill my mouth like a newly-learned word churned repeatedly between teeth and tongue, molded and committed to muscle memory.

Memory forces itself forward as the spice and sugar melt and my eyes close. I see black hair around alpine-lake-blue eyes, pale skin and pink lipstick, a loose ponytail, black blouse and skirt melting together with the cavernous darkness of sequestered thought, and they disappear into that same darkness, move around behind me, hands move opposite: left up my left arm, neck, and chin to cover my eyes, right down my right arm, to hip, belt buckle, and pants zipper. Meggy's voice wraps around my brain from behind and I feel her hands, covering my eyes, fiddling in my pants, her lips wrapping on and teeth nibbling my ear from behind, whispering the happy birthday song into my ear as wick-and-wax smoke meanders into my nostrils.

"Happy birthday, dear Merak," she whispers, "happy birthday," slowly, dragging it out, pulling each vowel to sentence-length, "to you." Meggy takes her hands back and puts on my glasses, a red velvet cupcake on her desk topped with an impossible sphere of buttercream frosting and a candle. "Make your wish," she says, sitting on the corner of her desk, legs crossed at her knees. In memory-darkness her room is empty void, dorm desk clear except a silver desk lamp with a dim, yellow-white incandescent bulb glowing onto the cupcake and a small circle around it that bleeds slowly into the memory space. Meggy, as though lit singularly from above, sits on her black and shadow-formwork desk that becomes an invisible, unembodied part of this moment.

The candle flame tilts sideways, disappears into a winding gray thread in the dim, incandescent lamp light.

"Well?"

"If I tell you, it won't come true." I hear my voice but I don't feel my mouth move.

Meggy leans in toward me, hair falling over her right shoulder and masking the blouse's open top buttons. "Or I can make it come true."

I smile at Meggy, break the cupcake in half, and she takes the smaller part. The frosting stays on my half and she reaches into it, taking fingerfuls as we snack slowly. When we finish, she slides open her desk drawer and pulls out a small box wrapped in blue with a black bow. I smile and she leans back a little, arms behind her, hands on the far side of her desk, and I unwrap my small present, the bow hand-tied, wrapping paper cut perfectly to size, folded clean-creased, the work of someone for whom perfection in the presentation of gift-giving is as important as the box's contents. This is her time, spent on me, slowly marking each cut and, I am certain, thinking of me as she planned and completed each step. Meggy works to make each moment one to remember, embrace, reflect on later as a small piece of some otherwise unattainable perfection. Each moment like this leaves me feeling increasingly like my imperfection is a hidden trap door in our relationship, something that we will eventually fall into with neither warning nor preparedness.

The box has a black, metal Fossil chronograph, blue face, simple and straight silver hands with thin iridescent lines, heavy, loose by about two links, which Meggy tells me we'll get fixed at the mall tomorrow. It is a significant step-up from the Jeep watch I had been wearing, with the elastic-metal band that snapped last week, and I let Meggy know that it's too nice, but that I love it already.

Meggy pushes the chair out from the desk and sits on my lap, legs around me. "What did you wish for?"

"That, um, that you didn't have anything on under your skirt."

"That was a wasted wish," she says, smiling and tilting her head to the side a bit. "Do you know what I wished for?"

I shake my head and Meggy leans in, hugging my shoulders, mouth at my ear, "that you forgot to bring a condom."

My lower jaw typewriters rapidly; my mouth feels like cotton balls. "I haven't without –"

"Neither have I," she says, and she slides her left index finger up my neck from shirt collar and along the underside of my chin to my lips.

"Well I don't know what George did to that burger," Rick's slightly high pitched, alto-soprano voice grabs me out from memory-darkness and I land seated in George's folding chair, burger juice on my chin, bun squeeze-broken and wrapping my thumbs, "but Merak loves it."

"That is an incredible burger," I concur.

"He should have called in 'The Meggy'," Amber says, arms crossed.

I look at Rick: "If the word 'scandal' comes out of your mouth, I swear to God you will walk back to Chicago at Spring Break."

‹◊›

In time, Jesse and George, outside on the shared walkway that connects the second-floor apartments and stairs down, smoke cheap cigars with the front door propped open a crack.

"Look, I wasn't mad at you, George. I mean I was, but for a few seconds only. I was, well that hurt to learn because I thought Jenny and I had something …" Jesse taps his bottle on the walkway railing, "other than what we actually had."

"For what it's worth, yeah, I assumed she was seeing a couple of other guys or so, but she never told me about you or anyone else."

"Do you think there were others?"

George takes a long drink from his beer, drains it, taps the bottle on the patio's old metal railing a few times and leans, the railing lilting forward as far as the loose screws and dangling washers designed to hold it to the building's wall allow. "There were for sure, but was it one or ten or a million, no idea. Maybe it was just us, by some random happenstance. And not for both knowing Merak, we'd have been none the wiser."

George and Jesse take large cigar smoke mouthfuls, and their moving cheeks show that they swirl the smoke around their tongues before exhaling. The smoke smells like a wet, sugar-coated rat running around with its fur on fire. "Kind of a blessing," Jesse says. "I was still hung up on her. It was time for me to move on anyway and, man, thank you." George gives Jesse a perplexed look, turns his face to look at him, cocks his head, narrows his eyebrows. "I needed to let go."

They stand on the patio for a while, lean on the railing, trusting it far more than I would. In time they crush their cigars on the metal railing and drop the butts in the dried, root-knotted soil of a dead houseplant in front of one of George's neighbor's apartments and join us inside. I hold my beer bottle up as they walk past and they clink it with theirs.

We know the house rules here, they're the same everywhere for us. George and I sit at the table and open two more beers. Jesse steps up to the sink and scrubs the plates and silverware, Amber rinses, and Rick dries them and stacks dishes in the drainer. George does not let anyone touch his cast iron, though, which he already cleaned and put away. In time we all sit back down, Amber walking confidently across the kitchen and living room to the table. Rule 1: If there's a disagreement, we work it out then. Rule 2: There are those who cook, and those who clean, and they are never the same. Rule 3: Clinking bottles, glasses, or cans means everything is okay.

"You learned the layout here fast," I observe to Amber.

Amber pauses, her hand on the chair before pulling it out from the table. "Standard layout. All the apartments built in all the towns here from the fifties to the seventies, they were built by the same guy, same floorplans. Sometimes reversed or mirrored, but the same. I've been in this apartment dozens of times."

"Similar apartments, you mean," George says.

"Yes, that's what I meant," Amber sits and Rick starts shuffling the cards. "I have an idea for a game. A get-to-know-you game," Amber says, smiling, face pointing between George and I.

Rick: "We're all ears."

Amber goes around the table points at each of us and says our names to make sure she knows where we're sitting. "Rick, then Merak, George, Jesse, and me, right?"

Jesse nods.

"Jesse is nodding, so I think that means yes," George says, and they smile at each other.

"Okay, well, we all know each other's first names. Do any of us know our middle names?"

"I know Rick's," I say.

"And I know Merak's," he replies.

"I think I know Merak's," George says.

"That's more than me," Amber says, and Jesse agrees. "Want to see if we can guess our middle names?"

"Wrong guesses do a shot?"

"George you lush, you had me at shots," Amber says.

Soon we each have an empty shot glass and George grabs a new, low-not-bottom-shelf tequila from his cabinet, filling each glass almost to surface tension. We all take a warm-up shot. "Rules?"

"Round robin, start with Rick."

"Why me?"

"My rules. Start to my left, person left of Rick guesses his middle name. After we all guess, either someone is right or not. If no one is correct, the person whose name we're guessing picks who they think is closest. Everyone else does their shot."

"If we already know."

"Sit out and drink," Amber says, smiling happily at me.

"Dude," Rick leans in. "I think your girlfriend is trying to get you drunk. Nice."

"Alright, Merak, you know Rick's middle name, so on to you George."

"No one is guessing this," I say.

"I'll guess it's, well let's see, Rick something Collins. What goes with Rick Collins." George leans in and squints at Rick. "Channel your middle name to me Rick, right here," he taps his forehead with his most recent empty beer bottle. Rick puts his index fingers on his temples, closes his eyes, and nods his head quickly at George. "Herbert."

"Herbert? Oh my God do I look like a Herbert? Fuck you. You need to take that shot right now. You will not be closest."

Jesse looks at Rick. "You have monogrammed towels. So I know it starts with a D. David."

"Oh, not it."

"Well that helps me," Amber says. "Donald?"

Rick looks at me. "I might guess Amber is closest. Donovan," I say.

"Rick Donovan Collins?" Amber asks.

Rick holds up his index finger, looks around at us, pretends to adjust a tie, and says in a falsely low voice, "Richard Donovan Collins the Third, thank you."

"That's a rich-person name," Amber exclaims excitedly.

"Very," I agree.

All of us, even Amber, take our shots and George tops them off. "You didn't have to do that," I say.

"I wanted to," she says. "Your turn, Merak."

I look at George who leans next to the table and pulls out another six pack of beer bottles, passing them around. We twist the caps off, dropping them with hollow tinks onto the tabletop, and set them next to our shots. He looks at me. "I remember one time you said it. Dangit. Um, Charles. I think it began with a C-H."

I look at Jesse.

"No hints? Wow, you suck at this game."

"Amber just made it up."

"You already suck at it," Jesse says. "Alright let's see. You're from a pretty poncey neighborhood. Not 'Donovan' poncey—"

"Hey"

"—but probably Christopher poncey."

"Amber?"

"Dangit, really?" Jesse and George pick up their shot glasses and down their tequila.

Amber faces me. "I don't even know of any other C-H names for boys."

Rick smiles and looks me right in the eyes as he says "who says it's a boy's name?"

"Charlie," Amber says, after some thought and a sip from her beer.

I face Rick, who points at Jesse. "Christopher."

"Really? Nice! My man," he looks at George, they clink beer bottles, "good hint. Kinda wish I hadn't already done that shot."

George tops off the empty shot glasses and we all do another round and I drink half the beer I just opened. Sounds outside begin to fade into mute audio blurs and discordant a-harmonious strings of noise. The apartment radiator sounds like its sputtering comes from a ventriloquist voice and the ceiling drops a few inches. George tops the shot glasses again and Amber turns her head to face him.

"Let's see if I can get a two-fer," Jesse says. "Let's see. George, what's your last name?"

"Packer."

"Whew, that's a hard one. George Packer. George Packer. George Nathan Packer."

George's eyebrows go up. "Interesting guess. Amber?"

"Let's see. Do your initials spell a word. I'm guessing yes. Andrew. I'm going with Andrew."

"Well, that's a guess," George says, looking toward Rick.

"What's your father's name?"

"Joshua. Never Josh, only Joshua."

"George Joshua Packer, no, I don't think that's it. But your dad was a reverend, so I'll go with Joseph."

George looks at me.

"Joshua."

George clicks his beer bottle into mine. "I am George Joshua Packer, and my father is Joshua George Packer."

"Gad – fuck," Rick says, drinking his shot then sipping his beer.

George doles out another round of shots and foam piles up in my throat, my eyes go to tunnels and the radiator click echoes in my head like a shout in a cave.

Jesse taps Amber's shoulder. "Your guess."

Amber faces him and scratches her chin. "Hmm. What's your last name again?"

"It won't make sense."

"That's okay."

"Hayden."

Amber sits upright. "I had it my head you're Hispanic. I kinda of figured your last name would be, like, Suarez or something."

"I'm half. Mom grew up in Jocotepec, a small town in central Mexico. She met my dad on his gap year and they hit it off."

"What's a gap year?" Amber asks.

"They're more common in Europe. It's a year between high school and college to go roam and hang out, but my dad did his between college and med school."

"Your dad went to Mexico from Europe?"

"Also Malaysia, Mozambique, Russia, and some other places. I forget all of them. It was something like seven countries, a month in each."

"Damn," I say. "That's a big trip."

"You okay, Merak?" Jesse asks. "What's a bing drip? But anyway, that's the story."

"Hmm. Jesse something Hayden, so your dad's Irish. Your name isn't super Irish, so your middle name must be. I don't know any Irish names. Steve. Is Steve an Irish name?"

"It is not," Jesse says laughing. "Jesse Steve Hayden I am not. I think it's fair to give you a second guess. Jesse is just my nickname. I don't go by my real first name. I know that's not much help."

Amber twists her lips on themselves. "Michael."

Jesse shakes his head.

"He's shaking his head, Amber," I say, and then finish my beer.

Rick looks at me, "what's a chain-king bread-ber, Merak?" he says, scratching his chin.

Amber faces Rick who moves his hand to his mouth, picks up his beer bottle and takes a sip. When he swallows, "she has the right idea. Sean. Sean's a very Irish name."

Jesse shakes his head and looks at me. I give him an answer, my head facing toward the table.

"Did he say Patrick, Parsnip, or plrthrergripnup?" Rick asks.

I nod, I think, hold my index finger up to signal the first. Or maybe my head is stationary, my hand on the table, and the building is spinning and collapsing around me. That's probably it.

"Is Merak drunk" Amber asks.

"Oh yeah. He's cut off," George says, and he guesses "Brian."

"Well, I think George is closest. It's Ian, and Brian at least has those letters in that order. My dad waned me to have a very Irish name.

Want to hear me try it – I struggle sober." Jesse asks to a resounding and approving chorus. "Lané Iain ÓhEidhin. Jesse is a nickname my mom gave me; no idea why, but she wanted me to have that name. I like Jesse Hayden."

"That's a mouthful," says Amber.

I reach for my beer, even though it's empty, and then my shot glass, but George takes it away. "You are past your limit," he says. Another round of shot glasses being filled around me, a couple of beer bottles opened and their caps roll and bounce through the dark corners that vignette my vision. The peeling laminate table and the plywood beneath looks like an old-timey, sepia-toned photo. Hands on the hair on the back of my head, "your girlfriend is up next, you lush," Rick says, pulling my head upward to look at Amber, and guesses "Delaney."

"How do I not know this?" I say. "I'm wildly in love with this woman, probably will marry her, I should already know this." I turn my face toward Rick. "There is a zero-per-cent chance she has the same middle name as Meggy."

"Did he just guess that my middle name is Megan?"

"I think so," Rick says.

Rick turns my face toward Amber, arms crossed, frowning, eyes closed tight and facing me. I was going to guess Dawn, because Amber Dawn is a good name, but I think I guessed Megan. No H. Definitely not because that was Meggy's full name. Meghan Delaney Ryan. But maybe it is Megan, and maybe that's why she brings Meggy up all the time. Maybe she thinks about her name and how it's my ex's name. Rick turns my head to face George, because apparently I'm drunk enough to be a puppet now.

George looks at Amber, confidence in his eyes. "Dawn."

"George!"

"Wait," Jesse says. "Did he guess it?"

"Take a guess, Jesse," George says.

"I was legit going to guess Dawn. Like, Amber Dawn, that's a great name. A very pretty mental image. Marie. I'll go with Marie. I think I heard once it's the most common middle name for women."

"George got it," Amber says, and everyone but me takes another shot. "Amber Dawn Clearly."

"Air," I manage, and Rick somehow understands. He and George pull me up, help me to the front door, and I walk to the patio railing, lean; it gives way, tumbles forward and my stomach slams into it and with a rush like water through a fire hose, beer and tequila and potato and Jenny Peters vomit sours and burns my throat, blasting like an emergency siren and tearing strips in my esophagus, exiting through my teeth in a wild spray that splashes in waves into a black pickup truck backed into the spot below me.

Rick and George work behind me, say frantic words I can't understand, my arms pinned back, head limp forward, more vomit, more splashing, handrail on belly, wobbling and loose, knees buckling, Rick tells me I need to force myself to stand, but I can't and he and George swing me sideways and lay me on my side on the walkway. My face presses into old wood and peeling paint, and the railing stretches ahead toward another building and night. Warm and wet beer foam and vomit drain slowly from my mouth, puddle warmly under my head, soak into my hair, and the dark vignettes around my eyes constrict and close and the darkness gives way to Amber, sitting quiet and alone on a chair in Meggy's void-space, alit from an unknown light somewhere.

"Do you still love her?" Amber's voice echoes, stentorian and direct, as though we sit in a small, metal box. She looks at me, eyes seeing me clearly, through me. Her stare focuses directly into my pupils and pulls the back of my brain, the part that operates with background programming and powers only reflex, into my mouth.

"I do." My voice also echoes, but less, my voice faint, but sure in what it says.

"More than me?"

"No. Differently."

"And me?" Amber stares at my eyes, I lock mine with hers, bright and brilliant and hued like the underside of a new leaf in spring.

"I love you more every time we're together." I struggle to push myself up to my hands and knees. Wherever we are, I'm inches-deep in warm, still water and when I move or talk it ripples away from me. Amber sits, arm's crossed, looking at my eyes, seeing me, her eyes directly in mine, aware and perfect.

"I will never forget her. More time will pass between when I think about her. She and I loved each other very much. Differently than you and I. Less some ways, more others."

"How so?"

"I don't ask you to forget your exes, Amber," I slam my right palm flat into the shallow water over and over, the splash sound echoing inside the chamber but the wave energy never bouncing back to me. I shift from a kneel to sitting in the water, feeling it soak into my clothes, and look at Amber, directly in her eyes. "I am in love with you and the life I will make with you. With Meggy, I was in love with the life she and I would have."

"I don't understand."

"It will take more work for us to build our life. I am in love with you and that work and I want that for us together. We'll have less handed to us. The life we make will mean more to us."

Amber stands and her footfalls in water echo in the small, metal space. She walks confident in high, black heels, foot in front of the other in a single line, legs crossing at her knees with each step, hips swinging as her legs move past each other. She stands next to me, squats, and puts her hand on my shoulder. "Tell me that, Merak. Don't ever wait to tell someone something important." Amber stands, walks past me and the light above her goes dark, my hands are on an old vinyl steering wheel,

Colander, muddy river water rising fills my mouth and the taste and feel of river grit, fish, and loose, black biomass fill my throat. Foam and churning water pulls Colander and I toward the riverbed below and the two small overhead lights above me flicker out. Amber's voice bubbles through the water, surrounds me and comes from inside my brain at the same time as the water rises to fill the last air pocket in the car, "you died in the river, Merak. Everything since was a dream in your oxygen-starved brain. It will be over soon in a bright, white light."

◇

Knees to stomach, scratchy all over, soft but scratchy fabric on face, cold below me, arms folded, hard on my side, dark but a small light, two small lights, overhead lights, water drips. Water. I'm in Colander's trunk. Water fills up around me, but I'm dry. I feel around the hard, cold space. I'm in my underwear and nothing else, a scratchy towel on me, an old couch cushion my pillow. The lights. One light, the kind that plugs into an outlet and turns on in the dark. The second is, what, no, it's a reflection of that first light in a mirror. I'm in George's bathroom, in his tub. It's hard and cold and my limbs feel locked up. With force and pain and movement that unleashes a wave of vomit stench that was trapped under me I toss the pillow and blanket on the floor, strip out of my underwear, and shower in the dark, accompanied only by the one light, its reflection, and a thin light line and periodic laughing from under the bathroom door.

I turn the water on hot and wait, embrace the cold that starts until the hot water pushes through the pipes to me. The cold water wakes me; my skin feels like it shrink-wraps my bones. I drink showerhead water as the post-drunk headache starts and fires like a cannon with each heartbeat. What do I remember? Burgers and a game. I remember us trying to guess each other's middle names. We got to Jesse, but was that it? When the hot water arrives, in much time, I shampoo twice, soap twice. Stand in the water, step around with my feet in the darkness and the water, feel the foot-step splashes on my opposite legs, the sound echoes in the small room. I grab my boxer briefs, wash them with shampoo, rinse, turn off the shower, wring the jockeys out well in a dry hand towel, and, when wrung, put them on still a little damp. My shoulders throb like I pulled them lifting something too heavy.

When I flip on the lights, eyes blinking to adjust, my clothes, washed and folded, rest on top of the toilet. I dress, hand-comb my hair to the side. I grab my black watch and look at the blue face, second hand ticking forward, unrelenting, nearly ten.

Amber and George sit at the table, talking easily about bartending and drink making, and eating scrambled eggs on toast. "Is that Merak? Did he survive?" Amber asks.

Strange wording. "It's me." I walk over to George's one semi-safe burner and make three scrambled eggs while some toast slowly browns in the toaster.

"I know the coffee won't be to your standards," George says.

"Don't care." I pour a cup, add some extra cream, drink it fast; it's not very warm and it tastes like I'm sucking on a lighter-fluid-soaked charcoal briquette. I make another, glad for anything that can cover the beer-tequila-puke taste in my mouth. When I join them, George asks Amber about any new cooking tricks and she shares a few, some one-pot and one-pan dish ideas he can make on his one good burner or portable.

"Thank you for dropping a blanket and pillow in there for me."

"Rick's idea. He and Amber got you out of your clothes and washed them in the complex machine for you."

"I appreciate that like I can't express." My eggs are fine, a bit rubbery and I put in too much salt, but on buttered toast it's hard to notice. I fold the toast like a taco and eat my food quickly.

"Amber said you guys are going sledding today?"

I nod. Amber smiles wide, teeth happy, eyebrows bright and raised, and nods fast and short.

"You going to be okay today, Merak?" George asks. "You, uh, you were in a bad spot last night."

"What happened?"

"I'll tell you on the way to the hill, at least the parts you aren't about to find out yourself," Amber says.

I give George's dishes and skillet a quick wash, hug George, thank him again for getting me to the tub, and we walk outside. The patio railing is near-sideways, broken from the wall to the wood column at the stairs. "Did you and Jesse come out here for another smoke and lean too far against that?"

George looks at Amber, eyebrows up, eyes wide, lips pursed. I look over the walkway and the truck below has a decent splash of yellow-brown and very chunky vomit in the bed.

"Oh damn was that me?"

George nods. "Rick kept you from falling over the side, but it took both he and I to really pull you back up. You were totally limp and vomiting and your arm slipped out of my hands. I think you woulda just popped some screws but when you went limp both you and Rick slammed into the railing and it just bent. Rick was like a damn ninja. He just squatted, kept his weight low, and that gave me the time I needed to re-grab your arm. We got you back on the walkway but man it was close. I really thought you were going over."

"I, um, I owe you a lot. Thank you."

George gives the space between my shoulders and gentle smack, and rests his hand there. "You need to thank Rick a lot."

"I promise I am not going to miss a chance to let him know how much I appreciate him."

12
Orange

Rick and I pack for spring break, debate if we should bring Irish-y shirts for St. Patty's day. Amber packed her rucksack for the week and plays an uncoordinated game of Goldeneye alone as Rick and I finish packing. She's going with us, really going. In the last week my parents have called nine times to ask about things that they need to do for her, what kind of food she likes, if it's a good idea to move all the furniture to the walls and have open space in the rooms, do they need to buy her brand of detergent? I don't know how this will go; I do know that of the five us of, Amber, I, Rick, and my parents, Rick is the one not nervous.

In time, car packed, on the road by seven to beat most of the students, Amber next to me and Rick stretched across the back seat, we leave Johnson County, heading north for Chicago, and Amber says that every moment now will be the furthest north she's ever been, and soon it will be the furthest from home that she's ever been, too. It will be that way the rest of the trip, until the drive home, Rick notes.

"Do you guys know any road games?"

"None that wouldn't give me an unfair advantage," Rick says. "I'm okay with winning them all."

"Oh?"

"Well, there's I Spy, which is where you have to go through the alphabet looking for things that start with each letter. Whoever finishes first wins. No duplicates."

"A – Amber, B – boy, C – car, D – driver, you need to catch up, Rick," she says pointing in the direction of the things she names.

"There's Punch Buggy, which is where whoever spots a VW Beetle first gets to shout 'Punch Buggy!' and punch everyone but the driver in the arm."

"These games seem wired to make me lose. I'll pass. What's out here?"

"Mostly farms, still," I say, the corn aligned in rows that pass us in endless, alternating valleys of leaves and dirt, open and closing like we're a zipper shuttle. "In a bit we'll take a bridge over Rend Lake. It's a nice, long bridge. And then we'll just basically cruise through farmland for about four hours. Deer Lake is almost to Wisconsin."

"Can we go to Wisconsin?"

"Sure. We'll pick a day for Milwaukee," I say. For a moment I wonder why; it's only Wisconsin, until I realize Amber's never left Illinois. "I know a place in Milwaukee with amazing margaritas."

Rick leans forward, a bright smile. "The slushy kind?"

"Of course."

"I'm down."

"Dude."

"I mean, I'm busy whatever night that is. But I'm really not. I'll be there. No take-backs." Rick leans back in his seat looks at me in the mirror, and then pulls his hand down over his face like he's shutting a window blind.

Amber sits upright when we cross the Rend Lake bridge, when the road sound changes. "Is this a normal sound?"

"Yup."

"How fast are we going?"

"A bit more than eighty."

"I think this is the fastest I've ever travelled," Amber says. "It doesn't feel that fast."

"We'll slow down in a bit. I'm trying to make some early time to get to the rest area before the coffee kicks in."

"Gross." Amber crosses her arms and faces the window. "Still a good idea."

"Merak," Rick says, "do you know Charlie Tutolt?"

"I do not." Amber concurs with me that this is a new name.

"He's a couple years behind us. Anyway, he lives up near 45 and 22, in Lincolnshire. Not too far from us. For fun one day he decided he'd rather take 45 all the way from Lincolnshire down to Cold Harbor, you know, instead of 57."

"That's, what, like ten hours?"

"More than fourteen. Lots of traffic lights, very slow, got stuck behind a tractor for like two counties, he said, which probably means two stop signs, but anyway, yeah, he wanted to do it."

"I like that he was counting distances in counties," Amber says, adding that should be a new thing.

"Probably a pleasant drive," I concede. "I'm no huge fan of Interstate travel, definitely prefer blue lines." A different kind of traveler takes blue lines, the numbered state highways that often run routes roughly aligning interstates. Interstate travel, like us, right now, at eighty-eight, forces the scenery to pass at different speeds with distance, constantly passing and hard to focus on, like trying to track a single blade on a ceiling fan. Interstates are not for travelers who enjoy the process, only for people who want the destination. I envy Charlie, a lot. Driving 45 from school to home sounds like a great day, a long day, a chance to see the scenery I usually pass quickly. I'd want to stay the night in Urbana, though, and take my time with two travel days photographing the small communities I'd pass, stop for snacks and meals at the little towns' stop-sign-intersection diners, meet the locals and chat with the waitresses who know the business of everyone but me. I don't enjoy the glances that some locals reserve for passers-though, however. People who stop to eat on Interstates, they want their food, their anonymity, and their destination. People who drive the state roads, who talk to the locals, who enjoy their time and travel, they want to meet, to learn, and to experience.

In time, and after our first break, I find a semi-truck keeping a nice clip at a bit more than seventy. I kill the cruise and let Federico coast down to pace it. About forty feet back, I match his speed, hit the cruise, and slide into the lane behind him.

"What just happened? We slowed down, the car started to shake a bit, and now it's a lot quieter and smoother."

I explain that we're drafting a semi and, once, while making this drive, I managed the entire trip from Cold Harbor to Chicago on a single tank of gas – half what I usually need – by drafting a semi the whole way.

"Amber, under your seat, can you grab the CD book?"

Rick looks at my eyes in the rear view. He's smiling.

"Do I get to choose?"

"Of course."

"DJ Random in the house, as they say." Amber unzips the large book. It could hold well more than a hundred CDs, but isn't quite full. Maybe seventy discs right now. She opens the book and reaches to a sleeve and stops. Two days ago I spent hours – hours – with a braille sticker printer I bought just for this moment. I labeled the artist and title of every CD's pouch. I hear her swallow and she runs her fingers over every disc on every page, methodical, clenching her jaw muscles, trying to hide a chin quiver. "Only Grandpa Arn," she stops, waves her hand over the book, closes it, and sits and breathes. I count her breaths, five, and she opens it, picks a CD, a good road-music anthology of the pop and rock I grew up on, and I tell her where to move her hand as she guides the disc to the receiver.

In some minutes, Rick lays down in the back seat, curls a bit, and reads a book, a suspense thriller about, Rick explains, a girl trapped in an RV with a homicidal maniac. It sounds intense, I say, as I notice soft snoring from Amber's side of the car.

‹◊›

Orange

I park Federico in the street in front of my home, Rick hops out and runs like a high-kicking gazelle to the front door for an emergency bathroom stop. "Welcome to 1327 Prairie Dew Court."

"Describe it for me," Amber says, resting her hand on mine.

"The upper floor is light blue siding that almost disappears into the sky on clear, summer afternoons. Downstairs, it's brick, oranges and reds in random order that my childhood mind used to search for patterns and shapes, like in clouds or the textures in popcorn ceilings. Rick, I, and some of my other friends, we scratched our names into the bricks behind some plants, making ourselves always part of this place. When my dog Tiddlywink died, we buried him under a new shrub and father mounted a brass plate there. He pretended not to know about the names we scratched in the brick when he saw them. This home is a maelstrom of memory where my parents fought, made up, where we had meals and watched TV, where I played in my imagination and the backyard. This is where I tossed sticks for fetch with Tiddlywink, where my father built a metal tube swing set and monkey bars for my friends and I, and where, a few nights my senior year when my parents were out, Amy would stop by and we would fumble uncoordinated and unguided through sex. This home is the place that fostered who I would grow up to be, never asking me to give back to it, knowing that our actions define our character and that, in the end, our character is our value. This home is the smell of baked chicken on a cold holiday afternoon, French toast or eggs in the hole for breakfast on Saturdays, the feel of cold vinyl flooring under bare feet, the thud of a refrigerator door closing loudly every time one of my friends grabbed a pop, and the tremor of thunder-shaken walls proving they would keep us warm and dry in the worst weather."

Amber squeezes my hand.

"We're parked in the street because, for some reason, mom's Tahoe and Dad's M5, which he named and will only call Giorgio by the way, are both in the driveway. I mean, I could park behind them, but I'd be blocking the sidewalk. That's not allowed for overnights. When you get

262

out, there's a curb with grass right behind it. Follow that in the direction we're facing now and the grass ends at the driveway. A couple feet off the driveway and sidewalk to the house are some short solar lights, so mind your cane. Everywhere you need to go to get in has grass on the right side. I'll carry our stuff and will be right there if you need me."

"Why did your father name his car that?"

"It's his seventh car – so he's on 'G' – and father likes disco."

Amber nods as she unfolds her cane, nervous and excited she explains, to find her way around somewhere new. This, she said, was something she did not get to do so often any more. Amber stands out of Federico's passenger seat and walks to meet me at the back. She feels the grass and curb with her cane, walking through the grass to the driveway. I carry my hard Pelican camera case in my right hand, a white and maroon duffel with Cold Harbor's mascot in my left, have Amber's rucksack slung around my shoulder, and push Federico's hatch closed with the duffel until it locks with a soft thud and click. Rick leads my mother and father out to us to meet Amber. "Don't worry," I lean in close to Amber where the driveway meets cul-de-sac, "they already like you. I know you're nervous and that's okay."

Mother and father walk to us holding hands, Rick runs up beside us and stands on my left, and the three of us walk up the driveway, past the cars, to where it meets the front door sidewalk.

"Can you describe your parents for me?"

"Father looks a lot like me, bit of thin, receding hair, dark brown and parted on the right, lots of gray at the temples and scattered around the top. He has a lot of worrier's wrinkles, forehead, eyes, cheeks, nose, and neck, stress from owning a business I imagine, but less apparent now since he put on some pounds the last couple of years. He has a slightly crooked nose from a high school dirtbike crash, a bit of a sloping chin; I get my jawline from mom. Father has, right now, a bit of stubble and he's wearing a button-down shirt and jeans. He has a small ponch that pokes out beyond his belt a bit. Mother is hippy, though pictures of her before I was born tell a different story, with a slightly rounder face than mine, a large-ish nose with a bump at the bridge, a cleft in her chin. She's wearing a robin-egg-blue dress with white buttons and keeps her red hair short in a pixie cut."

We greet my parents, us on driveway them on sidewalk. My father, facing me and mother facing Amber, smile like I have never seen before, and my mother greets Amber with a warm hug and her hands on Amber's shoulders while she says how excited she is to finally meet her. After incalculable minutes, I'm sure, for Amber as she tries to orient herself in a typical my-partents-talking-over-each-other-and-too-quickly-like-they're-competing-for-a-trpohy conversation, my mother asks if she can show us around the house.

I follow Amber, agreeing, inside, look at my father, and thumb toward their cars. "New project car in the garage?"

"Yup."

"Been a while," Rick says. My father sold the Ferrari, finally, after years of work, just over a year ago. He took the money and, struggling to find a new project car that he had any passion for, invested in a friend's real-estate trust.

"Well, I got a call about an interesting car, cheap and fun. I'll show you after lunch."

Inside, my childhood home unrecognizable with new furniture in a completely different layout than I knew, my mother leads Amber around the house and tells her about the rooms and the layouts. "Let me know if I'm giving too much, too little, or wrong details, Amber," my mother says. "You are the first blind person I've met. I tried to do a few things Merak suggested. But I am afraid I'll inadvertently say something offensive." Amber walks next to my mother and swipes her cane gently back and forth in a tight pattern to plot her steps. "We moved the coffee tables out of the centers of the living room, family room, and conversation nook.

The den is a bit messy, but that's not my room so don't take it up with
me."

Amber chuckles nervously, unsure of how to react. "This is a lot
of rooms."

"All the couches, seats, and end tables are on the left side of each
room when you enter, TV, bookshelves, etageres either on the right wall
or the opposite, depending on the room. The family room opens out to
the backyard patio, which you're welcome to enjoy, too. It's stone pavers,
slate, natural-cut; Merak says you know a lot about rocks and minerals.
We'll sit out there later since we're grilling dinner."

Eventually they make their way around the house to the kitchen,
where Rick, my father, and I drink cans of pop and make sandwiches with
chips for everyone. The kitchen, remodeled last year, has new stainless-
fronted appliances, a double oven where the pantry used to be, a large
island with a six-burner gas range and a large hood, and black granite
counter tops on all four sides except for the hallway that leads from the
kitchen dining nook into the laundry room and garage. My mother and
Amber sit at the small kitchen table, a U-shaped bench with central
rectangular table my father bought on a trip to Amish country, that they
had the nook built around. The kitchen smells freshly cleaned with a light
pine-and-lemon scent in the air. My mother, smiling, exhales and looks at
Amber, and Amber lets my mother know that we have a lovely home and
she appreciates the tour.

"So Merak tells me you ride horses?"

Amber seems surprised by the change in topic; she sits and turns,
faces quickly in the direction of us in the kitchen making lunch and talking
about sandwich toppings.

"She does," I say, not to confirm anything but to let Amber know
I'm here.

Amber faces my mother and starts to tell her about Sandstone and how long she's been riding, that she jumps him, too, and that he was her way to get around town growing up.

My father passes me a loaf of rye to start slicing and has Rick get the plates, condiments, and fixings. I, between slices of the thick, hard-crusted rye, pick up snippets of the kitchen table conversation.

"Oh yes, he's a good horse. It's all about trusting him… Jumping is never easy… Oh yes I've been thrown a couple of times, and that's always terrifying because I never know where I'll land… We taught him a few places to take me – school, a small apple tree grove, the grocery store and an ice cream shop where I could meet friends… Oh he doesn't want to get hurt, so he won't lead me into any place dangerous, like traffic." Amber fills in details about her life and I see my mother relax as they talk. It's too easy, I think, for people to become too dependent on others, and this is something I learned from my mother who kept control of her finances and, as my father grew his business, exerted financial control over it until Todd came along and she could take a job at another company and not, as she said, tax the marriage by never being apart. My mother, I suspect listening as she talks with Amber, shows relief-slacked cheeks and a calm smile to hear about how she is independent. Mother had worried that I could find myself in a situation where I would need to provide too much care for Amber, where she would become too dependent on me, and where that would put me in a place to decide if I would be a boyfriend or a caretaker. As they talk more, I realize that my mother isn't relieved to learn that Amber is independent so much as she's relieved to learn that I picked someone who wants to be independent. Being and choosing independence are different as one is a thing we are and the latter a thing that we do. Amber does not need me in order to live her life fully, but I hope that I make it better, and that's what my mother wanted to know.

My father eats his sandwich fast then sits fidgety at the table waiting for the rest of us. Amber and I slowly work on the sandwich we split, my mother telling us about her new job as a financial analyst for a small brokerage firm, my father quickly bringing us up to speed on his latest design projects, my mother asking Rick about his business courses. In time, and despite nervous fiddling and heel-tapping from my father's side of the table, we finish lunch and my mother, looking at my father, sighs-says "yes you can see if they want to look at the car now. Holy cow."

"What is this new project car?" Rick asks.

My father smiles.

"He's been dreaming of overhauling it for years," my mother says.

Father looks at her and, hands flat toward her, makes a double-tapping motion like he's patting potting soil flat. "Follow me out front of the garage for the big reveal."

Rick looks at me. Amber faces me. We stand, I take Amber's left arm in my right, and I decide to guess this car as we walk.

"Maserati?"

"That is my dream car."

Amber asks: "What's that?"

"Maserati Merak, it's the Italian sports car I'm named after."

"But that's not it," my father says.

"1986 911?"

"Gross."

"First-gen Mustang?" My father holds the front door for us and Rick sneezes when the sunlight hits his eyes.

"Nope, but solid guess."

"Old V-Dub Bug?"

My father stops, turns, his right eyebrow up, "I will write you out of the will and leave it all to Rick." Before we walk on, "one more guess."

I throw my hands up in the air "1930s Jaguar. That's it, last guess. I can't think of anything else you've ever expressed an interest in rebuilding. Except Colander." I wave my hand at the garage door and say "let's see it."

"His name is Antonio, not Colander" my father code-opens the middle door, his door, and parked in it is what looks like a large mound of muddy plastic bags, roots, and soils. To the side, behind my mother's door, is a car under a tan cover.

"I can't tell what it is under the cover."

"Look again."

The bags catch my eye, trapped in flat, horizontal lines, torn pieces of plant and mud-trapped rocks hang down over some kind of structure. Tan, like someone encased a giant brick in a cast made of plaster and mud. The horizontal lines seem to have structure and have mud well packed behind them. More plastic, what might be an old, muddy beach towel hangs over rusted and tire-free steel rims that rest on cement blocks. It's a muddy, rusted car with holes on the doors. The back, a chrome bumper, two mud-filled tailpipes with roots or something hanging out of them, two horizontal rear lights, visible only because they're under a thinner mud covering. Those strips above them, so horizontal, too perfect, like broad and flat stairs from the middle of the thing to the top; they look like mud and muck and biomass hanging on louvers on – louvers. Rear-window louvers with a branch stuck in one of the slats, rear-side window louvers, too, and when I walk to the car I see the driver's side window is missing. Above the front wheelwell, a wiped-clean spot, orange: Spitfire Orange.

Rick knows it before I do, and he swears.

Dizzy, not a spell but a lifetime of stored and hidden, pushed-aside and ignored dizzy rushes my brain like monster trucks over old cars. My vision focuses on the small spaces of orange and the louvers. Sound, but muffled like it's passed through a brick wall and a dozen pillows, maybe voices, maybe my name, or just a car engine on the next street. The garage floor rotates beneath my feet, turns upside-down and gravity pulls me from above, away from the cement but toward it now as the mud and orange spin around on top of me. Hands on shoulders and back, head gently set on pavement, sun through eyelids red and swirling. Amber says my name over and over four times then forty and numbers and repetition mean nothing and with each name her voice clarifies, rings, and resonates like the sound of a small, bass bell note played in reverse. Rick smacks my cheek and I'm looking up at all four of them, each saying my name, asking if I'm okay. Inhale and exhale, slowly, long breaths. Four more times. I am okay.

"That's Colander."

"His name's Antonio," father says pointing at me from above. "I got him back in January." Father reaches his hand down to me and helps me stand. "You have no idea how hard it's been to keep this secret."

I hug Amber when I'm upright. When, in some amount of time that means nothing, I step forward, Amber uses her cane to tic-tac the driveway behind me. I put my hand on Colander's spoiler and dust falls off the car and dirties my fingers as I trace the lines up to the roof above the passenger's seat, dented likely from rocks but looking as though beaten by hands. Holes. So many holes, only some I remember. Rims rust-welded to the brakes, axles rust-locked in their mounts. Holes from the wheel wells penetrate the trunk. Through the missing window the interior upholstery is cracked, reeks of mold and mud and rotted fish. The dashboard has cracked, been mended with mud, and the gauges are filled with thin strata of different-colored silt and sand. The hole in the rear seats shows a trunk-cave; holes in the trunk lid dust-form light spires that seem like supports and structure made by the metal that once was.

I look at my mother, who nods and walks back inside. My father is a smile I have never seen, teeth-to-ears, giddy like I've never known. He claps and bounces on his toes.

"Does it run?"

My father looks at me, stops bouncing, points at me, looks at Rick, "did you hear that?"

"I did."

He looks at Amber, "you sure you still want to date him?"

"Does it run?" she asks.

"I guess you do, and no, it does not. Never will again. The engine is a big block of rust. Some contractor on some river cleaning crew out in some small Colorado town calls me up last November, right before Thanksgiving. He calls me up and he explains they were cleaning garbage out of a river and pulled this and some old Caddy out. Also a bunch of appliances and stuff. He got my info from the plates, because the car was in my name. He asked if it was stolen, which I guess it was, technically, being my car. I asked if it could run, because silly questions run in this family, and he says 'uhhhhhhh, might need some work.' Anyway, long and short, I paid to have Antonio shipped back. Didn't figure he would be in this bad a condition or I might have told them to just scrap him. Haven't touched him, been waiting to see your reaction."

"You stole your dad's car, Merak? Why do I always fall for the bad boys."

"It was my car at the time."

"For like five more weeks and then you were getting Federico for college."

"Dude," Rick says. "You're a felon. Stealing cars and such. And from your dad, too. And after he's been such a good guy all these years."

My fingers run along the top of my glasses, massaging the short hairs where my eyebrows stop above my nose.

"It's water under the car, or maybe above. Get it? Anyway, I don't know. I got nothing. The point is, who cares," my father says, again giddy.

"What are you going to do with it?" Amber asks.

Orange

My father leans in to us, he smiles like a cat burglar about to describe an amazing caper. "Oh, I'm gonna rebuild it. From scratch, just like I wanted to do when Merak went off to school. Always wanted to do that. F bodies were never great, but they're simple, relatively easy to rebuild. Under the tarp I have a donor parts car, an ugly '76 Volare. There's a '78 Aspen I'm picking up in a week, too. They're simple cars and I've been learning carbon fiber casting for a work project. I might make the new body myself." He grins wide, spending a moment in his mind driving his yet-to-be made supercar. "It's going to be so dangerous to drive."

"I'll be right back." I walk slowly, as though I am playing myself in a videogame, the camera following me from behind, walking in a forced, seemingly unnatural cadence through the garage entrance to the house and upstairs to my room, slowly, careful steps. Closet. Old wood cigar box in back. Open, mementos from my trip, film canister of sand, some rocks, and Colander's spare keys. I take the steps downstairs in two bounds and my mother tells me not to do that in the house as I run through the kitchen, laundry room, and into the garage. In the garage doorway, my father, Rick, and Amber staring at or facing me, I walk slowly to Colander's trunk.

My father and Rick exchange glances. I put the key into Colander's trunk lock, turn it, no movement at first, wiggle and it grinds clockwise against rust and dirt, push down and in, and, nothing. It won't budge. I don't know what I expected. One more idea, and I turn the key as far right as I can then hit the back of the trunk with my fist. Something makes a noise inside the trunk, something falling or breaking and I can lift it. It fights, hinges rusted, lifting springs broken. Nothing. There's nothing inside of it but stink and mildew. I don't know what I expected, maybe I wanted to see if my two old duffels were still there, moldy and rotted piles of clothes and bag. I just needed to see inside the trunk. I set the keys on the garage workbench.

"I, um, I'll help Amber get settled in."

"Merak," Amber says, "are you okay?"

My father looks at us, "does she know about this car?"

I nod and Amber confirms she knows.

"Let's get your stuff upstairs to my old room," I say to Amber. "I'll take my stuff to the living room."

"You're adults, Merak," my father, eyes rolling, arms bent at his elbows, palms up, "you can both sleep in your room."

"It's a twin bed."

He shrugs.

‹◊›

Almost midnight, an evening of grilled chicken and brussels sprouts, sparkling wine and beers, laughing, stories, and catching up on the patio left me exhausted, my body fighting for sleep. Seeing Colander – I will go to my grave before I call that car Antonio – here, real, and intact-ish, forces my brain awake, excited at the possibilities. I imagine my father rebuilding the car, welding a steel frame, lowering an engine and transmission into it, wiring the parts together. I hope he can salvage the louvers.

Is building a car legal? He'll say, 'easier to ask forgiveness than permission.'

Will it look like it did? He'll say, 'I'm tinting the windows.'

Will I get to drive it? He'll laugh, let me take it around the block once.

Can he even do this project? He can. He has never failed at something he put his mind into. Best guess, four years.

I want to drive Colander to a mountain, with Amber. I know there are some in Colorado, tall ones, Pikes Peak, Mount Evans, I think, that I could drive up. I want to photograph Colander, new and rebuilt, shining orange and black-trimmed-and-tinted, parked on the outside of a hairpin turn, a valley or couloir behind, clouds movement-blurred in the sky, stars spinning overhead, lightning bolts in the background, I don't know yet, all of those, different shots, different times of day and night, bold and warm Spitfire Orange in front of a cool, blue day or night sky, or the purple hue of photographed lightning. I want to look at the photos and feel the colors and describe them to Amber. I want to rattle her in the car, punch the accelerator on a straight line to make her shout my name in a fury-excitement like she'll cry out my name that night.

"Merak," I thought Amber was asleep next to me, on her side, left leg over both of mine, right arm under my pillow, left arm on my stomach and hand in my pajamas waistband, her face tucked to my side. "Your heart sounds and feels like you're running. Are you okay?"

"I am. I'm thinking about Colander. I want to take you for a ride in it, maybe across country. Whatever Colander's going to be, it won't be the same car."

"Why?"

"My dad like fast straight-line cars. The M5, it's the fastest sedan on the market. It cooks. But it's a corner-friendly car, like Federico, believe it or not. That's what I like driving. Old muscle cars, they're straight-line cars. He's gonna pop as big an engine in it as he can and it'll be like strapping a jet turbine to a feather."

"Why'd he buy the M5 if he doesn't like cornering cars?"

"It's fast."

"How's he going to build a new car?" Amber wants me to talk myself to sleep.

"He'll make it from scratch. He's a very good welder."

Amber's body jolts. She must have had one of those almost-asleep-thought-I-fell-out-of-a-plane moments. But she didn't. "Your dad can weld?"

"Yes, and a lot of different stuff. Bar stock, square and round tube, carbon or stainless, even aluminum. When he welds up seams and grinds it all flush, you can't even feel where the welds were at. He's really good."

Amber mumbles: "Grandpa Arn is going to like him a lot."

They're both welders. Grandpa Arn welded mining equipment for his job, fixing cracked and bent parts of mine machines, working on engines and motors, pumps sometimes. He only gave it up because Grandma Helen died and someone needed to keep the farm running. "They both love working with their hands. I think you're right. When we graduate in a couple of months. We'll have my folks over to your house for a day."

"Your dad can chop wood," Amber's voice is soft, syllables mumbled and a bit sleep-mushy.

"Bail some hay."

"Tad can pull your dad over," she says as her breaths take a slow, methodic rhythm defined by a slight whistle in her nose. Seconds pass and her breathing calms my brain, slows my pulse, feels like the repetitious pumps of a dentist's nitrous machine as it brings on the tiredness and sleep that drowns away room sounds in bliss and light, ushering the inward sensation of imagination to run wild to form dreams existing in the semi-controllable boundary between consciousness and sleep.

《◇》

We take Route 131 north, Rick's idea, and since he drove, it works for me. Just past Russell Road he stops, announcing to Amber that we're in Wisconsin, pulling the car over to the shoulder.

Amber asks, "why did we stop?"

"There's a sign ahead of us," Rick says. "This is a huge moment for you. We need a photo of it."

"Won't do me any good."

"It'll do Merak some good."

Sign: a large, blue box, rounded corners, white border and text, a faded shape of the state in the top left: "WELCOME TO WISCONSIN" and "Kenosha Co." in the middle. Rick walks Amber up to the sign while I focus my F3 and dial in the settings. When he lets go of her arm and jogs over to me, I tell him it's ready to go and I join Amber by the sign. I put my hand around her shoulder and as Rick says "say cheese," she surprises me with her hand cupping my butt and my face and body jump into a surprised smile. Click.

"That look, Merak, on your face. I hope I got that. Okay, one more."

I give Amber a peck on the cheek and she giggles and slides her and around my waist. – Click –

"One more," Rick says, "in case I messed up the last two."

Amber reaches her hand into mine and I lean in to Amber and give her a long kiss with tongue-teeth flicking and lip pulling, and Rick takes another photo. We hop back into my car and pull back into the street before traffic catches us.

"You've been awfully quiet this trip, Merak," Rick says.

The backseat in Federico is fine and comfortable and I sit across it with my back to the driver-side window. I've spent the ride listening to Rick and Amber talk, to build the friendship that I want them to have since, things going as I maybe think I could potentially want them to go, Rick would someday stand beside us in a tuxedo, white tie of course, and, dabbing his eyes, glance from us to his date with some jealousy. I've spent the ride watching Amber, happy and talking with Rick, comparing notes on people they know in common, Rick telling her about the scenery of suburban Chicago, the restaurants to order food from. "Oh, I'm just happy to listen," I say.

"Thinking about the crash?"

I have been. A lot. But not so much about the crash, more about Colander sitting in a river, growing a cocoon of mud and dead leaves each year until some machine dragged him onto some piece of dry land, leaving him to drain and dry out in a yard, people working to identify him, a tow truck pulling him onto a flatbed, and a long road trip home. I think about my love for the sporty little Volare's looks, how much I enjoyed driving him, despite the many frustrations and hot, leg-skin-grabbing cracks in his vinyl seats. "I'm thinking of the places I want to drive and photograph Colander and what it must have been like for him on the riverbed."

"You're talking about your car like a person. I didn't think that was your thing." Amber is right.

"I didn't think so, either." When I drove the crappy old Sentra home from Colorado, it fought and spit and smoked and tried to burn itself apart, hating every inch its tires moved more than all the previous combined. Colander loved the road and the throttle opening, the engine pushing torque to the wheels. No, I don't think of cars as people. I do think of Colander as, I don't know, something inanimate with a soul buried in the workings of gas and oil in metal, spinning rubber and hot breathy exhaust. He deserved more than to be some rusting thing that fish called home. I hope that whatever life it has, if any, lives in the parts father moves into the new body. "I guess maybe Colander is different. Any other car that trip, I think, you two wouldn't be talking here now." Colander may not be a living thing, but I know my life I owe to Colander as much as I owe my thoughts, my aspirations to be better, to Rick and Amber. These two are my closest family and I am fortunate I could choose them.

Rick and Amber let me sit and think. They know that I have more to say, even if it isn't ready. Maybe I do, or don't. In silence, our brains think and conjure, cajole from the depths of the silent thoughts that guide our actions like a marionettist high above us silently dictating away our lives while gifting a perceived free will.

"I used to talk to Colander. I don't talk to Federico. I only ever swore at your Sentra. I hate that car. I want to watch it die on fire."

"Same here."

"I tried to kill it," Amber says.

Rick laughs.

In time we reach Milwaukee's lakeshore, marina, and yacht club area at Veteran's Park. Parked, we get coffee from a small coffee shop in an old stone building and walk along the water. We walk quietly and listen to the gulls screech overhead, gentle waves break immediately next to us on the breakers beside the path, our footfalls changing from chaos to coordinated in time with the waves' cadence. In the water, sailboats' masts and ropes creak and strain, a sound forged by calm wind and wave energy swaying the boats. We feel the breeze and smell the slightly-fish-and-algae-tinged Lake Michigan air as it pulls our hair up and back, caresses our faces, cups our jaws and necks, and kisses our lips with wave spray.

"There must be a lot of sailboats," Amber says. Their creaking, accompanied by a few sailboats' bells ringing, moves in advancing patterns over the water. "Are the waves doing that?"

"They are. The waves come in rows, today parallel to the shore. The boats lift and drop, like this," I hold her hand on its side, tilt it left, lift it, rock it right, and lower it.

"I get what the waves do, silly."

Rick looks at me, puffing his lips, glancing away, eyes wide.

"I just, you know," I don't know what I want to say.

"It's okay. Sometimes you explain things to me a bit more than needed."

Rick purses his lips, raises his eyebrows, nods lightly.

We walk northward along the lakeshore through the park, around to a stunning triangle bird-form of white, the Museum of Modern Art, a building that makes me want to photograph buildings.

"That's, I don't know," Rick says. "I think I like that building?"

"It's an amazing building," I say. We sit on a bench and look at the bright white triangle that dominates the park's otherwise smooth and wave-like grasscape and I lean in toward Amber. "Beauty like that never unites. Like all exceptional beauty, it divides us into camps of those who love it and appreciate it and those who, driven by jealousy or anger that we can't posses it for ourselves, despise it. People who love and appreciate exceptional beauty, they don't need to possess it because that love comes from the beauty they embrace within themselves. It's not just that this building is stunningly, physically beautiful; the thought that goes into buildings like this embodies the beauty of creative and purposeful architecture. It's white, like a seagull or a wave's frothy crest; triangular, like a ship's prow or a breakwater; dynamic, the top opens like birds' wings to shade the interior and so it looks different throughout the day; and at home, it grows out of the surrounding space and the shapes form into and meld with the shoreline and city beyond. This sort of thing, it is humanity refined, the capture and distillation of our best ambitions and intentions made manifest in a whited sepulcher of thoughtful design and striking outward form. I think the only thing more beautiful than channeling the creative mind into a form that shares beauty with the world is channeling the creative mind into our time with others and the sharing of our thoughts, hopes, aspirations, and dreams that form the core perceptions of self."

Rick holds his arms in front of him, palms up, "it's a building. It's nice, but really?"

Amber beats me to a response, "there's always something more worth finding, in people, in what we do, think, say, and build. When you find it, that's a huge reward."

I point at Amber, lips pressed inward, curled up a bit at the corners.

"You two are perfect for each other," Rick quips.

‹◊›

Over the span of some hours, we stroll to downtown, stop for water, browse local stores, and search for good music from bands we've never heard of. Milwaukee, to me, is something like ideal, a smaller city with quieter traffic, great food, and ample parks to walk around in and photograph. I love Chicago, of course, but the noise, towering buildings, echoing sirens, deep mid-day shadows on the streets, these are the kindling that burns into a self-conscious smallness, kin to but milder than the terror of inconsequentiality I felt the first time I watched the stars slowly traverse the night sky.

For dinner we stop at a food truck parked next to a liquor store on Water Street in downtown. When Rick volunteers to grab us a cold six-pack, Amber, unfolding her cane and tapping on the ground like she proposes a toast, proclaims with bold and stentorian confidence, "you boys drink what you want. I'm the designated driver tonight."

People in line around us hush and stammer. Amber smiles, faces me, happiness wrinkles appear in a flash and fade. "What? I've driven a car before," Amber says as all the mischief of her entire youth flashes in waves across her face and cheeks.

"You wrapped it around a bollard," Rick protests, his hands on his hips.

"And you were sober then, too," I add.

Our line neighbors, I think, find their way in on the joke when one asks, "did she really drive?"

"Oh yes, and she crashed. I think it's my favorite story from the last year."

"It was my car," Rick says. "Complete trash now, too."

"Rick, it was complete trash before I drove it."

"She's not wrong," Rick looks at our line neighbors, who, smiling or chuckling, return to their own conversations. Everything on the menu sounds amazing to Amber and our order reflects it: appetizers of potato skins, hot wings, and fried macaroni and cheese wedges because who knew such a thing could even exist and Amber's excitement at that idea led us to a double basket. I order Rick the truck's 'fries pile and burger' with cheese, a fried egg, bacon, and sprouts to be healthy; Amber finds the bratwurst with onions and mushrooms, side of waffle fries, and sleeping alone in my tiny bed interesting; I order a chicken burrito, smothered.

"Are you really going to sleep on the couch if I eat onions?" Amber and I walk to a bench by a bridge over the river to wait for my name and Rick pops the tops on our brown-bottled beers. Amber holds her bottle out and we clink the tops.

"Of course I will, onion breath."

Amber breaths on me.

"Well right now you just smell like beer, babe," I sip my beer and Rick takes the chance to step in.

"Things with your folks seem really good," Rick says, as the truck vendor calls my name for the food. We grab our beers and walk over the bridge and river to the River Walk and find a quieter place to sit, eat, and listen to traffic and boats passing.

The appetizers are packed in small, white paper bags differently sized for the various orders. Their over-pack bag has plastic silverware and paper plates. I put an appetizer assortment on a small plate for Amber and tell her to let me know when she wants more. "You know, they are. Their marriage counseling has really worked. The first two years of it were touch-and-go. But they worked on, mom told me, redefining shared goals, being open in their communications, actively forgiving each other for past mistakes, and re-learning to grow the last embers of love they had."

"Wow," Amber says. Rick nods at me, concurs that's great.

I take a bite from a fried macaroni and cheese wedge, which is so, so much better than I expected with a crisp and thick batter shell housing a core of hot, liquid American cheese that coats and fills thick elbow noodles. Hot cheese drips onto my chin. "Yeah. I think it was an important lesson for me. The key thing, they both said, is to understand that the other person is as much and as full as they are, with dreams and hopes that we need to respect so we can grow them and grow with them. My father keeps saying – I'm sure you've heard this, Rick – a rising tide raises all ships. So it's been good for me to learn that if they can patch up their mess and reinvest in who each other is, then shit, I can do the same, too." I look over at Amber and, with prompting, stack some wings on her plate and open us our second beers. "And I hope that means a lot to you, because I'm invested in you and us."

"Merak Cristopher Snyder, I do believe you are both getting tipsy and in love," Amber says.

"Amber Dawn Clearly, I believe you are getting even more tipsy."

"And more in love," she replies.

Rick leans elbows-onto-knees, hands fisted, middle knuckles pressed together to form a 'V' with his fingers, chin resting in that 'V,' "you two are just the cutest little buttons."

"Alright, Rick, we get it," Amber says, as she pulls a chicken wing bone out of her mouth, and she sounds like she says "aligitRigkweggetet."

We fill our stomachs with appetizers to try and calm the alcohol's effects on our dehydrated brains. I know it, Rick knows it, no way to know if Ambers knows it, but it's too late. The car ride home is going to be long. Rick eats wings, dropping clean bones on plate, and Amber does the same after working the bones with her back teeth a bit, and when Rick sees my wing bones, still with meat on the ends and sometimes in the middle, he points to mine then his and Amber's, back and forth a few times. "Look at your sad, sad wing bones with all that meat on them, Merak, and how clean Amber's and mine are. This, right here, is why the boys love us."

Amber laughs beer foam out her mouth.

"That's fair," I say, and Amber slaps my arm so hard I drop my (thankfully empty) beer bottle on the pavement as an old couple walks past. "My fault; slippery glass."

When we finish the appetizers, Rick volunteers to grab another six-pack for us while I unpack and serve the entrees. They come in large, white paper clamshells with stray fries poking out between the seams and grease stains soaked through the bottoms. I open Rick's burger first, "oh hell that thing is huge."

"Describe it for me."

"It's the size of one of those huge, squishy softballs and it rests atop a mixed pile of curly, steak, regular, shoestring, and waffle fries. This thing feels like it weighs more than a gallon of milk."

When Rick gets back and opens his clamshell his eyes go big and he mouths some swears.

"Brat?" Amber hands me her appetizer plate for the trash bag and brat and waffle fries land gently on her lap. My burrito, as large as a rolled-up newspaper, is drenched in a mix of red chili sauce and pan gravy and sprinkled with large pieces of cotija cheese. We should not have ordered appetizers. Or we should have ordered fewer. Or saved some to take home. Or, if we were smart, we'd just re-close these boxes right now. We are not smart.

Dehydrated and starting into her third beer, Amber is already not in any kind of shape to memorize where things on her plate are so I put her hands on the brat and fries. She eats leaned over and a bit messily. Rick stares at his burger, which seems to be as large as his whole torso.

"Dude, I have no idea where to start."

I shrug and cut into my burrito, mixing bites of chicken, rice, beans, cheese, guacamole, sour cream, lettuce, and tomatoes with the various sauces that fill my clamshell to the point that some drip over the edge and onto the sidewalk at my feet when I move my food around.

Rick starts eating his fries, showing a decided preference for the shoestrings. When he starts on the burger, egg yolk drips down the back and onto the pile. I grab a few fries with yolk drops, and learn I could be quite happy in life with a pile of waffle fries underneath some over-easy or scrambled eggs. We share our entrees freely with each other, fries and burrito, brat and burger, shared bites washed down with beers and jokes. When we finish, not finish but fill our bellies, we leave the clamshells on the back of a nearby trashcan in case, Rick suggests, someone who needs them finds them.

Milwaukee's River Walk takes us on a tour of downtown along the water, entombed in the sounds of periodic sirens, a freight train's engines powering up in a tunnel nearby, and the speaker-loud voice of a tour guide on a duck boat.

"A what?" Amber stops, tugs me and I whip around to face her.

"Duck boat. They're tour boat cars. Amphibious. They look like boats but they have wheels and drive on the streets, too"

"Can we do that?"

"We need reservations," Rick says.

"Shucks. Well, I want to do something, I love walking with you, Merak, but can we do something else tonight?"

Rick and I look at each other and grin. "Oh yes. We're going dancing."

Amber pushes my chest with her hands so hard I fall backward onto my butt on the sidewalk with a loud 'oof' as Amber says, "no way. We are?"

Rick reaches down to my hand. "We are."

"Rick," I say, dusting my butt off as Rick takes Amber's arm, "is taking us to a gay dance bar, The Engine Room."

"I know the bouncer."

"Rick," Amber says, "you and bouncers."

Rick fans his face, "it's the muscles, and how they can lift me up. Anyway, The Engine Room is having a Giorgio Moroder night. All Giorgio all night."

"Your dad's car?"

I laugh, "the guy the car is named after."

"So Merak is named after a car and a car is named after a person? Rich people are weird."

The line, around eighty people long, fronts The Engine Room's façade, original and weathered brick with a copper roof and gutters and small windows converted to displays for local artists' work. An old railroad locomotive repair building, The Engine Room barely contains the music, just loud enough to mask clear words from the people we pass. At the doors, large and new and wood carved with a stylized old-time locomotive on train tracks, Rick walks us up to one of the bouncers. True to his word, with a wink, blown kiss, and some kind of gesture that Rick makes while intentionally blocking my view, the bouncer waves us past the line.

Inside, the music pounds into our chests. The dance floor is large, painted black with lit circles that pulse in time with the music and change color. Long thin lines spaced like railroad tracks fan from the dancefloor through the bar and seating area. These pulse light in bundles toward the dancefloor. The dancefloor itself is recessed a few feet and towering more than thirty feet above it the entire club roof is a similar black and pulsing-circle finish in hanging rectangles that form a geode-like shape high above us. Columns from the floor to the ceiling with, again matching pulsing lights, carry the rail motif in vertical lines. Along the side, a bar made of thick and clear plastic tended by three men, built like Michelangelo sculptures dressed only in flyless knee-length boxer briefs, pour cocktails under pulsing neon lights. They top the drinks with cherries and speared fruit, smoke from a machine with some smoldering wood inside it, or thick whipped cream. The bartenders take orders, fill them fast, lean in to customers whose hands freely touch shoulders.

Most of the club is the dance floor, dark for the mass of bodies that covers most of it, their legs lit by the floor lights look like fireworks inside thin clouds. Behind it all, on a raised platform a story above the dance floor, a stunningly pretty woman with a tight top, large breasts that bounce far more than she, and long, red hair on top of her head – shaved on the sides and back – stands behind an array of turntables and keyboards. She blends music from records and samples, dances in time with the crowd, and communicates with points and hand waves at someone in a dim lighting booth. As she moves her hands, above the seething mass of women and shirtless men, a shifting waffle work mesh of lasers that form a roof of light over the crowd takes on different colors, shift hues, brightens and dims. Every few minutes, smoke machines on the ceiling hiss and drop a thick layer of raspberry-scented smoke onto the dance floor. Amber shouts into my ear to take her to the dance floor and I do. She stands in place, waves her arms above her head to the music.

I, not a dancer, lost like a child that followed a coyote into a forest, watch someone nearby who seems to know what he's doing and follow his moves as well as I can. Rick orders us drinks at the bar and, oh, he's made a new friend and he runs his fingers on one of the bartender's arms. Wait, oh shit he's flirting. I stop dancing. This is my first time in this part of Rick's world and it makes me very uncomfortable.

Music from the speakers shakes the sweat on my forehead as the DJ blends From Here to Eternity into Lost Angeles.

Amber puts her hand on my chest, runs it up to the back of my head and tilts it down to face her. She mouths, maybe shouts, who knows over this music, "what?" her eyebrows furrowing down.

I lean to her ear and, trying to compete with the beats and clicks, "Rick is flirting. It's weird."

Amber stands on her tip-toes, her shoulder smacking into my cheek, and she claps her hands excitedly. "I hope he meets a nice boy!"

Rick, holding three small cocktails above his head, dance-walks to the dancefloor, looks for us in the body-mass lit by alternating purple-red-white-yellow lights and flashing laser fans. The drinks go down smooth, easier than anything I've ever tried. It tastes like an oatmeal raisin cookie, like brown sugar caramel and cinnamon, rich and sweet and, wow, I want ten more.

Rick, Amber, and I dance and I watch and follow the man dancing a half-dozen feet away as the music changes, the DJ blending two songs with samples and, in time, while Donna Summers feels love, the dancer looks at me. He's muscular, defined abs and pecs, a rower's arms and torso, black jeans and a white belt lead to a – massive – crotch bulge and strong thighs that press the jeans' seams flat. His chest, back, and face, waxed or shaved hairless, shine and glimmer with sweat beads and streaks; he reflects the colored lights like a disco ball. His face looks like it was formed in clay, baked hard and defined, and given life underneath short dusty-blonde hair styled in spikes. When he makes eye contact with me, I already feel myself faltering in my dancing; I swallow. He notices and looks me up and down, takes in my black slacks and tucked in white t-shirt. Do his eyebrows raise as he looks away? Maybe?

Amber and Rick dance as she was with me, mostly in place and close, Rick's arms over Amber's shoulders and wrist-crossed behind her neck. As the next song changes, I feel a tap on my shoulder. It's him, gently rocking his hips and shoulders at me. He raises his eyebrows shortly, leans in close, "Tyler," washes across my ear and then face with warmth and the gentle softness of a midnight promise smelling of rum and citrus. I have no idea what to do, so I look at Rick. He looks at me and gives me a thumbs up, gestures a waving motion at Tyler. I lean in to Tyler, "Merak?"

Tyler puts his arms over my shoulders and presses his torso close to me, his ab sweat darkens my shirt. We dance for some songs, me casting furtive glances at Rick who really needs to help me out here. Rick watches me over Amber's shoulder, leans in from time to time to say something in her ear. Sometimes she shakes her head, another she throws it back laughing. These assholes.

The music transitions to something steady, clicks and pops, backbeats and rhythm, Tyler and his bulge on mine and oh my God my bulge is growing. I swallow and Tyler puts his chin on my shoulder. I turn my mouth to his ear. "I really hope you're using me to get to my friend," I point at Rick.

Tyler steps back, looks at me, at Rick, at my face, at my very obvious-now bulge, and just shakes his head while he points at me.

Fuuuuuuuuuuuuuuuuuuuuuuuuuuuuuuuuuuuuuuuuuuuuck.

Tyler reaches down to my shirt and starts to untuck it. I hear – over this music – Rick and Amber laugh. Tyler pulls my shirt up and over my head and I am somehow powerless to stop him. He helicopters it over us and tosses it somewhere. He looks at my torso, pale and sweaty, ribs popping skin and no real muscle, chest hair forming a loose mash around my nipples and funneling down my center-belly and navel into my pants, and Tyler nods, lips pushed out and pressed in a purse. I keep dancing and I keep glancing at Rick and, as the song ends, he strolls over and steps in, letting me dance again with Amber, whose eyes go wide when she presses into me, feels my skin, and asks if I'm secretly gay myself.

Rick and Tyler both pat my shoulder, laughing, as they walk past, getting more drinks Rick shouts in my ear. More songs, lyrics I don't understand or that don't make sense, instrumentals, and though I only lived eight months in the seventies, I feel as though Amber and I escape this time, this turning of the millennia, and dance in an era of heavy muscle cars, bellbottoms, tight shirts, and long hair. For a moment, I am my father and Amber my mother and we live in the exuberant promise of earlier decades.

But where is Rick with those drinks? They're taking a while. Turning Amber so I can face the bar, Rick and Tyler stand with our drinks in their hands, Rick drinks his and leans against the bar facing me, talking to someone on his right. Long black and loose hair hangs around her head; she's thin but in that fit and toned way that comes from daily gym time, a dark-blue top and black pants, slight hips and a strong jogging-built butt. It all seems … familiar. Rick waves, says something while he points at me. She turns, hair spinning up and into a sickle shape as she moves. The crowd between us splits like the Red Sea, chasming a straight line from my eyes to her eyes. I can't see them well for the distance but I know her eyes, blue like a sapphire in an alpine lake. My right hand reflex-grabs my watch. Meggy. I say it, can't hear it over the music.

What are the chances. I know they're still friends, but why would Rick point me out to her and while Amber is here. Rick downs his drink and starts into a second. Maybe Amber is driving us home tonight.

Amber tugs on my shoulder, pulls me down to stoop ear-to-mouth, hand on cheek. "If you're tired, we can go."

I nod, slowly and in a short up and down. Meggy looks at me, Amber, me again, and then turns her whole body to face Rick.

"Bathroom first?"

The Engine Room has a large, unisex bathroom, no urinals just stalls, the walls and doors are black with white circles that pulse in colors in time with the dancefloor, though the music here is much quieter.

"Are you staying in here, too, Merak?"

"I'll meet you right outside in just a moment." I stand Amber in front of an empty stall and find another one a few doors down. The lock slides into place quietly and I sit on the toilet seat, not for need except to hide and curl into a ball so small I can flush myself into the sewers and escape.

In some moments I hear Amber's stall open and she walks cautiously to the sinks, her cane on the floor, the near-vertical way she does it in crowded spaces. I'll need to leave soon.

Voice, soft and a slight nasal sharpness, long vowels, a word-pace like caressing hands in a slow massage. "Are you Merak's girlfriend, Amber?"

I sit up and rabid wolves inside my chest tear my organs apart.

Pause and quiet, sink water runs, soap dispenser. "I am. To whom do I have the pleasure?" Amber's hands rub together soapy under running water.

"My name is Meggy."

The water stops. Amber's voice sounds different; she must have turned, faced "Meggy?" Amber asks, pauses for some seconds, silent. "Did you just nod?"

"Yes." Meggy is quiet, perhaps confused.

"Nodding doesn't do me any good." Amber's words are short and finish sharply. She rinses her hands in the sink and a small motor whirs out some paper towels.

"I, well, I don't mean to be forward. I'm sorry to make you uncomfortable. I hope he's doing better and I just saw you here and wanted to … I don't know why I came in here. I hope he treats you like he did me."

The music softly backgrounds the conversation, quiet thumps in time with the lighted stalls. My forehead rests against my fingertips as Meggy opens her purse and her lipstick cap clicks off.

"Can I ask you something, Meggy?"

"Of course."

Amber pauses, starts with "Mer-," falters a moment. "Why are you at a gay club?"

289

Meggy laughs, her voice faster, slightly deeper, the nasality and long vowels of insecurity replaced with a still-alto-soprano but rounder, calmer tone. "The boys don't hit on me and the girls know I play for the other team. I can dance, get very good drinks, and not be hit on all night. Regular bars are awful for girls like us."

The two stand a moment. Water and a paper towel again, closer to Meggy. She'll be dabbing her lips.

"Like us?"

"Pretty," Meggy says. "It was good to meet you, Amber."

"Before you leave, Meggy, what did you like about him the most?"

"Oh God, I really just wanted to see Rick tonight… why do you ask?" After a pause, I assume Amber shrugs, "fourth date, we met for a late brunch and I suggested Mary Anne's. Know it? I figured. After, he's walking me back to my dorm, and he asked if he could take my photo that evening."

"He likes that."

"Yup. Immediately, I figured I had made a mistake. Photographers are too often creeps. My mom, she wanted me to model, started me in kids catalogs; seven, I think I was. Thirteen years of modeling later and every single photographer who had ever photographed me wanted me as a thing to make clothes, a necklace, watch, whatever look better. I was never photographed, just the stuff I wore. And some of them, the way they talk to us, it's so, so gross. I asked him what he wanted me to wear, but I figured that I'd just blow him off and ignore his calls after that. Merak," Meggy says my name a bit slowly and pauses; as she does my chest tightens, did she see my shoes under the stall, or do I just miss hearing her say my name, "Merak says, 'I don't care. I want to photograph you. I want a photo that shows who you are, and I might not even be able to do that today, but I'd like to try,' and no one had ever said that to me. I grew up a mannequin with a pulse."

"He likes to try and photograph people, even me, even though I can't really enjoy the photos. Did any of his photos, um, did they do that?"

"Capture me? A bunch, yeah. I remember one where I was sleeping in Federico's front seat, hair a mess, bare feet pressed into the inside of the windshield, bit of drool from the corner of my mouth. It won't ever be in my headshot book, but it's in my college album. That photo reminds me I'm not just a pretty thing to play photo dress-up. He did a series where I was drinking a chocolate shake and by photo, I don't know, ten maybe, I was so over it that I pulled the straw out of the shake and flicked some at his camera. That whole series was great, you can just see my expression go from playful to kind of exacerbated. Look, you know we loved each other. Would it help you to know the moment I knew?" Meggy, after a pause long enough for a nod, "I woke up in his bed at, I don't know, eight one morning and he's just looking at my face. It was weird. And I recoiled and asked what he was doing and he just says 'counting the freckles on your nose and cheeks and thinking of how you wouldn't be the same person without them. There's more of them on the right side. I was just thinking how that's great because it beautiful and imperfect. You'd be very boring to photograph if you were perfect.' He was focused on me. I'd never had that. I'd dated a number of guys and all they really wanted was to bang a hot chick, show off a model around their arms. Merak, well, he wanted to bang me. Anything else you'd like to know? Within reason."

"Lots, but maybe another time. I'd like to know why he broke up with you, and..."

After a pause, "And?'"

"And nothing. I didn't have another thing."

Meggy sets her purse on the counter, must lean against it, too, and shift some. "You get right to it, don't you? He likes that about you. But why ask me? Oh, you want to fact-check what he said. Whatever he told me when he dumped me, I never bought it. I don't remember it, even. Some bullshit. I think he got scared; what I mean is that he was scared by his own feelings." Meggy exhales and Amber breathes deeply. "His folks weren't such a good example for him and I think that sits stuck in his mind like a bee stinger you can't reach on your back," Meggy's purse slides off the counter and lightly slaps her leg. "I enjoyed meeting you, Amber, if we run into each other again, I'd like to say hi, if that's okay."

"It is. I would like that. Thank you," Amber says, her voice quiet, forced outward like the last air from a deflating balloon.

Meggy strides confident and long and she will be outside in a few steps.

"Merak," Amber says, "still loves you. It's … been a really hard thing for me. And what I wanted to ask was if you still love him, too."

Meggy takes a few steps back to Amber, these short and careful. "It's been almost as long now as we dated, so he's not on my mind every day, no. Some people, they stay in our lives even after they leave. Do I love him still?" Meggy pauses and I hear her breathe in and out deeply a few times. "He was the first, still only, boy that I have wanted to marry," Meggy's feet turn and she takes a step before stopping, her voice quieter and pointed away from Amber, "and I think I will always measure other boys against him." Meggy's strides track quickly to the door and, some seconds later, Amber follows her path, cane sliding with quiet 'sssstushes' back and forth on the floor.

When the door closes, I follow briskly, find Amber, and put my hand on her shoulder. Amber puts her hand on mine and, if I didn't know what had just happened, I'd worry about her expression, flat and resigned, yet somehow calmer than I've seen it before. Amber turns to face me, folds her cane, and traces her fingers between my ribs as she walks around behind me. I lead her to the bar where Rick hands us each a drink. I down it, motion to the bartender for another, down it, these things are good, settle up with a tip, and walk out of the club in time to see Meggy slide into a taxi and close the door behind her. Amber holds my sweaty, shirtless chest in one hand, grips my belt at the back of my pants with her other. Tyler and Rick stand next to us.

Tyler looks at Amber, "lucky," hands Rick a slip of paper, folded in half. Rick puts it in his back pocket and gives Tyler a hug.

"I'll see you next time I'm in town?" Rick asks.

"My number."

Rick blushes and tilts his head up at Tyler, who walks confidently up to him, grabs Rick's butt, lifts him to his tiptoes, and kisses him long on the lips. When they stop, Rick takes a moment to open his eyes and slide back to his heels. Rick waves at Tyler as he walks down the street.

I watch, aware now that I do not at all understand Rick's life outside of the terms we had defined until tonight. It makes me uncomfortable, both seeing this part of his life thrust into mine and knowing there's much of him I'm not ready to come to terms with, and my torso muscles twinge and gently spasm.

"Where's your shirt?" Rick asks.

"Tyler helicoptered it into the crowd. I just wish it wasn't so cold."

"Good to drive? I'm not so sure I can now."

"By the time we get back to the car..." I forgot about the car. We're parked at Veteran's Park. Dangit. We ambled around downtown Milwaukee so much that I don't know how far we have to walk.

In time and with alcohol-killing steps, stops at a small store for waters, and for Amber two bottles of sweet white wine to enjoy on the walk and then in the back seat, and with some getting lost in the city, we eventually make it back to Federico. I help Amber climb into the back seat, where she fades in and out of sleep as she drinks her second bottle of wine. When soft snoring comes from the back seat, Rick, no pause, "why were you in the women's bathroom with Amber?"

"There was only one bathroom."

"What? The men's was the other door."

"What other door?" Ugh. "Don't turn on the music, for a minute, please." Rick looks at me confused, I think, hard to tell in the darkness broken by the increasing then decreasing glow of overhead interstate streetlights. I need the quiet a moment. "Amber are you awake?" Nothing. I bring Rick up to speed on her and Meggy's conversation.

"I like you and Amber a lot, I mean love you really, as a couple. You're a good match. In a lot of ways, better than Meggy and you. But really for sure not in others."

"How so?"

"You and Amber, you're different than each other. This is you after your trip out west, you know, surrounding yourself with people different from you in significant ways. That was not you in high school. You before Colorado would still be with Meggy today. You guys worked and were good together, supported each other well and had common goals. I mean, come on, the photographer and the model? That was just a good start. Anyway, Amber and you are very different, but you seem to make it work well. But it is and will always be work."

"All relationships are work. It's work to have balance."

"It's never a perfect balance. Your and Amber's experiences and perceptions are just very different. Those things haven't clashed yet. That takes more than a year of knowing someone. You and Meggy, you came from very similar worlds, spoke the same social language, same expectations. Honestly, I don't even know why you guys broke up."

"I felt kind of trapped, like I was stuck in something I knew too well. I thought we'd become my folks."

"Relationships are like two different-size gears spinning together. Amber and Meggy, they're different gears, and you mesh with them differently. I think you and Meggy had some mis-aligned teeth. They'd have worked themselves out. You don't even know what misaligned teeth you and Amber have yet," Rick says and it sounds like an analogy I would make. "Look, I'm glad you have Amber, beyond glad. You have no idea how much I love her, too. She's great for you. Don't take anything I said otherwise, okay?"

"Did you know Meggy would be there tonight?"

"No. She knew you and I would be."

‹◊›

Home again, shortly before midnight, Rick and I help Amber to my room, and I make sure she sits on my bed and drinks a few glasses of water, leaning against me as she takes sips.

As Rick heads back out to meet friends, "hey, I owe you. I didn't even know it, but I needed tonight."

His eyes water at the sides. "Nah, man, you don't awe me anything. I promise."

Amber, finally finishing her third glass of water, flops on her back, "take me, Merak. Right now."

"Rick is still here."

"He can watch. It won't do anything for him because he's gay. I'm sorry, Rick, that was rude."

Rick at the door, eyes closed, turns his face to the bedroom floor. I shake my head slightly. Alcohol makes us who we are, clears away the mental filters we use to be polite and social. Rick looks back and me, gestures to the door, and steps out into the hallway.

"Let's get your pajamas on."

"No, take me."

I stand in front of her with my hands on my hips, holding her lightweight pajama bottoms and a night shirt in my right hand.

"Are you just standing there looking at me? I hate it when you do that."

At the bedside, I sit her up and help her with her shirt, boots, and jeans. "I need you, please, to help here a bit. Just sit a bit upright." She struggles a bit against her pajamas but, in a few moments, lets me put them on and I pull her up toward the pillow. I kiss her forehead and head to the door, planning to go get a sleeping bag and sleep on the floor here to keep an eye on her.

"Merak, tell me about Spitfire Orange."

My hand hovers over my door knob, fingers out like a catcher's mitt. How many hundreds or thousands of times have I grabbed this round, metal ball? How many click-lock twist-unlock repetitions have I given it as I beat patterns of child-terrible drum music into different parts of my door, embracing the hollow sounds and different musicalities the door produced when slapped strategically in different spots. In all those times, this is the first hesitation, the first unsureness, because I don't know. I don't know what orange is, besides my favorite color. I don't know how to describe it, nor where any of my other descriptions came from. I am afraid that I don't have anything. Maybe I gave all I had. Maybe that was all Amber loved and without it, I'm... what if I'm just a boring IT nerd who likes coffee and neatly-ordered wiring.

"Merak, if you left me here alone I'm going to dump you."

My head turns somewhat over my shoulder, moonlight sneaks past the sides of the blinds and dots the floor and walls, not in lines like the sunlight through Colander's trunk, just dots the shape of the blinds' edges. Light passes through the air to the bed and onto Amber's cheek and temple. "Can I think about it some until we head back to school?" Amber's snoring lets me know that will be okay.

In the hall, I close the door quietly. Rick stands in the hallway and though it's dark, just two plug-in lights to illuminate the floor, I know he's mad. I can't see enough of his face, but his jaw is set and his arms cross over his chest.

"That's just her drunk. That's not really her, right?"

"It's not her. You know that."

"That really hurt, the way she said that, dragging out the 'he's gay' like it's a crime."

"I know. I am sorry that she said that. I'll ask her to apologize."

"Don't," he holds his hand out. "She won't remember and it would embarrass her. Look, I'm used to it, just little small things that people say that, they usually don't realize, cut so, so deep." Rick looks at me, "everyone I know has done it at least a few times, but," he brings his hand up to his cheeks, left then right. "I'll be okay."

"Going back out?"

"Of course. I'll be back tomorrow. When will you need your car?"

"Whatever time the three of us go out for dinner."

Rick nods and walks down the hall, takes the stairs quiet but quick to the door. It shuts with a soft wood bump and the deadbolt clicks into place. My sleeping bag, used only once since I bought it two summers ago, is in the garage and, with it, I sneak back into my room, listen to Amber's soft and steady breaths, unroll the bag, grab a spare pillow, and sleep on the floor across the foot of my bed.

‹◊›

A soft knock on my bedroom door and hinges as it opens an inch wake me as my mother asks, "is everyone decent," tentative, her voice high-pitched and a bit thin, concerned she may witness something that will burn her eyes like bleach.

I sit up, look at Amber, under my blankets, and tell mom to come in. She looks at me with some confusion, then her head tilts back and, I imagine, the room must smell strongly of sweat and club smoke. With a long, deep groan I stretch my arms and legs out from me and bend my back forward. Last time I slept on the floor must have been that time in St. Louis with Meggy, Rick, and George at that hotel the night after Six Flags, so what's that, almost two years. My body feels as though I didn't sleep at all.

"We'll cook breakfast when you're both up," my mother says, walking backward out of the door and downstairs.

I open my bedroom windows for some air, climb in bed with Amber, and get a whiff of the smoke that lingers in her hair. Deciding this is not the morning for spooning, hip rubs, and a peck on the cheek wake up, I shake her shoulder slowly. Amber yawns, her mouth opening and closing dry like she's been sucking a paper towel.

"Are we at your place, Merak?"

"Yes."

"What happened?"

"We went dancing. We drank a bit much. You downed a bottle of wine on the walk back to car, most of another on the car ride home, all after a few cocktails and like four beers. What do you remember?"

"I remember grabbing your belt after I left the bathroom."

I'll take Rick at his word that he was past what she said very fast. I walk Amber to the shower, we strip each other and shower together, mostly so that I can help scrub her hair, wring it out, wash it three times with her, and then help with the soap, too, "many hands make light work, as they say," Amber points out.

Dressed and sitting behind English muffins, ramekins of fresh preserves, whipped butter, fresh fruit, and some scrambled eggs, Amber asks my mother about the church I was raised in, a question that warrants a placed-down fork, glances back and forth from my parents to Amber and I, and a pause.

"Totally common question down south, mom," I say, standing to get some of the pre-ground – shudder – coffee from the fridge to make something hot to coat my throat.

My mother explains that Amber is welcome to go to our church on Sunday, and that it's hard for her to find the words to explain it, but that experiencing it, that would be best. Amber agrees that she needs to experience what my younger life was like. I realize as I look at them talk, my mother laughing at an off-hand comment and putting her hand on Amber's, that shared experience builds relationships. So far, I have shared who I am with Amber, but only stories and anecdotes of how I got here. Amber, in inviting me to live her life alongside her, visit her home, Grandpa Arn, meet the people of her church who she would happily forget, she has opened up more to me than I to her. That took overcoming fear. Cowards, I reassure myself, never feel fear. This is my time to open up to her, and I am afraid.

13
Communion

Amber and I slide into Giorgio's back seat. When my father starts his car, air from the backseat's vents blows onto us. "Where's that air coming from?" Amber holds her left hand out to follow it. "Do you have vents in the back seat?"

"I do."

Amber looks at me, "you really hit the birth lottery."

"It's kind of neat, isn't it," my father looks in the rearview then puts his arm over my mother's seat, turning and backing into the street. He puts the car into drive and with the gas pedal punches us into our seats, eliciting a startled syllable from Amber.

Amber turns her head toward me, "now I know where you get that from." In the front rearview my father looks back at me, cheeks lifted and eyes squint, a happy, full-face smile and a thumbs up.

First Methodist of Deer Lake holds communion monthly and this happens to be that Sunday. Amber says she has never had a communion, that her church doesn't hold it, opting instead for the oil anointing.

"The what?" my father asks. "Like, with oil on the forehead?"

"Yes," I say.

"And altar calls?" he asks.

"The week I was there, yes," I answer.

"Do they handle snakes and swing from the rafters?"

"Richard," my mother scolds. "Apologize."

"Not the week Merak was there," Amber says, her hand in the vent air, fingers moving in it like they spin an imaginary coin. She turns her head slightly toward me and father's face reflects in her aviators as her left lip curls a little.

Communion

After a short drive through a few side streets and a short quest for a parking spot under a tree, Amber and I stand outside the large, white building, the sanctuary rated for more than 1,500 people, that near-fills four times a weekend.

Church dress was easy for me, a black suit, white shirt, and a red-black striped tie in my closet. Amber didn't bring any clothes that wouldn't draw attention at our church so my mother and she spent some time working to find a dress in the back of my mother's closet that could, with some strategic safety pins, fit without sagging. The dress, dark blue flirting with black, with a hidden zipper up the back, and gold, decorative-only buttons on the front and cuffs, fits Amber decently; being a bit more buxom than my mother, Amber fills the top more roundly. The neckline is lower than her flannels and the definition in her collar bones refuses to let my eyes go. Amber wears black cowboy boots, inlaid with horseshoes, in lieu of heels, because she's never walked in heels before, she explains. Mother says it will be fine and the look works well for her.

The church, like many others in the area, has a brick fascia and white doors, shutters, trim, steeple, and entry. "You're a back of the church family. Will everyone watch us walk up to the front for communion?"

"Not really, they'll be walking back to their seats or head-down in prayer. But you'll walk with me, I'll tell you when to put your hand on my shoulder, kneel next to me, and when you hear Reverend Beckett say, oh what are the exact words —"

My father turns around and looks from me to Amber, "for this is my body, eat of it, I think."

"It's in that vein," I say. "When he says that, hold out your hand and either he or I will place a small cube of bread in it. Then Reverend Tamerlin will come around with a large glass of grape juice, say the same thing but for blood and drinking, and I'll dunk your bread in the bowl, you'll open your mouth slightly when I pick it up, I'll put it in, and we'll stand and walk back to our seats via the outside of the sanctuary."

Amber nods.

"I brought you ear plugs. The organ is loud."

‹◊›

The organ is loud and low bass rumbles through our seats, vibrates the cushions and the hushed conversations that took place as congregants milled about on their way to their seats end before the third note. Bach's *Fantasia and Fugue in G Minor*, the bulletin indicates. Amber sits, tremors ripple up and down her torso like waves in a pool as the organist pushes keys and pedals, opens and closes the flaps that bring air to the pipes and send sound shockwaves to our ears. We four sit in the back pew, my father and I find the hymns for the day in our hymnals and, using the bulletin announcements as place markers, make it easy to flip right to them for the songs we will sing. When we finish, almost in unison, my father reaches to my mother to take her hand and I take Amber's hand and hold it on my leg.

The Sanctuary towers above us, necessarily high for the balcony seats above the narthex. The room, white with square patterns of pale blue framed in gold, adorn the wall and ceiling, designed by an acoustic engineer to meet the needs of the specific organ for which this room was designed and built. From the ceiling, six large chandeliers, mostly for decoration as their lights are dim and small, hang below the lighting workhorses, the many, many recessed halogen lamps. This room allows no shadows except under the pews and people. This cannot be an accident: the space, it casts away shadow, and so casts away sin; the light forces the room, and so also the congregants' souls, bare.

As the opening music plays, Reverends Drs. Beckett and Tamerlin, adorned in long white ministerial gowns with golden-brown trim up the center and around the neck, walk to the pulpits, one on each side of the sanctuary's main aisle. The pulpit on our left will be where the deacons, Mr. Buckner wearing a dark charcoal suit, and Mrs. Freeman, a pale-pink dress and a ring of red flowers in her hair, who walk down the main aisle now, will deliver the scripture readings. Walking in last, the choir, more than a hundred of the church's best singers, walks to the front in deep-red robes, split at the aisle's front, and walk around the pulpits to fill the choir boxes. The men sit on the left, women the right – bass to soprano.

Fantasia and Fugue continues for the whole piece, ending twelve minutes into service by my watch. Amber's hand squeezes mine and her face reflexes and spasms, her eyes blink to hold back some tears.

Mrs. Freeman steps to the right pulpit and welcomes us in opening prayer, her voice old and scratchy, scarred into the sound of a cheap coffee grinder by some decades of cigarettes. Mrs. Freeman is thin, bordering on frail, but when she begins the prayer, her voice finds purchase in her throat and, with calm confidence she leads us through one of the Methodist standards, and we bow our heads, ending with an "Amen." Mr. Buckner takes her place when she finishes and directs us to the first New Testament reading, his voice quiet and calm, round in the vowels and a deep baritone, First John 4, seven to thirteen, "Beloved, let us love one another for love is of God, and he who loves is born of God and knows God."

Mr. Buckner speaks and I turn to Amber, put my second hand on hers, and she leans her head slowly to me and onto my shoulder. My father hands mother a handkerchief.

"… if we love one another, God abides in us and his love is perfected in us." Mr. Buckner stops and looks around. "I apologize, I meant seven through twelve." The congregation chuckles a low rumble across the room, he smiles, and sits. Service continues through hymns, some the choir alone sings, others for which we stand and sing, and in time Mrs. Freeman takes the pulpit, her voice again timid and unsteady.

"Our second reading from the New Testament today, and dears you'll have heard this one if you're married," the congregation's rumble-chuckle joins us again, "First Corinthians thirteen, four to eight." Mrs. Freeman, her voice now again calm, confident, and even, takes us briskly through the passage with "Love is patient and kind, Love is not jealous or boastful," and ends, her voice catching on the last words, with "Love hopes all things and Love endures all things." She looks out at the crowd and smiles across the congregation before walking back to her seat. Dr. Beckett takes the pulpit and welcomes us. I whisper to Amber that this is the sermon and she sits in her pew straight-backed.

Dr. Beckett stands tall, wide in front of the room. His hair, a crown of silver with loose and random strands on top, rests round on his head. His face, circular and clean, wraps his eyes and gray eyebrows in the weight of age that creeps in with the succeeding injuries that slow us and, over time, build our bodies into plumpness. His robe fits tight on his round belly.

Almost fourteen years ago the congregation called him to service; I was seven and his first sermon spoke of God's need for Satan and how good and evil are opposite sides of a coin, forever forced to be one but never able to look upon each other. With time, tragedy, and, in his words, thoughtful meditation on the words of the Bible and not the words of the pastors he formerly admired, he mellowed and his tone changed, calmer in message and welcoming. Dr. Beckett proves that when people change for the better it comes only from their own desire nudged by the actions or words of others. His voice remains untouched by age and when he speaks he sounds like the largest and widest of the organ's pipes and his voice, too, sends sound and shockwaves through the room that jolt Amber with such force our pew-neighbors look at us with concern.

"Jesus said 'Ask and it will be given to you; seek and you will find; knock and it will be opened to you. For everyone who asks receives, and he who seeks finds, and to him who knocks it will be opened. Jesus," Dr. Beckett bellows, almost not needing his microphone, "preaches to us about seeking God and love. But where? Where is God? In whited spaces like these? God is not, to paraphrase my favorite apocrypha, in the buildings of man. Now to go fully off the farm," Dr. Beckett says calmly, "in The Gospel of Thomas, Jesus says that the Kingdom of God is within you and around you." He pauses and scans the crowd, some shuffle in their seats, shocked that a gospel they have never read was just cited, uncomfortable in this new experience. I suspect, though, many of the people around us should shift like this each time a passage is read. "How amazing and wonderful a thought, that the Kingdom of God is within you, that you need only you to commune with God, to know His Love. I guarantee that passage scared the pants off the early Christian church. It scares the pants of the modern church. Jesus himself tells us that we don't need religion, and how is that for a communion Sunday message?" The congregation laughs.

Amber fidgets and moves her hand back and forth on my leg, feeling the crease in my suit pants, then fiddling with my coat's surgeon buttons, undoing and redoing them.

Reverend Beckett continues in his sermon, a bit meandering and at times feeling lost, hammering and repeating that God lives in the love shared between people and reinforcing the earlier scriptures that no one need any intermediary. In time he comes to rest on the earlier First Corinthians, tells us that when we love we invite God into our lives, to commune with Him, and that, for him, the easiest way to do that is to hang his life on the Biblical quotes of Christ, to focus his study on those, and to live in the way that those quotes direct. Dr. Beckett's sermon ends with an amen, invitation to communion, and the organ playing a slow and soulful rendition of Brahms *Mein Jesu, Der Du Mich* followed by *Herzleibster Jesu* and, when Amber and I finally arrive at the front, we are in the final minute of *Herzlich Tut Mich Verlanger*. Amber kneels with me, and Dr. Beckett places the bread in her palm and says, "Jesus said 'take this for it is my body which I give for you'." And beside him Dr. Tamerlin speaks, "Jesus said 'drink from this, my blood of the new covenant,' please, dunk your bread." Amber picks up her cube and lifts it. Dr. Tamerlin sets the cup below it, "when you are ready." Amber dunks the bread, places it in her mouth, and I repeat the sacrament. Amber places her hand on my shoulder and I stand with her, my hand on her lower back. She walks this way with me around the front of the church and the far side of the pews back to our row. No one stares; we are anonymous.

‹◊›

At home again, mother and father change for a Sunday afternoon brunch with old friends, hug Amber and I long and tight. My mother holds Amber's shoulders, "not to presume anything, but I am glad I met you, and Merak is much different since he met you." Amber, flush red and twisting her boot's toe on the floor, thanks my mother. My father hugs her, too, shakes my hand and says he's proud of me. They wave themselves out the door, will see us at graduation, and remind me to drive safely.

"Let's go get you out of this old dress."

"Thank you, it's very scratchy."

I help Amber with the safety pins and the dress hangs loose around her. She massages her breasts and says she's glad they're not being pressed any more. She turns away from me, my cue to unzip the dress, and she lets it fall around her to the floor. She's wearing a comfortable bra and a cute, off-white pair of boy-cut underwear. She turns, puts her hand out and slides it down my chest.

"This is my parent's room."

"Then take me to your room. We made love on my childhood bed. We're going to do it on yours."

"Rick will be home any minute."

"Then you'd best not dawdle."

In my room, Amber takes off and drops her underwear on the floor. She takes off my clothes next and pushes me back in bed. After some minutes of hands and movement, curves and kissing, teeth and

306

earlobes, and a mild yank on her hair, she pushes my shoulders into the mattress, my head hanging back over the edge facing the window, legs toward the door. Amber reaches her hand between my legs and as her last finger curls I hear, too late, two footsteps and Rick turns brisky through my open door.

"God – Fuck – Balls" he shouts and walks out of the room, "at least shut the door and hang her bra on it, Merak," he yells, his voice echoing off the far walls before reaching us. He will be halfway down the hall and facing away from us, arms crossed.

Amber apologizes profusely and shuts the door. We dress, I hold her cheeks in my hands, kiss her long on the lips and she starts to laugh, and so do I.

"Nothing he hasn't seen before anyway," I add.

"Glad this is funny to someone," Rick says, door-muffled voice turning from agitated to a near-laugh, "because it doesn't do anything for me."

"What's he talking about?" Amber asks.

"I'll tell you later."

‹◊›

Rick loads Amber's and my rucksack and duffle into Federico's hatch. I give a fake wave and goodbye inside the door, as I explain later to Amber, just in case there are burglars around.

"Wait, isn't this a safe neighborhood. Isn't this early afternoon?"

"Oh, it is," Rick says. "This is suburban upper-middleclass folk, always worried that people want to break into their homes. So if you're leaving the house empty, it's especially important to make it sound like there are other people there."

"Is that why so many people here give their dogs people names?"

"Bingo," Rick says, pointing at Amber.

"Do your parents have a dog with a person name, Rick?"

"Rick comes from a different kind of rich. We're just affluent."

"What kind of Rich are you from, Rick?"

"The kind with a gated entrance, twenty-four hour attendant, and private police force," Rick says, looking back at our house. "I prefer affluent. Actually, I prefer less than affluent. There's less time spent making other people happy. Anyway, navigator picks the music," Rick says, paging through the CD case.

South of Chicago I run through a catalog of ideas that I had about orange for Amber. I play over some ideas I worked up the last few days but they all sound trite, and I drop them from my mind, full erasure, not worth keeping. Maybe she'll forget, and she does, until Champaign when Rick makes a comment about blue and orange team colors.

"Oh, Merak, that reminds me," Amber says from the backseat, as I look at Rick and curl my lips downward with excessive melodrama, "orange?"

Rick looks at me. "It's an honor to be here for this," and he turns down the music to near-mute.

I swallow and sip from a bottled coffee in my cup holder. Alright. "In our parents' eyes, and in those with which we will look back on our own lives one day, the years in which we know well enough to love our parents without pretense pass with the speed of a dragonfly's wingbeat. We move with neither warning nor time from that child to an angry, young version of the worst person we could become. And that period lingers like the stink of old chicken in a bagless garbage can, even when we start the slow and hard work to realize the best we have to offer others. In time, our parents learn to recognize us as adults, to treat us as equals, and let go of the parental superiority that defined the relationship till then. The first moment a parent treats their child as an adult gives us permission to find and become the best versions of ourselves. That numen sits our whole lives on our shoulders, like the toddlers we will one day ourselves carry above crowds while they love us without condition until the cycle repeats. We want it, that desire to be better, above us, aiming ahead of us, guiding us over the muck and the turmoil, froth and conflict of today to keep us tracking toward our best self, like the sun tracks in a lightly cloudy sky, warming our faces and bodies between moments of cool and shadow. Small steps broken up by large moments, the steady work to become better, both conscious and not, that is orange. It's my favorite color because it is the warmth of family laughter, the smell of cooking food on a holiday, the feel of our childhood bed on our back, and old photos of our parents seen for the first time in decades when we recognize in their faces, younger in those photos than we are looking at them, a reflection of ourselves and their hope that we would be better than them."

Rick looks somewhat away, his lips tightly pressed, curled back and between his teeth. His lower jaw twitches like a sewing machine needle. Amber faces the back of Rick's seat, fiddles with an empty pop bottle in her fingers. We sit shrouded in the sound of rubber on pavement, the muffle of the behind-truck air pocket, passenger-side tire whine bouncing back from a Jersey wall, soft engine whirring, and the faint bass line of whatever CD Rick had picked last. I let the quiet and white noise linger and I embrace it. This moment could not have been possible, I would have said, just a year ago. The silence, though, is not the silence of appreciation, but the silence of anger or jealously, and I realize that maybe some trite things about morning tea and drinks with friends may have been better.

"I owe you both an apology."

Rick nods. Amber sits motionless.

"This was a hard week for me. And I didn't think, at all, that it would be hard, or harder, for both of you. And I just rattled what was on my mind. I should have thought more about how you would hear it."

"It's okay," Amber says. "I got those moments from Grandpa Arn and Grandma Helen. I wish I could have had my folks for them, though."

"Rick?"

"Just don't talk to me right now, please." Rick faces away from me, looking out the window at the sprouting corn stalks.

I nod. And drive in quiet for minutes, past three exits before Rick speaks. "You got to see an old, rusty car, Merak. I got to spend the last week reminded that I'm not welcome at my childhood home and that my dad will never treat me like an adult. So thank you."

‹◊›

In Effingham, after more than an hour of car-silence, more than an hour of tire whine and wind noise and truck engines, I realize that words spoken carelessly arrive with the tact of a hurricane. And like a hurricane, our words can leave in their wake a swath of unrecognizable and hurriedly-destroyed piles. With my apology and a responding slight nod reflected in the passenger's window, we stop for dinner at a small burger joint, Griddlesticks, that George and I found on accident a year ago. Since then, it has become a standard stop on the way to school. The diner is older, built in the austere style of dustbowl-era buildings with few windows, floors that creak now, walls paneled over in wood maybe thirty years ago and due for a retrofit again someday far from soon, some taxidermy trophy heads of deer, full-bodied pheasant and fish, and some random antlers around the seating area. The bar's centerpiece, a coin-op pool table, re-felted since the last time we were here, almost always has locals playing a friendly, or not-friendly, game. Griddlesticks is the noise of conversation, the pause when newcomers arrive, clacking of pool balls, glasses and plates on trays, mugs set down too hard on tables, and old wood floors worn with smooth gullies from many decades' feet.

This is the sort of diner where it's easy to feel like an outsider, where the locals and regulars watch people who look city, who talk city, who drive city cars and wear city clothes enter and, throughout their meals, cast us furtive glances that let city know rural waits to be left alone again. This, however, never bothers me, as I think of it not being fear or apprehension but instead curiosity. I imagine they have, for me, the same curiosity I have for them, the nature of their lives outside this one chance meeting. Do they go home to a nice, large home or a failing old trailer and endless calls from medical debt collectors? Are they driving the reliable seventies pickup they got after high school and have since put two new engines and three new transmissions into, or are they the person who double-parked their shiny white 2001 F-350 with the dualies in the handicapped spot by the front door? I wonder what work the men and women in these diners do. I assume, and I know the unfairness here, though also the likely accuracy, that they own or labor on farms, work the railroad, or pull overnights at the abattoir.

One woman in scrubs, a phlebotomist badge from the local plasma donation place, sports-car-red hair, brown and gray roots inching out from her scalp like thousands of witches fingers, her place setting a house salad of fresh veggies and ranch dressing next to a steaming cup of coffee, sits next to an ash tray, ashes and two old butts, not hers. She glances at them every few minutes, maybe a desire. No, she looks, her eyes linger a bit, trace them up and down. She puts her hand on the table between her plate and the ash tray. She fights this, an addict who has quit and will struggle for the rest of her life. I imagine she's trying to rewire her brain, to associate her desire to smoke with a desire to eat salad instead.

Rick and I stopped there, the plasma place, two years ago on a spring break drive home to Chicago. We had no cash and we sold our plasma for twenty dollars each, enough to get us gas and road snacks. It took a long time and the phlebotomists ignored us. I imagine that job, seeing the same people selling plasma each month, dots of plasma-needle scars growing on their arms like Christmas lights on an ever-longer string, would drive someone to smoke.

At the bar, a man with dark hair, slicked back, a large, brimmed straw hat on the bar next to him, a blue work shirt and jeans with his name – Chester – and the logo of the local semitruck repair garage on the lapel, heavy leather boots, hands perma-dirty from converting time and strength into a living, watches Rick, specifically Rick, intently, breaking only when my eyes start to wander toward him. His look doesn't tell much, maybe he thinks Rick is pretty, or my boyfriend, and maybe he hates gays, or is gay. Does he fantasize about taking Rick into the filthy men's room or to his pickup truck cab? And if so, what does he want to do when they get there? With time and enough glances from me he pulls a magazine from under his hat and reads as he eats a chicken sandwich and tater tots.

Amber and I go over the menu; first I read the types of food and she narrows it down, next the names, finally a few descriptions and she settles on a ham and egg grilled cheese with tater tots and a pop, I the same. Rick, feeling a bit better, elects for their breakfast-all-day eggs, sausage, and English muffin. I excuse myself to the bathroom, stand next to Rick, we exchange a smile, and he doesn't flinch when I put my hand on his shoulder. Walking back, I hear he and Amber talking, his back toward me, and Amber says "it's not really that. I guess I like the poetry of it all, maybe?"

"But you're interested in what a color is?"

"What, oh gosh no. The world of the sighted doesn't mean anything to me. It's built around something I won't know. Imagine if, like, I don't know, some bird tried to tell you what it was like to have a magnetic compass in your brain so you could fly south every year. And how south is just an innate sense, or something. You don't have that now. Would you care?"

"I guess not. I don't really feel like I'm missing anything by not having it, either."

Communion

"And neither do I." Amber reaches forward and holds her pop glass, finds the straw with her left hand and guides it through the too-much ice to the glass's front. She lifts it up and takes a long sip. "It's not what a color is that I care about. When he describes them, it's him. I get to know more about him. He has been to see Grandpa Arn more than any other boy I've dated, and he always volunteers for work at the farm. That's something else no other boy ever did. And he is always early to take notes at class, never misses a single point, and they are so, so good. But more than that, he puts work and thought into these things, well most of them. And, well, outside of family, whenever people put work into me, it's 'cause they were paid to, like special ed teachers and tutors or whatever. It's rare that someone puts in the work for someone else."

For a moment, maybe a partial second or maybe long enough for our orders to be prepared, I don't know, this feels like a kidney punch. Why would I go to this effort if it isn't even something she's interested in. Quickly, though, I realize that, yes, this is her way to find out if I really am dedicated to trying to make our life together one that we can both access. She needs this to know that I'm not just a guy dating a tactile blind girl. She stays leaned forward in her seat a bit, facing Rick, and I wonder if she will ever trust that I love her and, if so, what would she do? I need this; she does not; if she ever fully trusts my motivations, Amber will stop asking me to describe colors, and I do not want that. Realization dizziness rolls through my head like a runaway truck: Amber is more important in my life than I am in hers.

"He can be kinda self-focused, I guess, not always thinking about some of the things he does and how they affect others, until it's too late," Rick says.

"But we all can be. And it's not common from him for that to hurt, and certainly not intended."

Rick concurs, "it's not."

"Merak," Amber says, "is a bullet ricocheting off the water. He's going to hit something sooner or later without even meaning to, and whenever that happens, it changes someone around him."

"You make that sound so bad."

"I just don't have a better analogy."

Rick shifts his legs, spreads his knees and sits back an inch before he leans back in. "To your second question, he was not like this with Meggy. That's not fair." Pause. "He was him. She would have said similar things. In high school, he was at ease with people like him. Then he went out west and now he is at ease with people different than him. Meggy and he have very similar backgrounds and interests. I think she wasn't the right kind of challenge."

I take a couple loud steps forward, afraid Rick will glance backward and see that I overheard them, and when I sit, "did I miss anything exciting?"

"I promise you, Merak," Amber says sipping her pop, "we did not talk about anything exciting," she says with a slight smirk that says she knows, from how short a distance I walked just now, that I must have overheard a lot.

We sit in silence a moment as kitchen smells of bacon, eggs, waffles, burgers, and chicken-fried steak weave through the dining area's air currents like a shuttle through a loom. The tapestry of food smells leads our stomachs to growl, noses to twitch, and, for Rick at least, his eyes to close as he inhales a particularly strong apple pie scent as a waitress carries a warmed slice past.

"So, how about God," Amber says, Rick and I turning to face her.

"What?" we say, almost together.

"Merak, we've been to each other's churches. It's time to talk the God talk. I should have asked this months ago, instead of assuming, but do you believe in God?"

My face turns and I look at Rick, who leans back in his chair, eyes wide and looking around the restaurant.

"Did I say something wrong?"

"No," I assure Amber. "We're just caught off-guard. But, like, how do you mean?"

"There's a yes or a no, either you do or don't."

"What," I ask, "if I genuinely don't know?" At this Rick looks my direction.

"Binary choice," Amber says. "Force a decision."

Belief lives in the poorly defined gaps within certainty, like water between rocks. But certainty, it's an obvious illusion our minds give us. Am I any more certain, I mean can I honestly prove without doubt, that the wood beneath my feet exists, and isn't just a brain-death fantasy? Certainty is, in many important ways, a belief we profess or share in a communion of observation-belief with others. Belief, though, has a strength that certainty lacks: choice. We believe because we choose to do so and that belief can change. Belief, at its core, remains mutable and malleable from our first inkling to the instant its fire fades from our minds. Certainty lacks that strength. No one questions if a rock is gray or red, round or flat, jagged or smooth because of course it is. "When I feel love for someone else, I feel as though something greater than us exists. Right now, I feel that with us three. Is that God? Sure let's call it that name – binary choice. Can I tell you with certainty what the nature of that beyond us is? No. I choose to believe it is good and loves us and is nothing less miraculous than the sentient embodiment of Love. And I don't think that just right now because that was what the sermon this morning was about." I cannot say for sure, but I think it would be sad if that doesn't exist and that, someday, all the best of us simply depart into a mist of legend and story, never to enrich the lives of others again.

Rick looks at his glass of pop, his lips pursed. Amber, head angled so she faces the ceiling, right ear toward me, listens intently, nods.

"I mean, that's just empirically and verifiably wrong," Rick says. "I'll spare you all the standard 'sick kids with cancer' and 'people are wantonly cruel so what kind of God do we worship if we're His image' arguments. No, it's quite simple, there is not because reality does not need anything beyond it. I can't see my way to a world where God is anything but a construct ancient people used to keep the problematic in line or explain the mysteries science has since unraveled. Good people exist because good doesn't need an outside force to make it so, and I argue good with an outside force is in fact not goodness at all. And we're probably all familiar with that argument."

As Rick finishes, two waitresses set our meals at our seats, ask if we need anything else, refill our pops from a pitcher, and head away. I look at Amber. "Your turn?"

"To eat? I concur," she says, feeling around her plate with gentle fingertips to find her sandwich and tot placement. When I press, she starts eating a tot, "can't hear you, eating a tot," Amber mumbles through part-chewed tot.

"Amber," this is me, calm, monotone.

She sighs. "If we had discussed this last night, the answer would have been different." She points to a tot. "But right now, tots."

14
Black

Amber holds my hand, almost pulls me, toward the carnival ticketing booth. The ground is soft, Mid-April-rain damp soil, pitted and uneven, and she seems more at home walking on it than she does in slippers in her dorm room, her feet tracking the known soil squish, uneven pits and pocks, and the textures that mimic so closely that of her own farm's pastures. Her face, alight like an excited child, "we're gonna ride the rides and play the games and eat corn dogs and funnel cakes and those caramel popcorn balls and the huge rock candy and deep-fried twinkies and –"

"I can't eat that much."

Amber points her face in my direction and her mouth spreads wide open in a happy grin. "I'll have your scraps." We buy the entry tickets and a number of ride tokens, too. Each ride requires a different number of tokens, which are just paper raffle tickets, to ride. The games and food stands just take cash. Most games are a dollar for some number of attempts at a thing, five for a bargain number of attempts, and my wallet is bursting with singles and fives. "This was always my favorite time of year," Amber says. "Spring Fair, seeing friends, sneaking away from the adults, even though I'm sure they let us get away from them, so we could go split a cheap beer – there's always some carnie who sells a beer to the kids – behind a ride. That was the best of being a kid."

"Do they have the same rides every year?"

"Oh yes. It used to be the same company but this year it's a new one, I guess. Walk me around and tell me what they have."

The eye-catching rides, a small roller coaster with steeply-banked curves called Static Shock, a drop-tower called Doom Pole, and a tall U-shaped roller coaster named Fighting Falcon where the train shoots up

and down vertical track, all have long queues. Behind these rides a long
stretch of game booths attract families and couples to toss rings, baseballs,
and water balloons; squirt water guns and fire BB guns; and use small
pumps to hand-inflate balloons until they burst. Each game has a caller
who wades into the crowd to attract cash-carrying players when the game
slows. The callers all wear ordinary clothes and some of them play the
slow games when people approach and ham up how much fun they have,
"win" big prizes that they carry around for a bit and then return. This
tricks a number of people. Behind the games, another row of rides, less-
exciting, attracts a smaller crowd. A pirate ship named Matey's Revenge
that swings back and forth and eventually upside-down, an elevated swing
ride called Hang-glider that lifts people up in swings affixed to chains as it
spins, and lastly Whirligig, a large black cylinder with a red glow coming
from the top.

Whirligig ends with a door that a carnie opens and the line-
waiters, eager for their turn, fidget as the last riders slowly exit. The ride is
a cylinder within a cylinder. The outer looks like a cauldron and the inner
is the one that actually spins. Inside the cylinder, blue pads line the walls,
each with the outline of a person standing upright, arms against the pads,
legs slightly spread. People file in and stand up against the pads as shown.
The door closes and the ride starts spinning. It begins slowly, a diesel
motor powering up, a chain drive clicking like a bicycle changing gears on
a hard uphill. The motor revs steadily faster and the chain clicks steadily
faster and the bucket spins steadily faster. When the bucket reaches a
speed and stays there, it starts to lift. As it does, a white blur around the
middle of the bucket, a white blur that had been covered by the ride's
shape before, rises above the walls in which the bucket rests. Finally
above the ride's protective walls, strobe lights flash on the white blur and
it turns into an animation of satyrs with spears dancing in a repeated
pattern. The strobes stop and the bucket tilts; the people inside, plastered
against the padded walls, tilt from being rotated vertically to what looks
horizontal. This lasts around twenty seconds and then the ride tilts back

to vertical, lowers back into the protective walls, and slows. The riders get out and, with the help of handrails, stumble to some seats near the ride.

"Same rides and games, just different names," Amber says. "That's curious."

"Want to ride anything?"

"Grandpa Arn never let me ride this one, which used to be called Dizzy Spell. Let's ride it."

Crap. The one ride I did not want to go near. "It looks scary."

"Oh, are you scared?" Amber rotates her face in my direction, chin brushing my arm. "Double…"

"Nope."

"Dog…"

"Quit it right now."

"Dare…"

"Do not even finish this."

"You."

I sigh. This rule dates back to childhood: "I can't walk away from a double-dog dare."

"Alright, yeah, let's do it." Amber claps and hoots, jumps in place a few times.

We wait in line for one more cycle of the ride but we're going to be first on the next ride. I tear off two ride tickets and hand them to a short, squat carnie who's more than a handful of years my senior, judging by the few gray hairs at his temples, and the sun-seared lines and wrinkles on his face. He wears a tight shirt and jeans and his muscles show through in strong relief. He smells of cheap, stale cigarettes and truck stop bathroom coin-op sprayer cologne. He lets us on with a smile and I guide Amber to two padded sections. We stand up against them as shown. I help guide Amber's arms and legs in place, and glance up to see her grin and blush as I do. Not enough people are in line to fill the ride so the carnie takes the last spot. Another carnie takes over the controls, much younger, maybe my age, and he operates the buttons and levers with precision all while scanning the riders pressed against the cushions. I look across the bucket at the far wall and notice that the pads do not go to the top, stopping at worn traction tape.

The ride begins to spin, slowly at first, steadily faster, steadily faster. I feel the rotational force fight with inertia and the padded walls as I'm pushed into the pads, my back flat and I work hard to slide my hand over to Amber to grab her hand. She squeezes it and shouts something about fun, a sentiment I don't share. We're going fast enough now that turning my head to face Amber rotation-pastes it into the pad. I can see she's shouting in excitement; diesel motor and chain, in growing and fading doppler-sound, pulverize her shouts in a seemingly endless cycle. The ride lifts and strobe lights outside it flash and a bright red light shines inside, and then it starts to tilt. Tilting my eyes upward, the fairground before me turns quickly into night sky and then parking lot lights before repeating over and over. And I feel as though the ground and sky and universe far beyond us spin and I'm stationary. The effect is utterly nauseating and closing my eyes, somehow, makes it even worse. I feel a bulge try and build in the back of my throat so I open my eyes again and stare at the space between the people across from me, which helps. I hear Amber say my name, I think. I roll my eyes toward her and the color starts to leave her face, forehead-down.

"I don't like this anymore," she shouts. "I might get sick."

I'm in the splatter zone. "It'll be over soon," I say, squeezing her hand.

The ride starts to tilt back into place and as it descends I hear the operator's voice say "who wants a show?" The other riders cheer.

When we're back to level, the ride does not slow down, in fact it speeds up, motor and chain sounds grow and fade behind us filling our ears then leaving, disorienting and maniacal. The carnie who rode with us pushes himself over to face the pads. He starts doing pushups against the pads. The other riders shout a count as he does twelve pushups.

"What do you think? How was that?" the young carnie shouts into the microphone so loudly his voice breaks into static. The riders holler, except Amber, who asks me when it's going to stop, asks me to make it stop, says she's definitely going to be sick, her face also force-molded into the pads and pointed at me. "Who wants some more?" The riders again cheer.

The old carnie presses himself into a crawling position on the pad and crawls up the side. When he reaches the end of the pad he turns, puts his feet and then his hands on the traction tape and forces himself into a standing position, arms out like a tightrope walker feeling a new cable's harmonics. "Give it up!" shouts the other carnie over the speaker, and the riders cheer like mad, except Amber, whose cheeks bulge and, yes, she is definitely my chipmunk.

The carnie stands and starts walking around the spinning bucket on the traction tape. "That's our man, Luke Wallwalker, we call him. The amazing, gravity-defying, physics-embracing wall-walking wonder man!" The carnie over the loudspeaker delivers in a loud, but practiced and sterile voice. Luke walks around the top of the cylinder as it spins and looks down at everyone.

Amber's cheeks shrink, a swallow I think. She heaves. Luke walks around the top of the ride and makes eye contact with every rider, waving or pointing at them. When Luke looks at Amber his eyes get a bit wide and he gestures a cutting motion many times across his neck at the young carnie, kneels, and as the ride slows he slides down the wall between Amber and I, his knee pushing my hand away from Amber's. I let Amber know the ride is almost over, tell her the ticket man is here to help. He says he'll walk us off first. The ride slows and stops far more quickly than the times we watched it. Luke and I grab Amber as she falls forward and walk her to the door.

At the door, my brain spins inside my head, still trapped in the ride's momentum, "I'm gonna fall, Luke," and I do, in the mud at the bottom of the exit ramp. Luke takes Amber and walk-drags her to a seat behind the ride, and I hear him say he'll be right back. I get to my knees and crawl around the ride, Luke walking next to me. "There's a trashcan on your right, metal with a lid."

Amber's hand finds it, flips the lid like a tiddlywink, and she throws up into the trashcan.

As we sit next to Luke, other riders walk-stumble-handrail-lean down the ramp. Some fall past the mud and into the grass laughing, others waddle away fighting dizziness like a skydiver fights gravity. Amber throws up into the trashcan again. The last of the riders exit and another, but smaller, crowd hands tickets to Luke, who follows them into the bucket.

The young carnie walks around to us. "You okay?" Amber gives him the thumbs up as she tries to puke again. "I'll hang out here for a bit and make sure."

"Thanks for cutting that ride short. You probably saved me from…" I gesture my arms in mirrored circles at the trashcan.

"My name's Zach. Did you like the act?"

Amber gives a thumbs up and I admit I did find it amazing.

"One of the guys who used to work for us, he could – shit you not – do a handstand while that thing spun. He had been an acrobat in some Russian circus." Zach looks at Amber and sees that while she's probably done puking she's still not feeling well. "Let's move behind one of the game booths. It's a bit quieter she won't be able to see the ride from there."

"I promise that's not my problem."

I point to my eyes and shake my head. Zach looks at Amber curious then back at me, a moment passes until he understands, and he nods.

"Quit gesturing at each other," Amber says, pushing herself away from the trashcan. Amber puts her hand on my shoulder and we stand and follow Zach to a bench behind a game where a caller guesses peoples' weight. While Amber takes deep breaths and pulls some gum from her pocket, I listen to the game. The caller, a young girl with bright blonde hair in pigtails and a denim jacket, guesses a weight, the person stands on the scale, and they get a prize based on how far off the caller is. Everyone wins because the prizes start at spot-on, get better the more the caller is wrong. As the caller names weights and gives out prizes: pattern. She groups people into four general camps, like rows and columns on a table, thin and fat, man and woman. She is well under with the women, the thinner ones by almost twenty pounds, consistently. With the heavy women, a consistent forty to forty-five pounds under. She never guesses more than forty-five pounds under. The men, especially the fit ones, she guesses within a pound, consistently. The heavy men she guesses over by around thirty pounds, consistently.

"That's some pretty consistent guessing she's doing," I say to Zack, gesturing with my thumb.

"Oh, man, she's not guessing. Notice how she has them all walk up the steps? There's a scale in the steps and the read-out is on the right side hidden behind the game's front wall. The guessing is all part of the show to make the women feel better about themselves and poke fun at the fat guys because they take it in exchange for a prize." Zach sits a moment, "well, not always. If we think someone is feeling really bad about their weight, some guy I mean, we guess low."

I think about Jesse for a minute and the pudge he's grown in the year I've known him, and I wonder if the heavy men can take it or if they just push that moment of pain down and pretend it's fine. Do they take their prize and resent it? "She's never off by more than forty-five pounds."

"Fifty pounds is the big prize, a life-size teddy bear. They're the only prize that costs more than the ticket. We're allowed to give away, at most, one per stop."

We sit on the back of the game's structure, a flat space used by carnies to access the back for maintenance, and Zach pulls three waters from a cooler, handing Amber and I one. The cooler has some waters but is mostly beers, cans of Shetland Lace, which sell in thirty-packs for less than a six-pack of my Killian's. The corner of the cooler has a red plastic cup with some singles and coins in it. "Don't tell anyone. We're definitely not supposed to give these out. But I figure you held it in on that ride and I didn't have to clean it up so thank you."

"Glad to oblige." Amber rinses her mouth out with water over and over. When she finishes, Zach hands her the third bottle.

"How long have you been doing this," I ask. "You seemed pretty comfy up there."

"Oh about ten years. Dropped out of school, got my GED, didn't need to study for it, and then left to do whatever. Whatever led me here. Here is full of the crazy shit, man. I am so glad this is my last season. I need to do more with myself. Owner's dropping me off at Sterling, Kansas, for college this fall. You guys in college here?"

"IT for me, Geology for Amber. Oh, my name is Merak, by the way," and I shake his hand.

"Nice to meet you, Merak. Never heard that name before and I thought I'd heard them all. But yeah, business I think for me. I learned a lot here about profit and loss, cash flow, sales, and how to make people enjoy giving you their money. The owner, Roy, took me under his wing a lot. It's been good. Roy was an aerospace engineer back in the sixties, spent his free time drawing up a carnival business plan and designing all these rides and games. All of them are his take on the classics. He loved carnivals as a kid, fondest memories he always says, the food and the games, the rides, the way the whole thing collapsed into train cars. All

Roy's rides and games, he designed all these controls so that we can make them more or less fair, more fun, more exciting, build the game play, make sure the jerks don't win, 'always weight the dice in someone's favor,' he says, 'and a fun guest having fun means good profit.' So, like, if a guest is a real jerk on the ring toss, we flex the board the bottles rest on," Zach says, putting his hands together at the palms and curling his finger tips up, "make the tips get closer, slowly so it's not easily noticed, but it's physically impossible for a ring to nest on a bottle because of the angle they land at. But cool guests, nice, or just, frankly, really cute, we have it go the other way," he says, bending his fingertips backward, "and it's about twice as easy to land a ring. We have buttons that control it all and some motors you can't hear over the noise. Squirt gun balloon pop, we control the water pressure to each nozzle. Baseballs and cans, electromagnets in the platforms the metal cans rest on. So," Zach leans in to us, "no one wins unless we want them to and that lets us control the crowd, the excitement, make the games more thrilling for friends and dates and, of course, make more profits. There's a lot of guys in the towns like this that, man, they will spend two-three-hundred bucks on baseballs just to prove they can take a ten-stack down. I'm sure, all things being fair, that they could."

"That sounds like cheating," I say.

Zach nods. "Oh yeah." He holds his finger up. "Sounds like cheating is the same three words as smells like money," he smiles. "That's Roy's saying."

"That," Amber says taking a drink, "makes me really mad. All the games I played as a kid, I never had a chance?"

"You probably had a good chance – the kids always get good odds."

"That feels even worse! Do you think I need help?"

I put my hand on Amber's knee and she pushes it off.

"Cheating is cheating, Merak, regardless the intent. Don't try and get me to hush about it."

Zach looks down at the ground, and I wonder what his brain tosses around in it. This man Roy, Zach's voice belies respect and admiration, not just for his business acumen but also that he is Zach's role model. Roy is either the closest Zach's known to a dad or, at minimum, a mentor who he loves like family. Zach's lips bend a bit down as he defends Roy, "he wants everyone to have a good time. Keeping the games fair, pure-fair, wouldn't give everyone as good a time. More people get prizes our way."

Zach's voice fades and as Amber lifts her hand I lean forward: "He designed the rides?"

"And built them, too, with some help. And his wife, May-belle, she was the marketing brain. She came up with all the names back in the day and all the alternative names. Like the one we were on, Whirligig, here was May-belle's genius. We call it Whirligig in The Bible Belt where family values are all this important thing, right. In the Northeast, we call it Spin-de-loo because I have no idea why but it's catchy up there. But in southern California, it's Hell's Cauldron because people can handle that stuff. It's Hades' Cauldron the rest of the country."

"Explains the dancing goat men in the strobe light."

"Bingo. But we used to call it Up-and-tip most places. All the rides got new names this year."

"I remember that name," Amber says curtly, face forward, hands around her water bottle. "Why'd you change it?"

"Whole company got sold. Roy owns it but really he owns a trust which owns an LLC that owns the carnival."

"What?" I am genuinely confused. I'll run this past Rick later.

"So," Zach continues, looking around to make sure no one is listening, "in New Mexico last year I was working the crowd, getting people on Up-and-tip. This huge dude, definitely pushing four bills, he comes up and he's all like 'I want to ride' and I'm all like 'uh, I think we're full' because I don't know if the ride can handle that. No one that fat had ever, in my time, asked to ride, and I'm all thinking this is gonna be like a towel in a washer full-up on panties. And bingo, sorry to spoil the story, it couldn't handle him." Zach leans in to us and gets a bit quieter. "So the ride's spinning and it's shaking just like that washer and, like, man, the damned supports break the weight-spreader boards and are drilling themselves into the dirt it's shaking so much. But the operator, he doesn't notice because he's not on the actual platform, he's at the control pedestal. So I do notice and I run over to get him to stop but by the time I can get there the bucket is up and tilting and this fat dude, he starts slipping along the pads."

"Oh damn," I say at the same time that Amber says "Shoot."

"Yeah. So the bucket gets up to about ten degrees and he falls though the air. Thank God, man, no one was in the spot where he landed. But he hits and the bucket bends over and slams into the cauldron. The motor chain breaks and the bucket is completely out of our control. Now, fortunate, the way that it broke it was just gonna free-spin down, but it has to stop is a specific place for the doors in the bucket and the doors in the cauldron to align. So when it stopped, me, Jose – you heard him as Luke – and a couple other guys we had to push this thing around until we found the door to go in and let all the people out."

"Did he die?"

"No, but he did get pretty well hurt. I don't know all the details, wasn't puking blood, had trouble breathing, overheard someone say those were signs of internal bleeding and a punctured lung. Sued the old carnival, which no longer exists. So Roy had these other trusts and they bought the property from the LLC for huge losses, for the judgement of course, and we reformed as a new company and hired the good staff back."

327

Amber sits in stunned silence a moment. "You just tell people this?"

"Merak doesn't seem like a talker." Zach looks at the ground in front of him, eyes flicking back and forth from the grass to Amber. He regrets helping her.

"You said it yourself, babe, people tell me stuff."

"You never tell me any of this stuff."

"I never tell anyone any of the stuff."

Amber turns and faces me. "We need to work on that."

Zach smiles. "But yeah, that's not even the genius of it all. Like the engineering, man, that's amazing stuff. I wish I had a brain to design things. So, Whirligig, it isn't really as scary as it looks. The cylinder and cauldron shapes make this spinning park look like a perfect cylinder and as it rises up the strobes distract people from noticing that it's got a taper. It's all these subtle angles. And then the passenger area lifts in the bucket, too, so the spinning cylinder tilt can be less and people still see over the top at the crowd. Twenty-two-point-five degrees, it's very precise. No one inertia-shoots out the top, but the angles make it feel like you're horizontal. All the rides have a bunch of little tricks like that. Static Shock, the seats are really low, like really, really low, like your butt is below the axles and the seats tilt back but the headrest is vertical so your head is really low to the rails and that makes it feel super-fast. It only goes twelve miles per hour at the fastest but people swear it's going fifty. Same reason a go-kart feels faster than a pickup. That's why the track on that has such deep U-shaped supports, but you never see how low the seats are because of the car's shape and because the undercarriage is painted matte black. That and the way the turns are banked, it feels so fast. Definitely my favorite ride here."

"Did that used to be called Nitroglycerin?"

"It did. We had to change all the ride names after the accident."

Amber looks at me. "I love that ride, too."

"So, yeah, Roy's amazing, man," Zach says to Amber more than I, "he's taught me a lot, really took me under his wing, said he wanted me to save for school and get direction. He works with people to help them be the best they can be. I gotta make him proud. He's taught me how to run a profitable business, taught me lots of tricks. I'm gonna miss him when I leave here," Zach looks past us, something on the game behind us catching his eye. "He's as much magician as carnie as businessman as engineer. 'A few little tricks and distractions and people will enjoy giving you their money, Zach,' he says. 'That's why people like magic shows. They're in on the act, just like the magician. They're having fun and they like to give this talented magician their money. Business is no different,' he tells me. 'In business, a bit of distraction and showmanship, people gladly handover their money.' Of course, no one wants to be had, but people love paying for a distraction. But not one single large big distraction. People notice those and they feel like they're being conned. No, lots of little tiny things that add up to a big distraction, and you can feed them these little tiny morsels for months and years on end and people will keep coming along for the ride. The angle of some bottles, shape of a bucket, dip in a track, placement of a seat, bank of a curve – people might notice one of those things, or even two, but without knowing all the little tricks people don't see how the illusion works. And because they don't see it they love it." Zach turns around, looks out and away from us, down a pasture at a distant string of headlights on 145. Zack focuses well past the horizon, not looking at the distance in front of him so much as the time, both before and behind, and he thinks, in the way of thoughtful self-examining people, about his life now and the moments that resulted in this moment. "Sorry to chat your ear off so much."

"Not at all," I say. "I enjoy listening." I smile at Zach. "It's amazing to me just how black the sky is out here at night. Even with Harrisburg about six miles north and the rides behind us. Man, I love stars. I love putting a camera out at night and photographing something in the foreground as the stars spin in the sky above, creating these white, blue, gold, and red circles in a black sky."

Zach looks at the stars. Amber looks at me and her eyebrows lift.

I exhale. "Black is impenetrable like a brick wall. It absorbs everything behind it, in front of it, and around it because it is all things and all colors together, blended into nothing unique and discernable, mixing and melding until they are indistinguishable and the same and nothing all at once. Black is the voice in your head that tells you to stand in front of the oncoming train, or the urge to walk on the thin ice of a freezing lake. Black is stray noise that sounds like a stranger calling your name when you're alone in a hallway. It is the way that headphone sound comes from inside your brain and it is that sound staying there, continuing and repeating after the headphones come off. It is that feeling on your arms when you know someone else is in a room when you thought you were alone, and it's the certainty that whomever it is does not have your best interests in mind. Black is the cold of your bed when you first lay down in winter and the void in the mattress where a dead lover used to sleep."

Zach looks at me, his jaw open wide.

Amber leans her head against my shoulder. "I really hope you're wrong about that, Merak, because apparently what I 'see' is just black."

I lean my head on hers, "when I dream, it's the thing I see the most. All my dreams happen in darkness. I wish I would never be tired again."

In time, Amber feeling better, maybe at peace with the games being fixed, Zach stands, shakes my hand, thanks Amber and I for not making him clean puke, and leaves. Amber and I sit on the back of the weight-guess game and I stare up and down her face's profile, eyes move flat along her jaw line, up and to her pale-but-for-light-rouge cheeks, along the angle of her nose and a small scar above the nostril, at the silver frames and temples of her dark aviator sunglasses, and along her ear above the blue and silver "X" earrings to the wild fray where hair meets air and fights against being tied into a nest of knots.

"Are you staring at me?"

"Yes."

"Why?"

Because I never challenge anyone on things. Not never, rarely. Because I need someone to show me that standing for principles is good and okay and that simply listening, remembering, and not challenging people may be the worse course, both for who I am and for forfeiting a chance to understand a difference more deeply. "Because I admire you and wish I could be more like you."

Amber sets her foot on the dirt and stands. "Aw, Merak, thank you. That's sweet. I like who you are, too," she says, holding her hand down to me and pulling me to a stand when I take it. As we walk from behind the game, the crowd noise, at a hard line where the game's wall ends, fills our ears with the cacophony of bells, whistles, shouts, laughs, wheels on tracks, motors, and rings on bottles. "Merak, people always talk to you, all these strangers. How do you not know everyone? You don't know anyone."

My feet catch nothing on the ground and I stumble, almost knocking Amber over, and we stop.

"Merak?"

I shrug. "I know people. George, Rick, Jesse, and you, for instance. Look, I don't need to know lots of people, just a few. That's enough. You can know all the people for us. How about that? I'm happy to just listen." As we walk, I hear a mother of two sons, a handful of feet ahead of us, explain that they can each play one game and ride one ride, and that's all the cash and tickets that she has for them. They are dressed in older, worn clothes with holes peeking into the sides and stitching of shoes, thin-to-thread-bare fabric at their knees and hips, and concert tour shirts from more than a decade ago. "Stay here for a sec, Amber." I let go of Amber's hand, grab our ride tickets from my pocket, and walk up behind the woman.

"Ma'am, as we were leaving, I saw these fall out of your purse." I say, and I hand her all our extra tickets.

"Oh no, those aren't mine."

"We're heading out and I'm certain these fell out of your purse."

She looks at me. Her two sons walk on and look back. She smiles and takes the tickets. When she gets back to her sons she says, "Surprise! I found the tickets I dropped," and divvies them up between the boys. She never turns around to wave, just to give a quick glance, and her boys spin and hop and shout that they've never seen so many tickets.

I walk back to Amber, who is standing in place, tilting her head and listening to the crowd as they mill about her, trying to make sure she isn't in anyone's way. "Let's head on back to your place."

Amber nods. "That was nice."

"Just wanted to tip the scales in their favor. I'm glad they can have a better evening."

"Than us?"

"Well, I didn't think or imply that. I don't think we're having a bad evening, just different than anticipated. I really wanted a jumbo pretzel."

"There's still time."

There's still time, and when we pass the last food stand before the exit I order two jumbo pretzels, one for each of us, mine with extra salt and hers with none, nacho cheese dip for mine and barbeque dip for Amber's. She puts her dip on my knee, just needs the pretzel to keep her stomach calm, and I eat mine in small, torn pieces, dunking them in sauce, putting each one in my mouth, and I picture myself in a new black suit, white tie and corsage, Rick, George, and Jesse to my side. Across from me Kerry, Short Amber, and Redhead Amber wear orange dresses and Kerry eye-flirts with George over Dr. Beckett's held-open Bible. George gives her a wink, glances at the cake, and mouths 'meet me later.'

When Amber walks toward me, white dress, flowers, eyes closed and head up, a walk practiced dozens of times until she knew the contours of the chapel floor through the soles of new, white boots. She steps in time with the organ booming the wedding march. Across from me Dr. Beckett says nice words about gathering together, the sharing of space, the fellowship of community, and the meaning of commitment.

And then I finish my pretzel, dump the loose salt on the ground, and we walk out of the fair and down parked-truck rows, past diesel-powered overhead lights with generators that whir and click overtop of nearby conversations, and an ever-present hanging in the air of acrid, nose-burning exhaust. "Hey, when's the pie contest?"

"Yesterday."

"How did Kerry do?"

Amber faces me and smacks my chest. "You remembered her pie?"

"Blueberry-blackberry compote with citrus and sea salt caramel? How would I forget?"

"Well, you'll be happy to know she placed second, her best-ever showing, just behind a raspberry-rhubarb pie with a lattice top. She did well."

"Did that thing I wrote help?"

"No idea. Kerry said she'd leave her husband and make you her plump little butter toy if you want."

My eyes go wide and dart anywhere that isn't Amber. "That is … quite the offer."

15
Cover

Amber's dorm room smells perpetually of laundry detergent and dryer sheets because the wind around the building pulls the shared-wall laundry room exhaust through her window. She and I sit at her laptop and work on a catch-all resume to hand out at tomorrow's career fair, an annual late-April event that heralds the end of the seniors' college careers. The student center gave us a flyer with some resume tips on formatting, content, and attaching letters of recommendation. Amber is in good shape. 3.6 GPA – great. Dean's List for multiple semesters – awesome. 4-H club volunteering – fantastic. Her resume is short, three-quarters of a page, and this concerns her. Mine is longer, she says, and I note that I had summer jobs, but employers aren't going to care that I can make coffee, "they will care that you've overcome blindness to succeed academically."

"How will they know I'm blind?"

"Well, the cover letter is going to explain that."

"Oh no, I don't think I want that." Amber puts her knees together and shifts them to her side, her loose flat sheet twisting around her.

"You're just going to show up on the first day without telling them?"

"I guess I thought I'd mention it during the interview?"

"Be honest, be upfront. Some employers will use it as an out if they think you'd be too much trouble. You don't want to work for them anyway."

Amber nods. "Am I too much trouble?"

"Always and it's the best kind," I say creating a new WordPerfect file for her cover letter. "Before we start on your cover letter," the student center gave us a guide on how to write one of those, too, "can we talk about, well, um, how do I ask this, can we talk a bit about this summer. We graduate in two weeks, not even. We have to be out of the dorms right after."

"What are you getting at?"

"I know we talked about this a while ago, but that time is really here. It's not just a distant idea any more. Are you planning to stay here or do you want to come up to Chicago?"

Amber looks straight forward. "I –" Amber's laptop fan ticks on and hums lightly "– are you asking me … I had a thought that Sandstone needs me."

"Because I had a thought."

Amber nods.

"We could go wherever. Grandpa Arn says there's no future for you here. There may be in Chicago. There are stables in my town."

"What if I get a job somewhere else? Or don't want to live in Chicago? Do we just put this on pause when we graduate and pick it back up someday, maybe? Maybe you can sleep on my couch until we find something."

"My back will be sixty-five by August if I sleep on your couch all summer. So, my thought was this, whichever of us gets a job first, we go where that job is. If neither of us get a job by the time we have to move out of the dorms, we pick a place that sounds interesting, pack up Federico, and go."

"What if there are no geology jobs wherever we pick?"

"You can teach geology for sure if you can't directly do it. We will find you a job. And if it is in Outermost Nowhereistan I will find something, whatever thing I need to do, just to be there, work any crap job if it means I see you after it every day. Besides, every place has a coffee shop."

"Outermost Nowhereistan needs good coffee."

"Is it a deal?"

"It sounds like you said you want to keep this going after we graduate, but took your time getting there."

Her laptop fan hums into a higher, louder speed, sounding like a soft, distant tornado siren, sound distorted by my arm next to the vent. No warning, no control, my chest tightens, muscles flex. My brain takes its time realizing what the sound is, just the fan, and letting everything know to relax. Amber is sitting straight, tilting her head, she's also trying to figure it out. "The laptop's fan. It scared me, too. And yes, I'm trying to ask that."

"Oh." Fan: hums. Overhead lights: capacitor whine. Wall: an off-balance washer in the laundry room. Hallway: laughter and running. Outside: a garbage truck lifts and drops a dumpster. "I don't think Grandpa Arn would approve."

"What happened to you not worrying about that? If we need a two-bedroom, we can find a way."

"Let me ask Grandpa what he thinks." Amber sits and fidgets her hands, knuckles and fingers flex and roll, a joint pops on occasion. She keeps her knees pressed tight together and hunches forward a little.

"I don't need an answer today. I just wanted to see if it still interests you."

Amber, facing the wall in front of her and not me, swings her left arm out, slaps my left arm with a solid 'thwack', "yes, yes it interests me. You're the one I'm worried about. I've lived on my own the last four years. You never have. You've never gotten see what life is like in your own space with just the silence of your mind to keep you company."

"I spend too much time in my mind." Amber is right. I have never lived alone, and I sigh and wonder if that means I might get antsy and itchy, resent the compromises in the space we have to make for her. "We can live separately if you want. I, well, it's more important to me that I be near you than on top of you." Living nearby, figuring out what I'm like by myself, sounds expensive, but maybe I need it.

"I don't entirely believe that."

"Amber, you know what I mean. We can live separately and move in together later, after a couple of years. Look, I just, you make my life better and I don't want to lose that just because of a job. I'll find something wherever you are."

Amber leans over and holds her cheek out for a kiss, which I give. "What does the thing say about cover letters? I want to really wow the companies at the job fair." Amber has softened this last almost-year, her bristly exterior peeling back, with me at least, most of the time anyway. She knew, somewhere in an aphotic, subconscious brain-nook, that she needed a good, honest cover letter. She knew, too, that her grades and her knowledge could land any sighted student, at minimum, many interviews. But a silent rejection, never even getting to the interview, that would hurt less than wondering if a job fell through because of her needs. All the bristle, the harshness, it protects her from being hurt by people who don't take the time needed to know her. It must drain like a broken pipe to always be outwardly brave or abrasive, preventing the good people from getting close just to make sure the bad ones don't.

‹〇›

Amber and I wake in her bed the next morning, her clock reads off the time and then plays a local pop rock station. We shower, Amber noting that her shower really is too small for this, dress, grab our resume packets, and head to the career fair. This is it, what we've worked four years for, the culmination of our college time. The next step is to find a job we love, work at it until we're old, retire happy with the career we led, and enjoy our graying years. I hand Amber the outfit she wants – red flannel, blue jeans, and the brown cowboy boots with the floral patterns embossed in them.

The career fair occurs annually in the school's recreation center. The space, the largest available on campus, converts to the aisles that house companies from around the region, sometimes further. Representatives sit on the indoor running track in temporary table-rows sorted by industry. The schools with fewer students, of course, attract fewer employers, and if we give out all thirty of Amber's resumes I'll be surprised. I brought fifty of my resumes, and the same number of George's, and I will run out. Amber asks that we start in the technology area so she knows what to do.

"So I'm your guinea pig?"

"Always and on everything, yes."

Each year the school hangs signs above the rows that look like street signs – Technology Boulevard and Plaza (because there are always two tech rows), Aviation Street, Journalism and Publishing Avenue, Construction Drive, Pharmaceutical Road, Mining Way, and, I have to imagine some student worker who designed these however many years ago had fun with this one, Business Parade. Rick waves to us from the Business Parade line. Jesse, getting here early is in Technology Plaza already and talking with someone.

In the two technology streets, students from my college line up to enter. My arms already tire and strain from carrying nearly a full ream of paper between my and George's resumes. George, now graduated, needed someone to sneak his resume into stacks. I volunteered, gladly. Strict rules of the career fair, only students graduating this year can submit resumes. So I put one of George's resumes behind each one of mine and plan to quite slyly take each double stack and set it at each booth. If they pick up my resume and hand back the second copy, 'oh, no, that's not mine, must be the last person's.' I worry, of course, that the booth operators will be inspecting resumes closely and will report me to the school for expulsion from the career fair. This would be disastrous for Amber, but she says she can accept the risk.

Our first five booths are resume drops only, no interviews and no reviews today. I drop my and George's resumes at each. The people manning the booths epitomize disinterest. They're different ages and genders, dress differently though comfortably. Most read books or magazines and just point to resume stacks for different types of jobs with their companies if anyone tries to talk to them. Two wear headphones and I learn they like Pearl Jam and Stone Temple Pilots.

At our sixth booth, a firm called PC Pro Group, I step up to the booth and a thin man with brown hair and a graying goatee takes my resume. He asks me to call him Pat.

"So, Merak, did I pronounce that right? Great. You want to be in computers. Do you know anything about retail? We direct sell and install hardware."

I explain my background working at a coffee shop and that my degree is in computer hardware and networking. We have a short and positive chat and he asks about how I handled situations with customers and if Amber was also in tech before looking at the line behind me. He sees the second resume and hands it back. "Not sure who George is."

I look at Amber. "Oh this is my girlfriend George. That's her resume."

"Thank you," Pat says, putting it in the stack with the others as we walk on to the next booth.

Amber laughs as we wait in line. "You just wish George was your girlfriend."

"I'd go gay for one of his burgers every night."

"Hey, now, I cook really well."

"You make amazing food, but those burgers," I sigh a lung-full on these last words: "Lordy them burgers."

Amber shakes her head and we continue around my rows until I run out of resume pairs. All around us, every booth: stacks of resumes. Someone a handful of years my senior carries two already-full banker boxes stuffed to near-busting with resumes out of the booth on a wheeled dolly, says to a woman many years his elder that he'll bring another box from the car. I have basically no chance of standing out: unexciting credentials, decent but not thrilling grades, no unique experience, degree from a fourth-tier IT school. Every career fair at every college in the country must have the same turnout, or better. My resume, and I by extension, are as memorable as a single, random sand grain on an ocean beach. Maybe Amber will have better luck. I bank my hopes for our future on her standing out.

Mining Way has a short line, only a few students. Amber holds my arm tightly as we wait. "You're going to do well. Be yourself. When you get up to a booth just hold a resume in your hands until they ask for it, hold it out and they'll take it even if only because they're polite, and then answer whatever questions they have. You'll be fine. I'll be standing off to the side so that I don't get in the way. When you're ready, just pat your hand on your hip a couple times and I'll come get you for the next booth. If you want your cane —"

"I do not."

"I'll be there. If the person on the other side has any body language that indicates they're ready to talk to someone else, I'll cough a couple of times."

The booth operators in this row spend more time talking to the students, getting to know them, their courses, and their resumes. Each new booth, person, or team who Amber meets first asks for my resume and then, when they learn she's here for them they have similar reactions of 'oh, of course' or 'well, that's wonderful to hear,' then they politely glance at her cover letter, glance at her resume and the bunch of professor letters. Most conversations are only a few seconds long and her resume gets some brief notes before being stacked. My forehead feels hot, red, and my chest tightens. Amber's a really good mineralogist. She knows this stuff pat and all these people write her off because she's blind, and they're not even trying to hide it. Maybe she was right and we shouldn't have

340

mentioned anything in her cover letter. Amber's growing discouragement seeps into me: What if no one ever sees how great she is, except me?

Two booths from the end, however, and the pattern changes. "Tactical Tectonics, mineralogy, mineral rights, mining, and subterrain investigations, Grand Junction Colorado," according to the booth banner, a dark-tinted and stylized American flag with bold white and gold text. Amber stands in front of an older man. His hair and eyebrows are gray and black, brown eyes slightly bloodshot, face clean-shaven but probably last night, and he wears a red flannel shirt, jeans, and brown cowboy boots. This seems basically perfect.

"Dawson Paul. Call me Daw," he says, shaking Amber's hand before taking mine.

Amber introduces us and Daw asks for her resume. Amber faces me, confused. "I watched you two come down this row. I know who's here for the job and I am very curious." Daw asks Amber to sit, walks around his table with a chair and holds it until she's felt the back and starts sitting. He reads her cover letter closely, and he's asking questions, taking lengthy notes. Amber answers, smiles, oh I hear a laugh! They're sharing a joke. The pattern repeats on her resume and they talk for some many minutes longer. I find a bench along a wall and sit, glancing around at the thousands of students lining up, milling about the booths, talking, visiting a vending machine getting precariously close to empty, and in time leaving. Most look exhausted, or disappointed. Daw calls out my name and I look over. Amber is waving at me. When I walk up to them, Amber says, "he does that. He watches people and observes them and completely tunes out to the world."

Daw and Amber stand and he thanks her for her time and interest. "Oh," he says" I just noticed that you have very nice boots." He puts his foot up on his chair. "Mine have patterns as well, dots and ripples. They are my daughter's favorite." His boots are very ornate. Amber runs her hand over them and feels the textures and seams under her fingers.

I tilt my head and look at his boots then at Amber. With a wave and many 'thank yous' we walk out of the rec center. Amber stops and holds me when we get outside. "His daughter has something called CVI – cortical cerebral visual impairment. She can see some colors and splotches, but her vision is very poor. He asked me some really good technical questions and I got them all right. He said that he'll see if he has a position for me, that his daughter comes in to work in the summer. I just don't even know what to say, Merak!" Amber jumps up and down, her hair bouncing.

"I think it sounds like we might be looking for an apartment in Colorado."

"Not yet. No promises. He needs to do some numbers, he said, see if he can offer me a job. No guarantees, but he said I was one of the most qualified applicants he'd met today, and the most interesting."

My head feels like it did when I stepped off Whirligig and my stomach fills with a lump. My body shears itself in two up the middle, equal parts terror and excitement about Amber getting a job before me. The excited half jumps and backflips knowing that, because it will almost certainly be harder for her to find a job, if she does get this job, things will work out more easily. And we could live in Colorado and hike and drive to mountain summits. I could give Amber a chance to stand atop a mountain this year, on our way west, to let her feel thin air fill her lungs and strong winds lash her hair into knots. But what about me? What if I don't find a job? What if Grand Junction isn't a hub for IT workers and networking? Maybe it is. I need to find out. Maybe I can target my search there.

"Merak, are you okay? We're halfway back to your dorm. You haven't said anything. Are you mad that I might get a job first?"

I stop and we turn, face each other without my hands guiding us. "What, no, just scared and surprised and planning and hoping and excited and trying to figure this all out."

"What if he only wants me to be an inspiration to his daughter?"

"Is that bad? There are worse things to be." Toliver Woods' tree shade cuts the late-April heat and humidity. Cicadas. Every year, spring through fall, with the cicadas. I do, I admit, enjoy the sound of their warbling, competing songs as different broods and groups vie for mates, for a while. I'm not certain I recovered from last year's overabundance yet, however.

"I want to learn to rock climb," Amber says, "and snowshoe."

"And snowboard or ski?"

"Let's not get carried away." Amber smacks my chest lightly with her hands. "But seriously, you can stand below me at rock climbing and guide me up the walls. And they have ropes, I'm sure, so I won't fall and die or something. And we can hike on easy trails in the summer, and snowshoeing should be a lot easier since the trails are all packed flat, right? I don't know if that's true."

"I don't know anything about climbing or snowshoeing. I guess we can learn together," I say, the future's weight bowing my shoulders like pine tree branches under snow, weakening my knees like the bending boards that hold up old buildings.

At my room, Jesse and Rick play Top Gear, tell me I'm not invited to the game but that Amber can play, and that's fine; I need to make some coffee. Water in kettle: heating; water in mugs: microwave; coffee beans: ground; pour-over and filters: sorted and filled. The kettle water makes pre-boil noise and it fades slowly, sounds like 155 — hey! 156, very close. Won't be long now. When the kettle beeps, I pour hot water into grounds, refilling the kettle when empty and repeating until all four coffees are full. In the time I focus on this, Rick, Jesse, and Amber have played three courses, Amber giddy when she crashes, ecstatic when she accidentally pulls in front of Jesse and gets sideswiped and her controller vibrates. I bring over Rick's and Amber's coffee, then Jesse's and mine.

Rick and Jesse look at me, then Amber, then me again. "How did it go?" Rick asks.

I gesture to Amber.

"Amber," says Jesse.

"Well," she says, "Merak handed out all his resumes. And George's."

"Hey, there ya go, Merak!"

"Guys, no, she's obfuscating." I put my hand on her shoulder.

"It just," she faces me, "it still seemed like you were a bit upset."

Rick and Jesse are concerned, share a glance.

"No, not at all – excited and planning."

"Maybe surprised?" Amber sets her coffee on my desk, brings them up to speed on her conversation with Daw. She speaks fast and her voice fills our ears like the rapid-fire beat of a hyperactive snare drummer, but more excited, more scattered. She misses some details and I ask her questions that lead to them. Amber motions with her hands, takes only a few pauses for breaths and coffee sips as she talks.

Rick and Jesse scoot forward on their chairs as they listen, hold their coffees and drink them in happy, nervous sips as Amber goes into some specifics on what the job would require. "Fieldwork would be exciting and I'd just need some of those things that protect from snakebites on your legs and someone to help me with rocky paths. But I guess most of their fieldwork is close to wherever they can park and it's mostly notetaking. I'll get to do some actual mineralogy." Amber bounces a bit, sets her coffee mug on my desk again, and claps with excitement. I set my coffee next to hers and sit down beside her with my arm around her shoulder.

"I," this is me, and I am lost in this sentence already, feeling like I have woken up in a strange meadow the morning after a night of heavy drinking, "am excited, so I just I don't even know."

344

"Merak," says Rick, "you have talked often about living out west and photographing canyons and stuff. You should be bouncing up and down on this bed, too."

"Well," Amber's cheeks turn red.

"Do we need to leave?" Jesse says.

"Guys, no, seriously, I am. I am so hopeful this works out. Just processing it all."

Amber sips her coffee and faces us, eyes closed and enjoying the warm mug in her hands. "I want Merak to drive us up a mountain and hold my hand in the wind and the clouds on top and we'll make out on the summit until the park rangers tell us it's enough and we'll find some nice mountain roads to take instead of the Interstate —"

"Merak may have had his fill of mountain roads." Thank you, Rick.

"— and we'll have coffee on every summit we can reach and eat at little restaurants and get beers and we'll stay in campgrounds and cook meals."

"That's a lot for one trip." Thank you, too, Jesse.

I look at Amber and she smiles and sips her coffee lightly, "that's the life I want to work for," I say. "I'm overwhelmed. I'm excited. I," I look directly at Amber, "am so overcome with how much I am in love with you and I will only be happy in the future if I have you there." Rick and Jesse look at each other, mouths in large, excited O shapes, they twist and lean back in their chairs and Jesse finishes his coffee in a gulp. "You know what. If you do or don't get this job. There's something else out there. If this comes through, we move to Grand Junction. If it doesn't, we pick another town out west and we move there instead. We're making this happen."

"When?" Amber asks, picking up her mug, finger over Peanuts' face, taking a long and shallow sip.

I look at the date on my watch, April 27. "We have to be out of the dorms on May thirteen at noon. So May thirteen at noon-oh-one we do it."

Amber drops her mug and the handle breaks off, Peanuts the hippo shears from the rest of the mug and spins across the floor; coffee spills. She screams and it sounds happy but I'm not sure until she throws her arms over my shoulders, momentum pushing my back into my desk. "Yes, of course I'll move out west with you," and she kisses me hard and tight.

Rick and Jesse get up, Rick grabbing the coffee mug parts, dropping them in the trash.

"Iberkermerg?" Amber says, still kissing me.

Rick: "I'll just duct tape it together."

16
Grand Junction

My phone rings early, just after six, my parents singing happy birthday. They hold the phone between them, unevenly and their voices alternate dominance, neither particularly on-key. They drag out the last few bars too long, too, and this is their annual ritual.

"You two know it's May Third all day, right? This could have waited until much, much later." My eyes aren't open and my voice sounds like a truck dumping manure in a ditch.

"We know," my father says. "I wanted to call you at five. So thank your mom for pushing this back so late. Look, we're just really excited because we wanted to let you know what we're getting you. We won't keep you long. So we are going to combine your and Rick's birthday and graduation gifts this year. We are going to buy each of you a car."

I sit up in bed and press the phone to my ear hard. "What?" I look at Rick in his bed, just waking up, eyes peeking at me through thin, sleep-crusty lid slits.

"Well, some asterisks. We'll buy it and cover the first ten thousand. You'll pay us back for any cost beyond that. We'll work out the terms later. So think of everything beyond you typical hundred-dollar birthday check as your graduation gift. Okay? And that means, of course, it's all contingent upon you actually graduating."

"He's going to graduate," my mother protests.

"I know. Just making it clear."

"Have you told Rick yet?" Rick wakes up at this, his expression concerned.

347

"You tell him," my mother says. "We're going to get going to work. But we wanted to wish you happy birthday and just let you know that we're thinking of you both."

When I place the phone into the receiver, gentle as though I'm afraid that I could break it and erase the conversation, I look at Rick, who sits up in his bed, and relay the call. He hops down from his loft to the floor, turns, walks animatronic to the window, opens the blinds and window and stares outside. This will not be Rick's first new car, his father having bought him one for his sixteenth birthday, another when some friends crashed his first car. The room's tile, cold under my blanket-warmed bare feet, helps me blink away sleep and whatever dream I'd been having. I follow Rick and stand at the window next to him. "Your parents treat me really well." Rick draws his right leg slowly back and forth in a small arc.

"Give them a call tonight, tell them that. They know you're appreciative, but I think they'd still be glad to hear it." Rick seems frail. I place my hand on Rick's sleep-damp shoulder, curl my fingers slowly and let the tips rest on his clavicle. He rests his hand on mine, looks away from me and up at the ceiling.

"Never," he pauses and swallows, "never, um, ever notice that," Rick stops, squeezes his eyes shut, holds them there, "that paint crack up there?"

"I have. I've been keeping my eye on it, making sure it's okay."

Rick, eyes pressed and not hard enough, nods a short, fast burst.

‹◊›

Sunsets arrive slow and late in Cold Harbor in May, later than in Chicago, our place in the state far further south, a bit west. The late spring evenings here let Rick, Jesse, and I throw a football around the agriculture building's lawn after we eat, enjoy slightly cooler evening air, and the last days we'll have as students. I don't know what I have ahead yet, and focus on what I do know: Rick will always be my brother; nothing exists more important than that. I cling to that thing, tight as an overeager child with a butterfly in their hands, smashing it to powder and guts and afraid to let it go.

I can't hold on long. What I don't know forces itself into my brain, rattles around like rocks in a tumbler. Jesse will live with his parents on the opposite end of Chicagoland, until he finds something and someplace better. George, and this worries me, what if George never leaves Cold Harbor? After our years being friends, I worry that if he stays here that it just ends. And Amber: We picked some backup cities on a map – Grand Junction, Boise, Carbondale, Cheyenne, and Denver. We'll find a place, a stable for Sandstone, and room to ride. We'll order pizza that arrives hot, go to comedy clubs, and she will make us thick stews. We'll put on bellies and sweat a lot more when we walk for it, too.

Jesse throws me the ball in a wobbly spiral. I step to the side and cradle-catch it. I toss the ball to Rick and it spirals, not perfectly but fine. Rick will land a job quickly and find a nice studio apartment. At least, that's what I believe. For certain: This time here, the five of us living so close together, having nothing between us but our shared time and friendship, meals and fellowship, these years we've had will be some that we look back on with great fondness. Right now we have everything anyone truly needs: a warm home, good food, close friends, shared time, and happiness.

When our hands tire, palms rough and dry from pig skin, and the mosquitoes start to find us, I let Rick and Jesse know I need to go meet Amber.

"Dinner?"

"Just a dessert, too busy with finals. We'll do an actual dinner at the farm this weekend."

Jesse, Rick, and I hug, and I head through Tolliver Woods, not knowing how many more times I will but that the number, always finite, is now low. Squirrels jump between tree branches, heading to their nests.

Soft whooshes, a few times, maybe an owl or some other night bird. Moths fly around the wood's one working overhead light; bats fly through the swarm.

Outside of the woods, the sidewalks radiate the day's heat into the evening-calm air, adding a physical warmth to the soft music of intermittent gentle breezes on treetops, the pops of building envelopes adjusting to cool, bike tires on sidewalks as the last classes end, and the distant hum of a freight train's engine powering up to move coal or cars or lumber through town to some other place.

Someone holds the building door at Amber's dorm for me, and when Amber answers her door she is bounce and joy, nervous and frenetic energy, excitement and amplitude. I'm not even inside when, swaying her hips and clutching her hands in a ball she tells me, in probably the fastest words my brain can follow, "I have such a great birthday planned for you tonight. I don't think you even know it. I don't think you're ready, or ever could be. Are you ready?"

"I don't think I ever could be."

Amber sits me down on her bed and tells me to close my eyes. Her desk drawer opens and there's some fumbling, some rustling of paper or carboard, no both, and the click and scratch of a match on striking surface, smell of sulfur and smoke, amber blowing out the match. "Hands up and flat?"

"They are now." She feels around for my hands with hers, tracing the hollows in my palms with a fingertip, and not because she needs the help finding them. "Don't open your eyes yet." A weighty paper plate rests in my hands. I hold the plate steady as Amber sits next to me, her bed's frame springs and the old dorm mattress sagging under us. Amber sings happy birthday to me, sitting on her bed, her voice and tea-scented breath awash across my face with humidity like summer evenings when the heat wraps the ground shortly before a gentle rain. After she sing-wishes me many more happy birthdays, "open your eyes."

"You know how to make me happy," I say, holding a small, plain paper plate with a jelly doughnut and a birthday candle.

"You know what to do."

Eyes closed again, I wish for Amber to get the job, for us to pack up Federico with our few things, to find a small apartment near a good coffee shop and her office, for Amber to succeed, to snowshoe, to climb a gym wall, for me to be alongside her helping her find her steps and handholds, and to pick her up when she trips. I wish for us to have warm summer evenings drinking wine on a patio as the sun sets. I blow out the candle and tear the doughnut in half.

As Amber and I eat the doughnut, raspberry jelly on our teeth and sugar falling on our chins, she asks what I wished for.

"Do you know what happens if I tell you?"

"That's a silly old wives tale. Tell me."

I take a small bite of doughnut. "I wished for you to get the job so we can move out west together."

"Hmm," she says. Finishing her doughnut, Amber stands, runs her hands over my knees to her desk as she passes, and plays a message on her answering machine.

"Amber, it's Daw, I have a job for you. Check your e-mail and let me know what you think." He ends the message with his phone number and I almost drop the plate and last doughnut bites.

"You did it. You got the job." My forehead feels like an ice cube melting in quick-time.

"I really hope you meant what you said about us moving out there together. I want that. I want us to move in together and to have a life together."

I am shock and silence and stillness and then I am not. Plate on desk, I stand and hold her hands and we jump up and down uncoordinated, mis-timed, shouting happily, our voices echoing at us in the small, concrete space, bounding around the air like the trapped waves of a small pond.

"Did you tell Grandpa Arn? Will he be okay with us moving in together?"

"I did and I didn't ask. He's going to be a long way away. He'll get used to it, or he won't. He won't be mad, might just grumble."

"This is going to be the best birthday I have ever had."

"I did get you something."

"A doughnut and a life together isn't my only gift? It feels like enough."

Amber hands me a small box, wrapped in checked wrapping paper, folds bulging slightly. I look at my watch, relieved the box is a bit too light for that. I undo the tape on the sides, the back, and put the paper gently in the trashcan. Inside is a thin cardboard box with a hinged presentation box inside of it. Before I open it, I finish my doughnut half and lick the sugar off my lips and chin. The presentation box is navy with gold trim at the seam, unmarked. I look at Amber, she faces me. "Did you open it? What do you think?" She seems nervous now that the unwrapping has stopped.

"I haven't yet. I, um, I –" I want to sit in this moment for a few more seconds and can't understand why the words plug my throat. "I want to guess what it is."

Amber nods.

"Money clip?"

"Guess again."

"Not a watch."

"I know better than to do that to you."

"Hmm. Okay. Let's work this out."

"Just open it, Merak."

I lift the box open slowly, eyes closed, opening them when the lid is up. Inside, resting on padded white fabric, a gunmetal-toned tie clip with a translucent blue stone oval reflects the overhead room lights. Various blue tones, hues, and gradients weave concentric, lazy lines diagonally across it. "Oh, Amber, it's beautiful." I may not need this often, but it is lovely and I cannot wait to wear it for the first time.

"It's labradorite. Rick helped me pick it out. He said it kind of reflects, iridescences, which is because of microcrystals under the surface. It's igneous, formed in cooling magma. That does neat things to crystal structures. I want you to look your best when you interview for jobs. I wanted it to match your watch, too."

"I will never need a second tie clip."

"Turn it over."

I read the back, "Love, Amber, 2001." The air in my lungs slowly leaves through my nose, and I sit, lungs empty some seconds, before my next breath. Resting my head on Amber's shoulder, her cheek nestled on and pressing my hair, "this is the life I want. Thank you."

17
Night Driving

Federico pulls up to the farm as the evening sun starts to turn the light around us warm and orange, reflecting off clouds that look alight like bonfires, and as the early hints of the blue and pink sunset to come move slowly from the east. Amber and I walk around to the front door and Grandpa Arn sits on the patio, in his chair, rocking slowly, listening to the police scanner.

"Quiet night, Grandpa?"

Arn smiles. "Tad's got 'un uhgent call. Some'un shov a tato into Ol' Jim's truck's egz'ust. Mayjuh scandal. Fiv'll get ten 'aht was 'aht boy Brad Tannuh'. He's a prankstuh." Arn turns off the scanner and waves his hand at the patio's wicker love seat. "Sit un' down. Gorjus' evenin'."

Sitting, Amber is a smile with flush cheeks and raised eyebrows, happiness wrinkles fan from her nose. Grandpa Arn looks at her, then me. "Whuz' 'aht suddin' dinnah' abut'? Yuh' tuh' ain't run ohf an' got married, did yuh'?" He smiles, seems almost hopeful.

Amber, hands on hips. "What? No. I," she pauses and faces me, slides her hand onto my knee and I hold it there while she faces Arn.

"Preg'unt?"

"Grandpa!" Amber huffs a short breath through her nose. "I got a job."

"Well, les' geh' sum steaks an' yuh' kin' tell me abut' 'aht." Arn slaps his knee, stands, tells Amber to, and gives her a huge hug, face a proud smile. His whole body changes, slacks and relaxes. His skin seems to soften, shoulders slide down a bit. He holds Amber's elbows in his hand and his eyes close and relax, as though a moment away from a nap.

《◊》

As Arn sears steaks in an old, smooth cast iron seasoned to glossy black by four generations of his family, he cooks the steaks with intent and method, 90 seconds each side, twice. The potatoes boil in salty water clouded with starch, and he uses some of that to make a simple gravy when the steaks finish. Amber gives him the details and when she tells him how far away it is and that she plans for us to move in together he stops stirring the gravy for a few seconds and nods, "aht's a gud' choice."

When the steaks have rested, potatoes been buttered and parsleyed, gravy drizzled, Grandpa Arn sets our plates out on the picnic table and I shoot two rolls of he and Amber serving and joking. Mosquitoes buzz around us as the evening's last blues turn dark and the early-night stars peak between clouds.

"Meruk', wud' yuh' lead grace?"

We hold hands, bow our heads, and over the smell of hot butter and fresh food we thank God for family, time, and the warmth of our shared communion.

‹◊›

In time and in darkness we head inside to clean the dishes. Arn hugs Amber, his eyes squeezed shut with thin, wet lines where the lids meet. "I uhm' suh' suh' proud of yuh' Ambuh'. Yuh's thu' bes' paht' uh' mah' life."

"I'm going to miss you, too, Grandpa. But I'm not gone yet. Graduation is tomorrow. I'll see you then. We're moving out May thirteenth."

"Suh' soon. Ah' wushn't really ready." Arn lets Amber go. He grabs my hand and gives me a firm shake then pulls me in for a hug. When he lets go, his hands on my shoulders, "yuh' look out fuh' her. Both of yuh' look out fuh' each othuh'."

Amber faces me then faces out to the pasture and the barn. "I'm going to miss this here, Grandpa. I'm going to miss you and Sandstone, until we can rent a stable, and the quiet and the people in town." Amber pulls her lips in her mouth and moves her jaw back and forth. "Is it wrong to be scared?"

"Normahl' an' right. Feauh' an' excitemun' of'n travel togethuh'."

"Merak, what are you going to miss?"

"I'm going to miss seeing you regularly, too, Grandpa Arn, and having evenings like this here, on this farm. I'm really going to miss the apple orchard. And bailing hay."

Arn rolls his eyes and Amber gently smacks my thigh.

"Yuh' both git' goin' befuh' it's gun' be too late gettin' back.

‹◊›

Federico nuzzles rocks up as we drive the dirt roads that take us back to the highway. I keep the speed low, enjoy the time. My camera, in its soft travel case, rocks quietly on the rear floor and I look forward to developing tonight's film. These will be photos worth hanging. Amber sits back in her seat and over the minutes we drive she is laughter and excitement, tears and facing the window, apologies and silliness. I am a belly full of downed electrical lines. The night entombs my headlights, looking like two small slivers of moon before us. Road dust and early-night's thin fog give form to the light ahead of us, disrupted suddenly by alternating red lights surrounded in their foggy glow at the railroad. I coast Federico to a stop a bit away from the slight but sort road incline to the raised tracks.

"If you just drove as fast as usual, we'd have missed this train," Amber jokes. She leans over and puckers her lips for a kiss. As we kiss, four large, black Illinois Central locomotives pass just thirty or so feet ahead of us, speed steady, engines rumbling like a pack of growling dogs. Full coal cars follow, the hopper cars' wheels squeal quiet on the tracks as they gently rock, pulled steadily through my headlights' twin circles.

"I am ready for this," I say, "and I am very, very proud of, and impressed by, what you accomplished."

Amber holds my hand. "Can I ask you to do me a favor, Merak?"

"Of course."

"One more color. Just one. Then we'll find new things for us, okay?"

"Okay. Name it."

"I want you to describe my eye color last, will you?" Amber opens her eye lids and I look into her eyes, staring past but through me, a disconcerting feeling as though she focuses on some other reality.

"I shall, and happily. On our way out west?"

Amber nods and closes her eyes, squeezing my hand. "Thank you. We'll find you something out there for you to describe, mountains or lakes or waterfalls."

"Bears."

"Mountain lions," she says.

"A yeti."

"You'll just make that up," Amber protests, lightly smacking my leg.

"Ha, well, you'll just have to trust me."

Amber shifts, leans back in her seat, then turns her torso to face me. "I do. Trust you, that is. Are you worried? Afraid?"

"Oh, I know, and I'm not really worried. I'm excited. I feel like I'm going to explode sitting still. I want to get back to your dorm, throw your clothes on the floor, and make love until we both completely pass out from exhaustion."

"So for like eight minutes?"

"You give me so much credit." A mid-train engine rumbles past, shaking the ground. I wonder if I've ever seen these engines before. I don't know how many they have. This one, 6252, is the number just a straight count? That seems like a lot. "I'm amazed by how much coal comes down this track. I don't even know how many hoppers have passed us. A hundred maybe?"

"It's around forty or so between engines, I think."

"But still, it's amazing to me how much of this stuff there is and we use it once and it's gone and there always seems to be more."

"That's why so many people around here used to work the mines. Machines now, they do most of the work, fewer people needed." Amber squeezes my hand. "Merak, I love your wonder for things, your curiosity. You say one thing at a time, but your brain must have a dozen or a hundred thoughts all competing for attention, all behind that one you're saying. You are chaos and symphony."

I put my hand on Amber's cheek and the electric motor whirring and ground-vibrating piston pounding of three engines pushing the rear of the train fill the car with echo and vibration. "This, for me, is as perfect a moment as I think I could want. No sense of rush, just excitement and nerves, anticipation."

"Is this going to be our life, Merak? Is this what you want?"

"Yes, so very much to both."

"Promise?" Amber smiles and I have never been this happy.

"I promise. Our life will be out west. Look, I have something I want to say," I start in as the last engine passes, but stop for the noise. When the final engine passes through the headlight circles, "it can wait till we're back at campus," I lean in, kiss Amber long and slow, ending with my tongue across her top lip, and all is bright and white and energy.

18
White

So, yeah, it's easy to say that white is just the opposite of black. You get black, well you can, by mixing all the colors or having none. Yeah, that confuses me, too. It has to do with emitted or reflected light, which is like the difference between speaking and hearing. Where black is, with something like paint, all the colors mixed together, white is, in terms of light, all colors mixed together. It is everything and it fills my mind full like a too-much-food dinner with friends. White is your hand in mine as we lay in grass on a small, damp hillside, the tingle up our arms when a warm hand holds our shoulders. White is the sound of an orchestra's first note when all the instruments are in perfect tune and a hundred perfect and harmonized notes exit strings, brass, wood, and percussion, and that note repeating over and over steadily and the air pulsing around it. White is the static of a radio breaking into voices. White is friends laughing at a joke, a fun game that we just made up the rules to, laying in a wildflower field in the spring and letting the scents of a million combined little flowers fill your nose. White is bright, and light, and energy.

Bright white surrounds me, wraps like a welcome blanket, breaking and taking night's darkness like a strong wind to an old, dry sandcastle. The train; it just passed. Wait, its headlights were off because that was the rear, just red lights were on. My face feels like road rash, like the first time I wore shorts and fell off a skateboard. There's a steady beep. Regular. My right eye is in black and my arms won't move. The light, whatever it is, hurts my left eye and I can't reach up to it. I hear myself grunting. Lights above, rectangles. This is not Federico. White drop-in ceiling tiles, the sterile and dead kind in offices. I hear myself mumbling Amber's name, but it doesn't feel like I move my mouth. My head can tilt. Pillow. Cheap and too-soft pillow, bit scratchy. Thin blanket. Where is my car? Where is Amber? I hear sound like mist rain on a windshield. No, like a pump. Spray pump, like glass cleaners come in, chlorine smell. Lifting my head, my left eye adjusting to the light finally, an orderly sprays a bottle in a white-tile room. What's her name; I know her. Chrissy, from Brumby's. I think, maybe, everything is so blurry and why aren't my glasses on? She sprays something on the floor.

"Chrissy," she freezes at her name, turns her head slowly to face me.

"How do you know my name? You're that barfly who George likes."

"Where's Amber?" Chrissy looks away from me, sideways, a door; her eyes won't meet mine. She looks above me, no, at the right side of my face, but I only see her out of my left eye. "The girl in my car. Amber."

Chrissy quickly wipes up a spot on the floor with some paper towels, ignores me, and leaves the room, letting the door shut hard behind her, waving her arms down the hallway. Oh my God. This is a hospital room and, head tilts, neck bends and I feel like a spear is shoved from my shoulder to my hip; my wrists are tied to the bed frame. I bend my hands and fingers, feel the edges of the Velcro straps, push at them, no grip or leverage to open them. Tubes and lines come out of my arms and the monitor beeping accelerates and, that fast, I have nothing but strapped wrists and immense whiteness above me.

The door opens and two men, one with a shaved-bald head and holding an ice pack to his face, another with short, receding hair and a graying beard, run in. The man with the beard tells me to stop struggling; he knows my name. "Dr. Sanders," he points to himself. "Dr. Colson," he points to the bald man.

I look around the room, Chrissy looks in through the door, sees me look at her, shuts the door and disappears down the hall. "What?"

"Merak," Dr. Sanders pulls a stool up next to my bed. "What do you remember about the last day or so?" He sits and leans in close to me, sits on what sounds like a wheeled stool. His beard is short, more just long stubble, gray at the chin and sides. His face, slightly soft, nervous but painted over with practiced compassion.

Day? Or so? "We left Grandpa Arn's home about thirty minutes ago. Where is Amber?" I struggle at the straps around my wrists, shaking the bed railings.

"I can't take those off until you stop fighting, Merak. Do you know what today is?"

"May seventh."

"It's the ninth," Dr. Colson mumbles.

"Frank, I got this," Dr. Sanders looks at Dr. Colson, watches him until the other doctor leaves. "It's the ninth. There was an accident. You were rear-ended at a train crossing by a truck."

"Amber."

Dr. Sanders looks to the wall and the floor. "You woke up asking for her about fifteen minutes ago, not really woke up, you were waking up from anesthesia."

"Don't say it."

"I am truly sorry. It's not my place to tell you this, but I am sorry. I am not someone who keeps others in suspense."

"You need to shut-up," I say, pointing my finger down the railing, fighting the Velcro to point it at Dr. Sanders. "This doesn't happen to me again. I had my crash. I'm a safe driver. I don't have another one. I need you to tell me this is just some new nightmare and she's fine and we're asleep in her dorm and I can't wake up." I turn my head, neck stiff, sore, and vertebrae-cracking away from him.

Dr. Sanders sits quietly and he puts his hand on mine. "I'm going to undo these straps. When you woke up earlier, you punched Dr. Colson in the jaw. Can I trust you not to hit me?"

"Amber, wake me up. Please shake my shoulders, Amber," I try to force air out my lungs but manage only a whisper, faint and whimpering like a prayer in the hands of an uncaring God. My chest is fire and pain, especially the right as I push up with my shoulders. The ceiling tiles are the generic type, white and with the small holes. One of the fluorescent tubes in a fixture in the hallway flickers.

Dr. Sanders undoes the strap on my right arm and it falls limply into the bed, the back resting against the cold, metal railing.

"When do I wake up," I say, teeth clenched so hard my jaw aches.

"Merak, you woke up a few minutes ago. You're at Cold Harbor Hospital in the trauma center. You were in an accident at a train tracks, rear-ended. One of the responding AACTs, sorry, air ambulance care technicians, told me what she knew."

"No, no, that's not what happened. We, I," what happened. "We left Grandpa Arn's. We left Amber's home. We," what happened next? Nightmare. "This is a new nightmare. I can make it end. Does Grandpa Arn know?" I ask, confident that this will shatter my brain-space illusion and in seconds I'll be asleep and warm under Amber's covers with her floral-scented hair in my face.

"I am told that the responding officers have notified her next of kin. Will knowing what I know help you?"

I must nod because Dr. Sanders starts talking.

"We called your parents after we got you stable. They're on their way. They should be here in a few hours." Dr. Sanders looks at me. "I am sorry I was not here when you woke up. I had intended to be. You started to wake up," hunching, he reaches over the bed to undo the second strap, and when he sits the cushion hisses. "You started flailing, yelling about a river, Amber, a colander, and you punched Dr. Colson in the jaw. Caught his cheek between his teeth."

"I'm sorry."

"Job risk. He'll be fine. I guess your brother and a couple of friends are in the lobby. Your folks called him. Want me to go get them?"

I must shake my head. "What happened?"

362

"According to the AACT, a pickup truck at high speed rear-ended you after the train passed, before the crossing gate lifted."

"My face burns."

"The right side of your face took glass shards." Dr. Sanders stops and looks at my left eye. "I'm a specialist in optical trauma. Do you know what that means?"

"Eyes."

"There was some trauma to your right eye. You will regain sight. I can't promise how much or when. Let me tell you your other injuries."

"Amber." Dr. Sanders looks away and puts his hand very lightly on my shoulder. I turn my head and stare at his blurry face as my eye burns, tears covering it and making his blurry form wiggle in the flickering light.

"Your folks are from Chicago, so if you're going back there, I know someone, an amazing optical trauma doctor –"

"Colorado. Grand Junction. Amber and I are moving to Grand Junction."

Dr. Sanders nods and puts his hand on mine. "I'll stay here with you for a moment." He presses the nurse call button and when Chrissy opens the door he asks her to get my brother and friends.

"We're moving to Colorado," I say. "She got a job. She did it and she proved to the people here she could get out."

"She did."

"We're," the bright lights dim as my left eye starts to weigh on my face, "moving." That's our life. We promised each other that would be our life now.

〈◊〉

Bright, pain again, face and eye. I blink as my eye adjusts to the light. Rick paces along the left wall by the door, door to wall, back, then the other wall until he disappears past my nose and then after a few steps

363

and a choking sound, returns with his right hand clenched hard at his mouth. He shoves his left hand in his pocket. George sits in the corner glancing at Rick, to me, the machines. Jaw set square and hard, he can't look at my face. I smell Jesse's cologne, something called "Night"; he must be sitting on my right. I look back to Rick and follow him with my eye through several paces until he glances at me.

"Merak?" Rick asks, realizing I watch him pace. He walks quickly over to the bed, eyes red and dry, lower lids puffy and dark. George and, when I turn to see him, Jesse crowd the bed and have the same dry red eyes, puffy lower lids. Turn, pain and neck-fire, face feels like sanded wood; their faces have no joy.

There is no Dr. Sanders. My arms are not strapped down and though they are hard to lift, I can. "Is it true?"

They exchange glances, lost on what to do, no guidebook. George, older, should know some advice that escapes our still-young minds, but he looks lost as a child in a corn field. Rick grips the rails on the bed, "it is."

"Mom and dad?"

"They know. They called from the road. Less than an hour."

"Grandpa Arn?"

George raises his hand. "He knows. Didn't leave his home yesterday except to take care of the animals. Tad's there."

I think I nod. Rick pulls a chair next to me and as he holds my hand he cries, mouth contorted like a hall-of-mirrors smile, bawling worse each time he glances at me.

"Jesse, how bad is it?"

"Dr. Sanders wouldn't tell us anything because we're not 'actual' family, his words. George and I aren't supposed to be here, but Rick couldn't do this alone." He shuffles a foot on the tile, but stands to my right. The bed jostles as though he lets go of the railing and then grabs it again. "Before we came in, Rick talked with Dr. Sanders, got him to look away from the nurse's station, and George distracted Chrissy. I grabbed your chart, pulled your record up on the computer, and read through it, called my dad and he told me what it all meant. They flew you in on a flight for life, both of you. Fucking hell, we were sitting," Jesse lets go of the bed, feet shuffle on the floor, and for a moment it sounds like he speaks away from me, "God, we were sitting at dinner, the three of us, and we heard them and," Jesse swallows, shuffles and his voice sounds directed at me again. Rick squeezes my hand and makes a circular wave at Jesse with his free hand. Jesse nods, "we looked up, put our heads down, and made a toast to hoping the people in them were okay.

"You have stitches in your face, probably a lot. You may have heard your voice is a bit mushy, which is the bandages. They had to remove a lot of glass. My dad said he'd take a look, tell you what to expect."

"Thank you, I might." I won't. This, here, is what I get for planning a future. I don't want to know what to expect, don't want to plan, to prepare or think. Just react.

George puts his hand on my right hand. "Merak," he looks me in the left eye. "Tad wanted me to tell you that Amber didn't suffer at all. She was gone when he got there, about four or five minutes after the crash."

"Did the train hit us?"

"Fuckin' T-T," George's jaw muscles clench, "and his stupid truck. He lost his license last week, too."

My body jolts, muscles clench and tighten in reflex and anger, Jesse puts his hand on my shoulder. "Relax. I wasn't done. You had some internal injuries, organ bruising and a liver hepatic avulsion. That's not good, means a laceration on your liver. It heals. Also broken ribs, right clavicle in two places, and extensive cutaneous – skin – facial, upper torso, and leg damage. So for your future self, relax and recover."

Why do I get a future self? I think I ask that, but no one responds. Rick is a mess. Jesse's face is solid like a marble bust, eyes distant and hollow. George looks at me and the door, the wall. "How," I look at George, "George, how did I survive? Why again?"

George scans the room and all our faces. "No idea."

19
Penumbra

I wake up slowly, laying on my left side, hips near the edge of my bed, bird songs and gentle lake waves pass through the room's open window. Morning, and I reach over to put my hand on Amber's hip or hand, to pull myself to the bed's center and feel her warm and pressing against my body and legs, and my hand drops onto empty mattress sending a waking shot of pain out from my clavicle as the broken ends rub together. Eyes closed, as long as I lay here in eyelid-shut black, I don't need to face today. I move my hand on her side of the mattress, up and down the space where she would have been sleeping last night. Oh God. It's real. My hand stops and at once I feel a wave like muscle cramps race up my legs, back, neck, and everything is paralyzed. I should cry. I haven't. My body spams and tries, but the crying feels like a wolf in a trap, stuck and tearing itself apart to get free. It will. I don't know when.

I spent three days in the Cold Harbor Hospital, mixing consciousness, tormented dreams of disembodied and frightened voices, and instant-passing hours after morphine injections like George mixes an Old Fashioned. I missed graduation. Rick and my parents packed my dorm; George and Tad packed Amber's as Grandpa Arn sat in her desk chair and fiddled with Mr. Sniffles.

Today Amber and I should have been celebrating and drinking; our last days in the dorms should have been making love followed by meeting up with everyone for some obscene and graduation-themed burger at George's.

After my shower, I, stiff, sit on the toilet, bend my right arm, cradle it in and loop the sling over my neck. Sliding and pulling my boxer briefs up my damp, swollen legs requires that I twist my waist and alternate which side of the elastic band my left hand tugs. My back lets me know it is unappreciative of my twisting and my upper right side feels like fingers in a heavy door. My legs, puffy Van Goghs of purple, brown, blue, and yellow swirls and circles with straight and harsh dried, red cuts, fight the underwear and I inch them slowly over many minutes. My legs throb as I move them, but I have lived this feeling, swelling-tight pants, impact-mashed muscles, before. This was not something I was meant to feel again.

Boxer brief band in place, I walk to my bed and Rick has me sit and lift my legs, sets my dress pants under them, works the legs around mine, and helps me pull them up. He takes off my sling carefully and I work my arm through my dress shirt. Rick faces me and buttons the buttons, and when I wince as he works on the top button, he skips it. Rick helps me tuck in my shirt and put my arm back in the sling. The movement causes my collar bone to flex and rub bone ends again.

"The top button?"

"Too tight."

"Force it."

"Merak, let me get a rubber band."

"This is for Amber."

"No one will notice."

"Rick."

Rick forces the top button into place and it feels like my voice box collapses under it. I breath slowly and help Rick flip my collar up. We walk to the dorm mirror, Rick under my left arm, helping me walk straight-ish there. He stands behind me to tie my solid black tie, standard over-under knot. It's not a Windsor knot, but it will have to do. This is my old Christmas suit. My father drove back to Deer Lake to get it for me. Having been tailored a couple of years ago when I was some pounds heavier, it would be loose except for all the swelling. My shirt, newer, fits too tight now and I feel it across my right ribs with each breath. I have no second option. I haven't much looked at myself in the mirror, glancing really only at the left of my face. My right side matches my legs, though the bruises that stare back at me more yellow. The scab-crusted stitches on my face cut through the skin, ear to nose tip, hairline to chin line, like aligned desert slot canyons seen from a mountain summit. The eyepatch the hospital gave me is black and rests behind new glasses, gotten at the place in the mall that makes them overnight, and the patch's point pokes through where the right lens should be. These frames will do until the patch comes off.

"At least I matched my suit and eyepatch," I say; Rick closes his eyes and weak-smiles, gallows humor not his thing. "I could stand here and delay until the universe ends and I will never be ready for this."

Rick, standing beside me, gently rests, no pressure, his right hand on my left shoulder before putting a new dressing on my face. I decide to skip a full wrap and opt for gauze pads that Rick tapes to bare skin.

"My tie clip is in my cigar box," I say and Rick walks to it, holds the box in his hands a long moment and opens it. He last saw this when he and Amber picked it out. "I'm sorry. I should have gotten it myself."

"No, no not at all." Rick walks behind me and takes the clip out of the box, holds it in his fingers as I did last time, reads the inscription and quickly puts it on my tie. He walks, near-jog, to my bed, sits and sobs into his hands. Amber meant as much to him as he does to I. Including Jesse and George, we were the closest family I could imagine having.

Sitting slowly and with care next to Rick, I adjust the clip, straighten it. Rick and I, our sorrow arrives in large, crippling waves that wash away everything except a mental darkness that feeds on our energy and, when the wave recedes, leaves us as empty as the dark spaces in my nightmares. "Let's get Jesse. Do you need him to drive?" I ask, and Rick nods. We learn strength, that which makes us from the inside outward, not for us but so we can share it and support others.

‹◊›

My mother pulls her Tahoe into the Pritcher's Funeral Home parking lot, parking to face a brick wall, the funeral home on my side of the car. Jesse parks the old Sentra next to us, backing in until the rear bumper taps a tree. It's a small building, Pritcher's, feels like it should be larger. Under a black-tile roof, white aluminum siding and blue shutters and window trim create, I assume, a calming exterior. Around the parking lot, I recognize Grandpa Arn's gray truck and Officer Tad's squad pickup; three other pickups, one white and two black, are parked away from the building. George pulls into the parking lot behind us, his old Chevy rattling over the drainage ditch grate at the entry. Rick, Jesse, and George exchange hugs, and I hear Rick introduce my folks as his parents; they concur. My eye fixates on the building's far corner, two concrete steps to a small concrete pad, a white-painted tube-metal handrail. There's still a chance all this won't happen, a chance that ends when I walk in. Maybe if I wait just a few more minutes Amber will push that door open, face the Tahoe, give me the double finger guns, and everyone will laugh at me and this will be the king of all pranks.

I'll wait here, just a bit, or longer, for that, yes. If I don't go in, she doesn't have to be dead yet. Oh God. I just thought that. That's it; that's real. Amber died and I was driving and she trusted me and I didn't watch out for her. She said it: If I had driven faster we would have beaten that train. Amber would be alive, telling me to be careful with Mr. Sniffles for our trip out west.

I pull the other rear door shut, worm my hand to the front seat and lock the doors. The back seat cradles me, fetal, finally the wolf has chewed its leg off and I weep till my eye patch feels wet. My voice sounds like something contorted, like noise travelling through a fan or a long pipe, "please, God, let me have died, too. Please let this all just be what I see when I die, God, please. Just please, God, have this all flash white and have T-T kill me instead."

"He locked himself in the car," Rick says, muffled voice through the glass.

The doors unlock, mechanical. The door opens and my father slides into the back seat. For once he's not in the rearview mirror but here, physical, his hand on my head stroking my hair. "We have some time," he says. "You will need to face this, but now, during, as long after as you need, don't hide what you feel or bury your pain. When you need to know what to do, do you know where to go?"

"You," my voice a wet whisper.

"Your mother, Rick, George, and Jesse, too. You have amazing friends."

"Is this where I hear I should look on the bright side?"

"There's not bright side to this and anyone who says there is, or tells you to cheer up, or move on before you're ready to, or some such thing, they just aren't able to be there with you when you need them. This is going to hurt for a long time, no way around it, only through."

I push myself up to sitting and look at my father. He reaches over and adjusts the tie clip.

"This is a very nice tie clip, son. Where did you get it?"

My mouth seals itself, twists and I bite my lip. If I say, I won't ever leave this car. The clip opens under my fingers and I hand it to him, inscription side up. He reads it, maybe three or five times, puts it back on my tie and leans forward, elbows to knees, chin to fists, forehead to headrest. In some seconds, "I can put a small pin on the back to make sure you never lose it, if you'd like."

I nod, breathe deeply twice. "I'm not ready."

"Neither are we."

"I need to do this."

My father sits up again, his eyes red and face puffy. "Yes. I am sorry for that."

Parking lot dust coats my shoes and inside my pants cuffs. A pebble that worked its way into my shoe presses into my foot until I shake it into the seam between leather insole and padding. My shoes and their dust seem to blend into the concrete steps, slide with the hard, flat, skich of leather-to-concrete. At the door, my father, right hand to my left shoulder, pulls the door open. No Amber, no finger guns greet us, just a small seating area with older furniture, yellow flowers in brass vases on end tables. And photos.

Around the entry on corkboards propped on easels, photos of Amber, many of them my photos. At the first board, an eight-by-ten print, Amber in color leans against a tree while biting a yellow and red apple, face tilted at the camera. On the second board the photos are smaller, 5X7, black and white, a sequence left to right wrapping three rows across the second corkboard, Amber rides Sandstone across his pasture and jumps a hurdle. Color again below those and Amber and I laugh in front of the Wisconsin sign, on the next photo we kiss.

Get through this, Merak. Face this: These times choose us, not the other way around. Circling the eight-by-ten, more color photos of Amber, Rick, George, Jesse, and I at the spillway, we eat burgers and drink canned beer in firelight. I study the photos on the rest of the boards more closely, them being new to me: childhood photos of Amber with a much younger Grandpa Arn, helping him feed chickens, holding a shop light as he welded some beams in the barn, and him hoisting her on to Sandstone, her hair, back, and legs muddy from a fall. My eyes linger on a series of Amber from around age eight to fifteen with a shorter woman, hair graying steadily as the series progresses, always the same short and fluffy perm, and through the photos they prepare meals, cook in the cast iron crockpot, and serve plates of stew or roast.

Left, Kerry, she glances at my eye patch and then the floor, holds her arms out at me and circles her hands as she walks briskly to pull me into a warm, powdery-perfume-and-dryer-sheet-scented hug. When she stands back, she leaves two dots where her eyes had been on my shirt. "Did you take all these photos?" Kerry wears a dark-red, ankle-length dress with a pattern of textures, buttons up to her collar bones, and a black shawl. Around her neck, a delicate silver chain with a small, black, drop-shaped pendant hangs an inch above the top button. Her hair is up, tied into a bun with some strays at the top of her neck.

"Some."

Kerry holds her hand up to the photo of Amber leaning on the tree. "This, you just, her and all your friends, they're just so right. This is what you need to do, Merak. God made you to photograph people like this."

I look at the photos. "They never really meant anything to her."

"Do you think that?"

"She told me."

"Oh, Merak," Kerry says, taking my left hand in hers, warm and balmy, skin cushy and soft, nails trimmed smooth and tips white in a French manicure. "She loved that you took time to photograph her. She told me, after that day in the orchard, how she knew you loved her because you would talk her through a photo, direct her on how to be a person in it. No one did that for her, Merak. You saw who she was, and look, here, this shot, and this one and all of these on this board, she's there." Kerry takes my face in her hands, the scabs on my right cheek like tiny hot coals under her hand pressure, and looks up at my eye, hers both wet with tears, puffy like down coats. After a moment, she lets go, looks at and squeezes my arm, before she shakes her head and walks to the chapel.

George stands at the wall, his forehead to it. "You saw them," I say, quiet, walking up to him, leaning my back and head on the wall next to him. Jesse and Rick look at the photos, Jesse's arm around Rick's shoulders.

"I did," George says. "Did you look in the chapel?"

The wall behind my head sways, or maybe that's just my head shaking.

"You should. Left side first."

The foyer's carpet shows wear and flatness where people walk from the door to the chapel's entry. The pattern, brown with red and orange pile bunched like ordered freckles, disappears behind my feet as I lean forward, walk some steps, face the chapel door, and look up. The chapel has rows of metal-framed seats, brass rails, and purple cushions. Grandpa Arn, wearing a charcoal suit with an older cut and a blue tie; Officer Tad, also in charcoal but new; Kerry, sliding one of her black, low-heeled shoes gently on the carpet; and my parents in matching black suit and dress talk to an old man with a thick, white beard, black suit and tie, and a gold tie clip. They point at seats, gesture at a small piano, and nod.

At the front, on a white pedestal, a light gray urn with a blue floral pattern rests between two photos, the right blocked by my eyepatch. Far left, a door to a small lawn behind the funeral home, propped open by a large rock, keeps the air inside smelling of fresh-cut grass. In front and near that, a large, twenty inches wide, two feet tall, Amber, shoulders up, so much larger than reality, smiles wide and broad with happiness-wrinkles pointing triangles to the bridge of her nose, her smile is happiness and brightness, her face in sharp, clear focus, and Federico's tan seat and The Bulbous Otter are blurry behind her. For moments I stare, her smile wrinkles, and I think this may be the only photo I took that captured them. At least I have one photo.

My head turns slowly, scans past the urn; to its right, another photo, the same size, faded and color-shifted slightly, a woman who looks much like Amber, more of a slope in her chin, her hair styled in a wavy and full-bodied eighties frizzy poof. She wears a red and black flannel top, sits in Grandpa Arn's recliner and holds a small, blonde-haired baby. She smiles and her cheeks squeeze her brown eyes into squints and happiness wrinkles fan away from the bridge of her nose. Her smile embodies the active work of hope, an ecstatic joy for the future, and a subtle undertone of fear and being in over her head. She cradles the small baby close to her chest like flames hold to embers. Amber, so tiny, faces the camera, happy, too, arms forward, open as though reaching through decades to me.

‹0›

Mr. Pritcher stands at the front, aside the urn, Jesus, the urn. Amber's urn absorbs all the light and sound of the room and Mr. Pritcher's voice becomes a mumble in a dim space as he speaks, says, I don't know, kind words or whatever funeral directors say, and, in some seconds or decades dictates the order of events to the crowd – words from friends, a homily and prayer from her reverend, and finally words from me and Arn. I fidget with three sheets of folded paper, quartered, that have nothing less than the weight of everything I've loved in the last year.

Grandpa Arn, Officer Tad, George, Kerry, and I sit in the front row. Behind us, my parents, Rick, Jesse, and Kerry's husband, a slight boy with bowl-cut dark-blonde hair, sit as Mr. Pritcher plays piano music I don't recognize. The funeral home chapel fills with people Amber's age and older, some are passingly familiar faces from her church. As the music ends, the room, loud with breathing and sobs, quiet of voices, warms with shared body heat. Over minutes, Kerry, George, Rick, Jesse, some people I don't recognize, and lastly Tad take the lectern aside Amber and share stories, fond memories, and the ways that she changed and bettered their lives. Tad, as he speaks, falters, his voice cracks, and he finishes when Arn stands next to him, arm over Tad's shoulders.

As Tad passes, I stand and shake his hand, unsure I heard anything he said. I sit slowly, Jesse stands beside me, aisle side, left side, holds my arm so I don't sit too fast. Mr. Pritcher plays another song and afterward, footsteps. The floorboards vibrate slightly with each flat, hard, leather-to-wood plap-and-slish. I turn and face Grandpa Arn, sitting forward unmoving, hands together in his lap, turning the funeral bulletin into a tube, unfurling it, and tubing it over and over. George's jaw muscles flex like he's chewing a bullet. Tad faces away from me, looks out the window. The funeral home's aisles are narrow, but not so narrow that when Joe Morris' arm hits my left shoulder, forces my arms together, sends waves of pain like dry ice pressed into the skin around my entire body, that it can be excused. Rick and my parents gasp; George looks at me and his eyes are unlike anything I have seen, pupils tiny and eyes wide and unblinking. George looks like rabid dog as his stare saccades between my eye and Joe Morris.

"Pardon me, Mark," Joe says, resting his right hand hard on my left shoulder. "I didn't see you there."

"Is okay," I mumble, and turn my face all the way to my left to meet Joe's gaze, locking my left eye with his right, embracing burning and stabbing around my neck, and smiling with lips-only curtness.

Joe, releasing my arm, walks to the lectern at the front of the funeral home and looks down at Amber's urn. He wears a black suit with dark, dark navy pinstripes, again pattern-matched, and black shoes of the same design as the brown ones he wore last time I saw him. This man's closet much be worth a small fortune. He wears a small, gold cross with rubies at the four posts' ends around his neck and behind that a white silk shirt and tie. He wears his hair back, combed and slick, and sets a Bible on the lectern. For a moment, I expect him to open it.

"My fellow mourners," Joe opens, eliciting feedback in the audio system until he turns off the mic. "My fellow mourners," more quietly, "Amber was a much-loved fixture of our community, a lovely young woman we all expected to see around here for her whole life."

Grandpa Arn mutters a swear and Tad puts his left hand on Arn's wrists.

"We will all, I'm sure, miss Amber's bright smile and the happy faces she gave us," Joe continues, gesturing to her photos, and if he noticed Arn at all he shows no signs. "God loves us all, even those who stray from his flock. We must, for ourselves, believe that God's love exists for ever, even when we don't ask for it. Can I get an Amen?"

George, already standing, "you can get the fuck out of here is what you can get." George walks steady as an oncoming storm to the lectern as Joe steps backward, eyes wide and eyebrows up like two frightened alley cats. Joe pushes the lectern at George, who steps aside to let it drop and it does, onto Amber's pedestal.

Photography makes time malleable. We photographers play with time, stretch and shorten it, freeze mud kicked up from horse hooves running quickly or blur the motion of stars over many hours and all that time-play happens in a single frame. Time affords no such malleability as it happens. The pedestal tilts forward as the lectern pushes it. Amber's urn leans backward, the bottom visible as it falls. I feel the pain; my side, shoulder, and legs burn as though muscle tears and bones rend free of tendons. My broken clavicle cracks like chicken thighs under a cleaver. This pain does not matter: Pain is temporary. Seeing that urn shatter: not temporary. Amber's urn is cold, ceramic, and hard and I wrap and catch it in my left arm like a football just inches from the wood floor. When I land, hard and on my side, the pedestal completes its fall onto my right side, corner digging in just below my ribs and I feel like a water balloon pops inside me.

George stares at me as his feet walk fast behind Joe to the door at the rear of the funeral home. The crowd behind me gasps and shouts uncoordinated noise. Pain is temporary, Merak – get up. My pants, so much tighter than earlier, legs swelling, they fight against my standing and I hear a seam tear. I prop myself on my left elbow, still clutching the urn, and my right foot finds its way under me. I hear a harsh, pained, and angry scream as I stand. It's close, inside my head and echoing in my throat. George and Joe turn; it wasn't just inside my head. Left foot, Merak, then right. Drag them if you need to. This is for Amber. Left and right, wood under shoes, my own worn leather soles step left and drag right across the floor's age-smooth woodgrain, krish-tud krish-tud. My feet sound as though from different people, legs respond differently, and with each step the pain tries to convince me it will not be temporary.

The crowd behind me: cacophony, a maelstrom of bedlam and panic, chairs knocked over and people shout and trip onto the floor. George: turns and faces Joe, pushes him through the door at the back of the funeral home. Joe: shock and stun, walks fast backward down the stairs with glances back inside. Someone calls my name behind me. Me: I step through the door and turn around, cradle Amber's urn in my arm. My father, Grandpa Arn, Tad, and Rick: at once they look me in my left eye and their expressions change, confusion-twisted eyebrows morph in turn into raised and fear-filled eyes. Tad starts to run for the back of the funeral home and my father jogs forward ahead of the crowd running for this exit. I slam the door with my right shoulder and a scream and use my good, left leg to pull the large rock that propped it open before to jamb it shut. My father, voice wood-muffled and masked by door on frame slamming, shouts something about not doing something.

The exit, a small wood patio, drops a handful of steps to the grass behind Pritcher's. George stands in the full sun, his shadow cast long and dark up to Joe's chin. Joe stands, facing him, taller, wider: George is a small, thin pole in front of Joe. When their eyes lock, "what's your plan, bartender?"

George moves like a monster trained in bar fights and back-street brawls. He brings up his left shoulder slightly and Joe, a reflex born of his own younger-year bar fights, raises his arms to George's left. George's right arm comes up, fast like a striking snake past Joe's mis-placed defense, and George's fist connects solidly on the man's jaw, up and back so hard his teeth sound like rocks dropped on pavement. Joe: dazed, falling, twists and lands face-first in muddy grass and a small red explosion leaves the side of his face like a tomato being stepped on.

"Fuck, George," Tad's voice behind us. Somehow he's alone, the chaos inside, he got through it, ran around the building to the front fence before anyone else. We are the only four people who saw that, Tad, George, Joe – if he even saw it – and I. The crowd starts to gather behind Tad and he hops the yard's fence and runs to Joe, turning him over. The man's head, the skin around and above his left eye are split open, bleeding in time with his heartbeat; Joe mumbles.

The grass, soft beneath my feet, warm and humid in the mid-May sun, lets me step with my left foot, drag my right to where Tad crouches at Joe and George stands over him.

"George, did anyone else see this besides us?" Tad whispers.

George shakes his head gently, almost imperceptibly.

"One-hundred percent?"

George nods the same way.

Tad stands, puts his hand on George's shoulder and turns him to face the crowd. "Folks, I'm sorry for the excitement today. We all know Amber would have wanted something a bit different."

Someone in the crowd shouts about Reverend Morris, if he's okay.

"George here," Tad says, stepping in front of us and projecting his voice to the crowd to stop their cross-talk, tells them the truth he wants them to remember: "George picked up on Joe's extreme sadness. Addiction never really leaves us alone. George knows someone who's had a few, comes with tending bar so long, I think we can all agree that's true, and so he knew Joe needed some air and was about to pass out. George tried valiantly to get Joe some fresh air and Joe fell down the stairs, hitting his head on a rock in the dirt. I'll vouch, Joe smells like the cheapest rotgut backwoods mash still in Kentucky. Now, if everyone could just go back inside, I'll make sure Joe is looked after."

Joe stirs in the dirt, tries to push himself up and falls.

"That's how a drunk person tries to stand," my father shouts. "I've been there a lot of times." My mother stares at him, mouth open. Father looks at Joe, then at George's hands, together and massaging his right knuckles, then to me, smiles just the right side of his face slightly with a wink.

Tad takes off his tie and motions to George to give him his tie. George rolls Joe onto his back and the men bandage Joe's face. I shuffle, like a bad-movie's least-scary zombie to the three men, George propping Joe's head slightly as Tad ties the neckties around the wound. My knees pop as I crouch and put my hand on Joe's shoulder. "You're awful and I'm sorry you have to wake up who you are every day." Tad's face and George's eyes turn toward me as I talk, as I rest my hand on Joe's shoulder. His eyes, open slightly, look at but not truly into mine. He has lost the piercing connection he made the first time we met, the hollow intimidation of a man who wants people to believe he can see their soul but instead sees only himself reflected in others' sunglasses. "Someday I will forgive you, but today is not that day," I say quietly to Joe, his eyes glancing around my face as though a bird trying to find purchase to land on a smooth wall. "When T-T hit us, Joe, I was about to tell Amber," I stare the man in his right eye, wide and surrounded by mud on his cheek, blood and two ties on his forehead, and messy, dirty hair, "that I wasn't ready to propose to her, but I wanted that to be our goal in Colorado. Today, I was going to stand in front of her family and friends and tell them," I put my hand on his shoulder, look into the forest in the distance, press my weight into his shoulder and grind mud into his suit and feel his shoulder blade teeter-totter on a stone in the ground, "that finding a good person, finding someone who makes your life better and worth getting up for, well, we were that for each other. You stole that from me. You stole that from Arn." I look into his eyes for the last time as I say, "we are our actions and the harm or good we cause others, Joe. That's the sum of our value. I'm sure you've heard 'hate the sin, love the sinner.' Joe, tell me, how can a man be separated from his actions? I'm sure you've read that we will be judged by our works." I look into Joe's eyes, his brow low and over his eyelids, nose scrunched on the right side, mouth slightly agape. "I believe, when our time comes, Joe, that we get to forget all the hurt we've caused others. For you, Joe, I hope that I'm wrong because, not matter how expensive your suit, how capped and bleached your teeth, there's no hiding that you are nothing more than a drunk who gets handsy with teenage girls. I do hope you enjoyed our chat about orthopraxy."

I press my weight into Joe's shoulder and he groans as I stand. George holds my arm and we amble, like a broken wind-up toy, toward the fence, Grandpa Arn, Rick, my parents, Jesse, and their empty hope something can explain the last few minutes. I look at Rick then to Amber and when he takes her my arm falls limp to my side. Pain is temporary, respite more so, and as my arm hangs tired, my body's pains, throbbings, and sorenesses tell me I am worse now than minutes ago.

My mother smacks my father's chest and hard. "What was that?"

My father looks at my mother, right eyebrow raised. "Merak and George needed me."

Grandpa Arn stands at the fence and looks at me.

"I'm sorry I locked the door."

"'Aht 'appen as Tad sed'?"

"He hit the important notes, if not all the harmonies," the top of the fence posts have texture, deep crevices of weathered wood, splinters and grain born bare by winters and summers destroying and graying the old, dead pine; a deep pit homes lichen and moss and for a moment I feel jealous of whatever tiny bugs live in the pit and don't bother themselves with the complexities of our lives. I look at Rick and my parents, Grandpa Arn and Jesse, back to George and Tad who have Joe propped between their shoulders, walking him toward the fence gate and to Tad's truck. The back of Joe's suit coat has torn along his left shoulder seam, around a large muddy stain. That can't be fixed. Jesse, no prompt needed, opens the truck door for them and Joe, flopping hard in the passenger's seat, rocks the truck like a boat in a marina.

Tad points at George, hand and finger shaking, not scolding but in fast, staccato tremors. "We're even."

George nods.

"Grandpa Arn," I look at the ground at his feet before looking him in his right eye. "Rick, George, Jesse and I, can we hang out with Amber one last time? I'll have her home before sunup."

Grandpa Arn nods.

I want to promise I'll take good care of her this time. "Thank you."

‹◊›

George's truck barely holds us and we sit uncomfortable, riding bumpy roads with shot struts, engine fighting age and old oil on the highways. My injuries flare with the physical pain of an unending fireworks finale on every foot of dirt road, side road, and even highway blacktop for the nearly two hours from Pritcher's to The Spillway. The parking lot is packed with students celebrating the end of the year. George parks far out on the grass, headlights pointed to the forest. He plays happy music, refuses to let me wallow in sadness.

"Celebrate that you had her joy in your life, Merak," he says. "Feel sad, but keep the good times in mind, too."

George's truck's hood warms the backs of my legs and butt. I hold Amber in my lap as my friends talk, some poppy ska quiet in the cab. When the song ends, I kill the music, set Amber on the car's hood, and stand in the glow of a headlight. I hold the folded paper in my hands, the words I wrote to read about Amber at her funeral. Joe stole this from me, from Arn. I look at the sheets, fold them, and tuck them into my suitcoat's inner pocket.

"I am going to miss the games that Amber thought up," I say. "She always had good ways for people to get to know each other better. I loved that she wanted to try everything, even when she sucked or knew she would probably fail, simply because doing those things let her have fun with friends. Amber needed us for help, sometimes, sure, but we needed her more – I needed her more – to show me that the world is far more than I ever saw. I will miss her steady and paced footfalls, how she fiddled with pencils or hemlines and buttons when she wanted to remember something." I stop, look at the grass below my feet, damp and dewy. My friends, when I see their faces again, walk through the grass to Amber and I. "The first things I loved about you," I say to Amber, "were your happiness wrinkles that fanned out from the bridge of your nose. I loved that you never let me guess your feelings, always showed them somehow. I always felt that gave me an unfair advantage, and I hope that I didn't use that. I loved watching you ride Sandstone and how you two talked through motion and gesture. I will miss your hand's warmth on my arm, the smell of your hair when your head rested on my shoulders, and knowing that when you held me like that it was because you harbored a deep and abiding happiness, different from the exuberance that wrinkled your face. Amber, I will miss basking in the light of your joy."

George steps forward to the urn. "Amber, I will miss your help when I make burgers."

Jesse next, "Amber, I will miss having a competitive video game partner."

Rick stands back from us, seems paralyzed, jaw set. He holds his finger up.

"Take your time," George says.

"Amber," Rick's voice fights to hide, to crack, fail, and flee from his throat. He forces air but it sounds like the fading breaths before sleep. "You were already my sister. No matter what, you were my sister. I will miss having someone to talk to when Merak is in the shower. I will also miss your sense of adventure and how even the most-simple things – like a trip to Milwaukee – became amazing through you."

The urn feels cool under my hand. "I love you, Amber, and I always will."

George and Jesse stand next to me, put their hands on the urn. "I love you, too, Amber."

Rick steps to the car, holds his hand out, it falters, he tries to move it to the urn, holds it in mid-air. With a swallow and a head bob his hand slowly moves to it. "I love you."

We stand around the urn for some minutes holding it. When the others let go, I hold the urn where they had and feel their hands' residual warmth. Rick stays with me, watches my hand on the urn and George and Jesse clean up the area. I take Amber's urn in both hands, untape and lift the lid and hand it to Rick. I pull an empty film canister from my pocket.

"What are you doing?"

The headlights, when I bend at my waist, cast enough light into the urn. Amber, gray powder ashes in a taped-tight plastic bag. Damn. I peel away at a corner of the bag and, once opened, I dip the film canister into her ashes, over and over in small scoops until I pick up enough to almost fill it. With the cap on the canister, I brush the dust on the outside of it back into the urn, close the plastic bag, and pocket my small canister of Amber.

"Merak," Rick says.

"I'm taking her to a mountain, Rick."

‹◊›

George drops Rick and Jesse at the dorms late, near midnight, and parks us in Grandpa Arn's driveway near one, parking behind Tad's truck. The front patio light is on and walking around the house I hear Tad's and Arn's voices, sitting on the patio, each sipping and setting a can of beer down on their chair's armrests as they talk. I stand next to the house, out of sight and listen a moment. This is it for me, the last time I'll hold Amber and I don't want to give her up yet.

"'Ah 'uh yuh' fuh' 'aht second 'copter. 'Ah didn'uh knuw' 'till yuh' tull' me."

"I know. You know if that," Tad stops. "Merak should be dead, too. If that train hadn't have had an engineer sitting on the back smoking, and if that engineer hadn't have been Terrance Bradley who grew up literally two miles from that crossing and knew exactly where it was to call it in on his radio," Tad stops talking and I hear his beer can lift, he drinks, and sets it down hard with a hollow tunk. "If I hadn't have been five miles away just patrolling when the call came in. I knew it, Arn, and I'm sorry when I heard the call red truck and black car. I knew exactly who was in both." Another beer can opens. "I had my squad at a hundred and forty on those dirt roads. I honestly thought T-T rammed them on purpose and I was rushing to try and stop a double homicide. He was blackout drunk again, passed out in puke in the grass by his truck. I tried to save her, but she was gone when I got there. All I could do was pretend I saw her breathing to get two flights. I knew I needed to tell you, not the scanner. I am so sorry I was too slow and too late."

"Yuh' did more' ahn' I coulda' asked all these yeahs'."

I shuffle around the corner to the front patio. "I brought her back safely this time, Grandpa Arn."

"Yuh' alwah's kipt' 'er safe, Merak," Grandpa Arn stands and hugs me gently, my body aching under his arms. "Ahn'thin' yuh' wun' say? Din'h geh' uh chance at Ambuh's service."

Arn's eyes and mine meet and then I look at Tad, his dusty-blonde hair, eyes like a mossy forest floor dappled in shade and light, and strong chin. "I have regrets. I'll mourn for a long time, think about her almost if not every day for the rest of my life. I wish I had told her more often that I loved her. I don't get to do that again."

"Same here," says Tad. "I also have regrets."

"We ahl' hah' regrets," Arn says, his hands on my shoulders, eyes toward Tad.

Tad glances at me and then away into the cloud-born night darkness that sits like a waiting dog beyond the patio's two lights. No one survives nearly dying, I want to tell him. The person I was just a week ago, if I talk about him it would feel no different than talking about a stranger. In my past, two previous versions of me, the one who died in the river in

Colorado and the one who died at that railroad crossing, stand at the end of their time and watch me intently, with, maybe, hope for who I can be and what I can build from the lives they lost. From each of those two moments, someone new and different walked away and into a disorienting and uncertain future.

20
Umbra

Cold, damp grass on my back drains warmth through my clothes. My right eye burns as though replaced by an ember that spills fire onto my face. The air thumps in steady rhythm, feels of that rhythm-pressure and smells like kerosene smoke. From the left, no detail, red and blue glow, a dew-damp hand in my left hand. People bustle and talk in voices that sound like trumpets with their bells underwater. The voices mix into the colored lights as sound becomes sharp and soft textures traced on my skin. Sound and light and coldness and darkness and rhythmic thumping air become one and with a loud cracking sound someone above me says "Arn is listening." The sentence drowns me in waves with each thump in the air.

Darkness holds me like a too-small sleeping bag, arms and legs pulled and pinned to the sides. Though I grip the hand in mine hard, try to reach as it slides, the hand pulls and drops from mine. I reach blindly, flail, and try to keep it in my fingers.

My bed, damp in sweat, blue pajamas soaked through along my sides, crotch, and back. I sit upright in the dark, faint moonglow between the draperies. It was a dream, but the air thumps follow me, cling like fingers pulled through dirt toward a cliff. I rock on the corner of my bed, back and side in the dorm room walls' corner, legs squeezed to triangles and knees to shoulders, "God please let me have my old nightmares back, please let me have my old nightmares back please let me have my old nightmares back" and Rick puts his hands on my shoulders.

"Merak."

I look at Rick, "please give me my old nightmares back."

Rick grabs me and pulls me into a tight hug that I fight. The moonglow between the blinds dims. My alarm clock casts a faint, red hue on the walls, now plain-white paint naked of posters.

"What happened. Where am I?"

Rick's face looks decades older, drawn and slack in his cheeks, concern melting into skin and he kneels on the floor in front of me. "You're in your room, Merak. It's," he reaches over and turns my clock "three-thirty-three AM. George dropped you off about an hour ago."

"I need to move my legs. I need some water." Rick fills a mug with tap water. "I never want to leave here. Please let me die here. I can't leave here." Rick says he understands, can't let me. He turns his desk lamp on low, sits with his face half in the dim glow-transition where light mixes with, fades, and eventually yields to dark. The tap water is warm, nearly too warm. "I can't go back to sleep."

Rick nods. "Neither can I."

"Ever. I can't go back to that."

Rick nods and sits in the unwavering, unyielding, and terrifying quiet that exists only in a dorm whose students have mostly gone home for the semester.

"I need clean clothes. I need a shower." I have no idea what I need. I think I needed to die in that crash. I think I can still die. Yes. Maybe that's what I need. I need to go back to that moment and die with Amber. Fuck you, Terrance Bradley.

"Take a shower. Get changed. We'll take a walk."

I leave the light off in the shower and run the water hot, so hot I know it turns my skin red. My nose runs slimy when I hold my face to the showerhead, covering my right eye and the stitches on my face with my hand. I wash my hair, slick with night-sweat slime, wince as shampoo gets into my eye and face wounds, tilt my head back into the water. When I exit the bathroom, dressed in loose pants that I can pull up with one arm, an undershirt, and my Illinois University Cold Harbor sweatshirt, Rick has the overhead light on, bright and blinding like high beams, and I shrink and crouch against the wall. The room smells of coffee.

Rick hands me a mug, warm and smelling of rich, slightly bitter vanilla and butterscotch notes. We drink our coffees in silence. For a moment, I forget the time, the darkness, the nightmare, and the confusion.

"Coat?" Rick asks, finishing his last sip.

"Laps till I collapse?" I ask, and Rick nods.

Campus Lake carries nature's music and the staccato of its own, tiny waves that caress the shore's pebbles. No birds chirp; maybe one or two fish break water to catch a bug; some spring peepers croak on the lake's far side, their night song carried distance on near-smooth water. Rick gives me time and silence. In time we exit the trees near our dorm to a crescent of path where the water meets shore. I tell him about what I recall of the dream, of the darkness and pain, the lights and voices becoming one with the air and tracing sensation on my skin, and someone saying that Arn listened. "I wish I had died in the accident, too. Every day since I think that it's not too late for that. Many times every day. Will it be like that forever?"

"I don't think so."

I swallow and nod, shallow, quickly. We walk. "I'm sorry that I woke you up."

Rick puts his hand across my shoulders and the muscles tighten, then loosen. "Merak, you can, for the rest of your life, wake me up whenever you need to. You're my best friend, my brother, and I love you, man."

My left arm finds its way around Rick's shoulder. This is his time to support me.

The crescent of trail along the beach ends and we enter more trees, letting each other go when my right arm starts to hurt. Dew droplets hang on the leaves' tips; the air smells of moisture, uncleared deadfall, and tree litter rotting rancid-sweet and filling my nose with carbon dioxide. It smells the opposite of the air after a storm, the opposite of hair in the wind, of skin and sweat and apple cores strewn on the ground.

On our second lap, we reach Campus Lake Bridge as the sun begins to alight the sky, thin morning cloud whisps beginning to glow, void above turning pale-blue and marching forward to drive the night away for a time. Rick and I stand on the bridge deck, the center, and lean on the railing from where so many times we heard saxophone music. Rick walks back to the shore and finds some smooth stones. We skip them from the bridge, not going for distance, not counting the splashes – as though we even could in this light. We skip them to break the night's silence, to hasten the light and noise of morning. Sometimes, the best thing a friend can be is there, quiet, reassuring, and a presence that holds dark-black aloneness at bay.

When the stones run out, Rick starts down the bridge, "it's okay," I say, and he walks back to me.

"One more night here."

"One more."

"I have to head home today," Rick says. I know. This sentence doesn't give me anything new; this sentence gives Rick a chance to see if I can survive the coming night.

"They're forcing me out at noon tomorrow. I want a bit more time. I'll make it okay."

"I'll see you again tomorrow night. I'll unpack the Nintendo first. We'll order a deep dish. Jesse said he'll be there to race go-karts."

We will, I twitch my head up and down, unsure if it even moves. I don't want that, though. I want to lie curled in my dorm bed in the dark, in silence, and imprisoned with my thoughts. But I can't; my friends need to help me and, more importantly, I need to let them. Tomorrow night we will all get together, we will play video games like we did; we will eat pizza and drink beer like we did. That night will end in about forty hours, though. I have a forty-hour stay of execution from being alone with my thoughts. My friends will be sad; they will move on in time. They will remember Amber fondly as their friend, my girlfriend, but in time they will think of her less often. People quickly forget the dead.

I will remember that Amber and I had a plan, a life we were going to live together, and that T-T took that away, and that if I had just driven like usual, he wouldn't have. I will miss taking her to a mountain, sitting after hours in the coffee shop near our home, enjoying Sunday brunch mimosas with new friends, and the old and quiet dog snoring at our feet until food scraps fall.

"The nightmares I had from the canyon."

Rick looks at the side of my face.

"Sometimes I go a few weeks without them. Sometimes its four and five times a night. All my dreams, even those that aren't awful, they always occur at night. I've never had a dream set in the day, at least not since Colorado. What does that mean?"

Rick looks out at the lake, as our shadows begin to form on the water and in a thin, low fog along the shore. "I have no idea."

"It's changed, too. I found an old journal. It's changed over time, gotten worse. That driver, he becomes people I love. My parents, Amber, you, Jesse, George, Meggy. All of you have been that driver, your faces wrenched in fear. I don't know what that dream tonight was. Never, never have I felt that, reacted like that. What if it changes? What if it gets worse? Sometimes I think I died in Colorado and this, this is what comes after." The lake undulates gently, an inch maybe as some very calm wind-energy, breeze-energy really, starts to build. "I must have been a bad person." A bale of turtles swims under the bridge.

"I do you no favors if I lie. I don't know how your dreams will change. For what it's worth, you didn't die in Colorado. You weren't, aren't, a bad person."

"It's my fault, Rick," the words stumble out of my mouth, thick and round, falling on the railing, resting obvious on the stone walkway. "I drove slow. I never drive slow. I wanted to savor the drive, the mark between our time here and there. I wanted to just look at her for a few more seconds after the train passed. I loved her and I loved that moment. I wanted to tell her that I thought we could spend our lives together, have kids. I was about to tell her. If I'd just hurried to get back, not been so stuck on taking it all in, we would have been past those tracks before that train arrived." How do I even say this. "I killed her because I was selfish for our time." The coffee burns bitter up my throat and I vomit into the lake. "How have I survived two crashes, Rick? I don't understand. It's not fair. It was my turn to die, not hers."

"I think, and I hate to say it, that you need to talk to someone who knows this stuff. I wish that were me, but it's not. I'll always listen. Knock on my door any time you wake up overnight." Rick looks up at the night, away from me, and I see his cheek, two lines of shiny silver-gold catching the rising sun's color. "I never had a brother. But, no, that's not right. I didn't have a brother until eight years ago. It took me a few years to realize it. If I had had a brother, he couldn't have been better to me than you. I couldn't have chosen better than you. I was really excited that Amber would be my sister someday. Look, just, things are gonna be dark. Think of me when you go there. I'll find a way to bring you into the light."

Birds start to sing their friends awake, to start their days looking for seeds and bugs. I want to ask, but don't; I know the answer. Rick knows that place well, the emotional umbra where our pain and fear meld. Rick never shared that. Our lives, at their darkest, can turn to and reach for a light if we know that a person, friend, brother – someone – is there.

"Merak, feel what you need to feel. It's okay to go to your emotions and lose yourself. Just come back from that place. Sometimes you have to lose yourself to find yourself."

21
Liminal

With a sharp pain that makes my teeth grind, my right shoulder hits the doorjamb at Brumby's. Tonight, George hangs up his bartender's apron the last time before driving to Chicago, his old truck and his few belongings, cast iron griddle on the front seat. Tomorrow he will move in with an old girlfriend, the day after interview for a job selling computers because I slid his resume into a pile. I'm early, won't attend his goodbye party later; I would kill the mood. A year ago, this bar's smell of acrid wood, decades of stale smoke, sweat, pickup lines and arguments, cheap scents used to hide body odor, spilled and spoiled beers, and the ozone that spews, crackling like pine needles in a fire, from the ceiling box felt and smelled like home. Today, the sensation chaos burns my sinuses like hot sauce, waters my left eye, and makes my nose a snot faucet into a cocktail napkin.

In the mirror, Chrissy sits, eats a slice of pizza, and drinks her Natural Light. She looks up between slices, sees me, makes brief eye contact with the reflected me. Her hand moves steady, lifts a lightly-used cigarette from her table's ashtray, and inhales long and slow. The smoke wraps around her head, rises slowly upwards, powerless except to show the air moving. Chrissy turns her seat, the back of her head in the mirror.

Across the space behind the bar, my reflection faces me and looks at the back of the liquor bottles. He looks up; does he recoil? His face looks aged and weary, but in my mind, no eyepatch, bruising, scabs, or stitches. In the mirror-life he leads, he never walked into the student center, never met Amber, still drives an old Saab, and will enjoy one more night at a bar with his friends. I want him to smile at me, to let me know his life is okay. I want for him a good future, happy and filled with friends, meals, video games, and time. The mirror me looks back with a slack mouth, furrowed eyebrows, curious and concerned, as though he wants to ask what happened. Fifty weeks ago we made separate decisions, simple and innocuous, that made us entirely different. I envy the me behind the bottles, the me who threw away George's paper slip.

George sits on the stool next to me, puts his beer-bottle-cold hand on my shoulder. Muscles tighten, hand remains, shoulder squeezed. "Today is because of you," he says; I know what he means but I hear it differently. "You got me to graduate, got my resume worked on, hid it in a stack. You changed my life. I'll be more than a town-favorite bartender throwing cheap beers and wondering what I could have done. You are the best friend I have ever had." Mirror-me and mirror-George shake hands, hug, and clink bottles.

I say thank you to be polite. I hope someday I can accept a compliment.

"Let me know if and when you need anything, Merak."

I nod. "I think, maybe just for right now, I need a beer."

George takes his hand off my shoulder and starts to stand. "I'll guess that you need a friend."

I might nod a little, or not; I don't know. I want to. Shortly, George sets a cold, water-droplet-covered bottle of Killian's in front of me, thin carbon dioxide fog hovers around the top like cool mornings on a warm stream. I put my hand on the bottle body, wet and cold like melting ice. The label, damp, glue loose, ripples like a bedsheet under my hand. George, hand on neck, presses the bottle into the bar top.

"Merak," George looks at my right eye briefly, instinctively, then locks my left. "Every man – every person – faces a moment that defines who they become. When that moment ends, they chose a path. No amount of work or time or prayer ever backtracks. Most people only recognize that moment years after it passed. You are, right now, lucky that you can recognize that moment as it arrives. Who do you want to be, Merak? Drink that, and another, and another, and keep on with it because you'll never have enough to quiet that voice you hear. Or find something in yourself, your friends, focus on the walk ahead and step into it. Take that drink, you take everything that comes with it."

"George, I just need a beer."

"I've seen this moment often, dozens of times over. Only ever stopped it once before. Count to seven. Decide what's best for the future you." George lets go of the bottle. "I'll get what you decide."

The goodbye party crowd trickles in slow as my bottle's water condensation drips to where glass meets bar top. The people bustle, talk, laugh, and joke; their lives, tonight at least, easy and painless as new shoes, as they walk and press shoulders, a living density moving and shifting in waves like an undulating and pulsing tide advancing and receding, move with the sound like the shores of ancient oceans across time. The movement jitters, twists on itself, orders and drinks, drops a glass, eats fried cheese and limp fries, spills ranch dressing on their shoes without notice, finishes drinks and orders more. They blur in the mirror like a vortex pulling the margins middle and the mirror-world spins, dragging me with and leaving me dumped and dizzy on wet grass; talk-noise blends into a fast, frenetic chatter of nonsense syllables, a made-up tongue that hides distinguishable sounds except the cracks of pool balls breaking, a beer tap spewing foam, and my barstool's rusty-chain squeal as I twist left and right. The noise builds like an approaching tornado, spins, grows, and moves like wave-energy on a small lake; the air vibrates in the rhythmic thump of bass-blast music; colored lights beam and blend into sound from the dancefloor. Pain and sensation ripple across my skin when a wild arm hits my right shoulder and drops me back into the bar as my back takes a hard bump from the dense, dark, ever-thicker mass of shoulders and shirts, hair and faces, perfume and cologne, smoke and ozone, faces that move in fast-time, and clothes colors blurring and bleeding together, pushing and undulating, dancing in a rhythm dissociated from melody and presence. My hand releases the bottle, somehow easily, and I dry it on a new cocktail napkin.

These are the people who know George, who will miss him for some weeks or so until they find another bartender to love. They fill the room, toast George over and over as an excuse for another round. They sip and gulp from clear plastic cups, beers and well liquors flow like echoes in a valley from the bar to trays to hands to mouths. The crowd noise builds into incessant ear-ringing, an eardrum-deep heat and pinch. I take a single, long, neck-draining swig of my beer, leave it on the bar, stand, and walk to the exit George's cheeks are a thin smile and his eyes relax watching me walk. The crowd slows to normal speed. Chatter from stray phrases, discrete words, reach my brain like sand through a sieve. I push through the reminiscing and laughing crowd that agrees that, after tonight, Cold Harbor will never be the same. I only see the crowd on my left; it looks flat and mashed like a pile of paper dolls made alive. They slide back and forth, barely a gap to squeeze through. My right shoulder bumps drinks and foods; marinara spills on my shirt.

The cool-humid Cold Harbor May night welcomes me with a breeze that offers no help with the sweat that makes my head a wrung-out mop. Moths under the building's lights cast small pavement shadows. Fifty or more people still in line to get in; this will be Brumby's biggest night. My ears ring and the lined-up voices become truck tires muted by after-rain asphalt, then metallic like wire brushes on a cymbal. I half-zip my jacket, pull the hood over my head, and walk. Streetlights, neon beer brand signs, and the moving dots of headlights reflect in the sidewalk puddles left by the afternoon's rain. The lights count off the blocks to campus' after-student quiet. I walk one last time through Tolliver Forest's clouded-night, deep-ocean dark.

⟨◊⟩

I will spend my last night here alone. Rick is in Chicago, Jesse at Brumby's with George and the crowd. My clothes, computer, and what remains of my camera all sit packed and stacked in cardboard boxes and duffels. I sit on my bed; warm light from the overhead light hard-lines harsh shadows from my things to the walls. From my cigar box, I take the small, plastic container of Amber and in my desk, a near-finished roll of masking tape. The roll has just enough to wrap the lid three times and when the tape ends I fold the masking tape down and over. Someday, when I'm ready to say goodbye, I'll remove this tape.

The small, plastic film cassette container of Amber sits on my desk alone, casting a short and straight shadow. Why do I have it? I don't know what I'll do with it. No, that's not true. Amber wanted to stand on top of a mountain. Damnit. Damnit. Damnit. I'm taking what I have of her to a mountain, letting the wind take her into a couloir, carry her into an alpine lake to rest and swim in deep, clear, water that lets the sun reach bottom rocks. What I have left of her will rest across a mountain slope to enjoy the sun and view until time turns the mountain into a valley again. I pick up the little plastic cylinder of ashes and put it back in the old cigar box I use for important papers, letters from my grandfather, and some mementos. Tomorrow I will shower, dress, sit in my mother's Tahoe, and ride home to Deer Lake. I'll have the summer to figure out if there is a next. Outside, lightning starts to flash and alights rain drops that land on the window.

I trace the cinder block lines of my dorm room wall with my finger, walking slowly around it and feel the smooth, rounded dip of mortar and dozens of paint layers. Spreading my fingers onto the bricks, the blocks' contours, dimples, and divots brush my skin one last time. This is one of the last times I will stand in a space I shared with Amber. Tomorrow, at Mary Anne's for breakfast, then my bedroom at home, that will be the last. Head down, fingers on wall, tear-water in eyes, will the future me be okay? Will he let Amber slip from his mind like a dream to protect himself? Or will he be stuck, unable to move on? I hope, for he and for I, that, like me leaving this dorm and this town, he will move past this year while part of it stays with him like the memory-feeling of paint-layered cement on my fingers when I pull my hand from the wall. I hope he will take Amber up high, put her on a rock, and watch the wind take her.

Morning, early, the overnight rain left the grass soggy and sidewalks deep-puddled. Sunlight crests the horizon, gilds Campus Lake's small waves in auriferous glints. Campus' quiet amplifies the soft waves lapping cedar knees, insects' calls, morning birds, and an airplane distant overhead. For now, the world exists for me only and it imbues a false peace and serenity which will not last long.

One at a time, I carry my boxes and duffels outside, stack them to wait until my mother pulls the Tahoe up. She'll drive us to Mary Anne's, absent another choice, for bad coffee, good food, and to start our drive. My father and mother will switch driving duties while I lay across the back seat, rest my eye, and listen to the road sounds to gauge our progress.

Sunrise starts in earnest with early gold light bouncing off thin, post-storm clouds in the clear, dust-free air that follows a good rain. As the sky turns pink and orange against a distant horizon bluer than I've noticed before, it reflects in a sidewalk puddle and in that reflection my father stands behind me.

"Are you ready for this drive? Can you make it? Do you have it in you?"

I am not. I cannot. I do not. "You're asking about every day after today."

"I am."

"I have moments where I know the best thing I can do is drive a car into a bridge embankment, and others where I see, I don't know yet, something else. There's no middle ground."

"There won't be, not for a long time. You got a shit deal. You made the right choice."

"Last night?"

"Fifty weeks ago." My father turns sideways, his right shoe kishes as he kicks the pavement. "You'll never forget her." He leans, turns, and looks over my right shoulder and into my left eye's reflection. "Pain,

Merak, never gets smaller. It feels smaller because you grow around it, become more than it. It … occupies less of you."

A waterdrop from a tree leaf ripples the puddle gently.

"Someday you'll be standing somewhere, I don't know, friend's apartment, company party. You'll look up and your life will change. That will not betray Amber, to find yourself, to live your best. I didn't know her well, but I know people and it's what she wanted for you."

I nod and he turns, takes a step, walks back close behind me.

"I hope who you become, that he's better than I am. Not a better version of me – the best version of you. Still flawed, but the best."

The clouds, now a warmer pink, warmer orange, yellow-edged with reds in their textures and folds, seem to move as the sun-cast shadows change. "I have no idea what you're talking about."

"I'm … hopeful for you, and proud. I needed to say that; you don't need me anymore."

I stare at the puddle-mirror. "I still need you."

"You need your real father, not the version you imagine in mirrors."

I nod in quick, small movements, close my eye. "I don't want to be alone."

My father lays his hand on my shoulder, "you won't be." His hand releases and his footfalls fade to silence. Some moments pass and a new set of shoes ka-tack ka-tack behind me, confident, flat leather on pavement.

"You didn't get them all right, I think. Sunrises are beautiful."

I bite my lip, lift my eye patch when tears build behind it, and let them drain down my cheek. I nod.

"Whole new day, isn't it?"

I stand over the puddle, let tears ripple the surface, dab my cheek and watch the moisture wick the fibers. "This reminds me of our ride on

Whirligig. It just feels like I can't get away, like everything happens like it did before but worse, so much worse. Each time around it's worse."

"Pain traps us in a circle, Merak, and it feels like we can't get out. And we can't, alone."

The sun rises over the cafeteria's roof, shines onto my face, warms my left cheek and I close my eye, let the sun's light glow red through my eyelid. "What am I going to do without you, Amber?"

"Merak, you loved me more than you have loved anyone else."

"Yes."

"I, well, I wasn't asking. That doesn't end. Feel what you need to feel, anger and sadness, denial and pain. Remember my laugh, our meals, and the feel of my head on your shoulder as we walked. I loved you, too, Merak, more than anyone else. You're even an inch or so above Sandstone."

I laugh. It's my joke, just in my mind.

"Merak, you are long hair in a strong wind, moving outside your control, flailing and stopping, whipping and spinning. In some ways, it's your choice to let it happen."

In time, Amber in the sidewalk puddle looks back, eyes bright with forest-dappled light, hair braided to pigtails and hanging over her shoulders, happiness lines fan from her nose as her face scrunches and smiles. "Do you want to know what happened?" Amber asks.

No strength remains inside me and I cannot; I cannot shake my head.

"Well, I guess the only thing left is to ask where you want to go."

Amber and I walk behind my dorm and stand at the middle of the short, stone bridge. Wind across Campus Lake moves the lakeshore cedars' branches. Birds fly low over the water. A fish jumps. I look back at my old dorm building, the window I looked out of, and I know, without hesitation or doubt, that if I could relive the last year over and over, from the moment I met Amber until now, that I would gladly spend the rest of time doing exactly and only that. I don't know if this is relief or sadness: No change exists for the past. We stand on the bridge, feel the sunrise warm our bodies, the wind move our hair, and we enjoy our time waiting for the sound of a parking truck and shutting doors.

Made in the USA
Middletown, DE
30 October 2023

41542170R00243